A Visit to Stoneybrook

Marina McLune

ISBN: 978-1-7393137-1-5

Cataloguing in Publication Data for this book is available from the British
Library

Printed and bound in Great Britain by Bell and Bain Ltd, Glasgow

Chapter 1:

'Don't You Want Me' – The Human League

There are people who leave a bad taste in your mouth – figuratively speaking of course. You don't actually taste anything, but you know these folk have left their mark when they leave behind something nasty in their wake. A bit like when a male fox marks its territory with his pungent pee to ward off rivals. Good for the fox, but not so great for whoever sniffs the stink he leaves behind.

Bad taste in your mouth; kick up a stink. How many more idioms could she think of? Lots. But this was physics, not English. Millie noticed the taste of wood, varnish and graphite in her mouth, after mindlessly chomping down on her pencil. She was chewing pencils a lot these days. Was this the reason 'bad taste' had popped into her mind? Or was it because the words had other meanings - boorish, callous, crude and smutty?

She sighed heavily and put down her pencil. There was really no point in trying to revise now that Giles was in her head. From experience, she knew the best thing to do was to pause and let the thoughts run their course. But how long would it take this time? In her mind's eye, she saw him waving to her at half-time. Meltingly gorgeous in his rugby kit, mud on his face after a scrum. She'd watch him play, teeth chattering, scarf wrapped around her neck, no questions asked. Any good girlfriend would have done the same, and when he was thrown down in a tackle, her heart would pound. Sometimes she'd even cover her eyes, too afraid to peek through nervous fingers, terrified she'd hear the scream of an ambulance siren any minute. And far too often, he would leave the pitch bloodied and bruised, and each time she anticipated permanent damage. A snapped leg could heal, and swollen lips would go down, even ugly cauliflower ears could be covered up with a hat or hair. But a broken nose? That gave her the chills. He'd never be the same again.

'Never be the same again' 'Never be the same...' the words kept repeating like an indigestible meal, over and over and over again, and each time they stung just a little bit more. The sting was opposite to the relief she felt knowing his face had survived one more game, the face that made almost every girl in her posh, fiercely competitive school melt, every time they saw it. He was the cream of the crop. Perhaps the most fanciable guy in the neighbouring boys' school and many girls hated her for being the cat that got the cream. He could have had his pick, yet he chose her, and to this day, she still didn't know why.

She stared at the blank page. 3rd June 1982. That's all she'd written after some fifteen minutes at her desk. Straightening up, her pencil flicking in her hand like a hummingbird's wings, she gazed out of her window. Not being able to concentrate made it a good time to lap up delicious scenery and savour early summer delights. The view could be distracting, invigorating and inspiring all at once, and especially inspiring when studying English, particularly poetry. The bucolic scenery had its way of igniting her innate creativity just like it had done for Wordsworth, Tennyson and Keats, and today, rather unusually for a working farmyard, everything felt hushed. There was no clanking tractor, buzzing chainsaw or rattling combine harvester. Even the cockerel was silent. But there was the occasional bleat of sheep interspersed with the comical cackle of geese to remind her where she was. Perhaps that's what made nature so inspiring and her home so beautiful. The peacefulness allowed the imagination to run riot and her artistry to flourish, at least that is, when exploring new possibilities rather than just reliving the past.

Her mother was right. 'Boys can mess with your head so wait until you're eighteen at least,' she'd said. So why then, despite such sage advice, did her parents not stop her from dating? Why did her mother just ban Giles from the house, as if that were a magic bullet, as if that would solve everything? If challenged, her mother Victoria would also struggle to give reasons for her head-in-the-sand approach. 'The relationship's not serious,' she told her husband, Cecil, and with him suitably disarmed, it was easier to then tell herself that their daughter's heady romance was nothing more than an innocent crush.

Picking up the pencil, Millie chomped down again on the soft woodiness between her molars. Definitely still bitter. Bitter like the unpalatable truth her parents had faced just twelve months earlier. Their youngest child and only daughter was becoming a woman. But Giles' parents were different. Unfazed, they welcomed her into their home with open arms, and that meant his bedroom. Sighing, she remembered the first time she stepped into that space. How he watched her, with quiet amusement while her eyes feasted on his environment, looking for clues as to what made him tick. She remembered the empty Top Deck shandy tins, the sweet wrappers scattered across his desk, the chunky A4 files filled with copious notes about the English Civil War. She remembered the bed, how springy it felt and its mustiness, like the sheets hadn't been changed in weeks. He didn't even bother to clear up discarded socks and dirty t-shirts from the floor. But so what? She didn't care. There was no stress, especially since even before they'd met, her doctor had prescribed the contraceptive pill. Monthly cramps can seriously interfere with exam success, so thankfully, that was another conversation she and her mother didn't need to have.

They both loved going to the pictures. With a dull ache, she remembered the time they sang along to 'Arthur's Theme (Best That You Can Do)' while watching the credits scrolling at the end. And then they saw *Endless Love*. Giles wasn't interested in soppy romances, so instead, they cuddled and kissed in the dark. 'You look like Brooke Shields,' he said huskily, biting her ear.

'Pull the other one,' she'd giggled back, trying to focus. The film was worth her full attention because it felt very much like their love story. Tragic, intense and passionate, the Romeo-like hero was seventeen just like Giles, and his Juliet, played by Brooke Shields at fifteen was a year younger than she was.

Remembering brought shivers, despite the balmy June temperatures. Then, wrapping comforting arms around herself, any unpleasantness was shooed away by her own touch. Like the characters in the film, her love story ended tragically but for very different reasons. But what did it matter now it was over?

Yes, it was over. Now she was thinking about that chilly January evening which heralded the beginning of the end. The phone rang, and after falling over her feet to get to it, she whisked it out of her father's hand, her heart pumping, her face glowing. 'I don't think we should see each other any more,' he said, sounding deadpan and as warm as a robotic 'Speak & Spell'. And so, with those impassioned words which came like a blow to her head, their *Endless Love*, ended.

Time to focus, Millie! Focus, focus, focus! 'Displacement is a vector quantity,' she mouthed, until her train of thought was interrupted yet again, this time by the whizzing sound of her mother hoovering downstairs. The comforting white noise encapsulated home and family, along with home-made crusty baked bread, hearty roast dinners and strangely enough, Pippa dolls - a sweet symbol of her childhood. Often, after skipping home from infants' and juniors' school, she'd come home to a waiting surprise. 'Thank you, Mummy,' she'd say, wrapping grateful arms around Victoria and holding her brand new toy. Those unassuming, fun-to-collect dollies, so cheap, compared to Sindy and Barbie were more than just a surprise gift, they were sacrificial love tokens from a cash-strapped farmer's wife to a beloved daughter. She didn't know that then of course, but she knew it now.

And her mother's sacrifices didn't stop there. Not when there was a desperate need for a shoulder to cry on following the break up of an intense six-month relationship. But first, had they really broken up? She sat at home and waited, fully expecting him to call again with his tail between his legs. He'd made a mistake. He'd change his mind. But the phonecall never came. So she made a brave decision one cold, wintry Saturday afternoon. She'd ring him. Why not? Within moments of picking up the phone she heard his father's deeply official voice at the end of the line. 'Lockwood Cottage,' he said. She opened her mouth and closed it. She opened it again, but no words came out. All she could do was put the phone back down and listen to her furiously beating heart. Would they guess it was her? If she dared to call again, would his entire family think her a laughing stock? Probably.

That was when almost overnight the farmhouse became like a mortuary. She cried in her room, she cried in the kitchen, the bathroom, the barn, the dining room, the sitting room - even the cow shed. Why did he do it? What went wrong? Why her? And whose fault was it, really? After she'd worn herself out with self-blame, and wearied herself, hating him to the hilt, it crossed her mind she might be being too simplistic. She smiled, baulking at the irony of a sixteen-year-old wishing for stricter parents. But now, a year older and definitely wiser, her eyes were opened to why stricter parents might not have been so bad after all.

Mums are easy to blame aren't they, but they can also be incredibly insightful. They know how to beat you with the iron rod of tough love, at least hers did. 'Enid came out of hospital yesterday,' Victoria sighed, exhausted by her daughter's dry, lifeless eyes. 'Here, take this and go see how she's doing.' Shrugging, Millie picked up the cake tin and dragged her feet round to her former piano teacher's home. Though, dulled with pain, Enid talked more over tea and lemon curd cake than she'd ever done sitting at the piano. She spoke about her childhood in the 1920s, her mother who was 'the best-dressed flapper in town,' and her eyes sparkled with pearls of emotion, reminiscing over her brief marriage to Percy before he went to war. So, bit by bit, in the stuffy little Clover Cottage sitting room, Millie noticed herself exhaling, releasing pain and inhaling, embracing peace. Mum was so right. Spending quality time with Enid taught her a valuable lesson she'd never forget. Forget yourself, lose yourself, find yourself.

A flurry of air flapped the pages of her textbook. Then, from her sash window, she watched lambs with springy tails, leaping and exploring their environment, without wandering too far from their mothers. At some point, they'd be weaned and in just over a year, she too would leave behind everything that was safe and familiar. It would take five years to qualify as a doctor and an additional eight to become a surgeon. Rubbing her eyes she refocused, and with her chin resting in her hands and an elbow pressed up against her old wooden desk, she began scribbling notes, slowly at first, then copiously, her head bobbing back and forth. Alternating between text and exercise book, she was absorbed once more, lost once again, only this time it was in a good way. She'd had a dream for so long, and medical school, university, London and a new life beckoned. Nothing or nobody was going to stop her realising her dream, not then, not now, not ever.

Chapter 2:

'Shipbuilding' - Robert Wyatt

Thursday 18th August 1983 and it was all over. Not for the first time, Millie reached into her pocket and smiling from ear to ear, pulled out the piece of paper with her A-Level results. There it was in black and white. 'Millicent Appleby, Biology - A, Chemistry - B, Physics - C,' *St Georges' Medical School, here I come!*

Poised to fling her arms out and spin around again, she focussed instead on how to celebrate this major step towards her goals. But while placing the results paper down on the farmhouse table, she could feel those troubling and counteracting emotions again, that uncomfortable feeling in the pit of her stomach which kept coming back whenever she found herself getting too excited.

Sitting down, her sentimental eyes began to take in the simple surroundings and notice the many things that were always just there, in the background. The pestle and mortar made from acacia wood, the ceramic mixing bowl, the crystal fruit dish, which today was piled high with conference pears. She picked up a hard, green fruit, felt its smooth texture, and then bit into it. It was a crisp and sweet early variety, just ready for the eating, and apples and pears, fresh from the farm orchard, had been her go-to snack for as long as she could remember. But when she moved to London, she didn't expect to come across a fruit tree for miles, let alone one from which she could just help herself. If saying goodbye to an orchard was going to be tough, the wrenching feeling she anticipated when leaving her parents behind, didn't bear thinking about.

It wasn't just Mum and Dad she was going to miss, but also her brother Dean, and sister-in-law Amanda who lived and worked on the farm. Taking another bite of pear, she cast her mind back to Dean's words as though they were said yesterday and not three years ago. 'Mum, Dad,' he announced after he and Amanda returned from their honeymoon, 'I've now left home.' The message, 'Give us some space,' seemed loud and clear, and so that's what everyone did including Millie, who stopped herself from visiting their cottage, Stoneybrook, too frequently. She glanced down at the fruit in her hands, eaten down to its core, wondering what it was going to feel like when she could no longer walk across the farm courtyard to wile away the hours inside Stoneybrook.

At least there was one brother and sister-in-law she didn't need to say goodbye to. Not only had she already done that a long time ago, but these particular family members were already distant, and the reasons for that were not just geographical or because Stuart, her eldest brother, was stationed in the army.

She left the kitchen and walked into the dining room, the place where her mother Victoria loved to entertain. No one could have imagined that within two years of joining, Stuart would be heading into a real battle, least of all her mother, and the news came as an almighty blow. The masterpiece, 'Shipbuilding' with its sultry double bass, and sauntering jazz progressions, spoke of the irony of a conflict nobody saw coming, and although the Falklands War proved to be short, it was nonetheless brutal with heavy casualties and many deaths. Stuart, however, returned to English shores largely unscathed, and this put an end to ten suffocating weeks of family anguish.

When he telephoned after he came home, everyone, absolutely everyone, was glad and relieved to hear his voice. It wasn't a long conversation, but better short and sweet than nothing at all. And for Victoria, it was like all her birthdays had come at once. It was with his mother that he spoke the longest, telling her how brutal the conditions had been and that trench foot was still a thing. She had been so sure she'd get to see her eldest son and wife soon after that, but to this day, more than a year later, a reunion was yet to take place, and what's more, there was none in the offing.

Millie stared down at the shiny, oak dining table, a piece of farmhouse furniture which brought back so many memories.

'It must have been a relief to give Stuart a hug when it was all over,' a dinner guest had once remarked, unaware her words cut like the silver knife in her hand.

'We've spoken but we haven't seen him since he came home,' Victoria admitted, eyes downcast. Feeling emotional, Millie hadn't thought about it until now, but her mother had been through a lot in a very short time. A son going to war, a daughter falling apart after a breakup and a family scandal, which still set tongues wagging throughout the village, even today. Scandal was a funny, old-fashioned word, Millie thought to herself, but there was no better way to describe what had happened to her family three years earlier. These days, they rarely spoke about it and everyone in the family had, by and large, managed to put it behind them, and at least Victoria could take comfort from there being no real enmity or hard feelings amongst her children. Even so, when it came to the Appleby brothers and their wives, it was much easier and much simpler for them to maintain a respectable distance. Hardly surprising then, that Stuart had only managed to make one brief visit back home in the previous two years and even then, he came alone.

Chapter 3:

'Better Love Next Time' – Dr Hook

Meeting up with Ursula over a Ploughman's was a great way to say 'goodbye' before they went their separate ways. On her way to the pub, Millie thought about how different she and Ursula were, yet they always got on. Perhaps it was because Ursula wasn't like the other catty girls at school, or perhaps it was because she and Ursula had both been through nasty breakups. Whatever the reason, Millie was going to miss her friend, who'd soon be in Scotland reading classics, while she was soon to be more than three hundred miles away in London, pouring over Snell's Anatomy with a real-life, bona fide, 'Alan from *Rising Damp*' human skeleton in her room.

Walking towards the farm gates, her gaze drifted towards fields dotted with caramel-coloured hay bales. Feasting on them with her eyes, she felt a stifling hollowness inside, noticing that just beyond, trees in varying shades of green were showing just a hint of her favourite season, autumn. Would living in London mean missing out on the delights of seeing the seasons change? Would the bright lights of the big city and colourful cultural delights light up the greyest of concrete jungles? She approached the farm gates but stopped when she heard Dean's radio. She'd listened to many songs over the years because her brother loved to work with his radio playing in the background. Even thinking the words 'On The Radio' reminded her of the Donna Summer hit of that title. But listening, she realised that currently playing, was Ultravox's 'Reap the Wild Wind' and instantly, she could see the stunning Seven Sisters coastal cliffs where the music video was shot, as though they were right next to her. That hollow feeling in her chest was now back with a vengeance. *If you want to qualify as a doctor, you can't stay here.* Lightly putting a hand to her chest, she opened the farm gate and walked through, reassured that she could come home for the holidays, Christmas, Easter, summer - every single one, if she so desired.

It just so happened that her stomach was growling like a lioness the minute she arrived at the aptly named Red Lion pub, and thinking about rich butter on crusty bread, with ham, Branston pickle, brie and cheddar, all washed down with Sussex cider, increased the belly rumbles.

She reached for the door but in an instant drew her head back. Without warning there was a sudden movement behind the etched Victorian glass and her arm was wrenched when the door was yanked from the inside. *What's happening? What's going on?*

Ursula emerged and stepped outside, looking like she'd seen a ghost. 'You're here,' she smiled sheepishly, standing in the way of the pub entrance, her voice high-pitched.

'Yes, I'm here,' Millie said, looking wary and peering over Ursula's shoulder. 'Is something wrong Urs?'

Ursula gently guided her away from the door. 'Don't go inside Mills,' she whispered, lifting her eyebrows, 'Giles is in there.'

For a moment, Millie's stopped breathing, then, it started again with a vengeance, slowly at first and then faster and more furious. Giles? Here? How come? She'd heard he'd moved away to the West Country. What the heck was he doing in Magham Down?

'I wanted to warn you,' Ursula said, lightly squeezing her arm.

'Yes, of course. Thanks.' Her voice dropped, before her eyes darted nervously again towards the pub entrance, terrified he'd emerge.

'What did he say, why is he here?' Her pumping heart and baffled brain needed to know more.

'He and his mates were doing a Sussex pub crawl last night and one of them wanted to come back here for lunch.'

'Oh,' Millie said, sounding deadpan now she knew for sure his reason for being there had nothing to do with her. 'Did he say what he's doing now – where he's living and all that?' She was trying and failing to sound casual and it was obvious that Ursula wasn't buying into it.

'He's an apprentice manager at a leisure centre in Bristol,' Ursula said. 'They're sitting near the door, so we won't be able to sneak past. Let's go to town and find somewhere else.'

Shaking her head, Millie explained that her mother had the car, and by the time they arrived in Hailsham by bus, few places would still be serving lunch. She also reminded Ursula of her long drive to Edinburgh in the morning, and so she had better things to do with her time, than to wander around, looking for somewhere to eat.

'Fancy a pot noodle back at mine?' Millie asked, mustering up a smile, but it was clear from the way

Ursula was wrinkling her nose that pot noodle was no match for a Ploughman's. What to do next seemed obvious. It was time to cut their losses and call it a day.

'I'm sorry things didn't go to plan,' Millie said, her eyes still hovering above Ursula's shoulder.

'Don't be silly.' Ursula jutted out her chin towards the pub door. 'It's that git in there that should be saying sorry, not you!' After eliciting a smile from Millie's face, Ursula then suggested meeting in the Christmas holidays for turkey with all the trimmings. 'Now, *that'll* be something to look forward to, don't you think,' she smiled.

At that moment, the pub door swung open and Millie's body froze, then loosened when a middle-aged couple emerged.

'Relax,' Ursula chuckled, 'he's got a huge plate of food. He won't be leaving yet.'

With a hollow ache, Millie felt torn. Should she slink away with her tail between her legs as though *she* were the one in the wrong, or should she face Giles head-on and show him who's boss? Shouldn't he know he hadn't destroyed her and that she was doing well without him? He really ought to know that she didn't miss him at all, and lifting her chin with 'couldn't care less' defiance, she was almost on the verge of staying. But, feeling Ursula's hand on her arm coaxing her to leave, her reluctant feet began to shuffle towards the bus stop. Ursula needed to get back to Eastbourne, and she needed to listen to sense.

'You look stressed,' Ursula said. 'Go home. The bus'll be here any moment and I'd feel terrible if he catches you here.'

Ursula was right again. Millie knew that seeing Giles was probably not a good idea, but if she did, it'd better be on her terms. She could just about cope with strolling past him in the pub, wearing a big smile and with her head held high. But the thought of him catching her off guard, standing at the bus stop or wandering around the village looking sad and miserable - now *that* was something she really wouldn't want. She'd hate it. Really, really hate it. So, after saying goodbye, and giving Ursula a hug, it was time to make herself scarce and head for home.

'Ursula, wait.' She turned back swiftly, feeling disappointed in herself. What she was about to ask was bound to be a mistake, but she had to, she just had to.

'Did...' she paused, 'did he ask for me?' A car drove by and her darting eyes watched it go past. Focussing on it, rather than on Ursula, helped relieve some of her tension. But the empty silence and the delayed response spoke to her fears, telling her everything she needed to know.

'He didn't ask for you, no,' Ursula looked up with sympathetic eyes, 'but I bet he would have done if we'd got the chance to talk more and...'

'We will keep in touch, won't we?' Millie interrupted, having heard enough and feeling numb.

'Of course,' Ursula frowned, surprised by the question. 'Friends forever, remember.'

'Friends forever,' Millie repeated, seeing the bus approach, and after it pulled up with its diesel engine choking out fumes, she lifted a hand to wave, and watched Ursula pay the driver and find a seat.

'Go now!' Ursula mouthed, her forehead leaning up against the glass, and with the bus pulling off with a splutter, she was soon gone.

Now alone, Millie walked along the country road, once again coming face to face with the Red Lion's creamy yellow walls and red tiles. The doors flew open but she didn't jump. She didn't even flinch. It wasn't Giles, but noticing her jaw clench and her body temperature rise, she felt ready for him. She walked on, resisting the urge to go back to shoot him a filthy look, or even better, confront him and show him up in front of his friends. She wanted to tell them what he was really like by slamming her fist on the table and letting it all out. She'd scream with fury, then she'd call him all the names she could think up, leaving him and them in no doubt whatsoever, what a complete and utter jerk he was. But, while all these fantasies swirled around in her head, the distance between her and the pub kept growing, and as it grew, her resolve to carry out retribution reduced. But perhaps the biggest reason not to go back was her self-awareness. Something inside was telling her something she'd rather not hear. If she were to see his face again, if she heard that spirited laugh, or saw his melting smile, then all plans for revenge might simply melt away, evaporate, disintegrate and turn to dust.

She reached home exhausted and hungry and walked to the front door with memories of the heady days of their romance. She used to sing along to 'Is That Love' by Squeeze, convinced she knew the answer. It *was* love, she was so sure at the time, and now with tears prickling her eyes, she bit down on her pain, determined not to cry. It was then, just when she needed it, she had an epiphany. Rather than the same old boring, been there-done that, self-pity, why not congratulate herself instead? Wasn't what happened just now exactly what she needed to prove to herself she was strong? She had literally just walked away from Giles, and as she headed over to the kitchen to hunt down that dreaded pot noodle, she knew it was time to leave the past behind and embrace tomorrow with a new-found confidence.

Chapter 4:

'Drowning in Berlin' - The Mobiles

A woman sits alone. In her hand is a spray bottle and by her feet a black bucket. Brush, broom, mop, bin, all close at hand. She is sitting on a plastic chair at the centre of a large room, surrounded by space, swallowed by it. Eager for her bed, but there is nowhere to rest. Her day is nearly done, and she'll soon be home.

She rises to her feet and touches her back. It aches but she can almost smile, because in the morning she'll see her children and right now, they're in safe hands. Squeezing out a rag, she begins her final wipe down, spurred on by the memories of one sunny June morning, fourteen years ago.

'What a beautiful baby girl,' an old lady smiled. 'Enjoy every moment, it goes too soon. What's her name?'

'Doretta,' the woman replied. She moved the pram in her hand, and the wheels rolled back and forth, lulling her little one to sleep.

'Doretta,' the old woman repeated, the friendliness in her eyes growing into tenderness. 'How amazing.' Then sounding wistful, her voice drifted away. 'That was my mother's name and I've never met another.' She stared at the woman. 'Do you know what Doretta means?'

'No.' The woman shook her head.

'Gift from God,' the old woman smiled. 'Isn't that beautiful? Just like she is.'

Gift from God. The woman looked at her sleeping baby. She'd named her after Doretta Morrow, a 1950s actress and singer, but until that moment, she'd had no idea what the name Doretta meant.

Back in the here and now, she realises that there really is no better name for her eldest child. Even after all this time she thinks to herself, that if that old lady is still living and if she were ever to meet her again, she'd tell her how appropriate the name turned out to be.

A sinking feeling invades her, now she is reminded of how much she owes to her daughter. Doretta always tucks the little ones into bed and reads them a bedtime story. She loves her brothers and sisters. Every single one of them. Even if the woman tried but failed to care for them all.

Stepping outside the community hall, she locks the heavy door behind her. Aching inside, wishing, wanting, she steps out into the darkness and feels the cool air on her face. Heading back to her home on the eleventh floor, she knows that she loves *all* her children, no matter what it looks like from the outside. She did all she could with what she had, and more, and she was always able to put food on the table.

She passes the bakery, pauses at the very spot where she'd met that old lady and remembers those parting words.

'Enjoy motherhood while you can.' The old lady smiled. 'Life is very short.'

'Thank you, I'll try,' the woman said, then asked the old lady for *her* name.

'I'm Maud, dear. And what's yours?'

Holding up a hand to wave goodbye, the woman smiled. Caring for a baby was exhausting, but she was happy. The sadness, the pain, the fears, were all yet to come. 'My name,' she said, glancing at her rosy-cheeked child, 'is Grace.'

Chapter 5:

'Change' - Tears For Fears

Kneeling on her bed, Millie shuffled across to her window and looked outside at the disheartening view. She thought she'd be used to the dull grey concrete, heavy red brick, and towering walls by now, but she wasn't. Her eyes, tired from studying, were again drawn to a wild cherry tree outside the halls of residence. Exhaling, she relaxed. This sapling was like a green oasis in a desert, providing her with endless visions of springtime - pearl-white blossom in delicate clusters amidst lime green leaves, and a blackbird perched within, its bright yellow beak belting out a song.

Outside her room, the stairs were hard and cold and the noise of students roaming around and slamming doors echoed through the building. But university was where it was at if you wanted a 'Piece of the Action' and she'd looked forward to it for so long. The grey-white walls in her prison-sized room couldn't dampen her spirits. Neither could the already full-on workload, or a hint of homesickness, or a disappointing Freshers Ball, which had taken place in a massive marquee where tuxedo-wearing men and women in flouncy dresses, drank, smoked and tried to hide their newbie nerves.

Her first weeks had great moments too. For a laugh, she'd raised her fist and shouted 'Power to the People,' *Citizen Smith* style outside Tooting Broadway station, before venturing inside Tooting market to explore and be dazzled by many international delights. She discovered breadfruit, plantains and fu fu flour, listened to the sound of chop suey sizzling in a wok, felt silky sari material between her fingers, and admired bright Sikh turbans. It was as if she'd won a round-the-world trip, and completed it in one afternoon.

Making her way through, reggae music caught her attention. She headed to the stall and there, a Rastafarian man with a knitted hat, heavy with dreadlocks told her the song was called 'Country Living' by the Mighty Diamonds. The soft melody and mellow beat took her away to distant shores, while the lyrics spoke of a man's love for a woman and his desire to return home to fresh, country air. She left the market munching on sweet baklava and reflecting on how the song spoke to her own longings for the Sussex home she'd left behind.

Back in her box room, she lay on her bed and tried to relax. Life was easier now she'd made a friend, Wahida who lived in the same halls. 'Call me Wah,' she said, as in the Mighty Wah who sang 'The Story Of The Blues'. It was a good thing Millie knew the song, because as she was soon to discover, Wahida lived and breathed certain types of music, and didn't suffer music ignoramuses gladly.

When Millie first entered the kitchen and saw the funky-looking girl with bobbed raven hair, dressed head to toe in black, she was slightly taken aback when she opened her mouth. 'I don't care how cute he is,' she said, with a Midlands twang, 'this is the last time I clear up after him.'

Initially confused, Millie realised she was talking about the guy who'd just left the room, and she watched the girl shake her head, pick up a cardboard Vesta curry packet and with a look of disgust, extend her arm and drop it into a bin. 'But then again,' she said, brushing away something invisible from her hands, 'I probably *will* end up cleaning up after him again because I *hate* mess. I'm Wahida by the way.'

The smell of instant curry was a far cry from the delicious aroma coming from Wahida's saucepan, and during the weeks that followed, enjoyable evening chats over dinner became a regular thing. Not much irked Millie about her new friend, but there was one thing that slowly began to grate. Despite coming across as feisty and cool, Wahida had a problem and it wasn't just her obsession with dirt. Her biggest obsession by far was with Jonas, a fellow student, who at first was affectionately nicknamed 'Goth Guy' by the two girls.

'Get a load of him!' Wahida said, staring shamelessly the first time Millie saw him. 'Now he's someone I could *really* do business with.'

Standing outside the lecture hall, Millie did as requested but had to bite her tongue. The guy in question was wearing a heavy black coat and was smiling and chatting to other students. Nothing exceptional about that. More unusual was his mid-length, dyed, jet-black hair, which fell like rat tails around his pale white skin. And if that wasn't enough to make him stand out, there was one final defining feature. He was wearing make-up. Thick black eyeliner, blusher-enhanced cheeks, and dark purple lips made him quite the unorthodox medical student and Millie stood, watching discretely, trying to work out how she'd managed to miss him up until then. Looking around, she could see that other students seemed nonplussed, but when she overheard one guy mumble to another, 'What the hell's going on there?' she realised she wasn't alone in finding him atypical.

'He's something else,' Wahida said when the time came to take their seats. 'I bet he's a goth.'

'I thought goths only wore black,' Millie said, before commenting on a bright tie-dye t-shirt, visible under his coat.

'True,' Wahida said, correcting herself. 'He's a New Romantic then.'

Again, Millie hesitated. It was almost 1984. Were New Romantics even still a thing? Had Wahida considered the possibility that Jonas wore make-up for an altogether different reason? One that might leave her out in the cold?

Shaking her head, Wahida had a confident smile. 'I have zero worries on that front,' she said, 'and anyway, make-up's dead sexy on a guy. Take Adam Ant, for example. I mean, wouldn't you?'

Shrugging, Millie listened to Wahida espouse the benefits of dating guys in touch with their feminine side. 'But what about your parents?' she asked.

'What about them?'

'D'you think they'd like him?'

Pulling out A4 paper from her satchel, Wahida placed it in front of her. 'My parents don't know I've dated English guys before and Mum would go ballistic. But she can't talk. She's a Muslim and my dad's a Hindu!' Before Millie had the chance to say she was thinking more on the lines of his unconventional dress sense than race or religion, Wahida had a question for her.

'Is *he* your type?' Wahida's eyes led her to a chunky guy with a shaven head sitting to the right.

'He looks like Buster Bloodvessel from Bad Manners!' Millie looked around, hoping no one had noticed her and Wahida laughing at this guy, but it was true. He really would look right at home dancing to 'Lip Up Fatty' on Top of the Pops. Lowering her head and still trying to hide her laughter, she noticed another male student looking at her, and he was smiling. Her heart fluttered just a little, because this was the third, maybe even fourth time she'd noticed him doing the same thing, and this time, she felt a nervous tingling inside. Had she managed to chalk up a male admirer so early in the game? If she had, was that really what she wanted? Wasn't medical school going to be challenging enough?

'Boys can seriously mess with your head.' Her mother's words came ringing back. But she wasn't sixteen any more, and if ever there was a time she ought to be able to handle a man in her life, surely it was now?

Chapter 6:

'I'm a Wonderful Thing, Baby' - Kid Creole and the Coconuts

'Yay, only one day 'til the weekend!' Tilting her head back, Millie rubbed her stiff neck.

'Thank goodness,' Wahida said, taking a deep breath, 'but first, we have to get through this.'

Separating into different groups, Millie and Wahida walked into the large clinical space and were instantly hit with a sickly pickle-like smell. It was formaldehyde, and it was used to preserve dead bodies. The dreaded human dissection day had arrived.

Swallowing hard, Millie composed herself. She was sure this would be a cinch because she wasn't squeamish. Nor was she a germaphobe like Wahida. She looked across to another group on the other side of the room and spotted her friend looking as cool as a cucumber. How Wahida always managed to look so unfazed was anyone's guess.

The moment arrived for Millie's tutor to unveil the corpse and when Dr Grantham pulled back the sheet she felt her heart pounding. Nevertheless, instead of looking away, she kept her eyes fixed on the departed man. Not too old, but not young either, his skin tone as grey as a tomb. Someone had remarked earlier, that by the end of the year, all that would remain would be decomposing body parts in a bucket for burial and Millie tried to steady her churning stomach in a room where the atmosphere felt stifling. To cool down she imagined walking through fresh fallen snow on the hills. Then she visualised the glow of a deep red sunset and felt gentle waves lapping her bare feet at the seashore while she unwrapped Cadbury's Country Style chocolate. Mentally ready to take a bite, she glanced down at the body again and immediately, all thoughts of food evaporated into thin air.

After overhearing someone complaining that Dr Grantham needed to get a move on and ignore an annoying student who kept asking questions, she listened to another student talking about phoning home after the session to tell their folks what dissection was like. The words 'phone home' reminded Millie of *E.T.*, the tearjerker which famously made grown men cry. Not Millie though. *She* didn't cry. Aliens weren't real, but when it came to keeping her composure when watching heart-rending true stories, that was a different ballgame altogether.

She remembered how she'd sobbed for hours after *The Elephant Man*. Life was harsh for this dignified, disfigured man living in Victorian London, but her tears were tempered by hope. During his short life, Joseph Merrick found comfort in his Christian faith. And he wasn't the only one. *The Hiding Place*, Corrie Ten Boom's harrowing holocaust account was another devastating story filled with hope. And to think she almost didn't read it, after Anne Frank's *The Diary of a Young Girl* had previously left her feeling low.

She looked down again at the dead body, curious about *his* life story. Had he had a happy life and did anyone miss him? Did he die fulfilled, or with regrets? A wave of sadness washed over her because she knew she'd never know.

Without warning, the sound of sobbing cut through her thoughts. Her head swung sharply, just in time to see another female student in tears, running out of the room, gripping her mouth. The girl's extreme but delayed reaction didn't surprise her because if it wasn't for her own efforts to control her thoughts, she too might find it all too much.

'Oh dear, there's always one!' Dr Grantham smirked, finally ready to begin. He formed his hands into a steeple. 'Let's get on shall we?' he smiled, rubbing his hands gleefully. She braced herself. *This is going okay, it's going to be absolutely fine.*

With the tutor's expert guidance, students began to take turns, dissecting arms and overcoming their 'this is the first dead body I've ever seen' trepidations. Millie was first in line, and getting stuck in was the tonic needed to melt away all remnants of anxiety. She was so focused, so engrossed in veins and sinews, she didn't notice when the tall, well-dressed chap slipped into her group. However, when she looked up and saw him, her up-until-then dexterous hands fell limp. *He* was the one who had been forever catching her eye, and right now for some reason, he was standing next to her.

'Not too distressing, I take it?' he asked, watching her every move.

'No, not at all.' Haphazardly, she prodded with the scalpel, then glanced up again. His eyes, framed by thick, dark, eyebrows were attentive. He seemed to tower over her. Perhaps it was because he was standing so close, or maybe it was because she was crouching down. Feeling uneasy she tried to focus and when she looked up again, she noticed his glossy black hair shimmering in the artificial light.

'Can I help?' he asked. He sounded nervous, despite looking suave and relaxed.

'Are you sure?' Her body tensed with conflicted feelings. She hadn't asked for his interference after all. But then, noticing her heart beating a little faster, memories of Giles came flooding back and her excitement grew. She was loath to admit it and it was a sad fact, but she was a sucker for a confident man.

He nodded crisply. It was then she noticed a flush of red around his face and neck. Maybe he was more nervous than she appreciated. She realised it must have taken courage for him to come over and offer to help and if there was any type of man she liked even more than a confident one, it was a sensitive guy. Flicking away unruly strands of hair, she felt flustered and wondered what to do. St George's wasn't the place to lose her head or lose her independence, but against her better judgement, she placed the scalpel in his hand. She noticed others in the group were watching, no doubt questioning why he was there. Then, she watched him skilfully lift a flap of skin, and separate the underlying tissues with the sharp implement.

'You'll find it easier to spot the veins under there,' he said sounding more assured. He handed the scalpel back. 'I'm Zane by the way. See you at the canteen later, maybe.'

Mindlessly passing over the scalpel to a waiting student, Millie wore an ambivalent smile as she watched him walk away. His 'see you maybe,' was polite but clear. 'Please be there,' would have been more accurate.

He didn't even ask her name, but she could tell… he already knew.

'I'm guessing you've heard of Professor Bridges,' another student said quietly.

Millie shook her head.

The girl student, who'd been watching the whole thing, was keen to tell her that Zane's father was an eminent cardiothoracic surgeon at St Barts hospital. His mother was also a doctor, a successful paediatrician. The girl said she reckoned that if anyone was going to come top of the class when exams rolled around, it would be Zane.

'Nice guy,' she said, chewing on gum. 'A bit up himself, but still, pretty decent if you ask me.'

Millie *hadn't* asked, but she was grateful for the information nonetheless. When the student began to talk to someone else, Wahida strode over and took her place.

'Yours looks neater than ours,' Wahida said non-emotively, looking down at the body. 'Anyway, can't stay long, but I wanted to get the low down.' She glanced intentionally across the room at Zane.

Millie shrugged, happy but conflicted, but now wasn't the time to fill her friend in, because Dr Grantham was approaching. Separating, she and Wahida began to look busy, but on the inside, she was thinking about Zane. She briefly watched him from a distance, slick, composed and slightly detached from others in his group. It was then she realised she wasn't instantly attracted, but that was okay. She'd fallen too fast and too hard in the past, and if there was going to be any hope of a relationship staying the course in a place like this, it needed to start slowly. She looked down at the cadaver, now with open incisions, somehow much less frightening. But she was still feeling daunted because there was possibly something scarier on the horizon. Nothing would stop her from achieving her goals, she wouldn't let it. But how could she face a guy, any guy, day in, day out, for the next five years, if anything were to go wrong?

Chapter 7:

'Food for Thought' – UB40

Term was almost over, and Millie sat in nearby Wandle Park thinking how well she'd managed her first months of independent living. Still, she was now more than ready to go back to Sussex for the Christmas break. Being away from home hadn't turned out to be nearly as painful as she thought it'd be, but during the last few days, she had become desperate for her mum's cooking. There were only so many varieties of toast toppings you could rotate - marmite, baked beans, cheese, sardines and so on, before boredom set in.

Wandle Park, her green oasis, was just minutes away from her halls of residence. She sat on a bench, crisp autumn leaves crackling beneath her feet, thinking how much a heart-to-heart with those closest to her was well overdue. There was so much she'd saved up to say. The wall-mounted telephone in the halls of residence was on the ground floor in an open spot where everyone could overhear your conversations. There was also no chair beside it, so you were forced to stand, and if this was all a deliberate ploy to stop students hogging the line, it certainly worked.

Watching her breath condense in the fresh, autumn air, she felt energized at the thought of a good chin wag with her mother, sister-in-law Amanda, and old schoolmate Ursula. Very soon, In her mind, the conversation with her mother began to play out.

'Remember I told you about Zane, the posh guy who went to Eton, and whose dad's a consultant at Bart's and mother's a paediatrician? Well, he's keen, but I don't know how I feel. He wants to take me out to dinner and the theatre. Fiddler on The Roof is on at the Apollo and you know how much I love the film, so I'm tempted, but I've decided to hold off, at least for now. I told him I've just come out of a serious relationship and need a bit more time. It's a lame excuse I know, but I had to say something. The truth is, I can't help thinking it'd make things so much easier if he were at another university, or at least another department or year group - just in case things don't work out if you see what I mean.

He's a bit flash, or at least he is when he splashes the cash. I don't think he means to show off, but some people can't stand him because of it. Like Jonas, the Northern Irish Goth guy who Wahida literally drools over (well, perhaps not literally!). By the way, when Wahida finally got talking to her Goth Guy, they really clicked because they're into the same music. I'm keeping my fingers crossed for Wah because she's so keen but I don't know how Jonas feels. Still, I'm hoping it's only a matter of time before they're coupled up. She says his accent's to die for, and it's 'Jonas this, Jonas that,' every evening. If only she'd shut up! But I have to admit, it's also quite sweet. I don't know how she manages to rave about him but still keep her poker face when he's around. Boy, I wish I had her composure!

Zane's not keen on Jonas. He thinks men and make-up don't go together, and he loves Thatcher, who Jonas hates, so they argue about politics constantly. Me and Wahida just keep out of it, and anyway, it's boring. It's funny because Zane likes me, and Wahida's obviously crazy about Jonas, so because me and Wahida are together a lot, all four of us end up hanging out at the canteen most days even though the men can't stand each other. It's hilarious!

Zane's quite a serious guy to be fair. The other day he said he'd like me to meet his Dad. I'd love to, I mean his dad's an inspiration and it would be great to pick his brains. Zane's been getting work experience with his dad in the operating theatre since he was seventeen, so he already knows loads about anatomy and human dissection. Meeting his Dad is a big step though, and like I said, I'm still not sure about how I feel about Zane.

Something else worries me. Zane said he always has to make an appointment in advance to see his Dad. Like really? His own father? He said it like it was the most normal thing in the world. I get that his Dad's an eminent consultant, but that's still pretty weird don't you think? And sad. But Zane doesn't seem bothered. He went to boarding school when he was six and said it toughened him up. He said he didn't see his parents for weeks on end and got used to it. No doubt his mum and dad worked hard to get where they are today, and I'd be lying if I said after spending years qualifying as a surgeon I'd want to stay home with the kids like you did Mum, but sending my little'un away like that and for so long? No way. I just couldn't do it. Zane also said something about me meeting his Mum but at the moment seems more keen on introducing me to his illustrious Dad. Apparently, his Mum also works long hours and I wonder if he has to make an appointment to see her as well.

Some people say Zane's aristocratic airs are an affectation and that he does things for attention. I'm not sure that's true. He holds the door open for me and stuff like that, and yes, sometimes it's OTT, but it's also nice to know chivalry isn't completely dead. The other day he stepped aside and opened a door for a girl. Then he twirled his hand to invite her to walk through, like some sort of Musketeer or Cavalier. A couple of guys laughed, and I don't think Amy - the girl - was impressed. I feel bad for him because now they've started calling him Zane the Insane, and it reminds me of when Clarissa started the 'bitch with an itch' thing when I got hives in PE. I hate bullying, as you know. Clarissa and a few other girls got so nasty after I started going out with Giles and I thought I coped well at the time, but some of the things they said still hurt.

Sometimes though, I have to admit, Zane doesn't do himself any favours. Last week, for instance, he said he'd rather jump off a cliff than be a GP. It was in the common room, and no one, I mean no one laughed. Sure, becoming, say, a neurosurgeon or cardiologist is a big achievement, but being a family doctor isn't exactly a fail is it? Horses for courses, that's what I say, and if Zane was a horse, he'd be a thoroughbred!

One thing no one can accuse him of is being mean. I actually think some people hang around him because he buys them lunch and stuff like that. The other day, two young lads were doing 'penny for the guy' in the street, and Zane gave each of them a pound coin. You should have seen their little faces light up! I don't think they'd seen a pound coin, ever, despite it being in circulation for - what - I reckon it must be about six months now.

It's awful to think anyone might use Zane. I'd never do that. But maybe I'm stringing him along because I don't want to burn my bridges, even though I'm pretty sure he's not for me. That sounds bad, but honestly, for now, I just want us to be friends and surely, that's not a bad thing. I'd hate to hurt him - ever. I know how horrible that feels.

With the one-sided conversation in her head now over, she felt a light breeze across her face. She hadn't realised there was so much to say about Zane, but still, she mustn't neglect telling family and friends what else was going on in her life. How tough studying was, for instance, or how she almost got a Lady Di haircut after getting bored with her barnet. 'Wahida told me to go for the wild and funky Bananarama look instead,' she'd say, 'but after she said how much back-combing and hairspray was involved, I just couldn't be bothered with any of it.'

Before returning to her room, there was one final place to go. She'd already told everyone at home how excited she was to discover the River Wandle. Nestled within the urban sprawl, it was her little haven and her escape from the daily rigours of academic life. It was where the sight and sound of rushing water rejuvenated her soul.

Taking an easy breath, she stood up to make her way over to her favourite spot in all of South London. But when it came to fully recharging her physical and emotional batteries, there was no better place than home - her real home. And she simply couldn't wait to be back there for Christmas.

Chapter 8:

'All Those Years Ago' - George Harrison

Enid's granddaughter Lauren sat on the sofa inside Clover Cottage and yawned, before taking a swig of Earl Grey tea and mindlessly opening the Kays catalogue on a nearby coffee table. While flicking through its pages, it suddenly dawned on her how unusual she was. Most folk would pack a paperback for a holiday or an overnight stay. Not her. She preferred to lug heavy mail-order catalogues around instead. But there was nothing wrong with being unusual, and she had never been into words. Pictures were her thing, and these pictures were like having a department store at her fingertips.

Halfway through the pages, she came across something and her heart raced. Shiny, patent red court shoes. How come she hadn't seen *them* before? Should she? Shouldn't she? She already had a similar pair. But these were much nicer.

Sinking back into the sofa, she yawned again and touched her head. The drive to and from Northampton was exhausting and had left her with a headache, so maybe she ought to take the train next time. But how many more 'next times' were there going to be? She stared at the shoes and enjoyed another rush of endorphins. That was it, she'd made her decision. She deserved it and was going to order them the minute she got back home.

It wasn't easy always being the one to drop everything to drive for miles, especially when owning an antique shop and bringing up two kids who ran her ragged. Thank God for her husband. What would she do without him? They'd had their ups and downs, but throughout their ten years of marriage, he'd kept her sane, and what's more, he was fully on board with what she was doing for Gran, one hundred per cent.

She stood and reached over for a piece of paper sitting on the top of the piano. 'Vertical compression fracture,' the handwritten note said. The doctor had later explained it meant a crushed bone in the spine. The news came as a blow. Ever since Gran broke her hip she'd been on medication for osteoporosis, so everyone thought the condition was being managed well. No one knew how or when this new fracture had occurred, and no one could quite fathom how she'd managed to carry on like normal, teaching piano and doing other everyday things.

Lauren's jaw tightened. Her Gran was being infuriatingly stubborn when she said things like, 'I'm not having strangers in my home.' It was high time they put their foot down. She didn't want home help and maybe that was fair enough, but Gran needed support, whether she liked it or not. But who? Everyone lived too far away, and as much as Lauren wanted to, she just couldn't do any more. She had a business to run and a family to look after and because Gran had stupidly turned down the invitation to move in with her, another solution was desperately needed.

Lauren was no stranger to finding solutions. She'd learned early how to take responsibility. Before checking on Enid, she opened her grandmother's display cabinet and took out a gold-framed photograph. It was one of her and Ben as children and she looked at it wistfully. She was wearing shiny brown t-bar shoes and had a big red ribbon in her hair. He was in shorts with thick, long grey school socks. Both smiled sweetly and although *he* didn't smile nearly as much these days, he was still sweet. He was still her baby brother Ben. Lauren shook her head and smiled. Twenty-four was hardly a baby, but when her mind drifted back to the old days, he was still that little boy. She remembered pulling him by the hand, telling him to stop being naughty over and over again. She struggled to recall whether he was screaming because he didn't want to go to school or because he didn't want to go home. Either way, he was kicking up a stink - again.

Years later, when she was twelve, Ben went missing. She remembered her mother panicking, racing around the nearby streets frantically looking for him. Lauren felt like her mother's saviour when she presented a mud-caked Ben to her after finding him hours later, playing alone on disused railway land. She never forgot the look in her mother's eyes that day she brought him home. 'Thank you Lauren babsy,' she'd said, too weak, too exhausted to smile. Her mother, notably weaker since the day Dad left, had struggled to leave the house for many years.

Lauren checked her reflection in the mantlepiece mirror. Her straight, dark hair was still scraped back into a tight bun and nothing, not even a single hair was out of place. Her tense shoulders relaxed, just a little, and smoothing down her plaid skirt and adjusting her pearl choker, she reflected on how the customers in the antique shop expected class.

Heading towards the narrow cottage stairs, she wondered if Gran was finally awake. Still, it was better to be dosed up with morphine and sleep for hours than be doubled up in pain. Touching the bannister, she mounted a step, but before going further, she noticed a shadow at the front door. Then the doorbell rang.

She opened the door to see a young woman with a pleasant smile on the doorstep.

'I'm sorry, but are you a pupil?' Lauren asked, her voice apologetic. 'I thought I'd cancelled all lessons for the week.'

The girl's smile dissipated. 'Cancelled?' she shook her head. 'Oh, no, I used to be a pupil, but I'm not any more. I've come to see Mrs Griffiths.' She paused and raised her eyebrows. 'Is she okay?'

Lauren's sparkling blue eyes dulled. 'She might be sleeping, although I'm hoping she's awake by now, so feel free to come in... um, you are...?'

'Millie,' she said, gently closing the front door behind her. 'I'm Millie Appleby from Hillbrook Farm.'

Chapter 9:

'Party Party' - Elvis Costello

Millie's fingers glided adroitly across the piano keys, her spirits lifting with every ascending note. She hadn't realised until now quite how much she'd missed playing the piano. When at school she had found it hard to find time to practise, so quickly gave up lessons, but these days playing felt like a luxury, along with all the other comforts of home. Seeing her old teacher Enid the other day, looking so frail after her recent fracture, was both sad and sobering. But at least she'd been in good spirits, no doubt because she had her granddaughter Lauren there to help her. It was great to meet Lauren, and although she'd seemed harried at the time, she also came across as caring and warm.

With her strength renewed and her mind rejuvenated, Millie was ready to go back to university to start the new term. She was looking forward to seeing Wahida again. How was she feeling after what happened at the end-of-term Christmas party? Was she *really* as nonplussed as she had seemed when they'd said goodbye, before heading their separate ways?

Reaching up to the sheet music balanced on the music rack, she turned the page, convinced Wahida was fine. She always managed to keep her head. How she had handled things that night Jonas invited them both to a friend's Christmas do, was proof of that.

Millie thought back to that day when she'd been so sure it was going to be Wahida's night, judging by how she and Jonas had seemed closer than ever that afternoon. They'd spent ages in the common room chatting about New Order, Echo and the Bunnymen and other favourite bands. They concluded that Orange Juice's 'Rip It Up' was fantastic but also very mainstream; they both thought The Icicle Works' new single, 'Love is A Wonderful Colour' was brilliant; and they debated who was the most innovative and under-rated, The Associates or Visage. And so it went on. Millie listened, munching on a wagon wheel, feeling warm inside. How sweet that they both liked a song about love! This might go somewhere tonight, she thought, thinking ahead to the party.

Back in the here and now, Millie closed the piano keyboard lid and headed for the kitchen. Her mother was out, and had left some cake she'd baked the previous evening from homegrown pumpkins. Millie's mouth watered, recalling the smell of spice filling the kitchen, the taste of juicy sultanas and the softness of cake, fresh out of the oven. She was ready for another slice.

Sitting by the kitchen table, she nibbled on a piece and while sipping from a glass of milk, her mind went back to the moment she and Wahida arrived at the three-storey student townhouse. They had turned up late, after getting the address muddled up, and when they did eventually arrive, 'Christmas Wrapping' by the Waitresses lifted the atmosphere in an otherwise dim, smoky room. The house was packed with people. Some were sitting, most were chatting, many were drinking and a handful of brave individuals danced.

Wahida scanned the room, looking for Jonas. Neither she nor Millie expected to see Zane as he hadn't been invited. After chatting with other students and moving to different floors, the two lost each other in the crowd, and by the time they met again, they'd both found Jonas.

Munching on some more cake, Millie remembered how, after they'd separated, she'd spotted a room in front of her with the door slightly ajar, darker and quieter than the rest of the house. She walked in, and it didn't take her long to realise this was the "smooching" room where the music wasn't nearly as loud, but in dark corners, couples were making their own "sweet music" together. Looking around in all directions, she drew back in surprise. *Flippin 'eck, these people ought to get a room.* Then, turning towards the door she did a double take. She caught sight of something, or rather someone, out of the corner of her eye.

The black hair, pale skin and fashionable dress sense were unmistakably Jonas, but when a person's face is so moulded to another's and the two are writhing and pawing at each other, it takes time to recognize someone. She stood for a moment, trying not to stare.

Then, quite unexpectedly, Jonas separated from the clinch. He'd spotted her.

'Millie,' he smiled, looking intoxicated, although not from alcohol. 'You made it!' He took a swig from the drink in front of him.

'We just got here.' Clearing her throat, Millie looked around, hoping *not* to see Wahida and thankfully, there was no sign of her.

'This is…' Jonas turned to the woman he'd been snogging and snapping his fingers closed his eyes, 'this is… uh, um…'

My goodness, he can't even remember her name!

Helping him out, the girl stepped in to introduce herself, then, with a blank expression, she pulled out what must have been a battery-operated mirror because it lit up when she flicked it open. While watching her top up vibrant pink lipstick, Millie couldn't help thinking she didn't look like Jonas' type. Not like Wah did. This girl was certainly no goth.

'Is Wahida here?' Jonas asked. Millie nodded. 'Good,' he smiled, 'because I can't wait to tell her I've outsmarted her, *yet* again.'

Millie raised her eyebrows and tried to work out exactly what he meant. Meanwhile, his lady friend pulled out the brush from a tube of black mascara and proceeded to paint her lashes.

'Wah couldn't name a single song with lyrics about a medical condition,' Jonas explained. 'Tut tut. That just won't do when she claims to be a medical student who's also into music.' Millie listened to Jonas' lively Northern Irish accent say the word 'maa - dicle' and the way his 'do' sounded so much like 'dye,' was also cute.

'Well, I've got a song for her,' Jonas grinned. "Water on Glass' - Kim Wilde.'

Having finished applying her make-up, the woman snapped her handbag shut, and although unsure if it was because of what Jonas had just said, Millie noticed that with her tousled, highlighted hair and pleasant pout, his companion looked a bit like Kim Wilde herself.

'It's about tinnitus,' Jonas added, still focused on the song. 'Can you hear my head full of sounds, and all that,' he said, paraphrasing the lyrics.

That was all very interesting, but Millie had other things on her mind. The only sound ringing in *her* head right now, was Wahida's voice saying how wonderful Jonas was, and the only thing in her mind's eye, was Wah's face when she was hit with the bad news. But little did she know she wasn't going to have to say a word, because not long after leaving Jonas and his new friend behind, she found Wahida sitting on the stairs, sipping from a can of Lilt, and in an instant, she could tell she already knew.

Relieved not to have to break the news, Millie's shoulders eased, but she needed to say something.

'I've just seen Jonas,' she began tentatively.

'Me too,' Wahida said, sounding surprisingly relaxed.

Millie blinked. 'Did you speak to him?'

'No, he didn't see me.'

Millie opened her mouth and then paused. 'I'm sorry,' was all she could think of to say. Then, something happened next that she didn't quite expect. An odd smile began to spread across Wahida's face.

'Look,' Wahida said, putting down her drink, her voice artificially bright, 'haven't you ever got off with anyone at a party before?'

'What, me – personally? No, actually,' Millie said, 'but...'

'Well *I* have,' Wahida interrupted, 'and it *really* isn't a big deal.' Still smiling, she turned away and reached for her drink.

Not a big deal? Millie's jaw dropped. *It would be for me!* She decided *not* to ask Wahida how come she was so certain this wasn't his new girlfriend, and how she was so sure it was just a casual encounter. Later, when Jonas and his new acquaintance hardly exchanged two words, and he and Wahida re-engaged in music trivia banter as though nothing had happened, Millie began to think perhaps Wahida was right. She also doubted herself, thinking that maybe, just maybe, *she w*as the weird one. Perhaps *she* ought to loosen up a bit and, assuming Wahida wasn't covering up her true feelings, Millie envied her a little. If only she could be more relaxed like her friend, then she might not get so easily tossed about and buffeted by her emotions.

They left the party in the early hours under a wintry night sky, and having watched Wahida for a while, still obviously crazy about Jonas, still holding on and hoping, despite what had happened, Millie realised she could never be like that, and neither did she want to be. The Sheena Easton song 'One Man Woman' described her to a tee, and one day, she hoped to fall in love with a one-woman man. Surely that wasn't too much to ask?

Chapter 10:

'January February' - Barbara Dickson

A woman sits by the telephone, with deep, dark circles around her eyes. She picks up the phone. She puts it down again. 'I can't,' she mouths. 'I just can't'. Did she even need to do this? After all, she was still managing fine. She'd got through another Christmas and had bought *all* her children something they'd really wanted. Saving up for a special gift all year was *her* way of showing love. It was *her* way of saying how much she wanted them *all* to be together one day. Christmas was over and because of her love for the festive season, she believes she doesn't have a problem with winter. But in recent years, January and February have felt like her coldest, darkest months. The time of year she feels most lonely, when the entire world feels bleak.

Taking a deep breath she puts a finger to the dial. She watches it spin. Zero. One. Seven... the clicking sounds add to her sense of unease. Soon, she hears ringing and her muscles twitch.

Click. She tenses. A female voice responds and her tone is soft and instantly calming. 'Hello, this is the Samaritans. Can I help you?'

The woman closes her eyes, then she turns to look out of the window, briefly watching the rain falling.

Pearls of water droplets race to the bottom of the framed glass, uncannily similar to the warm tears on her face.

'My name is Naomi,' the voice says, 'would you like to tell me yours?'

Silence. The woman hesitates, nods but then shakes her head. She forgets it's impossible for the person on the end of the line to see her.

'You don't have to tell me your real name,' the Samaritan reassures, 'any name will do.'

'I'd rather not say right now.' The woman hears her own voice sounding shaky. She's still unsure why she's made this call. How could this person help? Why was she even bothering to speak to her? What am I *really* feeling? Loneliness, worry, fear, burnout? Gripping the phone tightly, her hand clammy, she realises she's feeling *all* of these things and more. Most of all, she feels regret. She regrets not studying harder at school, she regrets falling in love with the father of her children, but most of all, she desperately regrets not being able to cope with the children alone. She thought she was strong, but now she knows differently. Now she knows she's a failure.

'I...' she begins. 'I...'

'Please take your time.'

She does take her time. Then the words come, and as they flow, so do the tears. The volunteer listens with an open heart. She doesn't sound surprised by anything. The woman exhales gently. Being judged is still one of her biggest fears. She feels she deserves judgement and no one is able to convince her otherwise. Why shouldn't people judge her? She judges herself.

With her heart poured out, she feels lighter, so now she has another regret to add to the list. With daughter Doretta being too young to share her burdens, she'd bottled things up for far too long. She should have made this call a long time ago, but at least she'd done it now.

'Please remember if you'd like to speak again, we're always here, day and night,' the volunteer says.

'Thank you.' The woman's smile is small and imperceptible, but the Samaritan volunteer senses it because the relief is palpable. 'Thank you,' the woman says once more. 'Thank you, Naomi.'

'My pleasure…' The volunteer's voice inflects and the woman takes a deep breath. Rejuvenated and refreshed, she is willing to reveal her name at last. 'Grace,' she utters, feeling much less afraid. 'My name is Grace.'

Chapter 11:

'Take That To The Bank' – Shalamar

The British Rail train coursed through the countryside like the Casey Jr. Circus Train in Disney's *Dumbo* and Millie's eyes flickered with the changing scenery. Her eyelids felt heavy, worn out by an increasingly punishing workload and she desperately looked forward to the Easter break. She spotted a bird of prey gliding high above a field of oilseed rape. Was it a buzzard or a red kite? Either way, its wingspan looked magnificent. Now and then, she'd focus on the simplicity of a rustic barn or the grandeur of a country estate and everything she saw was like the perfect antidote to forthcoming exam pressures. Zane wasn't stressed. So far, he'd glided through tests and exams with ease. But not everything was easy for him. Fiddling with his red dickie bow, there was a tinge of sadness in his eyes when she turned down his offer, yet again, to meet up in the holidays. Forever the perfect gentleman, his parting words were, 'See you next term,' and he said it without any audible frustration. Glad it was still a slow burn, she found herself steadily warming to him even though she was keen to tell him that a bow tie on a man his age looked ridiculous. If things were to ever develop beyond a friendship, she would need to break that to him gently.

'Tea? Coffee?'

The tempting clatter of the catering trolley filled the carriage. She could murder a chocolate, Cabana or a Banjo maybe, but train refreshments were pricey and her student grant had to stretch until the end of the year. She watched the grey-haired man and his trolley rattle past, until they were out of sight.

'Oh blow it.' Relenting, she jumped to her feet and decided to treat herself. *I'd better take this with me*, she thought, grabbing her large holdall.

When she caught up with the man in the next carriage, she spotted a familiar face. Was it? No, surely not. Yes! It was Lauren, Enid's granddaughter. And there was a small lad sitting on the seat next to her and another fidgety little person in pink shoes sitting opposite. Quickly guessing those must be Lauren's children, Millie squeezed past the trolley man and headed towards them, beaming.

Too distracted to notice Millie, Lauren scowled at the little boy, who was pouting. Reaching into a Fortnum and Mason bag, she pulled out a yellow and blue packet. This seemed to work magic, because the boy's scowl instantly became a smile and the two children sat up straight, arms folded, waiting patiently.

'Happy now, Mr Sulky Pants?' Lauren said, handing over chocolate bars. She poked out her tongue, then, after looking up, did a double take. 'Millie!'

The little girl was clutching a cabbage patch doll, and she too looked up with a big toothless smile. The boy, however, lost in the world of his Bandit chocolate bar, paid scant attention to anyone.

'You can stand it with Bandit!' Lauren chuckled, repeating the advert's slogan. 'I came prepared. The kids are a nightmare in the car so, this time, I thought

I'd take the train. They keep telling us "this is the age of the train" on telly, don't they? Anyway, what a surprise seeing you here, Millie. These are my little brats - sorry, I mean my sweet little angels.' Holding out her hand she introduced Hetty and Oscar.

Hetty's pigtails swished as the carriage bumped along and while sitting down next to her, Millie thought it was sweet how Oscar nibbled on his chocolate as though it were a delicacy. She smiled at Lauren, noticing how once again, her fastidious dress sense contrasted with her fun-loving persona.

'I'm seven,' Hetty announced proudly, 'and Oscar's five. Did you buy chocolate from that old man?' she asked.

Millie shook her head. 'No, because I saw your mummy and I'm very glad I didn't. His chocolate's very pricey.'

Deep in thought, Hetty took another bite of her Bandit bar. 'Daddy says, Mummy likes expensive things and she's going to break the bank,' she piped up unexpectedly.

Narrowing her eyes, Lauren let out an awkward laugh. 'No, Hetty darling. When I bought that jacket Daddy said, "That *won't* break the bank." Honestly,' she said turning to Millie, 'I bought a Burberry jacket once and Malcolm pretended to faint. What are sprogs like? Spilling out all your secrets!' She ruffled her son's hair and smiled. 'Hetty talks for England, but Oscar's more like his dad. He doesn't say much, but he takes everything in.'

Speaking for the first time, Oscar had something to declare. '*I've* got a piggy bank,' he smiled, 'and *I* haven't breaked it.'

'You mean *broken* it, silly,' Hetty giggled. Oscar returned to the important business of demolishing his chocolate bar and Millie and Lauren smiled knowingly at each other.

The train sped through the countryside and their conversation became just as lively. After Lauren asked about university, the first thing Millie wanted to know was how Enid was. Lauren filled her in. 'Gran's doing better than anyone thought she would,' she smiled, then her face grew even brighter. 'My brother Ben's moving down from Sheffield to live with her in September,' she said. 'It's final!'

Millie felt a spark of positivity inside her chest. At last, someone would be caring for Enid.

'My uncle Ben plays piano just like Gran Nan,' Hetty smiled.

'And he can play a sazzi phone too,' Oscar piped up.

'Saxophone, silly billy!' Hetty giggled, correcting her brother once more.

While Lauren wiped Oscar's chocolately hands with tissue paper, she just happened to mention casually that Ben had been in a pop group which had split up and that he was ready to start a new life. 'He's managed to get a job teaching music in schools and will stay with Gran, at least for the time being.' Her eyes softened with relief. 'It will be good for them both.'

Pop Group, Millie repeated in her mind, *how interesting - Wah and Jonas might be impressed, although it probably depends on what sort of music.* She glanced out of the window. *Uncle Ben* she repeated inside and the image of the Afro-American Granddad on the rice packets sprang to mind. She smiled. *This* Uncle Ben sounded a little different and she wondered why

Enid hadn't said anything about the prospect of her grandson moving in when she visited four months back. Whatever the reason, she was very happy for her and glad to have bumped into Lauren to receive the good news.

'Polegate station already!' Lauren looked up with a start. 'Hey sprogs, grab your stuff. We're getting off.'

Millie picked up her holdall. 'My Dad's meeting me at the station,' she said. 'Do you need a lift?'

'Are you sure? Thanks so much!' Lifting her suitcase, Lauren breathed a light sigh. 'I've lost the bus timetable, and I thought we might be in for a long wait.'

Stepping off the train, Millie said it was no problem and then, she was given a surprise invitation in return.

'Are you coming to Oscar's party at Gran Nan's?' Hetty asked, tippy-toeing in her bright pink jelly shoes. 'He's already had his birthday but Mummy said he can have *two* parties.'

'I'm five!' Oscar waded in.

'I know,' Millie smiled, 'your sister told me. Are you *really* inviting me to Oscar's party?' Millie asked Hetty. The little girl nodded.

'Millie you'd be very welcome,' Lauren said. 'It'll be tomorrow afternoon sometime,' she lowered her voice to a whisper, 'but don't raise your hopes, it's not a *real* party. It'll just be the four of us.'

Millie felt a small hand clasp hers, and Hetty looked up with a big smile. They stood in the car park, warmed by April sunshine, waiting for Cecil to arrive. 'Thank You', Millie said, singing internally the song with that title by the Pale Fountains. Indeed, there was much to be grateful for and it was very good to be home.

Chapter 12:

'Get Out of Your Lazy Bed' – Matt Bianco

'I'm coming,' Millie hollered, yanking the covers over her head. Being woken up by Joyce's high-pitched voice felt maddening, but why shoot the messenger? After all, it wasn't the landlady's fault her mother was ringing painfully early on a Friday morning. What time was it exactly? She turned her head and peered at the glowing red numbers on her digital clock - 08:10. Stepping out of bed she stretched and tried to get her sluggish brain in gear. Perhaps that third Bacardi and coke during last night's evening out with the girls wasn't such a good idea after all.

Sitting upright on her bed, she lowered her feet and scrunching her toes felt the soft woollen rug beneath. It had been quite a change to move into a real home after a whole year of institutional living in a university halls of residence. She and Wahida's grey-haired landlady handed them an extensive list of house rules on the day they moved in. "Clean up after using the kitchen, don't stay out after eleven without prior notification, keep radios and music low, label food in the fridge, no visitors after ten," and the grand finale - "absolutely no male visitors upstairs!"

'I'll be spending every day at Jonas' then,' Wahida had said. Millie rolled her eyes. *Same old Wahida!* Rules aside, the rent was incredibly reasonable and despite the restrictions, their new home was much cosier than the halls of residence they'd left behind.

With her mother still waiting on the end of the line, Millie threw on her dressing gown and dashed downstairs.

'Hi Mum,' she mumbled, after picking up the receiver with a yawn. Her mother's voice was cheerful but also measured. She asked if Millie was okay.

'Sure, what about you, and how's everyone else?'

Had she heard the news?

'No.' For some unexplained reason, the moment she said the word 'no', her ear began to tune into the sound of a television in the next room. A reporter was speaking. Her heart began to beat a little faster. Having recently decided to avoid the news altogether, she hoped she wasn't about to hear anything that might take away her peace.

'The IRA bombed a hotel in Brighton during the night,' her mother said. 'The government was at a conference and lots of people are dead with many more injured.'

Raising her eyebrows, Millie listened quietly to the news that the Prime Minister, Mrs Thatcher, had narrowly escaped with her life. This happened in Sussex, her home county, and if it could happen there, it could happen anywhere. There was no mistaking that the reach of the ethno-nationalist conflicts in Northern Ireland, also known as 'The Troubles', was spreading far and wide.

'I just wanted to let you know we're okay and to remind you …' Victoria paused, 'to take care.'

At that moment, as if sent to give her mother something more to worry about, the loud siren of an emergency vehicle roared past Joyce's house. Its earsplitting siren soon faded into the distance and Millie returned to the conversation, wondering how safe she really was. And her family, how safe were they? Dean, Cecil and Amanda occasionally went to Brighton on farm business, but she told herself to relax, the likelihood of something happening on that scale in the same place twice was minuscule. Besides, it was the safety of one person in particular that was at the forefront of everyone's mind, especially her mother's - Stuart.

So far, her brother had not been involved with the conflicts, because for many years, the government had preferred to employ police rather than the Army, in an attempt to "normalize" the situation. Millie listened to the tone of her mother's voice, knowing full well what was going on in her head. Even before this attack, things were escalating. How devastating it would be, if after getting through the Falklands War, Stuart were to be catapulted into the heat of conflict yet again.

After reassuring her mother that Stuart would be absolutely fine, Millie said goodbye, but the very instant she placed the handset down on the hook, she turned around with a jerk. Joyce was standing beside her, seemingly from nowhere, with a frown which emphasised the tiny creases around her eyes. 'Terrible state of affairs!' she said tutting. 'Awful isn't it?'

Sensing from the look on her face that Joyce had been listening to the conversation the whole time, Millie smiled as best she could, and clenching her jaw, returned to her room bemoaning the lack of privacy.

Stepping inside, she decided not to reach for the radio. It would only depress her, and besides, her mother had filled her in. A violent assassination attempt. The British Prime Minister and her entire cabinet almost destroyed. Not even Guy Fawkes, almost four hundred years before, had managed to wreak such havoc. While opening a drawer, she made a mental note to ask Jonas for his take on things. Being from Belfast and hating the sectarian violence, she was sure he'd have something to say about it.

How was it possible that more than three hundred years after the English Civil War, Catholics and Protestants were still at war with each other? She shook her head, it was all to do with politics, and for someone like her who didn't align to any one political party, or consider herself a Conservative like Zane, it was baffling. But on a day like this, political allegiances didn't really matter, did they? It was a dark day for everyone.

Relenting on her resolve not to listen to the news, she flicked on the radio. Perhaps she would understand things better if she paid attention to what was going on. But after listening for a while, she soon realised she'd made a mistake. Instead of answers, she had tuned into a chilling message issued by the IRA.

'Today, we were unlucky,' the statement said. 'But remember, *we* only have to be lucky once. *You* have to be lucky, always.' The words were spine-chilling. Evil must be real. Why else would a person murder and glory in it? Yes, Guy Fawkes tried to pull the same stunt, and his lack of success was still being celebrated these days. But he lived in ostensibly uncivilized Stuart England under the reign of James the First. This was 1984, nearly 1985, and supposedly a civilized modern Britain.

Thinking about people hurting one other made her mind wander back to the day Giles ended their relationship. She put away her nightdress, remembering the day he dropped her like a hot brick, the day he turned away, even after she'd given him everything she had to give. She closed the drawer, again reflecting on the IRA's chilling words, struggling to grasp how people could be so cruel.

The title of the China Crisis song 'Tragedy and Mystery' summed up her conundrum perfectly. Why people chose to do certain things was indeed a tragedy and a mystery to her. But, another band named after an Asian country - Japan, and the title of *their* hit, 'Quiet Life' might suggest an antidote, pointing to a better way to live. Qualifying as a surgeon didn't sound like the fastest way to a quiet life, but being a doctor felt like much more than a career. It was a vocation and in a way, something she didn't choose but something that had chosen her. In other words a mission, a purpose and something that kept her going when things were tough.

Turning off the radio, she got up from her bed and opened her wardrobe, and with each second that passed, she felt stronger in her resolve. When faced with a world full of sadness, she had a solution. A skilled job could literally save lives, and as clichéd as it sounded, make the world a better place. If this meant she would sometimes have to say goodbye to a quiet life, then taking a deep breath, Millie decided that was a price she was more than willing to pay.

Chapter 13:

'Favourite Shirts (Boy Meets Girl)'
- Haircut One Hundred

Turning the steering wheel while chuckling to herself, Millie pictured how comical Wahida had looked, screwing up her face and picking her way around the farm as if stepping on broken glass. Poor Wah, so terrified of getting mud - or worse - on her shoes. But seriously, how was someone so germ-obsessed going to cope when required to treat patients with bodily fluids oozing out of every orifice? Still, at least Wahida wasn't put off to the extent that she didn't want to come back in the summer. 'I'll bring Zane with me next time,' she'd threatened, but instead of taking the bait, Millie was glad she'd decided to ignore that comment. And wasn't it hilarious when...

WHAM!

Millie's thoughts were cut short, her body thrown violently forward, and after a terrifying crumpling sensation, the car screeched to a halt.

In the silence, she lifted a shaky hand to her chest and tried to stay calm. Finding herself still securely strapped in, relief washed over her like a wave. She touched the tight strap across her chest, glad that seatbelt wearing had recently become mandatory, happy she'd always adhered to the motto, 'Clunk, click, every trip'.

The feel and the noise of the impact still resonated, and looking through the windscreen, she caught her breath as she reached down to put a stop to the idling drone of the car's engine with one turn of the key. When she finally left the vehicle, what struck her most was the calm, muffled stillness of the wintry air surrounding her. Everything was peaceful, the antithesis of what she was feeling inside. She'd hit something, that was obvious and she told herself not to panic. It couldn't be a person, surely not this early in the morning. But what if... She felt nauseous. Please let it be some*thing* and not some*one* she begged, walking slowly towards the front of the vehicle. When she got there, the first thing she felt was relief, then intense sadness. Putting a hand to her chest, she felt her heartbeat slow, and she peered down at the sight before her eyes, dazed.

A lifeless body, larger than a man's, was lying in the road. It was a majestic-looking fallow deer, fawn coloured with a white underbelly and spotted back. Its antlers spread out like the open palms of receptive hands. Stepping closer, she shook her head in disbelief. She'd never seen such a creature this close before. 'Poor thing, poor beautiful thing.' Words repeated like a mantra kept her rooted to the spot. She found it difficult to bring herself to look elsewhere, even when she heard the sound of a car pulling up slowly behind her.

Snapping out of her stupor, she quickly began to feel her tension ebbing away. Someone had arrived, and so she was no longer alone with the fatality. She squinted in the face of bright headlights and listened as the engine was switched off. To the east, she could see the bright aurora of a dawning sun peeking above the horizon and this too was calming. *I'm okay*, she thought to herself, *and everything is going to be okay*.

He stepped out of the car, and her muscles tightened, ever so slightly. Almost instantly, she knew exactly who he was, even though she'd never seen him before. The road they were on led straight to her village, and when someone new moves in, you know of them, even if you no longer live there full-time, more so when you've heard so much about them, more so when subconsciously, you were excited about meeting them.

He looked nothing like what she'd imagined. There wasn't even a hint of rock star about him, although admittedly his thick cable knit jumper was very Haircut One Hundred. It was invitingly warm, beige, soft, and cried out to be touched. *For crying out loud, get a grip!* Realising her mind was doing irrational things, she pulled herself together, thinking the prang must have knocked her senseless and turned her brain to mush.

He said nothing, but simply walked straight past to the front of her car, unsmiling, his eyes focused on the cervine casualty.

'We'll have to move him,' he said, breaking the silence. In those brief words she detected a Yorkshire twang reminiscent of *Last of the Summer Wine* and other owt, nowt and nay-lass sitcoms.

'You've quite a bit of damage.' He rubbed his jaw, then lifting his eyes, he scanned her for visible signs of injury. 'Are *you* okay?' he asked.

'Me?' she flustered, placing a hand to her chest. 'I'm fine.' Suddenly feeling chilly, she briefly wrapped her arms around herself and watched vapours from her breath condense in the air. To make driving easier, she had removed her coat at the railway station after saying goodbye to Wahida. Thank goodness her friend was now on her way to Leicester, and not caught up in this.

'I'm Millie,' she said, finding her voice at last, but he didn't immediately register her words. Instead, he was crouching down, looking preoccupied, examining the stag's hefty, solid frame.

'Sorry,' he said, rising to his feet. 'Ben, Ben Bradshaw.' He held out a hand and she grasped it. It felt warm when everything around her was cold. The handshake was firm and brief, suggesting he didn't have a lot of time for pleasantries. He had work to do.

'*Ben.*' She repeated his name slowly and inaudibly, and she didn't tell him she already knew. She watched him stoop and grasp an antler in each hand. Then heaving, he began the necessary task of removing the obstruction from the road.

'Can I help?' She bit her bottom lip, knowing there was no way she possibly could.

Smiling narrowly, he shook his head and continued to haul the stag slowly across the road. She watched, saddened by the unresponsive eyes on a once majestic beast. She imagined it running wild, darting through woodland and glade, alive and free. It must have weighed at least 150 pounds, yet Ben was making light work of moving it. Her imagination began to shift gears, and now she could see him hurling the animal, caveman style, across his shoulders, gripping it tightly by its legs and carrying it like a weary hunter bringing home the kill. But with his altruistic face and dusty fair hair, he was far softer looking than a traditional caveman type. She chuckled silently. This was no club-wielding macho man. This was no *Rambo* or *Terminator*. Slightly ashamed of where her vivid imagination was taking her, she opened the car door and reached for her coat. Just at that moment, she heard him hoist the deer into a ditch by the roadside with a groan. He'd done it, and to her mind, in sorting things out so easily, he'd elevated his status to a minor hero. *Be sensible Millie, be sensible!* She slipped her arms through her sleeves and buttoned up her coat.

'He'll be gone soon,' he said, striding towards her, brushing his arms,'thanks to the foxes and crows.'

'And badgers,' she added quickly.

They stood eye to eye, and he was now close enough for her to inspect his sweater discreetly for signs of debris, dirt or bits of fur. She couldn't find anything. His clothes weren't spoiled because of her. She could relax.

'It just ran right out in front of me,' she said, feeling the urge to justify herself.

'These things happen,' he said, his voice consoling, 'and you're not hurt, that's the main thing,' he paused and eyed her curiously, 'although you do seem shaken up.'

'Do I?' She lightly raised a hand to her cheek and it felt cold to the touch even though she felt hot. Something about the way she was feeling disturbed her. The way her heart thumped reminded her of a painful past. She thought she'd learned from her mistakes and wasn't at risk of becoming infatuated, ever again.

She inspected the crumpled bonnet and bumper. The car was quite old but even *she* could tell that it wasn't in the best shape following the impact.

'It's nothing that can't be fixed,' he said, reassuringly.

'I don't think my parents will be happy.'

He smiled a little. 'I'm sure they'll be more concerned about you. Are you sure you're okay to drive? I don't mind leaving my car here and taking you home.'

'Really?' she hesitated. Now was the time to confess that she was fine to drive. But if she did, they'd have to part company right away. Then what? Would she get the chance to see him again before going back to London? 1984 was almost at an end and New Year's Day was just around the corner. She felt twitchy, thinking that before she knew it, it would be back to the grindstone - lectures, tutorials, tedium, repetition, hard work. Time was of the essence, so yes, she was going to accept that lift, but first, she was desperate to put him in the picture. It was high time she told him his grandmother used to teach her piano, that she knew his sister and had even met his niece and nephew.

'I went to Oscar's birthday party in April,' she smiled proudly.

'Really,' he arched an eyebrow, his smile halfway between amusement and disbelief. 'Oscar had a party? Here?'

Nodding with enthusiasm, she began to talk avidly, all the while trying her best not to come across as an excitable puppy, despite feeling like one.

'Small world,' he concluded, then he turned towards the road. 'I'd love to chat more, but don't you think we'd better move your car?'

Feeling silly, Millie thought she'd needed a wake-up slap around the head. She had been going on and on so much, she'd completely forgotten that the car was still blocking the road!

'Would you like me to move it for you?'

She nodded and looked up at him, her eyes blinking coyly. She felt slightly bad about playing helpless, but needs must, and it was working fine so far. He held out his left hand for her car key and he wasn't wearing a wedding ring. No surprises there, because Lauren hadn't mentioned a significant other, but a welcome sight nonetheless. What's more, all through their encounter, Millie thought she'd picked up subtle clues that he might be interested. But she couldn't be certain, at least not this early in the game.

With all her senses heightened she felt energized, but she knew she needed to be cautious. At best, this could turn out to be a bit of holiday fun, and at worst, it might come to nothing at all. That's what she told herself, trying to avoid the extremes of, 'he's the one I've been waiting for', versus, 'he's going to destroy me like Giles did'. Jumping the gun to conclusions either way was a very bad idea. He wasn't quite a perfect stranger because of the tenuous family connections, but what did she really know about him? Nothing. When it came to what was important, she didn't know him from Adam.

Still thinking far more about him than she ought to at this stage, she watched him move her parents' car to a safe place, and when he got out, her admiring eyes watched him walk towards her again. He was about to take her home. Should she invite him in? They'd only just met and that might look a bit too forward.

With her parents' car out of the way, he seemed more relaxed. He began to talk with enthusiasm as the two walked back to his car to lock up. They lingered by his vehicle and he kept talking. The conversation was about roadkill, and Millie listened keenly. She'd never had a conversation with anyone about roadkill before. He told her that he once came across a young deer that had been killed on a quiet country road. 'I picked it up and threw it in the boot,' he said. 'I didn't have a clue what I was doing. Deer was venison, that's all I knew.' He smiled when he told her how he'd managed to muddle through and how surprised he was to discover how tender and tasty venison was, after he'd prepared and cooked it.

Millie's eyes grew wider. She'd never eaten roadkill before. Living on a farm meant there was plenty of home-reared meat, but even if that wasn't the case, eating roadkill seemed so…she wasn't quite sure what. Rugged? Unwasteful? Unusual? Certainly, *something* on those lines.

'What about the deer *I* just killed?' she asked, looking over towards the ditch.

'That big guy?' Ben shook his head. 'I'm guessing he'll be tough and stringy, so I think I'll pass.' She agreed, finding his waste-not-want-not mentality combined with culinary discernment very appealing. Soon, the topic moved on to hunting. He asked if she'd ever hunted. She told him she hadn't, but that her brother Stuart often did, at least he used to. 'He's in the army now,' she said, feeling the smooth metal of Ben's car against her skin. She told him that when Stuart had lived at home, he'd hunted pheasants, ducks and other game birds, 'and was very good at it as well,' she added, now feeling more relaxed than she'd felt for some time.

They stood in the morning light, not wanting to go anywhere just yet, a bright winter sun starting to warm them a little. He talked with excitement about his scouting, and air rifle club days and said he'd hunted grey squirrels, rabbits and pigeons.

Squirrels? Playfully, she glanced up at nearby trees, just in case any of the bushy-tailed, nut-eating cuties were eavesdropping. He assured her that squirrel was tasty, but despite being adventurous, she wasn't keen. Maybe this guy was more of a caveman than she'd realised. But cavemen didn't teach music in schools, did they? How was he enjoying his new job so far? But before she could ask, he asked her what *she* did for a living.

'A medical student,' he repeated slowly, looking slightly in awe. 'You must be very clever.'

'No,' she said hastily, 'not really. I just work hard.'

He nodded, and after a moment's silence, both knew it was time to move on. Neither said a word, but instinctively they made their way to her parents' battered car, just a little further along the road. Feeling inspired by what they'd shared so far, her legs felt restless, knowing there was so much more she wanted to say.

They reached the car, but before getting in, they turned their heads towards the rattle and chug of a vehicle approaching from behind. Millie instantly recognized the person in the driver's seat and lowering her head, she wished it was someone else.

'Young Millie, is everything okay?' A man's voice, louder than the car door slamming shut behind him, echoed through the air, smothering the delicate song of a robin.

Horace, (a.k.a. Farmer Hutchinson), was rushing towards her, concern etched on his weather-worn face while his wife Agnes sat silent and still in the passenger seat. Millie's heart sank, but nevertheless, she hitched up her shoulders and did her best to put on a smile.

'I hit a deer,' she said, watching the senior but sprightly man inspect her vehicle. 'There was no time to stop, it just appeared out of no-whe...' her voice trailed off. She looked at Ben, then at Horace. Then she looked at Ben again. Something was wrong, very wrong. What was going on? Each man was eyeing the other like an angry bull snorting at a toreador, and to an outsider, it looked as if they were squaring up for a fight.

'This is Ben,' she said, clearing her throat. 'He stopped and helped me. Ben, this is Mr Hutchinson, a close friend of the family.'

'You bet I am!' Horace glared with pursed lips. Ben looked away, his jaw tense.

Millie's eyes bounced back and forth between the two, and she tried to hide her fluster and confusion. Whatever was going on, she hoped it wasn't *that* important.

'Ben was going to give me a lift,' she said, sounding casual.

'That won't be necessary.' Horace held up a firm hand. '*I'll* be happy to take you, in *our* car. I'll drop the wife off at Betty's first, then after dropping you off, I'll come back here on foot to fetch your father's car.'

It's actually my mum's. Millie opened her mouth, ready to correct him, but nothing came out.

***

There was plenty of small talk on the short journey home, with Millie trying not to make it too obvious she was being distracted by the Ford Cortina on the road in front. *I could have been with him*, she thought ruefully.

Ben's car wove in and out of the country lanes which brought to Millie's racing mind the mellow *Follow You Follow Me* by the band Genesis. She couldn't shake off the feeling she had met someone special, but love at first sight didn't happen in real life, did it? But still, there was something, she could feel it. She hadn't felt this for Zane, or even Giles for that matter. With Giles, it had felt like instant attraction wrapped up in teenage angst. But today there was more, an immediate connection, an unexplained affinity that was loud, yet subtle and unspoken at the same time. She felt stirred up inside, knowing it was hard to put into words, the best explanation being it felt akin to the moment a switch flicks on and light floods a room. Reflecting on this, one Genesis song inside her head quickly morphed into another. 'Follow You Follow Me', became, 'Turn It On Again'.

'Shame he's related to the piano teacher.' Horace cut into her thoughts when Ben's car turned into the road leading to Clover Cottage, disappearing from view. '*Enid's* not a bad sort.'

'Mrs Griffiths is lovely,' Millie said, her searching mind still trying to decipher the reason for Horace's hostility. 'Do you know Ben at all?' After her gentle prodding, she waited with bated breath for Horace's reply, hoping finally to get to the bottom of what was going on.

Turning briefly, Horace gave his wife a knowing look. Even from the back seat, Millie could tell from Agnes' stiff posture that her taut face gave nothing away.

'Know him? Naah,' Horace said, shaking his head. 'But one thing I *will* tell you, although I'd rather not go into details,' he glanced at Millie in the rearview mirror, 'I met him on just the one occasion before today, and believe me young lady,' he grimaced, 'once was more than enough.'

Chapter 14:

'Don't Tell Me' - Blancmange

Feeling compelled to prepare for her return to St Georges, Millie found herself mindlessly throwing together items of clothing in the quiet of her farmhouse bedroom. It stood to reason that if she started to pack early it would gear her up, and by the time the holidays were well and truly over, she might actually be looking forward to going back. At least, that was the theory.

She stopped for a moment and felt her shoulders sag, just a fraction, then reaching inside her wardrobe, she pulled out her blue denim Lee Cooper jacket. Folding it, she carefully placed her most trendy item of clothing inside her holdall. Everything about the 'Don't Be A Dummy', Lee Cooper TV advert was cool - the slogan, the song - everything. Still, wearing a jacket didn't automatically make her cool, and when it came to being 'with it', Millie knew she still had a long way to go. Wahida was her guide to all things fashionable, and having been persuaded by her to ditch the American tan tights once and for all, her friend had brought her up the coolness scale, at least a notch or two.

Millie stopped packing for a moment and looked around, noticing for the first time how dated the pink floral wallpaper now looked. Still, her room brought back so many memories, memories of hard work, happiness, helplessness and hurt. *Don't Be A Dummy* she repeated inside, and lifting her head, she resisted the temptation to put herself down. In the past, *she'd* been a dummy for sure, but she was older now, and this time, she knew what she was doing.

What a shame the collision had happened *after* Ursula returned to Scotland. Millie would have relished giving her old school pal a blow-by-blow account of the whole shebang. But, shrugging her shoulders, she reasoned that perhaps it was just as well Ursula had already returned to university. From experience, Millie could guess what her friend's reaction would have been, had she told her what had happened. Most likely, it would have gone something like this: 'So Mills,' she would begin, 'let's get this straight. You crashed into a deer and some random bloke you happen to fancy got rid of it for you and now suddenly he's Superman and you're Lois Lane?' Millie smiled, imagining how Ursula would then throw her a classic "What you talkin' 'bout Willis," (Arnold from Different Strokes) stare. And to be fair, she probably deserved it. If there was one person who knew how to slap her into shape, it was Ursula, and although they'd had their fair share of fallouts, at the end of the day, Ursula always had her back and had stuck up for her when other girls had gotten nasty. They also had so much in common. For a start, neither had wealthy parents, but were considered bright, and that meant they were both given sought-after scholarships to cover the eye-watering fees at their prestigious private girls' school. And during their seven years there, the two had gone through so much together.

Ursula deserved happiness after what Gregory had done to her. Millie cast her mind back to two sixteen-year-olds, giggling in class, in love with love. When Ursula, out of breath with excitement, told her, 'Gregory's asked me out,' just weeks after Millie had started going steady with Giles, it felt as if they were both walking in sync on cloud nine. 'You do realise you're *Gregory's Girl* now,' Millie said one day, amusing herself. After that, they had a laugh, replaying their favourite scenes from the movie. But within six months, instead of laughing, Ursula was crying. Discovering you've been two-timed with the school bully is very humiliating, and when Millie and Giles split shortly afterwards, the two girls bonded like never before over their failed relationships.

Millie even wondered if she craved Ursula's approval even more than her own mother's sometimes. 'If you ever go out with another scumbag like Giles,' her friend once said, 'then please, Mills, do me a favour, and don't tell me about it, 'cos I won't be listening!' Since then, it became an unspoken rule that if a new man came on to the scene for either of them, the other would vet him thoroughly.

Recently, Ursula surprised Millie by giving her thumbs up to Zane, even though according to her, he sounded 'like a toff'. How could he be much worse than most of the boys they'd known at the boys' school, and what was Millie's problem anyway, when she was used to being surrounded by 'poshos'?

'That's exactly it,' Millie remembered, retorting with a sigh, 'I'm sick to the back teeth of them!'

Ursula laughed at the time, but when talking about Zane much more recently, Millie was surprised to see her looking more serious. 'He's keen, even after all this time,' Ursula said, looking Millie straight in the eye, 'and that means, he'll take care of you, Mills.'

Millie hesitated, not knowing what to think, or how to respond. Perhaps Ursula was right. Perhaps Wahida was right. Perhaps the whole flippin' world was right. Maybe she shouldn't look a gift horse in the mouth and just maybe, she ought to give Zane a chance.

Through a single-glazed, sash window and in the silence of her room, she noticed the distinctive cackle of fieldfares flitting past over leafless hedgerows. Soon, the sound of redwings flying across open pastureland was audible too, their gentle twittering intermingling with the fieldfares' call.

Sighing deeply, she zipped up her holdall and lowered it onto the floor. Then, lying back on her bed, she slipped her hands behind her head while resting in her true feelings and comforted by the sounds of nature. The truth could be very beautiful indeed, and she couldn't ignore a growing realisation. Sinking deeply into the softness of her pillow she knew things were different now, because shortly after the conversation with Ursula about Zane, the crash had happened. And on that day, she met Ben, and everything changed.

Chapter 15:

'Walk Out to Winter' - Aztec Camera

How was Enid? Was she managing her pain, and had she avoided any other fractures?

Despite her best intentions, Millie hadn't quite managed to carve out time to visit her old piano teacher, during what had turned out to be a very full-on Christmas break. Most likely, Enid was doing just fine though, especially now that she had a live-in grandson to keep an eye on her.

Millie strolled along the quiet country lane, noticing a growing tension. Should she? Shouldn't she? Why not drop in to Enid's now, right this minute? She stopped, paralysed with indecision, knowing that if she did just turn up at Clover Cottage, it might look suspicious. What if someone, somewhere got it in their head that she had ulterior motives, now that Ben was living there?

'What do you think I should do, Conker?' She eyed the lively border terrier wagging his tail by her feet. Conker had been a companion to Millie's Great Aunt for almost two years, and whenever her elderly relative visited, she'd bring the cute canine with her. Millie looked forward to seeing his teddy bear face and taking him out for lengthy strolls - something her great-aunt struggled to do these days. And on this particular day, Conker's need for exercise provided the perfect excuse to get out of a mucky job. Being the studious one who lived away from home, Millie was rarely expected to do farm chores, but dagging was an exception. Just before lambing was the ideal time to dag, and her family needed all the help they could get, but however much she wanted to help, removing caked-on or sloppy poo from sheep backsides in freezing animal pens just wasn't much fun. 'Thanks for getting me out of that one, Conker boy,' she smiled slyly, arching an eyebrow.

Strolling past a hawthorn tree, she noticed round masses of green leaves on its bare branches. Mistletoe was very distinctive, and with eyes still staring upwards, she questioned why a parasitic plant growing in sinister-looking clusters with poisonous berries was so closely associated with romance and kissing. But, when she thought about it some more, it didn't seem *that* ridiculous. Romance, kisses and even love could be deadly poisonous. Giles had taught her that lesson only too well, and with a sinking feeling, she walked on, but being reminded of Giles also made her feel somehow lighter, because she realised how little she thought about him these days. She was no longer that insufferable bore who would talk about him ad infinitum to Ursula and her mother. Yes, it was looking as if she'd finally gotten over him.

Pressing ahead with Conker by her side, and with a fresh wintry wind blowing through her hair, her mind drifted back to when she hit the deer on the road. She recalled being driven home by old farmer Horace and how grateful she was to both her parents for hardly batting an eyelash when they saw the damage. She could almost taste the hot chocolate and feel the heat of the mug which her mother had placed in her hands, hoping it would calm her down. But little did Victoria know that her daughter's jitters had far less to do with the accident and much more to do with thinking about the person she'd met in the moments that followed.

When Millie had told her family what happened after the crash, she'd made a concerted effort to curb her enthusiasm when talking about Ben. After listening to the whole story, Amanda smiled and said that neither she nor Dean had met him, or even seen him yet, but he sounded nice, while her mother (who had seen him once in the village shop) said that if she should bump into him again, she'd thank him for being so helpful.

However, largely thanks to Horace, Millie's father Cecil seemed rather less enamoured.

'He's trouble.' Those were the exact words Horace had said soon after he'd dropped Millie home. After declining Horace's offer and recovering the car himself, Cecil stood inside an icy cold garage, trying unsuccessfully to readjust the damaged bumper while Millie looked on guiltily, feeling horrendous about saddling her parents with extra expense. Seemingly determined to hang around the farmhouse, Horace stood by her side, telling Cecil repeatedly how fortunate it was that he had happened to be passing by. It wasn't until Millie left the garage to visit the bathroom that he took advantage of her absence to fill Cecil in properly.

'Why exactly is he trouble?' her father had asked, genuinely curious, but Horace's reply didn't give much away. 'I'll tell you more over a pint,' he replied, 'but for now, mark my words, that chap won't last five minutes here, not with his appalling attitude and behaviour.'

Millie subsequently listened to her father wondering what on earth Horace had meant. Why did he say Ben's attitude was bad? She couldn't imagine, but then again, she'd only met Ben once, but what exactly had he done wrong? She gritted her teeth with frustration. *Horace, tell us more, please!* Then, realising her father's acquaintance probably had no idea what he was talking about, she relaxed. Horace didn't live in Magham Down but in a nearby village, so how could he possibly know so much about Ben? Frustratingly, no amount of cross-questioning her father could help get to the bottom of the damning report, and besides, she needed to be careful. It really wasn't a good idea to give her father the impression she'd flipped over Ben - a stranger, who Horace had just roundly condemned.

'You'll just have to wait to find out I'm afraid,' her father said, once Horace had finally left, surmising Horace probably assumed Ben's background in the modern music industry automatically made him a troublemaker. Millie wasn't convinced though: she had been able to tell by Horace's and Ben's body language that day, there was much more to it than that. And when it came to her father and cantankerous farmer Hutchingson, how come *they* got on so well? She asked Cecil precisely that, and he explained that while he didn't exactly consider the overbearing old man his best buddy, he did have *some* redeeming qualities. 'He hates seeing anyone out of work,' Cecil told her, 'and he takes on more labourers than he needs but *still* pays them all a decent wage.' Then her father summarised his and Horace's camaraderie in one simple sentence. 'Us farmers stick together,' bringing the subject matter to a close.

With her mind now back to the present day, Millie found herself in Featherbed Lane and dangerously close to Clover Cottage. 'Why are we here?' she asked Conker. He was the boss and knew exactly where he wanted to go. Squirming a little, she knew there was no excuse for hanging around Enid's house hoping to bump into Ben accidentally on purpose. But if the guy was truly as bad as Horace made out, surely it was better to find out sooner rather than later? She felt a tug on the lead as the excitable pooch raced ahead, and following swiftly she hummed Nik Kershaw's 'Wouldn't It Be Good'. It *would* be good to see Ben again - in fact, not just good, but fantastic.

Soon she approached the familiar row of small Victorian cottages and felt her heart pounding. *I'll just walk past quickly.* Those were her conscious thoughts, but underneath there was another voice saying, *it's still the holidays, he's a teacher, so there's a chance I might see him.*

It was quiet on the approach, even though Millie had heard from her mother that it wasn't only the sound of a piano coming from Clover Cottage nowadays, but also the smooth notes of a saxophone. Another cold wind blew across her face and she paused, thinking how much she'd love to hear him play the sax. Lost in thought, she failed to notice Conker had stopped suddenly, and when he started barking, she quickly and abruptly snapped out of her daydream.

No Conker, quiet, shush, please! She spotted a fluffy white cat sitting on a wall, and with his eyes fixed on it, Conker was now refusing to budge or quieten down. Red-faced, Millie couldn't believe how a dog who wasn't normally this noisy had chosen this moment to draw attention to them both. Cringing, she had no choice but to accept that what was intended to be a quick dash past had now turned into full-on loitering with an accompanying racket. After the cat jumped off the wall and out of sight, she glanced apprehensively at Enid's lounge window and was relieved to see no sign of twitching at the lacy net curtains. Breathing more easily, she wondered if she might get away with it after all, but then, a small voice inside said '*Look up*'. Taking a peek upwards, she saw a shadow, then a movement, and letting out a gasp, she just about found the self-restraint not to cover her mouth. '*What did you expect?*' said the voice in her head. '*This is what you came here for, wasn't it?*'

Ben was standing by an upstairs window, looking right down at her, and there was nowhere to run, nowhere to hide. He wasn't smiling, at least, not in the way she would've hoped or expected him to, but thankfully, neither were there any signs of irritation, negativity or a bad attitude, despite Horace's warning. Instead, he looked - how could she describe it - forlorn. Lost. Somewhat like a prisoner, locked up inside a tower. The corners of her mouth relaxed, and feelings of embarrassment slowly began to evaporate. His wistful look was disarming, and if this were a fairy tale, the roles would be reversed. He'd be the damsel in distress - a male equivalent of Rapunzel and she'd be his knight in shining armour. Wanting to giggle with relief, she pressed her lips together - after all, she'd hate him to think she was laughing at him. But, when she noticed him smiling back, she could tell he knew *something* was tickling her. For a moment, she just kept smiling at him, but when she glanced down at her great-aunt's dog, she noticed the true source of Ben's amusement. The naughty pup was cocking his leg and doing a big wee, right on Enid's smart brick wall! Realising Ben was now laughing at her canine companion's antics, she closed her eyes briefly, silently thanking Conker for breaking the ice with his very minor indiscretion. Once the amusing moment was over, she and Ben both stood there, as though locked in a stalemate. If only he'd run downstairs, throw the door open and invite her in, but as the seconds continued to tick by, that appealing prospect began to look less and less likely.

Was Enid at home? Probably, but Millie reasoned that now wasn't the ideal time to knock on the door to find out, not when she had Conker with her, and certainly not when Ben had just watched her from an upstairs window without inviting her in himself. And why should he? He wasn't obliged to. Encouraged by knowing that at least she'd managed to raise a smile, she decided it was time to move on. He was bound to know she was interested by now, but even so, it wouldn't do to look too desperate, would it?

'Goodbye.'

'Bye,' he mouthed, holding up a hand, with a hot smile that cut through the chilly air. She took a few steps forward, and then walked on, happy but disappointed, still wishing he had run downstairs to say hello, still regretting they didn't get the chance to continue where they'd left off, right there, right then, outside Clover Cottage. But for now, it was time to forget their little dalliance. Even *she* was aware that getting excited about a man she hardly knew was slightly idiotic, as was losing her head. It really was a classic case of 'been there done that', and with a hand still holding on tightly to Conker's lead, she headed back home and back to reality.

Chapter 16:

'Back on the Chain Gang' - The Pretenders

This is Millie Appleby's being back at University pros and cons list: 6th February 1985

Pros

1. The River Wandle. I love how the sound of trickling water somehow almost manages to drown out cars, buses and roadworks. Back home there's all the peace and quiet, streams and rivers I could want, so I'm not sure this is much of a pro.

2. Wahida's a great housemate, even though her OTT cleanliness gets on my wick sometimes.

3. Zane's a nice guy, doesn't bad-mouth anyone, even when they're nasty to him, and he's clever and lends me his notes when I've almost fallen asleep from boredom in lectures.

4. And he fancies me. Should this be a separate pro? Is it even a pro at all when I still don't feel the same? But, being liked by Zane means treats - lots of them, like the time he took me, Wah and Jonas out for a six-

course slap-up meal at a Michelin-starred restaurant. Trying posh grub like foie gras, monkfish tails, fillet steak and dessert wine for free was definitely a pro. Also, everyone's getting along so much better. Zane's not annoying Jonas half as much now he's keeping his Thatcherite and anti-socialist views to himself and Jonas isn't rubbing Zane up the wrong way so much either, now he's finally ditched all that make-up (and in my view looks <u>way</u> better because of it).

5. At uni I can watch the Jonas and Wahida love saga unfold (<u>if</u> it ever does, that is, because it's so blooming slow in coming).

6. In London I can do cool things like go to nightclubs. Except, this is probably a con because I hate them - the music's way too loud and dancing solo in a crowd in the wee hours feels like torture. It's nice that Jonas likes inviting me and Wah to the trendy ones but I didn't like the Limelight and The Wag Club was rubbish when that bouncer almost didn't let me in. I guess I don't look trendy enough. But that's fine by me, because I'm not going back. You can guarantee Wah will keep going though. Any excuse to be with Jonas, even though she finds Friday and Saturday all-nighters killing.

7. Being able to pop out to a corner shop that's *Open All Hours* for a bar of chocolate whenever I fancy it.

Cons

1. A big fat heavy workload that's getting heavier by the day.

2. The 'Dog Eat Dog' attitude of certain students.

3. Hate to admit it, even to myself, but I'm definitely feeling a bit homesick.

4. It's winter and too cold to sit for long by the river, but at least Joyce's house is warm.

5. Joyce is a prying old bat.

6. There are too many cars around.

7. Not many people catch your eye or smile back at you.

8. I miss 'My Old Piano'.

9. Sometimes I'm desperate for Mum's roast beef or Toad-in-the-hole, or her Shepherd's pie and rhubarb and apple crumble, plus I'm totally sick of toast with whatever's left in the cupboard.

10. I'm fed up with trying to stretch my grant money and bored with living off baked beans at the end of term.

11. Ben. He's in Sussex, and I'm here - but that's not really a con, because I've no idea if he's even worth getting to know. At least, not yet.

I think I'll stop there, because with seven pros and eleven cons, I can already see what's starting to come out tops. Like it or not, I'm stuck here for another three and a half years, and if I carry on with this malarkey, I might depress myself. I want to have sweet dreams tonight, not nightmares!

Chapter 17:

'Rock 'n' Roll' - Status Quo

A woman opens up her Abbey National savings book, closes it again, and then clasping it to her chest, lifts happy eyes towards the ceiling. She is beaming and she is dreaming. She remembers her phonecall to the Samaritans more than a year before, thinking it was just what she'd needed to help her carry on, to keep moving forward, to stop herself giving up. She closes her eyes, amazed that savings with interest which grew so slowly, could suddenly add up to something big. For far too long, it felt as though she was drowning. Then one day, her head was just above water. Then soon after, she found herself treading water, until now, she finds herself swimming at last. All this, just by putting aside a little here and a little there.

The woman sits in the warm living space of her council flat, thinking that now she has all she needs to take that final step. She now has just enough to cushion her transition from one job to another.

She thinks of her children, *all* her children and she's glad that the ones inside her home are tucked up in bed. They're well-fed and happy, and when they're happy, she's happy. She begins to realise she feels happier than she's felt for a long time. She's so happy in fact, she could dance. Her restless legs are itching to dance. Why doesn't she? It's only ten o'clock, maybe some of the children are still awake, Doretta, her eldest, is bound to be reading. Whoever's not sleeping, why not get them out of bed? Then, they could all dance to her favourite music. Some good old-fashioned rock and roll would fit the bill. 'Mummy's going to be a nurse one day,' she'll say. 'Not for a long time yet, but I've started the ball rolling. Let's have a party!' The woman shakes her head and laughs quietly. It's a school day tomorrow, so she can't risk a racket waking those children who are already asleep.

'Mummy's going to be a nurse one day,' she repeats to herself. This is something Doretta already knows and she'll tell the younger ones tomorrow. Then her mood changes abruptly and she stops smiling. She fears she's being overly ambitious. She isn't clever or good at exams. She wonders if she'll ever make the grade. State-enrolled nurse, state registered nurse, SEN, SRN, she rubs her forehead knowing there is so much to learn, and in the world of nursing, so many things have already changed. Some people say SENs don't get the appreciation they deserve, some say SRNs are better. But the woman doesn't care if snooty people look down on her. It doesn't matter what kind of nurse she becomes, or what sort of nursing she does. All she cares about is swapping her cleaner's overalls for a nurse's uniform, *any* nurse's uniform. She simply couldn't wait. She doesn't have qualifications, but she's used to working long hours, and best of all, she isn't too posh to wash, or too clever to care. She could make even the filthiest room shine. All she needed was a mop, a jaycloth and some polish. She'd cleaned enough toilets in her time, now, it was her time to wash patients instead, to dress them, change their sheets and provide their meals. It was just doing what she'd always done, just being a Mum. It would hardly feel like work at all.

The woman's daydreaming eyes sparkle again. Yes, one day she was going to be a nurse. All she had to do was keep trying and keep working hard. For now, her plan to be a ward orderly and work in a hospital environment was plenty. Perhaps learning from the nurses around her would help when her time came to begin the journey to become one of them.

Holding up the job application form in her right hand, she looks at the boxes already filled in. The nice lady at the job centre helped her, but there are still more sections to complete. Tomorrow, she'll post it and wait. She sighs and her legs start to jiggle again. How long before she hears back, how long before she knows?

Her mind returns to yesterday, and the nice lady at the job centre. *So friendly, so unlike the others. She asked me so many questions. Questions she didn't need to ask.* 'What ages are your children?' 'Oh, how lovely that the youngest has recently started school.' 'You now feel ready for a new direction?' 'You'd like to have a career in nursing one day. When you're ready, come back and we can help you with that too.'

Thank you, the woman thinks in her heart, *Not just for helping, but also for being interested in me.*

With three fingers, the job centre lady dragged the application form closer. 'Ward Orderly at St Helier Hospital,' she smiled. 'Let's start with your name, shall we?' The woman didn't hear her for a moment. She was distracted. *Ward Orderly at St Helier Hospital.* The title sounded so grand, but she knew in reality that it wasn't. It's a working-class, domestic job, and there are no airs and graces attached to it. But it felt grand to her because it's what she'd set her heart on. And if she got it, it'd be her first hospital job.

'Your first name is?' She remembers the nice lady looking at her with her pen poised. The woman also remembers she'd said her name earlier. The nice lady had forgotten, but it really didn't matter, the woman was just grateful that someone in an official setting took the time to talk with her. Took the time to treat her like a person and not just a number on a list. The woman looked up and repeated her name. 'It's Grace,' she murmured with a simple smile. 'My name is Grace.'

Chapter 18:

'Duel' - Propaganda

It was far too chilly to linger on the wooden bench, so pulling her soft, woolly hat over her ears, Millie set off on the short walk towards home. When she arrived back at her lodgings, she walked through the front door hoping to see Wahida, but instead, her landlady stood in front of her, gripping the phone. 'Hold on a minute Mr Appleby, she's just walked in,' Joyce passed the telephone to Millie before she'd had the chance to put down her bag or take off her coat. 'You're lucky,' the landlady smirked. 'I was just about to hang up.'

Just give me the bloomin' thing! But, instead of saying what she was thinking, Millie took hold of the handset and sat down hesitantly on the soft cushioned seat by the telephone. Her father didn't usually ring and he didn't like chatting on the phone if he could help it. 'Is everything okay?' she asked him, feeling slightly on edge.

Listening to her father speak, she was soon reassured that everything was very much okay and he was simply ringing with some news. The minute Millie heard the information he began to relay, her eager ears perked up. This was what she'd been waiting for. She looked back over her shoulder, glad to see Joyce wasn't hanging around, although of course that was no guarantee she wasn't listening.

Cecil began by telling Millie that the previous evening he'd bumped into Horace at the pub and the first thing Horace had said, was, 'Keep Millie away from that bounder.' Millie chuckled. If Horace thought there was a real chance she and Ben might get together, then that was surely a good sign.

'So let me get this straight,' she said, slowly repeating her father's words, 'according to Horace, Ben marched up to him and his gang and shouted "Stop!" at the top of his voice?'

'Indeed,' Cecil said.

'And that's it?'

'I believe so.'

Millie let out a short, sharp laugh. 'Good on him!' Far from being successfully warned off and repelled by this so-called troublemaker, she felt proud of him. Horace had said Ben was totally out of control, yelling at the top of his voice, and very aggressive, and she didn't believe a word of it. Why? Because the moment her father went on to tell her the reason Ben had told Horace and his gang to stop, she understood everything.

'You know, love, I'm no fan of Horace,' Cecil's voice sounded sullen, 'but do you think it's right that a man who's lived here five minutes is telling people what to do?'

'But Dad, they were hare coursing! I don't agree with it and neither do you!' Realising she was being loud, she lowered her voice. Just then, she noticed the living room door move a fraction and she pursed her lips. What was the betting that Joyce was listening to every word?

Trying to forget about being overheard, Millie rubbed the back of her neck. Perhaps there was some truth to her father's words. She knew he hated watching dogs chase and rip hares limb from limb for a bet, just as much as she did. She knew his hope was that they'd escape every time, but she also knew he had a point. Did Ben *really* have to be so confrontational and bolshy with total strangers? Perhaps not, but there was one thing she *was* sure of. It didn't matter whether you were talking whippets or greyhounds, hare-chasing dogs were certainly not, to quote a Kate Bush song, 'Hounds of Love'.

She didn't know whether to be amused or horrified when visualising Horace's angry, affronted eyes and had this been the eighteen or nineteenth century, you can bet your bottom dollar he would have challenged Ben to a duel, just to save face and to restore his honour.

'So there you have it,' Cecil said, winding up the conversation. 'Now you know why he's a troublemaker.' Still laughing lightly, Millie could tell by her father's intonation that he was being slightly tongue-in-cheek. But at the same time, she detected a slight reservation in his voice, and it concerned her a little. 'Look, love,' he said, about to make his opinion clearer, 'no matter what *we* think, there are still plenty of folk who enjoy killing hares for fun, and for good or ill, and as much as I hate to say it,' he paused, 'upset Horace, and you upset a lot of people.'

Reflecting on those highly disconcerting words, Millie almost didn't register her father saying, 'Goodbye,' and after a quick chat with her mother during which her distracted mind struggled to pay attention, she placed the phone on the hook and wandered towards the kitchen. *Upset Horace, and you upset a lot of people.* The words kept coming back, and the troubling thing was, she knew her father wasn't joking.

She put the kettle on and memories of what had happened to old Jerry Baker's hay barn sprang to mind. The barn mysteriously burnt down five summers ago and it happened just days after Jerry had been shirty with Horace in the Red Lion pub. Jerry had said in no uncertain terms that hare coursing was 'barbaric', and had threatened to report Horace to the police for the damage it had caused to his property. Barely responding, Horace apparently kept his cool but coincidentally, within days, the so-called accident happened. Strangely enough, Jerry didn't utter a word after that, let alone approach the police, at least that's what everyone believed. Dismissing a heavy feeling in the pit of her stomach, Millie took out a milk bottle from the fridge and poured some into her mug. She lived in a tight-knit community, there was nothing wrong with that and rumours were just rumours after all. Opening a packet of rich tea biscuits, she took one out. *It's only gossip*, she thought, taking a bite, *Horace likes to throw his weight around, but surely he doesn't have it in him to do anything that dreadful.* Shaking her head she reached for another nibble. *No, he could never do anything so vicious and so vile.*

Turning her mind to much more pleasant things, she glanced at her watch. Robin of Sherwood was on TV in a few hours and she was looking forward to the ethereal theme tune by Clannad and the on-screen chemistry between the dishy lead actor, Michael Praed who played Robin Hood, and his winsome Maid Marion. But for now, it was back to her room and her books and deciphering the difference between respiratory alkalosis and respiratory acidosis. She grabbed her mug and headed upstairs, still unable to shake off an uncomfortable feeling inside. Why did she care so much about Ben? Why would it even matter to her if the whole village turned against him, or even the whole world?

Twisting the knob on her bedroom door she stepped inside, laid down her bag and sat down at her desk. *Boys can seriously mess with your head.* With a frown, she harked back to her mother's words. But Ben wasn't a boy, he was a man, and she wasn't a girl any more, she was a woman. Would it matter to her if he made enemies? And being a grown-up, wasn't he capable of taking care of himself? Right now, it was time to take care of *herself*, to get her mind back in gear and to focus on what *really* mattered.

She opened her textbook and picked up a pencil. London was a fabulous city, but she wasn't here for a joy ride. Before she could write anything she was distracted yet again. Both Ben and Zane had romantic potential but when it came to Ben, if nothing came of it, she'd lose absolutely nothing. She wasn't even friends with him, not like she was with Zane. With the pep talk over, she felt lighter, and at last began to make notes - *respiratory alkalosis induced by hyperventilation can have hypoxemic, pulmonary and iatrogenic causes.* It felt good to be concentrating on her work again and with every minute that ticked by, she came closer to coming to a decision. Perhaps, at least in the short term anyway, avoiding getting serious with *any* man and keeping, or at least *trying* to keep an emotional distance, was the way to go. That was the safe option and while pressing her thumb against the sharp point of her pencil, she began to accept, albeit with a degree of reluctance, that the less danger there was in her life right now, the better.

Chapter 19:

'To Cut a Long Story Short' - Spandau Ballet

With a carrier bag in one hand, Millie pressed Enid's doorbell, took a deep breath and stepped back. She waited. Enid was bound to be in because she usually was, but swallowing nervously, Millie also appreciated that this time, it might not be her old piano teacher opening the front door. Although she *had* imagined the scenario of seeing Ben standing in front of her, somehow she'd forgotten to prepare for a negative reaction. What if he looked at her with a 'what are *you* doing on my doorstep' face? The last time he'd seen her was in January, and it was now April. Would he be surprised? What if he didn't smile? Might he seem nonplussed or confused? Would he think she was pretending to visit Enid when really, she was there to see *him*? Gripping the bag a little more tightly, she began to wish she'd thought this through.

When Enid slowly began to open the door, Millie breathed more easily again. But when feelings of relief were overtaken by a strange sinking feeling, she reassured herself that all was not lost. Ben might be somewhere inside. He might yet still be there.

'Millie, lovely to see you.' Enid's warm smile on her small frame was welcoming, but stepping inside,

Millie's heart ached when she saw how her former piano teacher was more stooped and looked even frailer than the last time she'd seen her. 'I hope I haven't come at an inconvenient time,' she said with a fading smile.

'Of course not, dear,' Enid said, 'you've caught me in between pupils so it's actually a good time, and remember, I said you could drop by whenever it suits you.'

Sitting on the sofa, Millie's sad reaction to Enid's frailty lessened when she noticed the sparkle in the elderly lady's eyes. It was the same sparkle she'd seen a year earlier at Oscar's unofficial birthday party. In fact, she'd never seen Enid smile so much than when her granddaughter Lauren and her great-grandchildren were there. And now Ben was living with her full time, so clearly having family around was good for her. Was Ben going to walk into the room at any minute? Trying to be discrete, Millie's eyes flitted around surreptitiously, her senses alert for clues to suggest he might be home.

'Ben's out and about,' Enid said, her words sharply insightful. Wriggling in her seat with embarrassment, Millie nodded. How come Enid had dropped Ben's name in so casually when the two had never spoken about him? Whatever the reason, it felt quite good.

'These are for you.' Millie placed the biscuit tin she'd been carrying on the coffee table. 'Mum made them this morning.'

Enid released the spicy aroma of cloves and nutmeg into her tiny living space when she opened the tin. 'Easter biscuits, how delightful! Please thank Victoria for me. We need a cup of tea to go with these delicious-looking bickies, don't you think?'

After a while, having declined Millie's offer of help, Enid slowly walked back into the lounge carrying a pot of tea and two mugs on a tray. Millie watched her pour, amazed that those same awkward looking fingers were so nimble on the piano. While biscuits got eaten, one by one, and the tea flowed, so did the conversation. Enid told Millie how much easier her life had become since her 'lovely grandson' had moved in. 'But,' she said, 'they - and by that I mean the grandchildren, forget I've looked after myself for the best part of forty years, and just because I've had a couple of fractures, they act as if I'm incapable of being left alone.'

'I guess they're concerned.'

'I know, and I'm fortunate. Ben didn't have to move all this way to live with me, but it's only for the time being, until I sort myself out.'

Millie watched Enid's face turn sombre. 'It might take a while, but I *will* get back on my feet, Millie,' she said. 'I have to. I don't want to be a burden to anyone.'

Resisting the urge to jump in with a trite 'I'm sure you're not a burden' type of response, Millie chomped down on a biscuit and waited for Mrs Griffiths to say more. Soon, Enid was telling her that she rarely saw her daughter, Ben's mother, who lived miles away in the Shetland Isles, which was 'her choice', and neither did she see Ben's father, whom she referred to as her 'former son-in-law' who Ben had left behind, up north. 'He misses his son terribly,' she said, nibbling on a crumbly biscuit, 'but I dare say he'll manage just fine.'

Millie's eyes drifted across to Enid's old family photos proudly displayed in a cabinet. Everyone knew she was a widow, and Millie glanced again at the beautiful black and white, pre-war picture of Enid as a bride with her dashing groom Percy. Aware that he'd died in the war, Millie had always been keen to hear more, but Enid never went into details and Millie didn't ask, fearing the whole subject might be too sensitive.

There was another photo that took pride of place inside the display cabinet. She'd first seen it at Oscar's birthday party and could hardly have missed it because of its size and position, blocking out the others. Set inside a large gilt-edged frame was a picture of two children: - a girl aged around ten, a boy, perhaps five, both smiling, one softly, one brightly, one fair, one dark, both wearing old-fashioned clothes, both quietly content. When Millie glanced at it this time, her immediate thoughts were that they'd both changed a lot since they were young, but you could still tell who they were, especially the boy, who still had that same understated smile.

'Yes, that *is* Lauren and Ben when they were youngsters,' Enid said, proudly.

Just at that moment, the distant sound of a car door closing filtered through an open window and Millie's heart beat a little faster. *He would've parked closer* she reasoned, *It can't be him.*

'Ben was in a band wasn't he?' she asked.

'Yes, he was.'

'What sort of music?'

What was that? Her heightened senses thought she'd heard footsteps outside, and with the unmistakable click of a key sliding and turning inside a lock, she was left with little doubt, Ben was home.

'He's back,' Enid smiled. 'Perfect timing. He can tell you all about it himself. Breathing through her mouth and telling herself to relax, Millie kept her eyes firmly fixed on the lounge door.

It didn't take long, just a few seconds perhaps, and Ben was in the room standing right in front of her. The moment he stepped in, he stopped and their eyes met. She looked at him with an easy smile, a smile that said her being there, in his grandmother's lounge, was the most natural thing in the world. And it was, wasn't it? Visiting Enid was nothing new, and besides, taking lessons at that piano was something she'd done for many years.

After lowering his raised eyebrows, his face relaxed again, as though quickly getting over the surprise, and when Millie heard his voice, that light, steady, unruffled voice, she too felt calmer. 'Great to see you again, Millie,' he said, looking at her with a casual intensity.

Enid's grey eyes began to bounce between the two. 'And this time,' she smiled, 'there's no deer blocking the road.'

What did Enid just say? Millie glanced at her old teacher, open-mouthed. *Well, I never,* she beamed inside, surprised that Enid hadn't let on for one minute that Ben had told her about the accident.

Still feeling warmed by what she'd just heard, Millie watched Ben grab a biscuit before sitting in the chair opposite. Then, munching quietly, the conversation began with him asking Millie how she was.

'Not bad,' she said, trying to keep still and playing down her excitement.

What about university?

'Hard work!' she explained.

And what about the car?

'It survived,' she chuckled. Keen to turn the conversation around, she thought of a question, and when more started to flow from her lips, it soon became a deluge. How was his job? How well did he know Sussex? Did he like Magham Down, and then, the six million dollar question – why did he move here in the first place?

He hesitated and Millie looked on vacantly, wondering why he looked uncomfortable, but she soon relaxed as the answer became clear. He'd moved to support his grandmother, but obviously he didn't want to embarrass Enid by saying that in front of her.

Ben shifted in his seat a little. 'It's a long story,' he said eventually, 'mostly to do with work.' Millie leaned back, remembering Lauren saying he needed a new start, so maybe there was more than one reason for the move. Thinking it was time to leave that line of questioning, she asked about his rock band, only to find out it wasn't a rock band after all.

'We played blue-eyed soul,' he said. Tilting her head, she listened curiously, having never heard that expression before. Although a new one on her, it sounded cool and very mellow, but also surprising since she'd always imagined Ben to be on the rockier side of pop, rather than a James Brown or Blues Brothers 'Soul Man'. And his eyes? So much for blue-eyed soul because *they* were definitely brown, a light, warm brown, like the sort of aromatic cinnamon or spicy cumin you might find in a Marrakech marketplace. The band was called 'Sheffield Fusion', he told her, but since Sheffield was a long way away from the US of A, they never quite managed to pull off the Philadelphia sound of The Delphonics or The Stylistics. 'But still,' he said, with a playful spark in his eyes, 'we tried our best.'

The Delphonics, Millie chewed over the name of the band, then remembered they'd released, 'Didn't I (Blow

Your Mind This Time)' as well as the delectable, 'La-La-La-La-La-La-La-La-La Means, I Love You'. She shut her eyes briefly, thinking if *that* was the sort of music Ben played, she wanted - no - she *needed* to hear it.

'Were you famous?' she asked, curling inwardly the moment she heard how stupid she sounded.

Politely, Ben shook his head. 'No,' he said, 'but we did almost get signed for a record deal.'

A record deal sounded like quite an achievement, so perhaps her question wasn't so daft after all.

'That seedy lifestyle just wasn't for him.' Enid's out-of-the-blue comment turned both their heads and after taking a sip of Tetley tea, Enid added that she'd recently seen an episode of *World In Action* about corruption and bribery in the music business.

'Really Gran,' Ben said, 'I missed that one, but I *did* watch an episode of *Nationwide* about record company reps buying up records to manipulate sales.'

Tutting, Enid shook her head. 'What do you expect from an industry awash with sex, drugs and rock and roll?'

Gently biting her lip, Millie tried to hide her surprise. She'd never heard her taciturn piano teacher come close to saying the 's' word or mention drugs before. She looked at Ben, only to catch him staring at nothing and smiling awkwardly.

'You wanted nothing to do with all that rubbish, did you?' Enid asked, looking at him solidly and waiting for his validation.

'No.' Without warning, he rose to his feet and slipped his hands into his pockets. 'I'm afraid I've got to go.'

Looking up at him, Millie felt hollow. Why so soon? Hadn't he only just arrived? Would she see him again before going back to university? Did she care? After throwing him a forced smile, she knew the answer to that one, and it was a clear and unequivocal 'yes'. She *did* care.

'Do you know Jill Mason?' he asked, turning to her unexpectedly.

Jill Mason? Her eyes widened. *Oh my gosh, <u>everyone</u> knows Jill Mason.* Holding back from verbalising her thoughts, Millie remained visibly nonplussed, even though she'd just heard Ben mention a name she neither expected nor wanted to hear from his lips.

'She's invited me and a bunch of others for lunch,' he said with a tight smile.

Jill Mason! Still managing not to say anything bad, Millie's poker face belied an awareness that Jill was easily the most desperate femme fatale in the village. The song 'Maneater' was surely written just for her and now, it looked as if she was trying to get her mucky mitts on Ben. A lunch get-together was just a ruse, because Millie had never known Jill to play the hostess to anyone. One thing was for sure, if Jill was wheedling her way in, it might be an idea to back off now. That girl could be very determined, and Millie wasn't up for a fight. Still, there was hope. Surely it wasn't going to be difficult for Ben to resist her charms and trying not to look amused, Millie thought of another Hall and Oats song that was bound to come into play soon. 'I Can't Go For That (No Can Do)'. If Ben didn't think the same after spending just an hour or two in Jill's company, it'd be a wonder.

Millie was surprised Mrs Griffiths hadn't warned her grandson off, but then again, Enid often seemed blissfully detached from village life and probably had no idea that Ben was walking into a lion's den.

'Have a nice time,' Millie said, pretending she meant it, and Ben gazed at her with a wry smile, as if he could see straight into her lying heart.

The mahogany wall clock ticked away until Enid broke the silence. 'I'm afraid I must also say goodbye to you, Millie,' she said, heaving herself onto her feet. 'I've got a pupil due here any minute and I need to visit the bathroom first. Thanks again for coming, it was lovely to see you, and please, don't forget to thank Victoria for those delicious biscuits.'

Enid slowly made her way up the stairs, leaving Ben and Millie alone. For a delectably brief but awkward moment they stood, avoiding eye contact, until Millie knew it was time to leave the room. She walked ahead of her attractive escort, and when she arrived at the front door, she paused.

Squeezed into the tight space, they were now standing face to face and he was so close she could smell him. Lemony and fresh, it was a fruity, citrussy, soapy smell. He reached over to pull down the handle on the door and she breathed in deeply.

He opened the door and smiled. 'What's your dog's name?' he asked, watching her step outside.

Confused, Millie blinked. 'Oh, you mean Conker,' she said, sounding flustered. 'Conker's not my dog, he's my Great Aunt's.'

'Tell Conker he's welcome to take a leak here again, any time.' Ben's brown eyes darted towards Enid's front wall. 'Neither me or Gran hold it against him.'

After another round of awkward but delightful smiles, it was all over, and stepping through the metal gate, Millie heard the front door shut gently behind her. She walked away slowly, feeling happier but also oddly more weighed down than when she had arrived. It was then she noticed a gangly youth approaching her with piano music in his hands. He walked straight past, and turning her head, she watched him pull down the latch of Enid's gate, step towards the door and reach up for the bell.

She found herself wanting to swap places with the lucky lad and wishing *she* had an excuse to ring the bell again, only this time it wouldn't be Enid she was keen to spend time with. Then, like some magical coincidence, it happened. There was nothing in her hands, and she realised she might have the perfect excuse to go back. Her mother's biscuit tin! She'd left it on the coffee table. About to turn on her heels, she stopped abruptly. Wait a minute. Would her mother care if she didn't get the tin back? Not likely. But going back for it seemed like the perfect excuse to see Ben again, right here, right now. Still hesitating she continued to deliberate. Was it worth it? It wasn't even seeing him again properly, and if she did go back, it was risky. He was in a rush to go to lunch with you-know-who, plus Enid was teaching. What if she rang the doorbell only to be greeted with an irritated face? So should she risk it? *You bet*!

With legs almost running back down the lane, she opened Clover Cottage's metal gate and pressed the bell hard. Now fully committed and with a heart beating furiously, she already regretted her decision. How stupid it was to be bothering Ben, or worse, poor Enid, who struggled to walk and was busy, but she didn't have much time for regrets because almost instantly, the door flew open, and there he stood, with a smile as warm as an equatorial sunset and a biscuit tin in his hands.

'I guess you've come back for this.' Smiling, he handed it over. 'You came at the right time, I was just about to shave and get changed.'

The sound of piano scales resonated through the air, flowing, circulating, just like the heat now spreading through her face and her eyes glided upwards from his chin to *his* eyes as well as the rest of his face. *I wish you wouldn't get rid of that stubble*, she mused, walking away with the tin in her hands, *I'll have you know, matey, I think it's incredibly attractive.*

Chapter 20:

'Lady Love Me' - George Benson

'Millicent Appleby, are we keeping you up?'

Jerking to attention, Millie lifted her head to see her professor's eyes staring down at her and it didn't feel good. Not since school had anyone called her by her full name, and the sharp sarcasm in his voice made her feel like a naughty school girl, only this time - worse. Her face tingled and she glanced back skittishly. *Why embarrass me like this?* All eyes, including Zane's, Wahida's and Jonas' were on her, and it wasn't fair because she hadn't even been sleeping. It was okay to feel drowsy after studying late, wasn't it? She'd forgotten that burning the candle at both ends never paid off and being 'Under Pressure', as in the Queen and Bowie song was no excuse for making that mistake all over again.

'What did I just say about the branches of the facial nerve?' The Professor's voice was gentler this time, which did little to alleviate her shame. In fact, his softer tone implied all the more that she ought to be pitied. He didn't wait for an answer, which was just as well, because she didn't have one, and as though feeling some remorse for calling her out, he lowered his gaze and moved on.

'As I was saying before I rudely interrupted Miss Appleby's slumbers,' he smiled, pacing the room again, hands behind his back, 'exams are in a little over six weeks, and I want you *all* to pass first time.'

Later that same day, after carrying out tedious microfiche research in the library, Millie sat alone inside a study cubicle, poring over a textbook, trying to commit to memory definitions, formulas and medical terms that were just not sinking in. *What's wrong with me?* She straightened her shoulders. Nothing probably, and it was far too early to panic. She'd get through, because studying was the one thing in life she felt able to control. She pulled out a strip of Orbit sugar-free gum, unwrapped it and soon felt the cool peppermint on her tongue. Hoping the gum would help her concentrate, she repeated in her mind, *I'll get through.* Didn't Wahida say that a mate of hers in the year above had warned her that things rachet up in the second year? If so, she wasn't wrong.

With the short-lived sweetness in the chewing gum all but gone, she thought back to the Easter holidays. Since returning to university, she'd become accustomed to replaying the highlights in her mind, just like a favourite film, and right now, once again, she was back inside Stoneybrook, her brother and sister-in-law's cottage.

'Please don't say anything to Dean, will you? Not that there's anything *to* tell.' Those were her words to Amanda after sharing some of what had happened during her visit to Clover Cottage the previous day. Amanda promised not to breathe a word, and leaving Stoneybrook on a high, Millie was glad that her favourite sister-in-law had managed to carve out time for a chat, which wasn't always easy at that time of year.

In the silence of the library, Millie discarded the tasteless gum, wrapped it up and reflected on how much she appreciated living on a farm, especially during the Spring. Lambing time was a period in the farming calendar which kept everyone busy. Her mother would be in the farmhouse taking care of meals and other needs, while Cecil, Dean and Amanda worked around the clock inside the sheep pens, sometimes dealing with the loss of a stillborn lamb or a ewe dying during labour, which was never easy. But the joy of hand-rearing orphans, and watching ewes bond with their young, or with foster orphans after losing their own, was second to none and made the heartache and hard work all worthwhile. With a faraway smile Millie sat in the library thinking how few people had the opportunity to grow up seeing sheep mothering and nuzzling their young and keeping their offspring close. But it wasn't all moonlight and roses: the first time she'd heard a ewe's mournful bleats after losing her lamb, it had really hit her hard.

She remembered once, when very young, looking at the ewes curiously and asking her father if the 'daddy sheep' ever helped the 'mummy sheep'. With a subtle smile on his face that she could still see in her mind's eye, Cecil cleared his throat. 'Mr Ram has one quick but very important job,' he said, 'and now he's not needed so much.' Readily accepting the explanation, it took some years to fully grasp what her father meant, but there was one thing she did know at the time. She was glad to be a girl and not a lamb, because she loved spending time with *her* daddy. In that regard, nothing much had changed since then, and she was still grateful for her father's love.

A father's love, with eyes still drifting away from her notes, she tried to remember where she'd heard those words before. Ah yes, it was while watching *Jesus of Nazareth*. At Easter, there would usually be a biblical drama on the television, often playing in the background in the farmhouse lounge. She couldn't explain why this time she felt keen to watch the whole of this epic series and was struck by the many farming analogies and references she'd never noticed before. 'Feed my sheep', 'the good shepherd', 'the lamb of God', 'sacrificial lamb'. It all tied in with lambing time and her farming background, and while she sat at the library desk, she remembered again the goosebumps, the unexpected feelings of privilege and the warm sense of connection.

Not everything about the series was as appealing though. Herod killing children, John the Baptist's head on a platter, and of course, the crucifixion. Even though she knew how the story ended, when the credits began to roll she felt a knot inside, optimistic because good ultimately triumphs over evil, but also just a little bit saddened and afraid. Why, she asked herself, did there have to be so much suffering and death along the way, both then and now? She sat in her wooden cubicle, with its high sides designed to block out visible distractions, wishing they could also block out the distractions in her head. Would she *ever* be able to concentrate? Not now when the words death and suffering had infiltrated her mind, reminding her of the terrible images of the Ethiopian famine on the TV. With a lump forming in her throat, 'Africa' by

Toto came to mind, and the beautiful melody about a beautiful land gave her hope that some day, somehow, she might be able to do something for someone suffering in the world, wherever that might be.

She looked down at her notes again. There was one thing, or rather one person she could think of that was guaranteed to switch her thoughts over to something more positive, and that was Ben. Up until now, she'd tried to be careful not to think about him too much, but right now, when unable to focus no matter how hard she tried, why not give in, just this once? Had it been a mistake to tell Amanda and her mother that she liked him? Hopefully, she hadn't given either of them the impression she was over-excited. It was far too early for that.

'You did the right thing,' was Amanda's response, when Millie said it took all her strength not to say anything when Ben said he was having lunch with Jill Mason. 'He'll find out what she's like soon enough, and when it comes to her being a threat,' Amanda smiled, 'I really don't think you need to worry.'

Her sister-in-law's encouragement was very welcome, but clenching her jaw, Millie remembered what Amanda said next which had taken her by surprise. 'Does that mean you've made up your mind about Zane?'

Zane. Millie put down her pen, recalling that it wasn't until she'd heard his name that day, that it suddenly dawned on her that she'd spent ages talking about Ben, without even giving Zane a second thought. But it wasn't until she'd closed Stoneybrook's wooden door behind her and walked back to the farmhouse that she realised the implications of her failure to even consider him. She had to admit, it really did say it all.

How could she be so unbelievably dismissive when it was Zane's own scrawly handwritten notes in front of her? It was common knowledge that doctors had abysmal handwriting, and his scribbles were just one of many indicators that he was heading towards a brilliant career. Yes, for many reasons it was evident that he was going to be an excellent physician and all thanks to him and his kindness in lending his meticulous notes, she was able to catch up after the disastrous tutorial during which she'd been too tired to concentrate. She felt her body stiffen. *What's wrong with Zane and why does he have to be so flipping nice to me all the time?* And now she found herself thinking back to what had happened the previous week, after which most normal men would have probably moved on and called it a day. But not Zane.

When he had asked her out to the pub that day, she had been feeling particularly worn down by revision. It was also a Friday evening and she fancied a change of scenery, so the thought of heading out for a drink rather than going home was particularly appealing. It wasn't a dinner date, or a trip to the theatre, or anything like that. He'd given up asking her out on a proper date, so she felt she could relax. Surely it was okay to let her guard down for a little while, and what possible harm could it do to join him for a quick after-college drink? Staring at his handwriting she sighed, thinking had she known what would happen that night, she would have thought twice about saying yes.

He said he'd pick her up in his car, and even then she didn't think much about it. Everyone knew about his shimmering grey Porsche, or the 'Silver Dream Machine' as she liked to call it, only not to his face.

Before that evening she'd never been inside it, and when she finally plonked her behind on the shiny, black leather seat and looked around at the plush, high-spec interior, she knew that despite its sumptuous appeal, she couldn't be swayed. She didn't intend to be here more often than she needed to be.

After spending the evening talking mostly about college and exams, she finished her gin and tonic and headed back to his Porsche. At some point, she couldn't remember when, the song 'In Your Car' by The Cool Notes popped into her head. Perhaps it was because the lyrics were 'you wanna get me in your car to love me, but you won't get far', or something along those lines, that it sprang to mind. But Zane was too much of a gentleman. *He* wouldn't pull a trick like that. Walking towards the vehicle, he was in a musical mood himself. Certain it wasn't her imagination because she had a good ear for music, earlier that day she was sure he had been whistling 'Waiting For A Girl Like You', by Foreigner, almost every time she went near him. And now, later that same evening while walking together to his car, he was whistling a different tune, The Police's 'Every Little Thing She Does Is Magic'. It seemed he was trying to tell her something.

Still sitting in the library, she squirmed when she remembered what happened after he'd pulled up outside Joyce's house, and opened the car door for her. As they stood at the gate, ready to say goodbye, his sudden jerky move towards her came from nowhere, and his plump lips making a beeline for hers took her by surprise. She bit her bottom lip just thinking about it. Was it bad that she instinctively turned her face away? Was it bad she offered him her cheek instead? Was it bad that deep down she knew that had it been Ben, her reaction might have been quite different?

'I'm sorry Zane, I don't think I'm ready for this.' She remembered how flustered she sounded, after scrabbling around to think of something appropriate to say.

'No, please Millie, don't be sorry, *I'm* the one who should be sorry. That was terribly boorish of me and I apologise.'

'No, don't be sorry, it's fine.' She hated seeing the mortification in his eyes that he was trying but failing to hide.

'No, I ought to have given you a warning first… if you get my drift, but … I hope we're still friends.'

Warn me? Millie hoped he couldn't see her amusement. *How sweet! What kind of guy thinks he needs to warn you before trying to kiss you?* Giles would never have bothered, not in a million years.

'Of course we're still friends, don't be silly!'

Had she reassured him? She really hoped so. She watched him run his hands through his thick dark hair while noticing that his full cheeks, that gave away his love for exquisite food, were looking very flushed.

She knew what Ursula was going to say when she told her about this. 'Mills, you need your head testing. Remember what I said, give the guy a break. Not every man would still be keen, even after all this time, and that means he'll take care of you.'

Ursula's advice was a million miles away from what used to be her mantra at school. 'Treat them mean, keep them keen', but Millie forgave her for the change of heart, knowing she'd only adopted that mindset after Gregory had cheated on her. Going on the defensive helped her friend cope and was her way of trying to avoid getting hurt all over again. And when it came to

Zane, Ursula was probably right. Millie listened to the whirring of a photocopying machine, which for a brief moment distracted her from the whirring thoughts in her own mind.

'He'll take care of you Mills.' Yes, she was sure Ursula knew what she was talking about. And yet, feeling rotten inside, Millie had to acknowledge that instead of responding in kind, she did something she'd promised herself she wouldn't do, at least not if she could help it. Rejection hurts, and that was something she knew more than most, yet here she was, doing it to someone else, someone as nice and as kind as Zane. But still, surely leading him on would be far worse?

Come on, concentrate! But it was no use, she was just too tired to focus. Better call it a day then.

As she stood up, she decided to prepare for the next seminar which was less than half an hour away, but first, she needed another coffee. She walked away from the library still thinking about Zane, still feeling torn, wondering if it would be so wrong to keep him in reserve - assuming he was willing to wait of course. Was it wrong to keep a guy hanging on, just a little longer, just in case? Of course it would be wrong. Her eyes widened, how could she even think such a thing and what kind of girl would treat someone like that? She knew she wasn't that sort of girl and Zane was a gentleman. Surely, the least she could do was act like a lady.

Chapter 21:

'Romeo and Juliet' - Dire Straits

Parked on the edge of a grass verge, Ben tugged at the handbrake and turned off the engine.

There was a sense of Deja Vu, when Millie stood rooted to the spot in the lane outside Clover Cottage, wondering if she was looking as obvious as she felt, standing there like a lemon. 'I've popped round to see Enid,' she'd say, and fortunately, it happened to be true, so he'd better believe her.

'Hi,' he said, striding breezily towards her. 'I'm guessing you've come to see Gran?'

'Yes,' was all she said. What else *could* she say, after he'd pre-empted the line she'd mentally rehearsed? He didn't look surprised to see her. Instead, sounding bright, he told her they'd just come back from his sister's in Northampton. He'd dropped Enid off in town and was going to pick her up later. 'But now,' he said, looking restless, 'I need to stretch my legs, it's been a long drive.'

'Fancy a walk?' she asked, thinking on her feet and suggesting they head towards Herstmonceux Castle together. When he said yes just seconds later, it began to feel surreal.

She couldn't have imagined the summer holidays beginning like this, even though, after passing her end-of-year exams with flying colours, it had already started well. She'd driven home to Sussex with her father in the passenger seat and her possessions in the boot. Ten weeks of bliss! And she couldn't wait to reconnect with friends and family and get back to nature. When she hit the motorway and gathered speed, thoughts raced around her mind like motorbikes on a Brands Hatch circuit. At some point she was hoping to see Ben again to get to know him better, but she never guessed that a mere two days later, she'd be walking and talking with him in the Sussex countryside.

With tense, excitable footsteps, she headed through country lanes, orchards and green fields and the more they talked, the more she relaxed. How were Lauren, Hetty and Oscar? Was Enid feeling better? Why was she in town? To see a chiropodist. Must be a new practice because the old one closed down ages ago. No amount of questions phased him, and when *he* uttered precious rare jewels of communication, she hung on his every word. They made their way across a field, blades of wheat crunching beneath their feet and then stopped for a minute to admire the ochre-coloured grain all around.

'Your Gran *did* mention that your Mum lived on a remote croft on the Shetland Isles,' Millie said, looking at the golden expanse surrounding them, 'and it sounds idyllic.'

'I don't know about idyllic,' he said, 'but it's definitely remote, and because Mum and Gran don't have much to do with each other, they're both cool with that. In fact,' he smiled half-heartedly, 'Mum doesn't have much to do with anyone. She's been living alone, with no mod cons in the middle of nowhere for years, and she's never been happier.'

'Do you and Lauren see her much?'

Ben gave Millie a steady look. 'From Sheffield to Aberdeen it's a seven-hour drive and from Northampton add a couple on top, then it's an overnight ferry from Aberdeen.' He raised his eyebrows. 'Does that answer your question?'

'Yes, I guess it does,' Millie said.

'Mum moved there to "find herself" after she divorced Dad,' he said, 'but the trouble is, after she found herself, she dropped everyone else. Seriously, she loves living there, but it takes a certain kind of person to live somewhere so isolated, and that's definitely Mum.'

Glad that Ben had chosen Sussex over the Shetland Isles, there was one burning question in her mind. Had he got to know anyone in the village yet?

'I'm going fishing with Alan, Alan... I think his surname's Carter. We're going on Tuesday morning. Do you know him?'

Millie's eyes brightened. Alan was a great guy, and talking of fishing, she felt relieved that despite getting off on the wrong foot with Horace, Ben wasn't a fish out of water. He'd made a friend, and a cracking one at that.

'My brother Dean reckons it's hard to find good farm labourers these days,' she said, 'but Alan's definitely one of them.' Still being warmed by the sun, the two went on to discuss how it was no secret that Alan's wife was expecting baby number three and money was tight. 'Dad and Dean would love to give him more work,' Millie said, 'but our farm just doesn't make enough money, unfortunately.'

Talking of friends, or rather foes to be exact, she had a burning question.

'How was lunch at Jill's?' Turning away, she pretended to study the electric blue flowers of some nearby vipers-bugloss while waiting for an answer with bated breath.

'A bit of a disaster to be honest,' he said, smiling through gritted teeth. 'No one turned up but me.'

'You don't say,' she said, with more than a hint of irony in her voice, 'I never would have guessed.'

Ben lightly scratched his head, 'Jill's a bit,' he paused, '– how can I put it? Let's say, she's a bit full on.'

Somehow resisting the urge to respond with a 'you don't know the half of it', Millie instead thought of a clever reply which might garner some much-desired information. 'And, what would your girlfriend say about Jill?' she blurted out clumsily, immediately thinking the question wasn't so clever after all.

He stopped walking briefly, then he continued on, turning towards her before turning away again and the warm flicker in his eyes seemed to say, 'I was talking about fishing earlier, but who's fishing now?'

Stopping again, he shifted sideways and instantly Millie felt uneasy. *Why has he stopped and what's he doing? Perhaps that girlfriend question was a step too far and he's finally gone off me.* She cowered inside, convinced she'd shot herself in the foot, but the magical two words that came next, quickly put her mind to rest.

'What girlfriend?' he asked.

The title of the song 'Wonderful' by Mari Wilson (with The Wilsations) summed up her reaction in one simple word. But after she exhaled, her relief turned into embarrassment when looking past his shoulder she saw what was there. They'd arrived at a wooden kissing gate. The reason he'd stopped had nothing to do with her being flirty at all. How silly of her. She ought to have realised because she'd passed through this gate numerous times before, but for obvious reasons, she'd forgotten it was there this time.

'After you,' he smiled, extending his hand.

Sliding past gingerly, she pushed the arm of the barrier and slipped through into the enclosed area, then out to the other side. Ben followed on, timing it just right. Too soon and they'd be hemmed in together, trapped inside the tiniest of spaces. Thinking the same thing at the same time, they looked at each other, both wondering if that would have been such a bad thing.

After walking side by side up a gentle incline, they stopped to take in the view. Thanks to Lauren, Millie already knew Ben's age, but did he know hers? Staring ahead, she thought about the pop video for 'Hang On Now' by Kajagoogoo. In it, a young girl, even younger than she was when she first met Giles, falls in love with an older man, the lead singer in the band and a performer in the music industry, just like Ben used to be. She relaxed. He knew she was at university, so he must have some idea of how old she was, and the age gap was hardly massive.

As expected, he seemed completely nonplussed when she casually dropped in that she was twenty. 'I was twenty-six in March,' he replied, frowning playfully, 'I can't believe I'm pushing thirty.'

'Hardly!' Smiling with relief, she mentally ticked another concern off the list.

They walked on, and the more open fields they crossed, the more he opened up. She felt for him when he revealed how his father's gambling addiction led to his parents' divorce when he was little. Then, going even deeper, he shared how growing up in a single-parent household with little to live on made him hate his father, before finally making peace with him in recent years. 'We're good now,' he said, with the gnarly roots of an ancient oak tree forming a solid base beneath their feet.

'Are your parents still in contact with each other?' she asked.

'Not any more,' he said. 'After Dad gambled away the house we moved into a council flat. I was only five or six at the time, but Gran told me only recently that when we were being offered a place, Mum didn't care how rough the neighbourhood was or how far it was from the city centre - none of that mattered. The only thing she cared about was that it was as far away as possible from where Dad was living at the time.'

Millie thought she could sense some disquiet, or at the very least, disappointment behind Ben's easygoing tone of voice. Sadly, it sounded like there was little hope for his parents' relationship, and while clearly, his mother was happy where she was, might his father fancy joining him down South one day?

'Eeh by gum, nay lass,' Ben laughed, striding beside her, 'Dad's a proud Yorkshireman and set in his Yorkshire ways.'

Covering her mouth she giggled like a child. Normally, Ben's accent was so subtle she couldn't even detect it, so hearing him speak 'Yorkshire' was very funny. Still, they'd just been talking about something serious, so now felt like the right time for *her* to share something difficult. 'I don't know if you've heard,' she began slowly, 'but our family also went through a rocky time not long ago.'

There was a look in his eyes that instantly told her he knew exactly what she was referring to. 'Yes,' he said quietly, 'I did hear something, but not from Gran.' She could tell he was keen to reassure her that Enid hadn't gossiped, and knowing Enid, Millie had little doubt he was telling the truth.

'Your family has nothing to be ashamed of.' His words and his smile were like a soothing dock leaf on a stinging nettle rash. 'I try not to care what people think,' he added. 'There's just too many other things to worry about.'

She nodded. That was true in theory of course, but in practice? The scandal that had rocked her family happened well before she'd had the emotional strength to shake off what people might say. Her fourteen-year-old self couldn't bear seeing loved ones gossiped about, ripped apart and their personal lives put on display in front of the whole village - indeed the whole world - at least, that's how it'd felt at the time. But that was in the past, and things were good now. 'And,' she said with a broad smile, 'in the words of the Bard, "*All's Well That Ends Well*".'

She'd hardly finished speaking when Ben stopped abruptly, spotting something out the corner of his eye.

'What's that?'

'What's what?' She followed his gaze.

Putting a forefinger on his lips he crouched down, inviting her to join him.

'Look,' he said, pointing to a movement in the undergrowth. 'See that little guy?'

She focussed. At first nothing. She focussed some more. Then a rustling sound. There it is! She let out an excited gasp.

'It's a shrew,' Ben smiled, 'a common shrew.'

'I know,' she said, now able to see it clearly, 'I'd recognize that snout anywhere.' She paused, 'But how can you tell it's a *common* shrew?'

With keen eyes still on the cute mammal, she listened to a long list of facts. Whether common, pygmy or water, Ben certainly knew his shrews, their different tail lengths, colourings and sizes. As for her, all she could see was teeny weeny black eyes, tiny ears and velvety fur, and before she knew it, it had shuffled off and was gone.

'How come you know so much about shrews?' she asked, rising to her feet again. Then it dawned on her. 'Don't tell me,' she smiled - holding up her hand, 'Boy Scouts?'

'Aye, you're not wrong,' he said, with a hint of Yorkshire once more. 'We had an Akela who was like a Dad to us boys.' He paused. 'Aye,' he repeated, 'Akela was like the Dad I never had.'

There was another pause, during which Millie registered unspoken sadness, then looking livelier again, Ben continued. 'Anyway, this Akela was really into wildlife, and he showed us how to make traps, so I've caught quite a few shrews.'

'Trap?' she frowned a little.

'No,' he smiled, 'it *is* a trap, but it isn't cruel, and I always set them free.' He turned his head to catch her eye. 'Perhaps I can show you how it works sometime.'

'I'd like that.' She felt a flush of heat as they strolled on, their footsteps in unison, side by side. She couldn't believe how well this was going. He wanted to see her again.

'You really know your stuff,' she said, thinking the time had come to broach another sensitive subject. 'No wonder you loved that hare so much.'

He was quiet for a moment then, turning his head a fraction, he didn't quite meet her gaze. 'Oh, you heard about that,' he muttered, his shoulders rigid.

Trying to show her acceptance, Millie smiled gently, all the while hating that he now looked uncomfortable and it was all her fault. 'Don't worry,' she said, 'I would have done the same.' She wanted Ben to know she wasn't in the least bit interested in Horace and his cruelty, and steered the conversation back to something they both liked talking about.

'That shrew was so cute,' she said.

He seemed tickled by her words. 'Cute but vicious,' he scoffed. 'Ever seen a shrew fight?'

She shook her head.

'You said something about the Bard just now, so I'm guessing you like Shakespeare.'

She nodded.

'So you know all about *The Taming of the Shrew*, right?'

Pausing for a second, she soon knew what he was driving at. 'That was a woman not a *real* shrew, but point taken.'

They stopped for a minute to catch their breath.

'What about you?'

'What about me?'

'Do *you* like Shakespeare?'

Ben shook his head decisively. 'No, not really. But poetry's cool. Song lyrics are a bit like poetry don't you think. And what about you?'

'What about me?' she teased, pretending not to know what he meant.

'Are *you* into poetry?' he asked.

'I *adore* poetry,' she smiled, 'especially Keats, Wordsworth, Shelley…the romantics.'

Breathing in deeply, she thought she could detect the subtle scent of fresh chamomile flowers crushed underfoot.

'So you're a bit of a romantic then?'

She stopped in her tracks, and tilting her head she turned towards him, making no effort to hide she was picking up on his flirting.

'You don't have to answer that,' he said.

Walking on again, she hoped that just by the way she'd looked at him, his question had been answered, silently and ardently.

They stepped onto a small wooden bridge, enjoying the semi-silence of a breeze caressing the leaves of a nearby beech tree and from this vantage point, they could see curved hills in the distance, and cows grazing lazily in a nearby meadow. Curious as to what was below his feet, Ben cast his eyes downwards and saw through open, wooden slats, water flowing into marshland ditches fringed with reeds and scattered willows. Side by side, they leant against the parapet, admiring the view, their elbows almost touching.

'Can I ask something?' he said, looking directly ahead.

Feeling a burst of inner energy, she tried to control her movements and her voice. 'Yes,' she said, pressing her palm against the smooth timber barrier and waiting with bated breath.

Opening his mouth, he closed it again, then, turning away, smiled and shook his head.

'Go on,' she coaxed, 'what were you going to say?' Turning her head, she studied his handsome profile, looking for clues.

He hesitated, then straightening up, turned to face her again. 'Shall I compare thee to a summer's day?' he asked softly.

One, two, three, four – the beautiful seconds ticked by, and then, he took one step away from the edge of the bridge looking slightly embarrassed, but he couldn't take the words back now. 'Sorry,' he mumbled, gliding a hand through his fair hair, 'that was cheesy.'

'I *love* cheese,' she said, thinking that somehow, the words of the Bard sounded even sweeter coming from his lips.

Naturally, effortlessly, they slid back into position. Then, while leaning against the wooden parapet and still mirroring each other's body language, it occurred to her, why stop there?

'Thou art more lovely and more temperate,' she began slowly, reciting words she'd learned by rote for her O'level English literature.

'Rough winds do shake the darling buds of May,
And summer's lease hath all too short a date,
Sometime too hot…'

She stopped and wrinkled her forehead.

'I can't remember the next line,' she said, her cheeks on fire. She made herself look him in the eye wondering how she'd cope if she noticed any sign of rejection, but after bravely turning to face him, she found nothing. All she felt were the shimmering sun rays on the back of her neck, the physical manifestation of the warmth, acceptance and connection she was feeling.

'Millie,' he said at last.

'Yes,'

'How fast can you run?'

She blinked and looked bemused. 'Not very, especially on a hot day like this.'

'I've got to go,' he lifted a sleeve, and glanced at his watch, 'or I'll be late.'

Her hands fell at her sides. How had she forgotten to remind him to pick up Enid?

Before preparing to run, he turned around. 'Thanks for a great walk,' he smiled, and his eyes told her he meant it.

Raising a hand in farewell, she watched him sprint away, and shrinking into the distance, he was soon gone.

She wandered back to the village the way she'd come, with every excitable step reminding her that time passed far too slowly. At the top of a hill, she could see Magham Down. Set within a secluded valley, the honey-toned and muted grey houses nestling within emerald green trees drew her towards home. Somewhere amongst it all was Ben, unless of course, he was already in his car on his way to town, weaving in and out the quiet country lanes, just as he'd woven indelible and enduring pathways right through her beating heart.

Chapter 22:

'Go Wild in the Country' - Bow Wow Wow

Horace pulls out his gun from under his bed and his heart thumps. The pace quickens and he rubs his hand along the smooth wooden stock, fingers gliding across the silken wood. Only the best walnut from the South of France would do. Only the best. Staring down at the barrel, he admires the glint and how the silvery metal shines. It feels exquisite; it looks exquisite. His lips turn upwards and he grins. It *is* exquisite.

Feeling in control of everything, lock stock and barrel, is a good feeling. It's the way he likes it. He puts a finger on the trigger and raises the weapon to eye level.

Bam! Bam! Bam!

Almost falling off the bed, he erupts into child-like laughter. Suddenly, he's a boy again and he's playing his favourite games: cops and robbers, cowboys and Indians, battlefield soldiers. For a moment he can forget about being a respectable citizen, an admired member of the community, a pillar of society. But why forget and not revel in the fact that the farming community, the rural community, *his* community, love him? Grinning again, he bares his crooked teeth and admires them in the wardrobe mirror. It's a fine thing to know people like and respect you, and magnificent when everyone says what a solid man you are.

It's a privilege to be a farmer and for a farmer, it's his birthright to own a gun. *There should be no stipulations or restrictions to hinder or to stifle this right* and as he thinks these thoughts he breathes deeply, feeling the patriotism rise within the cavity of his chest.

'Rule Brittania, Brittania rules the waves,

Britons never, never, never shall be slaves.'

But if that's true, if Britons are not slaves, why do so few in this magnificent land of ours, a land of hope and glory, have the privilege of being able to own a beauty like this? Touching the gun once again, he questions with incredulity, how a man can hunt without one. *How else can he rid himself of pests and vermin? And how else*, he smiles, baring his teeth again, *can he eliminate every form of lowlife that exists on this planet?*

Lowlife, he repeats, and his inner voice grates on him. He thinks of Ben, and gripping his gun, his insides burn. People don't have a clue, do they? They think they do, but they really know nothing, zilch, nada, nothing at all about farming life. What does a jumped-up, wanna-be rich and famous cretin such as him, know about living in the countryside? Horace lifts the gun, and his bloodshot eyes stare down the barrel. *Sunny Jim knows nothing*, he smiles, *nothing at all*. He laughs out loud, but this time it isn't the gun bringing him pleasure. Or maybe it is. Stupid people, ignorant people, people like that, are very entertaining. They make him laugh.

Putting his baby away, he says goodnight to her. He must leave his bedroom, he has work to do. He rises from the queen-sized bed, turns off the light and walks away. The hare coursing season begins again in earnest next month, but that doesn't mean he won't be taking out his beautiful shooting iron before then. It may just see the light of day if the timing just so happens to be right.

Chapter 23:

'The Longest Time' - Billy Joel

After placing the handset on the receiver, Millie lifted her head, feeling strained. Zane was making a real effort to sound casual, but there was an intensity at the other end of the line. She didn't want to be unkind and it was good of him to phone and ask how her summer was going, but she didn't realise how much she *hadn't* wanted him to ring until she heard his voice. And then, when he suggested meeting – in London, in Sussex, anywhere - she didn't know what to say at first. 'I'm still not ready', or 'let's take it slow', perhaps? No, she first started using the 'take it slow' line two years ago, so you really couldn't get much slower. One thing was certain, giving him the cold shoulder or being nasty just wasn't an option, because they were friends.

'I'll speak to Wahida, it'll be great to meet,' she said, trying to sound upbeat. She was stretching the truth of course, but she wasn't being completely dishonest. She valued Zane's friendship, and moreover, burning her bridges before Ben was in the bag was stupid. She was experienced enough to know that a guy can seem interested, only for things to fizzle out, and even if they don't, even if you start going steady and believe he's in it for the long haul, you could be sorely mistaken and in for a shock.

She gazed out of the landing window to see gorgeously fine weather, the sort of day when sunlight illuminates every dark corner of your world. It was ten days since she'd seen Ben. Had she allowed herself and her emotions to get carried away or counted several chickens before they'd even come close to hatching?

Until this morning, whenever the telephone rang or there was a rap at the front door, she'd leapt with expectation, only to deflate like a ruptured balloon. Would he *ever* call? But, in saner moments she knew she was being over the top. She hardly knew him, plus, he might still be interested because ten days wasn't *that* long. One thing was for sure, she wasn't going to Enid's. No way! Turning up to Clover Cottage now would look desperate, and desperation was never, ever a good look.

Wandering around the farmhouse somewhat aimlessly, she tried to look forward to another day of freedom. Ursula was abroad, so she couldn't meet her, but there were plenty of other things she could do. She'd been meaning to read George Orwell's 1984, and since it was now halfway through 1985, she ought to get a move on. There was always the piano. With no grades to work towards, or schoolwork eating into her practising time, playing was more of a pleasure these days. And what about the pictures? She paused, thinking it was hard to visualise a dark cinema without imagining Giles' arms wrapped around her. Snapping out of it, she shook her head, and as in 'The Last Film' by Kissing The Pink, tried to remember the last film *she'd* seen. It didn't matter how long ago it was, because she knew she lacked the courage to go alone. Heading over to Hailsham Picture House all by herself just wasn't going to happen, not today.

Feeling lonely was silly when she was never actually alone and at least one member of her family was around, somewhere within the farm's four hundred or so acres. And of course, there were also the animals to keep her company, including their beloved border collies. But, amazing as the sheepdogs were, they weren't very pettable, nor were they allowed into the house. Still, later today, there was another four-legged companion to hang out with, because her great-aunt was paying them another visit.

***

The sun was still shining when Millie grasped Conker's lead, said rushed goodbyes and slammed the farmhouse door behind her. Tuning into herself, she consciously slowed down. Why was she in such a hurry? The answer came straight away. If she should bump into Ben, and there was no pretending she didn't hope that she would, racing towards the village centre wasn't going to increase her chances of seeing him, so she might as well relax.

With her aunt's scruffy little dog by her side, she passed a wildflower meadow which was a riot of colour and the magenta-pink flowers of rosebay willowherb stood tall against a grass verge heavy with yellow and orange common toadflax flowers. Ben *wasn't* ignoring her, she told herself, soaking up the floral brightness, and he wasn't arrogant either. Horace was wrong.

Stopping outside St Mark's church, she turned on the outside tap for a drink, and, after splashing her face with cool refreshing water, cupped her hands and slurped. 'Conker', she said, watching his ear twitch, 'wasn't I good not going past Enid's? I deserve a choc ice, don't you think?'

On her way to the village shop she was greeted by several folk. Mrs Yalden was keen to share how her husband was becoming more, 'thick of hearing,' which was the Sussex way of saying he was going deaf, and the gardener who everyone called 'Old Boy', told Millie how amazed he was by how many 'bishop barnabies', aka ladybirds, there were this summer.

By the time she'd arrived at the village shop, there was still no sign of Ben. Tensing with frustration, she began to question whether he *ever* came into the village centre. Dang it. She stopped herself from slapping her thigh in public. Why not just go round to Clover Cottage and ask him out and be done with it? And if that turns him off, so what? She shrugged unconvincingly, telling herself he wouldn't be the first man to go off her.

'Now Conker,' she said, pointing at the pooch, 'be good and wait here. If you see anything, cat, rat, squirrel, I don't care what, no chasing, okay?' Conker cocked his head to one side which she took to mean, 'message received and understood', and after tying his lead to a post, she entered the shop to the familiar jangle of the bell and exited just minutes later, with an ice cream in her hands.

'Stop looking at me like that - you're making me feel guilty. Ice cream isn't for dogs!' Then, after taking another lick of creaminess, she felt her heart race when she noticed a familiar figure coming up the hill. 'Look Conker,' she whispered with excitement, 'it's Lauren, Ben's sister!'

'Millie!' Lauren waved enthusiastically, a stylish jute macrame bag dangling in her hand. 'How's things?'

'Fine thanks.' With Lauren now standing by her side, Millie could smell a strong perfume that completely overpowered the subtle scent of creamy mock orange flowers nearby. She thought that Lauren's scent smelled identical to the new Christian Dior fragrance, which a shop worker once doused her with inside Dickens & Jones department store in London's Regent Street. What was the name of that perfume again? Ah yes, that's right, 'Poison'.

'How's things with you?' Millie asked.

'Great.' After making a beeline for Conker, Lauren began to pat him vigorously. 'And how's this little fella doing?'

'Conker's doing great. He's not mine, he's…'

'I know,' Lauren interrupted, 'Ben told me all about him.' Crouching down, she fussed over him, and Conker rewarded her with excitable leaps and tail wagging. 'I gather he likes to do wees in strategic places,' she smiled.

Millie felt her belly flip. For Ben to have mentioned all this, he was obviously talking about her, and that *had* to be a good sign.

'He didn't tell me he was a border terrier though,' Lauren said, 'and that's surprising. He knows I've got a soft spot for them.'

Before she could say she felt the same and thought border terriers looked like cute, grumpy teddy bears, Millie watched Lauren's blue eyes lose their sparkle.

'Did Ben tell you about Teddo?' Lauren asked, her hands briefly falling away from Conker.

'Teddo?' Millie shook her head. 'Was he a border terrier?'

Lauren nodded. 'Yes, and not only that, he was *my* border terrier - well Dad's actually.'

There was a pause, interspersed with more pats and affectionate strokes. And then came the story. When Lauren was seven years old, she began, Teddo was her world, even when he reeked of fox poo and even when he threw up over her Mum's new carpet or made off with Lauren's faggots and mash and left her without any dinner. 'Ben was too small to love him like I did,' she said, wistfully. Then, after a pause, she told Millie that Ben couldn't remember the morning they got out of bed and their mother said their dad and Teddo had gone. 'I asked if Teddo was coming back, even before I asked about Dad,' Lauren said. 'To me, it made sense to ask that at the time, because Teddo was always at home, in my lap, or on my bed - he'd be somewhere around, whereas Dad - well, Dad was hardly ever at home.'

Ben didn't remember any of this, she went on to say. All he remembered was having to pack up his toys, leave the house and start *another* first day at school. Lauren's smiles were heavy as she sped through her story. A new house, a new area, a new school, a new life and her eyes flickered with every detail she shared.

After she'd finished, Millie felt like reaching out to hug her, but instead, they just stood, facing each other in the centre of the village square. What Lauren had said happened so long ago, but clearly, seeing Conker was bringing everything back, and while watching her pet him, Millie visualised a five-year-old Ben, looking like he did in that photo in Enid's lounge and wondered just how much all this had affected him. He wasn't unscathed, that much she knew, and by a few things he'd said, it was obvious that he'd been buffeted by those same metaphorical waves that had drifted his mother and his big sister far out to sea.

'You're ridiculously like Teddo,' Lauren smiled, embracing Conker in her arms, still lapping up his nuzzles and affectionate leaps, 'I wish I could spend more time with you cheeky fella, but right now, I've gotta go I'm afraid.' She rose to her feet and thumbed towards the shop. 'It's a long old drive back up to Northampton. Lucky old me, Malcolm's cooking tonight, but Gran *still* insists we take snacks just in case the car conks out on the way.' She rolled her eyes. 'It had better not break down because it's almost brand new!'

Now reminded that Enid had said she went away to stay with family each summer, Millie had just one question on her mind. *What about Ben? Was he staying behind?*

'Must run,' Lauren said, 'but before I do, can I give you a word of advice?'

'Yep.'

'Stay away.'

What? Those two words were like a bolt out of the blue, and although she managed to stay silent, Millie couldn't help but raise her eyebrows. Why was Lauren staring at her like that? Stay away from what, from whom? She couldn't possibly mean Ben, could she? Was she warding her off, like Horace had done, or maybe Lauren wanted her to leave Ben alone?

'From the trap, I mean.' Breaking into a smile, Lauren seemed amused by the confusion she'd just created.

'Ben said you're keen to see it, but I'd keep well away from it if I were you.'

'I, I *am*, keen - to see it, I mean,' Millie stuttered with relief.

'You have *no* idea what might turn up in that thing,' Lauren flapped a hand, 'and unless you're also into diseased vermin with disgusting long tails, I'd pass. Personally, I've not got the stomach for it.'

Just at that moment, one of the ladies in the village sauntered by with her poodle, and grabbing Conker's rein tight, Millie shushed him when chaos threatened to break out.

'Ben promised to keep rats and mice away from me years ago,' Lauren said, shouting to make her voice heard over the barks and trying to calm Conker down, 'and, touch wood,' she tapped the shop's oak window frame, 'so far, he's kept his word. Still, I keep telling him his obsession with those nasty things is the reason I left home.' She laughed, but her smile turned into a horrified grimace when Millie told her about her various encounters with rats and mice around the farm.

'I would have loved to have grown up on a farm like you,' Lauren said, looking reflective. She took a deep breath. 'I can see…' she paused, then stopped and Millie tilted her head, noticing a quiver in her voice.

'Sussex has been good for Ben. My baby brother desperately needed a fresh start and…' She paused again and gave Millie a tentative smile. 'I've not seen him this happy in a very long time.'

Not knowing what to say after that, Millie swallowed hard. 'Safe journey,' she said, eventually, 'and I hope Enid enjoys her break.' Lauren stooped down again to give Conker a goodbye cuddle, and Millie, knowing it was now or never, finally decided to say what was on her mind. 'Is Ben going?'

'No, Ben's not coming,' Lauren said, matter-of-factly. 'Now Gran's got someone at home to keep an eye on things while she's away, she's making the most of it.' Then, she arched an eyebrow and looked directly at Millie with a mischievous smirk. 'But, while he's taking care of the house, who'll be taking care of *him*?'

Millie could hardly believe her ears. Was that a hint? Was Lauren really giving her a thumbs-up and her seal of approval? Fighting an overwhelming urge to head over to Clover Cottage, there and then, she said 'no' to the gravitational pull. Instead, when Lauren stepped into the village shop with the bell ringing behind her, Millie looked at the milky white walls of this quaint historic building feeling at ease with the world. There was something lovely about Lauren, even though at times she came across as too much of a 'Material Girl'. But still, clearly, she had a big heart, especially for family, and especially for her brother.

'Come on Conker, I should have taken you home yonks ago.' Millie walked away from the heart of the village with a skip in her step, feeling emboldened, upbeat and also slightly emotional. Granted, she hadn't seen Ben, but as far as she was concerned, it was mission accomplished. Lauren had given her all the grounds for hope she could wish for, and with Enid soon gone, who knows? Maybe now she and Ben would get the chance to spend some time together, inside Clover Cottage, alone.

Chapter 24:

'Love on a Farmboy's Wages' - XTC

Not many people these days could appreciate a hay mattress, but Millie certainly could. She lay back in the barn, hands behind her head, and sank deeper, listening to the crinkling and rustling. The forage underneath her was tightly packed and unyielding, however, being nature's answer to luxury bedding, it was also surprisingly elastic and accommodating. She could sleep for hours on it... for hours, and although marrying a farmer didn't make you rich – her mother and Amanda could attest to that - life on a farm supplied riches in a plethora of other more meaningful ways.

It was a hot August day that had drawn her to the barn's coolness, and with its doors flung open wide, light streamed in. A sunbeam warmed her face, lighting up her brown eyes, flecked with green, and she looked through the open doors to the world outside. Rising downland in the distance, its pastures past the peak of viridescent lushness, was tinged with golden hues, and flopping backwards again, fully supported by the hay bale, she felt content and at peace.

Since seeing Lauren in the village, too many days had passed without hearing a peep from Ben, and with Enid away and no legitimate reason to go round to Clover Cottage, Millie had grown tired of waiting. She'd also worked herself up into a tizz, managing to convince herself that she'd misread the situation. If he was so slow about it, he probably wasn't that interested, and so she was coming to terms with letting go, telling herself what will be, will be.

She couldn't take all the credit for her newfound attitude. Four days earlier, and finding herself dangerously close to 'losing it', she headed over to the new bookshop in town, scoured the shelves for a self-help book and walked away with *How to Love and Be Loved* by Dr Paul Hauck. She read the whole thing in just a day, and it pumped her up with some much-needed advice to bolster her self-esteem. No more one-sided relationships, no more falling for a guy before he'd declared his interest, and no more over-sharing - and for her, that meant not saying too much, not even to her mother, Ursula or Amanda. The result of all this? She still liked Ben, but if he didn't feel the same, she felt much better able to move on and take it in her stride.

Was it the sausage rolls or the copious amounts of Kia-Ora she'd had for lunch that made her eyes feel heavy? Either way, very soon, she started to drift off to the sound of rustling in the trees, the mooing of cows and the occasional bark from the sheepdogs. She dozed, but only very lightly, and before long her slumber was interrupted by an unfamiliar sound. The steady crunch of footsteps grew closer and louder. Listening attentively, she could tell it wasn't her father's, or her mother's and it sounded too heavy to be Amanda's. Was Dean back already? But actually no, it didn't sound like Dean either. The crazy idea that it was Ben, come looking for her, entered her dozy head. *Ha Ha*, she chuckled silently. The moment she decided to forget him, had her wish come true?

The sound of footsteps stopped just outside the barn and sitting up, she raised a hand to her forehead to shade her eyes from the sun.

Squinting, she saw nothing at first. Then, almost falling off the haystack, she gasped. There, in the farmyard, looking totally lost, was none other than the man himself, Ben. Yes, she blinked, it really was him standing there, right here on the farm. What is it that people say about something happening when you least expect it? She'd never paid much attention to that saying, at least not until now. He was looking slightly lost and holding something box-shaped and wooden under his arm. *I think he likes me. I think he actually likes me!* Just managing to avoid tripping over the bales, she rushed over, just as he was about to move on.

'Hi!'

He turned swiftly and then walked towards the barn. 'Hi. I thought I'd heard something in there. I guess it must've been you.'

'What a surprise!' she flustered, brushing hay from her blue dungarees.

He turned towards the farmhouse. 'I knocked, and your mum answered the front door. She said, you'd be somewhere outside.' Looking hesitant, he paused. 'She was on the phone, so I was sorry to interrupt her.'

Swiping her hand dismissively, Millie rolled her eyes. 'Mum's forever gassing on the phone, it's fine.' Then, glancing at the wooden object being carried under his arm, she invited him into the barn, to lay it down somewhere. He followed, and for the first time, she realised the tang of silage and manure with top notes of oak wood might not be to everyone's taste. Personally, she loved the smell of animal quarters, and at the very least, she hoped Ben wouldn't mind it.

'I'm assuming this is the famous trap,' she said, looking directly at the wooden box after he'd placed it on a hay bale. She put her hands on her thighs, bent down a fraction, and peered into its small glass window. 'Thanks for bringing it over.'

'No problem.'

'Can I feel how heavy it is?'

'Sure.' Lifting the trap, he placed it into her hands.

Taking hold, she felt its lightness and the pine wood's uneven texture, then she pushed a curious finger through its trap door.

'You see the little nail inside?' he said.

She tipped it on its side and peered in, 'Yes.'

'That's the hook for the meat, bread, cheese, whatever... depending on what you want to attract.'

She stepped back a fraction. *What do I want to attract?* The answer was simple, the answer was obvious, but at that moment it didn't have much to do with small mammals.

'Then the critter steps onto this bit,' he continued, gently taking it from Millie's hands and stepping closer. Now shoulder to shoulder, he opened the trap door, and both leaned in to take a look inside. They bumped heads lightly, and pulling back, they glanced at each other with 'we can't go on touching accidentally like this' vibes.

'As I was saying,' he said, clearing his throat awkwardly, 'it goes inside through here, and when it steps on to here, it grabs the food, then the door shuts behind it.'

'You made this yourself?'

He nodded.

'I'm *so* impressed.'

'Really? Thanks. Talking of food,' he said, 'have you just eaten?'

Opening her mouth, she looked a little confused by the question. 'I… *did* have lunch, but about an hour ago.'

'Let me guess. Eggs?' With a quick flare of his nostrils, he glanced down at the top half of her dungarees.

She looked down, and sure enough, starting from her tee shirt, right down the top of her denim dungarees was a large and crusty yellow trail.

'That wasn't lunch, that was breakfast,' she confessed with an uneasy grin.

'And, let me guess,' he smiled, 'you had a salad for lunch?'

Oh no, what now? She thought for a second. 'Yes, I did, watercress actually.'

'That explains it.'

'Explains what?'

'Why there's something green stuck between your teeth.'

'Where?' Inviting him to help her out, mouth clenched, she bared her teeth.

'There.' Smiling, he pointed to a tooth and she rubbed her tongue across and waited.

'Still there I'm afraid.'

After she repeated the action, he shook his head, so, kissing goodbye to any remaining decorum, she poked around with a fingernail, until she felt something come loose onto her tongue.

'Thanks,' she said, hoping this was the end of the messy Millie show.

'Anytime, and it's always good to be told these things.' A patchy smile spread across his face. 'Once,' he began with slow deliberation, 'our band was performing live at a music venue. All was going well, but then, during the interval, a guy came up to me and said words no performer wants to hear.'

Millie looked and listened, keen to know what he said.

'"Hey mate," he said to me, "your flies are undone".'

The moment Ben finished his story, she peered down at his crotch. She couldn't help it. It was automatic, a reflex. Then, she began to giggle idiotically.

'I'm sorry,' she laughed, covering her mouth.

'Me too. I mean, don't get me wrong. I'm all for letting it all hang out and everything, but there's a time and a place.'

That was it. If there was one thing Millie found annoying about herself, it was her inability to control the giggles once they took over. Smiling, Ben stood by and waited out the silly laughter now sounding throughout the barn. At some point after starting medical school, she'd made the decision that such behaviour wasn't fitting for a soon-to-be doctor, but boy, did it feel great to enjoy a belly laugh again.

'Good of him to tell you,' she said, trying to calm down.

'Yeah, and rather him than a groupie.'

'Groupie?'

When Ben explained exactly what he meant by that, it soon wiped the smile off her face. She didn't quite like the sound of 'Female fans, always looking for an excuse to get with a band member' and 'girls who follow you around when you're on tour'.

She looked at him, feeling uneasy, weighing up his words. Nothing he'd said was particularly bad, at least it didn't make *him* look bad. And just because an offer was on the table, she reasoned, didn't mean he ever took it up. He didn't fancy Jill Mason, so perhaps he was never interested in any of those girls either.

'Sounds like you were a popular guy,' she smiled, unconvincingly, 'but then again, what girl doesn't love a rock star?'

He tipped his head back. 'I thought I told you I wasn't a rock star,' he smiled.

'Okay,' she snorted, 'blue-eyed soul artist then.' The sharpness in her voice easily gave away her jealousy and made her cringe. *He must think me utterly ridiculous.* 'Anyway, tons of people in the village think you're a rock star,' she added in a half-hearted attempt to deflect, then teasingly, she narrowed her eyes, 'especially all the single girls.'

Basking in her light flirtatiousness, he shrugged nonchalantly. 'Too bad,' he said. 'I guess I'm just going to have to suck it up then.'

Smiling, she watched his facial expression edge towards serious. It was as though he was about to announce something, something lovely, just like he did on that sunny day when they stood on the bridge together.

'I'm here because…I want to tell you I'm going up to Macclesfield tomorrow to see my Dad.'

She didn't move. She waited. Was that it? Still smiling through gritted teeth, she'd thought they were finally getting somewhere, but now he tells her he's going away. With Enid at Lauren's she'd also hoped they might have the house to themselves at some point, to talk and get to know each other, if nothing more, for now at least.

'I've not seen Dad for six months and he lives on beer and crisps so I like to keep an eye on him,' he said, picking up on her disappointment.

'Are you away for long?' she asked casually, lifting her brows.

'Four days. It's a punishing drive, so I usually stay longer, just to recover, but this time,' he paused, his eyes focussed on hers, 'I'd really like to spend more time around here.'

In the silence, she began to breathe more easily again. *Only four days, just four days.* She'd already waited weeks. She could wait just four more days.

'I'm leaving this with you.' He glanced at the trap, and after advising her to place it strategically somewhere around the farm, he had further instructions. 'After you've caught something and had a good look at it,' he said, slipping a hand into his pocket, 'just lift the door to set it free.'

'Okay.'

Thrilled, but at the same time feeling somewhat bereft, she thanked him and quietly led the way across the barn before they both stepped outside into the sunshine.

'See you soon,' she said, when they reached the farm entrance. 'Safe journey.'

Hesitantly, his head lowered a touch. Then, he stepped through the gate, and slowly began to walk away.'

'Wait!' She called, and he turned swiftly. Nervously touching the gate with her hand, she felt the warmth of steel heated by the sun.

'I'm free on Wednesday,' she said, realising she'd wasted enough time. 'We could go for another walk or…'

'Or, I could cook you dinner,' he chipped in unexpectedly.

'Really?' she gripped the gate a little tighter, glad of something to hold on to, grateful for something to keep her steady.

Nodding, he smiled some more, enjoying watching her eyes dance. 'Your place or mine?' he asked. 'But if it's mine, it'll just be us I'm afraid. I'm sure Lauren told you Gran's staying with her for a couple of weeks.'

Millie's pumping heart was battling against her will. Playing games wasn't her style. Even so, it was imperative to pause before responding because it was essential to give the impression that she had to think about it, even just a little bit. 'Yours, if that's okay,' she said when absolutely sure the timing was right, and with the farm tractor whirring in the fields behind them, she closed the gate after him and whispered her goodbyes.'

Chapter 25:

'Music and Lights' - Imagination

She loved this time of day. That mystical hour when the sun no longer shone, but there was still enough light plus a stillness in the air, which covered the earth in a slate blue overcoat. Twilight was when the daytime wildlife clocked out, hung up their proverbial workwear, settled down for the evening and handed over their shift to the creatures of the night.

Millie made her way to Clover Cottage, carrying a bottle of Cabernet Sauvignon and the mammal trap in a cotton bag. All she'd caught was a cute little mouse in four days, but it had worked, and she strode along, basking in her success.

The wine was a 'thank you' to Ben for cooking and she intended to sit back, relax and enjoy a glass or two, and afterwards, dawdle home on a clear summer night.

Dusk descended quickly, and it was almost dark when she arrived to a warm glow coming from Enid's lounge. She took a couple of controlled breaths, opened the black metal gate and mounted the short step to the front door. She was nervous. Why? She could be herself with Ben. That much she already knew. But tonight, things felt like they'd stepped up a gear or two.

Going for a walk was one thing. Being alone in that cosy cottage at nightfall was a different ballgame. What went through her head when she thought about being alone with a man? She tutted, feeling frustrated with herself. Now wasn't a good time to remember Giles and the hours they'd spent together, or feel those emotions which could oscillate between passion, regret, longing and despair. Forget about Giles. Ben was nothing like him and seemed in no hurry to get physical, but raising her hand to the doorbell, she questioned what she'd do if Ben *did* make a move tonight. She really liked him, but was she ready? And if she was, how far would she, should she go? If he wanted to get too close and she said 'no' would he hate her? If she said 'yes' would he hate her even more? She rang the doorbell and tried to breathe steadily.

Just at that moment, a rich smell of bolognese and béchamel sauce wafted through the downstairs window, luring her inside. They'd spoken on the phone just before he'd gone away, so she knew he was cooking lasagne, and the mouth-watering aroma quelled her nerves, at least until the moment she saw his shadow behind the glass.

'Hi.' The door swung open and he stood in front of her with an easygoing smile. It was the same reassuring, comforting smile that he had when they were in the barn together. Feeling a lot calmer, her inner tensions began to disappear. 'Come in,' he said, turning around and leading the way.

When she stepped inside, the interior felt very familiar but also very different. She'd been inside this cottage so many times, but only in the daytime, and only after Enid had opened the door. *Enid's not here. How weird is that?* Millie looked around before hanging up her cream, double-breasted jacket on the wooden coat rack by the door. She knew Clover Cottage would be warm inside, so she'd chosen to wear her mint green, puff-sleeved, polka dot dress - which had just the right balance of comfort and style. She'd hummed and hawed about whether to go for dressy or casual, but after Ben had caught her scruffy and unawares in the barn, she decided to make an effort. Adjusting her sleeves, she lamented that he seemed far too busy to appreciate her efforts just yet. *C'est la vie. Maybe he'll notice later.*

'Nearly ready,' he called out from the kitchen.

'Can I help?'

'Nope. It's all in hand.' She slipped quietly into the kitchen and watched him slide on thick oven gloves, and she kept watching while he opened the oven door, releasing a blast of heat and the gentle clattering sound of an enamel lid, lifted by steamy, bubbling sauce.

'It's really kind of you to cook,' she said, trying to make conversation. 'No one's ever cooked for me before. Well, um, no, I don't really mean that,' she spluttered. 'Mum cooks all the meals at home, and my friend Wahida at uni, she did an amazing Bengali biriani once - what I mean is, no man has ever, - no,' she touched her furrowed brow, 'what am I saying? That's not true, Stuart, he's my oldest brother, he likes cooking and he used to cook loads.' Wincing, she saw Ben trying his best to keep up with her chaotic rant. Perhaps it was time to shut up.

'What about your Dad?' he asked, inviting her to sit down at the table. 'Does he cook?'

'Dad?' Chuckling, she pulled out a chair and shook her head. 'No way! Mum says he'd burn a salad given half a chance!'

They laughed a little, then after closing the oven door, he glanced at her. 'I *had* to learn to cook,' he said, placing the oven dish in the centre of a small wooden table. 'Either that or live off baked beans and Campbell's soup. Lauren was a lousy cook and Mum was too lazy.'

Millie thought Lauren sounded like a kindred spirit and she could also see where his mother was coming from. She smiled, thinking their inadequacies were her gain, because thanks to them, Ben was going to dish her up something special tonight. He began to talk about a culinary repertoire which had come about through necessity, and she started to salivate. Nepalese, Thai, Mexican... he'd perfected them all. His friends, who'd dubbed him 'The King of Spice', would go round to his place instead of the local takeaway. 'But Gran's not so keen on what she calls "exotic foods", so I tend to go easy on spicy meals these days and when *she* cooks, it's usually kidneys, liver and bacon or,' he paused, looking like he was about to heave, 'tripe. So you can see why *I* prefer to do the cooking.'

Millie looked at the delicious meal in front of her, relieved never to have encountered the nauseating smell of pot-boiled tripe inside the cottage.

'You didn't fancy doing something spicy tonight?' she asked, staring at the lasagne's meltingly golden, cheesy crust.

'I thought I'd play it safe.'

'I *love* a bit of spice, me.' Instantly, she curled back with embarrassment, realising she hadn't meant for it to come out *quite* like that.

Wearing a hidden smile, he quietly pulled out cutlery from a drawer. Then, after stopping to think for a second, he removed the garlic bread from the oven, reached into the fridge for a salad bowl, and, after taking out two etched crystal glasses from the kitchen cupboard, placed them next to the bottle of wine. 'Thanks again for bringing this,' he said, picking it up and reading the label.

'No problem,' she smiled.

'Ah, yes,' he said, standing up again and tapping his forehead, 'water.' Reaching into a low cabinet he took out a glass jug.

'No, let me get that.' Gently lifting it from his hands, she gave him a firm smile. Then, walking over to the sink, she placed the jug under the brass tap, turned its handle, and instantly the sound of rushing water filled the air. Moments later, she headed back to the table with the jug in her hands filled to the brim with water she was trying not to spill. On her way, she squeezed past and brushed up against him, ever so slightly. There was only room for one worker in this tiny kitchen and feeling the goosebumps and the hair rising on her arms, she could suddenly see why he'd declined all her offers to help. It all felt very up close and personal, and without catching his eye, she turned her head towards him as, standing by the table, he pulled out a chair and sat down, looking slightly redder than before.

After a quiet pause, he lifted a large kitchen knife from the table and slowly began to cut into the lasagne. In so doing, he unintentionally drew attention to his attractively patterned long-sleeved shirt, and after sliding a huge portion onto her plate, he began to light a single white candle. She breathed in the characteristic, sulphuric aroma from the match while staring at the flickering orange flame.

'The wine's really full-bodied,' he said, finally able to sit back and relax.

She smiled, then closing her eyes, savoured a rich, satisfying mouthful.

'If only *I* could cook like this,' she said dreamily. 'My compliments to the chef.'

'Thanks,' he said, placing a humble hand to his chest in acknowledgement, and then he frowned. 'Drat!'

'Is something wrong?'

'I forgot to defrost the dessert.' Heading over to a freezer compartment, he pulled out something disproportionately large for the space it had occupied – a big cardboard box with an unmistakable brown and red design.

'*Sara Lee* chocolate cake,' she gasped, 'I'm a chocoholic.' Then her shoulders dropped. 'But they take ages to thaw, don't they?'

He scanned through the instructions. 'Slicing it might help.' After tearing open the box he gave her a cheeky, disapproving look. 'A doctor with a chocolate addiction? Tut tut,' he said, shaking his head.

'Could be worse,' she smiled.

'I guess it could.'

Guided by the soft glow of candlelight, he began to cut through the frozen dessert. Chocolate shavings crackling under the chef's knife and the wait for the anticipated last course to defrost, provided a perfect opportunity to enjoy conversation just as sweet. When, forty-five minutes later the cake still hadn't thawed, they dived in anyway, agreeing that half-frozen gateau was surprisingly tasty, and between mouthfuls, Ben talked about his trip up North, his father, his old friends, and how he wasn't in touch with his former bandmates any more. Millie listened, enjoying how he was doing most of the talking and thinking how it made a really lovely change.

By the time half the gateau was gone, she was much more knowledgeable about the music industry and what it was like to 'nearly hit the big time'. He promised to dig out a demo tape or two for her, if he could find them. 'I haven't seen any since I moved and I have no idea where they are.'

Dinner all but over, he suggested retiring to the living room. 'After you,' he said, blowing out the candle.

Picking up her wine glass, Millie rose to her feet, wondering if she was brave enough to say what she was thinking. Should she? *Go on, go for it.* 'I'm glad you didn't make it big,' she said, stepping into the lamp-lit room, 'because you wouldn't be here today if you had.' While congratulating herself for her bravery, she sat down on the dark green sofa and watched him perch on the armchair opposite. *Why didn't he sit here, next to me?* Clasping her hands on her lap, she ignored her disappointment.

'You're right,' he sighed.

Forgetting what she'd just said, she tilted her head, 'about…?'

With an odd smile, he breathed in. 'You said, I wouldn't be here today if I was famous and that's true, because I'd probably be dead.'

For a moment, there was silence and she looked at him, unsure if he was joking or not. *Why dead?* 'I didn't mean…' her hand ran across the smooth upholstered sofa, 'what I meant was, you wouldn't be *here*, in Sussex – not that you'd be dead.'

Smiling slightly, he didn't look as if he'd been trying to be funny. 'Sorry, I must sound so melodramatic.'

She shook her head.

'And I hope I haven't freaked you out.'

She shook her head again.

He placed his wine glass down on the coffee table and sighed. 'My time in the music industry was… I guess, it *was* fun while it lasted but,' he looked down briefly, 'but it was also… put it this way, I don't for one minute regret leaving that crazy, hedonistic world behind.'

Sitting tight, Millie began to process his words. *Crazy, hedonistic world. What does he mean*? She looked for clues, but his eyes gave little away, so she began to rely on her imagination. Wild parties? All-night benders? Female fans in hotel rooms? Getting high? The more she thought about it, the worse it got. She glanced over at Enid's artificial chrysanthemums. Plastic and dreary, they were a dull shade of orange, with dusty petals, and twisted leaves. Even so, they were more beautiful than the thoughts running through her head right now.

'Are you sure you don't want me to wash up?' she asked, glancing nervously at the kitchen door.

'Definitely. I'll tackle that later.'

He smiled awkwardly, then she smiled back just as awkwardly, but very quickly she could see that the man sitting in front of her was no crazy hedonist. If he was, once upon a time, he wasn't any more, and feeling lighter again, her head began to settle down. There was plenty of time to find out more about his old life, the life he was glad not to be living any more, but tonight was all about getting to know each other, as the people they were today.

'What made you want to be a doctor?' Ben asked, doing the job of changing the subject for her.

She picked up her glass and took a sip of wine. 'I was involved in an accident.'

Jerking his head upwards, he looked surprised, and immediately, she knew it was time to tell her story. It was the same story she'd told many times over and the one that began with Granny, who lived on the farm. It was the story about a granny who taught her so many valuable things, who showed her how to make delicious chutneys, quince jelly, relishes, elderflower cordial and every other country preserve imaginable. It was a story about a granny she loved.

'Once,' Millie began, her eyes lively, 'Granny made sloe gin and gave me a taste. Well, one night, I sneaked into the kitchen and I gulped down a whole lot, all at once. I must have been noisy, because Mum walked in and caught me red-handed, and she wasn't happy at all!'

'Uh oh,' Ben narrowed his eyes disapprovingly. 'How old were you?'

'Eleven,' Millie said, 'but I wasn't just being naughty. I loved science and it was an experiment. I genuinely wanted to study how many drinks it took to get drunk.'

'And how many *did* it take?'

'How was I supposed to know when Mum cut the experiment short?' she laughed quietly. 'I was in the dog house for days, and Granny was told never to give me anything like that again,' Millie paused, 'but it wasn't her fault.'

Ben smiled soberly. 'I'm guessing that wasn't the accident?'

Looking more serious, Millie shook her head. 'No,' she said, 'that happened a few months later.' She took a deep breath and began again. 'One day, me and Granny were making jam. We… by that I mean Mum and Dad, my brothers and me, noticed for a while that she was getting clumsy and dropping things - stuff like that. The doctor said it wasn't Parkinson's or anything, he said it was just old age, but Mum and Dad weren't convinced.' Millie lifted her wine glass, but she didn't drink from it. Instead, she put it down again with plaintive eyes. 'Granny's hands started to tremble more and more, and everyone kept telling her to be careful, but she wouldn't listen. One day in September, just before I went back to school, we, I mean me and Granny, were in the kitchen making blackberry jam. She said, "Millie, it's like liquid sulphur." She said it wouldn't be safe in my hands. She kept saying it and *I* kept saying, "No Granny, I'm old enough, really, I am".'

Pausing, Millie frowned, and this time, after picking up her glass she drank from it. 'Even at that age, I was dead scared she'd hurt herself. I wasn't worried about me. I didn't think anything was going to happen to me, not until Granny knocked over a jar.'

Grimacing, Ben sucked in his breath, listening to how Millie's life changed in a split second. He listened to her talk about the bubbling jam and the melting sensation on her inner thigh, the searing pain, the blackout, and later the throbbing, the burning, the weeping wound and finally, the surgery. 'It's really weird,' she said, 'but whenever I think back to what happened, just before I was unconscious, what I remember most was Granny's confusion. I can't forget how she kept looking around the kitchen as though she'd lost something and only when Dad ran in, did she seem to realise what had happened. "What have I done, what have I done?" she asked over and over and over again. "Cecil son, what have I done to young Millie?"'

Still sitting in silence, Ben listened with heavy eyes. 'I had a skin graft,' Millie said, keen for him to know she was now fine. Then, realising she still hadn't yet told him the reason she had decided to become a doctor, she finished the story. 'Queen Victoria Hospital is famous all around the world for its plastic surgery, and that's where I had my skin graft. It's just up the road in East Grinstead, how amazing is that?', she smiled broadly. 'All the staff were great and the medics didn't only save my life from sepsis and all that, they couldn't do enough for me. After that, I just knew I had to be a surgeon, just like them.'

Still listening with admiration, Ben noticed her eyes become glassy, and his face slackened in response. 'If only they'd been able to fix Gran as well as me,' she mumbled. 'But I knew that couldn't happen. Her problem couldn't be fixed with surgery and...' she stopped abruptly, 'you know what, I don't think she ever forgave herself for what happened, but just like that time I drank the sloe gin,' Millie blinked, 'it wasn't her fault.'

For a moment, there was an unhappy pause. 'Did she get better?' Ben asked, lifting his lowered eyes, guessing what the answer might be.

Feeling disquieted, Millie looked around the living room. She could see paper doilies, crocheted chair backs, lacy armrest covers and other visible signs of being in an elderly person's home.

'She died a year later,' she said, sounding as hollow as she was feeling and slowly realising why Enid meant so much to her. Ben and Lauren were incredibly lucky. They still had their Gran.

'Did having a skin graft mean you avoided a scar?' he asked, lifting his voice.

She shook her head vigorously. 'I wish! No, I've got a whopping great one – here take a look.' Without giving it a second thought, she hitched up her dress, revealing an area of taut, slightly pitted skin around five inches across on her inner thigh. She hadn't looked at the scar for a while, and for a moment was lost in thought, noticing it had faded a little. She pressed it gently, and then, feeling her stomach take a weird tumble, she suddenly realised just what she was doing. The act of pulling down her dress again was accompanied by a horrible sinking feeling. *I can't look at him, I can't look at him, I can't look at him.*

She looked at him. That's when she saw his face was turned away, and after initially feeling even more embarrassed by that, she slowly began to take comfort from it. *At least he's not leering. That would've been awful, in fact, far, far worse.* She tried to relax a little. Okay, she'd been an idiot and had literally parted her legs in front of him, but she was pretty sure he hadn't seen anything he shouldn't have, and besides, loads of people had seen her scar - friends, family, her ex of course. She'd never felt shame when showing it off before, so why this time? Smoothing down her dress and straightening up, her tensions began to subside because he was no longer looking away. And while they gazed at each other and neither said a word, she was even more relieved to detect a measure of tenderness and warmth in his eyes.

'Aren't you going to play me that thing?' She pointed to a shimmering, golden instrument leaning up against the piano.

'Would *you* like to have a go?' he asked.

She hesitated. 'I'd love to, but I've never played a saxophone before.'

'Then it's about time we put that right, don't you think?' he smiled.

Lifting the conical body, she followed his expert guidance, positioning her mouth just so, breathing in, blowing out, sounding horrendous. Think battered horn on a rickety old car, or a choking goose perhaps. Hoping to improve things, and quickly, he lifted it from her hands, showing her the right way to blow and gave advice on alien words and concepts like embouchure, altissimo and intonation - all to no avail. Giving up, she flopped back on the sofa, hoping just to lie back and be romanced by one of the most sultry instruments known to man. And when he began to play, she wasn't disappointed. Cushioned by softness, she closed her eyes and drifted to distant shores. 'Ee ba gum!' as they say up North, he did sound fabulous.

'Any requests?' he asked. She tried to think, and the first song that popped into her head was 'Echo Beach', Martha and the Muffins. With its bright, soaring saxophone solo, she'd love to hear that one. But what about the twirling sax in Dean Friedman's 'Lucky Stars' or even better, the sultry, jazzy solo in Kool & The Gang's 'Too Hot'? But there was one song with arguably one of the best saxophone solos of all time, that kept knocking on the doors of her mind.

"Baker Street',' she said with a crisp nod, 'could you play 'Baker Street' please?'

Without hesitation, he lifted his instrument and put the single reed mouthpiece to his lips. She waited, trying not to wriggle too much with excitement. Could it really be this simple? She asked him to play something and he just played it – without any music? The answer was a resounding yes, and soon she sat in awe, hardly moving a muscle, listening to his near-perfect delivery of one of her favourite songs of all time.

'Bravo, bravo.' She clapped with enthusiasm and he bowed playfully. 'You're very talented,' she said, 'and you've got a super eclectic taste. I bet you've got a fantastic record collection.'

'Why not take a look?'

Pulling the strap over his head, he carefully placed the instrument down and headed towards the record player. Following him, she noticed the clock on the wall. Ten already. She couldn't believe it. Where had the time gone? She'd told her parents not to wait up but guessed one of them might, even though she was now an adult and an independent woman living in London. There was one thing she knew for sure, she didn't want to leave. Not yet, at least.

She could see several record sleeves in a cupboard and he crouched and flicked through before picking out a 7-inch track.

'The Stranglers,' she said, catching sight of the distinctive style of the artists' name on the record sleeve. 'I didn't think you were into punk.'

'You just said my taste was eclectic, didn't you?' he smiled a little, quietly popping the record onto the player.

'I'm guessing it's 'Golden Brown' and that's not punky at all.'

He stopped moving and stared into nothingness. 'It's *not* 'Golden Brown',' he mumbled, 'and do you know what that song's about?'

She shrugged. 'Something bad probably. It's funny but I've never really been bothered by lyrics, even if they're dead stupid or make no sense to me, although I have to admit, if there's tons of swearing or stuff like that, it can put me off.'

'Well, I hope you'll like these lyrics, because this one is for you.'

Her head felt slightly dizzy, and it wasn't the wine. *This one's for you. He just said this is for me. This could be very revealing.* The record sleeve was now on a high shelf above her head, so even if she wanted to cheat, and have a sneaky look, she couldn't. Twisting a ring on her finger, she tried to keep her eyes away from the turntable and waited impatiently for the song to start.

He slowly lifted the needle and the record began to spin. Then, after carefully placing it down on the shiny black vinyl disc, the characteristic crackle began.

With heightened senses, she listened first to an electric keyboard introduction and then the tune began simply and evocatively. So far, so good, and so far, not very punk but definitely beautiful. Then the tuneful vocal started, and as the song progressed, advancing towards the chorus, the punk elements began to kick in, in earnest. 'Strange Little Girl'. Millie listened to the singer, asking this 'Strange Little Girl' where she was going. It was pleasant and interesting, atmospheric and almost otherworldly, but why had Ben chosen it for her? Opening her mouth as though surprised, she pretended to be affronted.

'I'm a strange little girl, am I?' she laughed.

He looked amused, but didn't say a word. She was used to that. And that wasn't the only thing she was getting used to. She was also getting used to having to push things along a bit, so she knew exactly what to do.

'Dance with me,' she said, holding out her right hand, 'before I go.'

Listening to the song, they both breathed in deeply, and silently, she watched his chest rise and fall, but much to her surprise, he didn't accept her hand, at least not immediately. Instead, he stepped closer and took hold of her left hand first. Then, moving closer still, he pressed an open palm against her right hand and raised it to shoulder height. Inside she felt exquisitely unsteady, listening to his unspoken message which seemed loud and clear. *From now on, I'm going to lead.*

They danced. Hands touching loosely, circling, shuffling, shifting, moving gently to the music. Was it okay to rest her head against his chest? Yes, it was okay. It felt warm against her face and the trace of shampoo scent in his hair reminded her of green Bramley apples, picked fresh from an orchard. Eliza Doolittle in *My Fair Lady* could have danced all night, and Millie knew the feeling, because so could she. But the crackle came all too soon, the needle lifted, and the record stopped spinning.

Their hands separated, and he took one step back.

'Thanks for dinner,' she said, almost scared to look him in the eye. She knew it'd be a dead giveaway and that if she did, he'd see just how much she wanted to feel his lips. But why would that be such a bad thing? Maybe she should look, and keep looking. 'It's been amazing,' she said, staring into his eyes.

'Can I walk you home?' he turned to the window. 'It's so dark out there.'

'If you're sure,' she said, a little disappointed her tactic hadn't worked. Then, looking towards the window herself, an entertaining thought popped into her head and a smile morphed into a chuckle.

'What's up?' he asked, looking confused.

'Why didn't you draw the curtains?' she giggled. 'I mean, if Jill Mason saw us dancing just now, she'd murder me!'

Unsure if it was awkwardness that had prompted her to say something so unfunny and pointless, she felt incredibly grateful for Ben's willingness to smile and politely go along with it. It was time to go because lingering wasn't a good look, and slowly, reluctantly, she made her way to the coat stand and slipped on her jacket.

'It's chillier now, so you'll need it,' he said, picking up his house keys, ready to go.

***

She could have walked with Ben forever, but the short distance between Clover Cottage and Hillbrook Farm just didn't allow for that. So, she spent those final moments beside him, imagining, dreaming about what it would have been like to sleep with him that night. But not in that way, not yet. She was thinking about *literally* sleeping with him, on that sofa, inside Clover Cottage, leaning up against his shoulder and drifting off into dreamland with him by her side. Wouldn't that be special? She smiled at her secret thoughts. 'I Love You When You Sleep' was a beautiful song by Tracie Young, and Millie hoped it wouldn't be too long before she could say those words to him.

They stood at the entrance of Hillbrook Farm with the moon glowing overhead like shimmering silvery galena. It was a waning moon, but Millie's passion hadn't waned, far from it. If anything, she was fired up. One evening with Ben wasn't enough. Dancing with him wasn't enough, and it was going to be very hard to say goodnight.

'I'm fishing with Alan tomorrow, but I'm free in the morning if you're on for another walk.'

Nodding, she exhaled. Not only did he want to see her again, but this time, he was also doing the asking. They faced each other, outside the farm gates and quietly, patiently, she waited. And she waited some more. But that kiss, that much longed-for kiss, never came. Tonight's not the night, she thought, slinking away after they'd said their goodbyes. She reached for the front door with her key and turned around, just in time to see the darkness engulf him. The kiss would just have to wait, she told herself again, closing the door quietly and dreaming of tomorrow.

Chapter 26:

'If This Is It' - Huey Lewis and The News

Rain was forecast and there was dampness in the air, but since Millie swore by the maxim, 'there is no such thing as bad weather, only bad clothing', it didn't matter to her. What's more, not even a deluge could dampen her spirits, not today, perhaps not ever. She turned over in her bed and opened her eyes feeling hundreds of butterflies fluttering inside, then, sinking back into her pillow, her face shone. She had a little surprise for Ben. They'd talked about so many things the previous evening, she'd clean forgotten to mention that her aunt had left Conker with the family for a few days, and they were going to have company on their walk this morning.

Some minutes later, when strolling into the kitchen, she bit down on a smile before joining Victoria at the table. Then, picking up a box of muesli, she poured some into a bowl while her mother watched silently, wondering when to speak.

'How did it go?' Victoria asked, sounding matter-of-fact.

Before responding, Millie held her breath. Should she or shouldn't she come straight out with it? Should she confess to how well things had gone last night? *Yes, why not?* Looking as pleased as punch, she gently placed her spoon down.

'Mum,' she said, noticing the knowing look in her mother's eyes, 'I like Ben. In fact,' dropping her shoulders, she sighed dreamily, 'I *really* like him.' Just at that moment, there was a gentle nudge against her leg.

'Hey cheeky, how ya doing?' She reached down to ruffle Conker's coat and looked up again, only to be met with misgivings in her mother's eyes.

'Take it slow, I know,' Millie nodded, trying not to roll her eyes with frustration. In her keenness to get to know Ben, it felt as if her mother was trying to put a dampener on things, even though she did actually know that wasn't true, and having slipped in late last night to find Victoria too bleary-eyed for a full-on conversation, all Millie had said was that she was seeing Ben again this morning. Since there was no time to discuss things now, her mother would have to remain needlessly concerned, for that bit longer.

'I just want to say… Look, if he's right for you,' Victoria began, sounding wary, 'he won't rush you into anything.'

Millie stopped chewing and looked up with a sardonic smile. *Rush me?* She felt like saying, *I wish, or as Del Boy Trotter likes to say, Au contraire!*

'Don't worry,' she said instead, giving her mother a watered-down version of her thoughts, 'Ben's not like Giles, and if you're worried because of what Horace said, don't be, because I really don't believe a word of it.' Standing up, she tucked her chair under the table and grabbed a slice of toast.

'Aren't you going to finish your breakfast?' Victoria asked, sounding surprised.

'I'm not hungry.' Attaching Conker's lead, she headed for the door. 'And Mum...' she spun round when she reached it.

'Yes, Sweet Pea?'

'Please don't worry, I won't let anyone hurt me again. I promise.'

Victoria said nothing. Instead, alone and in silence she picked up the used bowls and spoons, and when she heard the front door slam shortly afterwards, she knew her daughter and youngest child was gone.

'I hope not,' she mouthed, staring vacantly at the kitchen sink. 'I really, really hope you don't get hurt, Sweet Pea.'

Stepping outside, Millie breathed in deeply. The air was fresh and moist, and the day was rich with promise.

'I hear you're off out to see your fancy man,' Dean grinned, sharpening a hand tool on the farm's drive.

'News travels fast!' she said, rushing towards the gate. 'Can't wait for you to meet him, but can't stop now – I'll be late.'

***

When she and Conker arrived at Clover Cottage, Ben was already waiting outside and the moment she saw him, a heart that was already beating fast, quickened its pace. *Don't be an idiot Millie, just play it cool.* He began to walk towards her, and the instant she got a better view of what he was wearing, she relaxed.

'Spartan!' she said, covering her mouth and pointing at his bare legs. Didn't he realise there was a good chance of rain and that they'd be wading through waist-high stinging nettles? Chastising him light-heartedly, she shook her head while suggesting, 'Wake Me Up Before You Go-Go' style shorts were not a good choice.

'I get hot and sweaty,' he said, 'and anyway, who says I can't handle a few stingers?'

'Famous last words,' she muttered, admiring his stoicism but thinking he might live to regret it.

No one would have believed they'd parted less than twelve hours earlier because there was still so much to talk about. Comedy for instance. Ben was a die-hard Monty Python fan, whereas *she* preferred easy-to-watch family sitcoms, like *And Mother Makes Five*.

'Lovely jubbly,' he said in his best cockney accent, when they stopped to take in a magnificent view.

'Funny you should say that,' she laughed, telling him she was thinking of Del Boy from *Only Fools And Horses* herself, that very same morning.

Despite all they'd discussed up until then, there still remained an elephant in the room - previous relationships. She had tried to broach this thorny subject by mentioning in passing she'd had a boyfriend while still at school, but got the distinct impression he thought it was just a childish thing. The conversation had moved on, but now they were closer, she wished she'd been braver. She needed to tell him that Giles was much more than just a childhood sweetheart, but bringing it all up again right now just didn't feel right.

Stopping to touch the frayed petals of a ragged robin wildflower, she knew it was also too early to question *him* about previous relationships. They weren't even officially a couple yet. 'I was shy around girls at that age.' That's all he'd said when she'd mentioned a boyfriend. Desperate to dig deeper, she'd held back, so the questions remained. How many relationships had he clocked up? Were any of them serious? Were there any flings or one-night stands? Remembering what he'd said about groupies and a crazy lifestyle, she tried to swallow away an uncomfortable sensation in her throat. Conker's entertaining antics were a lovely distraction from these thoughts, and they both burst out laughing when he rolled over to perform his famous belly crawl.

They stopped for a break and leant their backs up against the smooth, pearl-grey bark of an ash tree while Conker sniffed around the tree roots.

'How are they?' she asked, looking over at his legs.

He rubbed his calf and thigh, smoothing down fawn hair. 'It stopped stinging a while back. Still itches though.'

She glanced at the angry red patches and raised her eyebrows.

'I know, I know, you were right. Shorts were a bad choice,' he said.

There were so many cool things about Ben. Talented, kind, easygoing, not to mention gorgeous, but his hit-and-miss dress sense wasn't cool. Pairing a formal shirt with shorts was an interesting choice for a country walk, and, glancing at his lean pins again, she realised it was lucky she was partial to men on the skinnier side, unlike Ursula, who liked brawn.

It was humid, and although there were clouds in the sky, it didn't look likely that the forecasted rain was going to materialise. Millie pulled out a bottle and two plastic cups from her bag and offered Ben some cool water. After they'd refreshed themselves, they were ready to move on.

'Aren't you hot?' she asked, removing her rain mac and putting it away.

'That's nice of you to say!'

'Say what?'

'You said I was hot,' he said with a cheeky grin.

After repeating her words silently, she stared back with an incredulous smile. 'I didn't say *you* were… I said, aren't you… oh never mind, you know full well what I meant.' She gave him a playful swipe. He ducked and they laughed together a little more, but while they continued to walk in step, the conversation took on a slightly more serious tone.

'Dad worked for Viners cutlery,' he said. Millie nodded, saying she knew Sheffield was famous for the steel industry. Ben told her his father had worked there for almost forty years, until the recession, or rather, Thatcher, imports and privatisation, cost him his job. 'And now,' he said slowly shaking his head, 'Dad thinks he's too old to get another job, and is very happy living off the state, boozing and sitting in front of the box all day. But as I said, even before that, he was never responsible with money because he'd gamble it all on the horses and the football pools.'

'I'm sorry,' Millie said, wishing things had been different.

'Don't be. In some ways losing his job was the best thing to have happened to him because it finally got him to kick the gambling. With so little money, he had to choose between gambling or booze, and he chose booze.'

With Conker setting a fast pace, they stopped again to catch their breath.

'Maybe that's where I get it from,' Ben said.

'What?' Millie asked, her voice tentative.

'My laziness.' He smiled awkwardly. 'That was the best thing about being in a band. I got paid to bum around and basically do what I love. The trouble is, being a loafer doesn't pay the bills, does it? And now I know what it's like to have a real job, it actually isn't all that bad.'

Fanning herself, she tightened her grip on Conker's lead. He'd be off like a shot the moment she let her guard down, but getting distracted was going to be easy. Ben's sharing and light flirting threatened to absorb all her attention. Then, suddenly she noticed his hands fall loosely. She looked at his face. Something was up.

'I'm too much like my Dad, unfortunately,' he said, his tone of voice quieter.

'I know, you just said you were lazy, but you've had casual jobs, and you're working full-time now. That doesn't sound too lazy to me.'

'It's not just laziness,' he said.

Millie looked at him wide-eyed and feeling twitchy inside, waited to hear more. 'You told me why you left the music industry, but… did you move here for any other reason, apart from your Gran needing you?' Oddly, she felt like she needed to ask this question, although she didn't quite know why.

He swallowed thickly, and his bobbing Adam's apple looked more prominent and much more noticeable than usual. 'I spent years hating my Dad,' he began tightly. 'When I were a lad, some nights I'd hear our Mum crying in bed when she thought I were asleep. But it wasn't until I were older I realised there were days she'd go without dinner to buy me and Lauren shoes, or borrow from The Provident Man who turned up at our door and charged crazy interest.'

The way he said 'our' sounded very Yorkshire. In fact, all of a sudden, he was more Yorkshire than ever. It was as if talking about his childhood had made him regress to the accent of his youth. There was silence, and Millie bit her lip, desperate to hold his hand. But instead, keeping her composure, she tightened her grip on Conker's lead.

'I grew up,' he sighed, glancing at his feet, 'and that's when I stopped hating my Dad, because despite all he'd done, despite him ruining everything, I understood him better.'

There was a pause while Millie's curious eyes looked into his. 'Why?' she asked, quietly.

'Because...'

Still looking at his face she tried to remain unflustered, but behind her relaxed smile was a hammering heart. Then came the word. Just one word from him, which hit like a heavy bulldozer.

Addiction, addiction. She repeated the word inside her head. *He said he understood his father because of an addiction.* Everything around them was quiet, apart from the chirping of crickets in the surrounding grass, and swiping her hair back, she told herself there was nothing to be concerned about. Most people were addicted to something. Coffee, TV, exercise and some people were workaholics. Workaholic, yes, that sounded a lot like her. There were many days when studying had helped her get through a crisis. And chocolate, of course, plenty of chocolate. She stared back, wondering what Ben's weakness was. The suspense was too much, and she *really* needed to know, right now. Far too distracted to notice Conker crouching down with his ears pricked, the next thing she felt was her hand being jerked forward, followed by a big tug on the lead.

'Conker no!' Free at last, the energetic dog pelted down the hill at breakneck speed, and holding out two desperate hands she bounded after him, almost tripping in the process. 'He's probably seen a rabbit or something,' she gasped, and within seconds, Ben had overtaken her.

'I'll get him,' he shouted, before disappearing into a dense thicket.

***

She just managed to catch up, when Ben finally came to a halt, and leaning over and placing a hand on each thigh, she panted fiercely and waited for her heart rate to slow.

'You should have stayed where you were,' he said, 'I'd have brought him over to you.'

She felt lighter and breathed more easily, knowing Conker was safe, but where was he? She looked around. Where were *they*? Going by the clueless look on Ben's face, he didn't know either.

Out of the corner of her eye, she spotted movement. Then she heard the tell-tale sound of a frisky dog accompanied by the ominous sound of splashing.

Oh no! That's all I need. Border terriers were notorious for being stinky when wet, plus she didn't have a towel. Stepping aside, Ben motioned with a gallant wave, clearing the way for her to deliver some choice words to the naughty mutt.

She walked lightly, her footsteps cushioned by crunchy twigs and spongy soil before stopping for a moment, to feast her eyes on a woodland floor carpeted with luscious ferns and emerald green bracken. Then, raising her eyes, she looked up to see a canopy of trees growing ambitiously towards the sky.

Where *were* they? She asked herself again.

'You're going to reek of wet dog!' Ben called after her.

'Don't I know it?' Reaching out, she took hold of Conker's lead. 'I'm amazed you didn't get tangled up,' she scolded, 'you're very naughty - hey – stop that!' It was too late. A vigorous shake of wiry, grizzle fur, covered her in water droplets.

Throwing frustrated hands up in the air, she sat down on a large log by the water's edge.

Ben approached quietly from behind. 'Mind if I join you?' he asked gently.

'Please do.'

She shuffled across the oak trunk to make room. There they sat, side by side, listening to the gentle rhythms of nature in this unknown copse. She breathed in the moist, earthy air and caressed damp moss, soft and spongy, like a vibrant green fleece thrown over her woodland seat. Then looking down, she was glad to see Conker sitting quietly by her feet and no longer spraying water.

'Where are we?' Ben looked straight ahead, arms crossed, thumbs gently tapping his forearms in quiet contemplation.

'I have no idea, but I'm guessing this stream feeds into the Cuckmere River,' she said.

He picked up a stick and threw it, and it hit the water with a light splash. Making no effort whatsoever to chase it, Conker stayed firmly stationed at their feet. 'I think he's worn himself out,' she said, feeling somewhat bushed herself.

'So, thanks to you, old fella, we're lost,' Ben smiled, and after scolding a weary Conker, he slipped his rucksack off his shoulders and pulled out an ordnance survey map.

'Hold this for a sec, will you,' he said, delving into his bag again.

Watching him pull out a compass, Millie clamped her lips together and stifled a smile. Now it was plainly obvious he took the Scouting motto, 'be prepared', *very* seriously.

The needle pointed north, their village was east, and it was approaching midday, so the sun was to the south. This was all helpful information. Then, taking the map back, he peeled open its folded pages.

'Here's Magham Down,' he glided a forefinger along the silky paper across numerous contour lines and landmarks, 'and I think this is where Conker made a dash for it.' He paused for verification.

'Looks about right,' she nodded.

'I think we're here.' He pointed decisively at a specific location on the map.

'Greenglade woods.' She did a double take. 'Never heard of it, it must be private.' Then she noticed a public footpath running through the middle, which made it even more surprising she hadn't come across it before. Scouring the map together, they bumped heads again. How was it possible to be this close and not kiss? Millie just didn't get it, and that all-too-familiar tingling sensation was almost enough to help her forget. Almost, but not quite. As beautiful as this place was, it was time to feel uncomfortable again. Yes, she thought, glancing at Ben. It was time to revisit that earlier conversation.

'Before Conker ran off,' she began slowly, 'you mentioned… addiction.'

Quietly he fiddled with his shirt sleeves, and for what felt like ages, said nothing. Then, sharply, he turned to face her.

'I had an addiction.' His face melted into a frown. 'Heroin, Millie,' he said finally. 'Until about two years ago, I was addicted to heroin.' Turning his face away again, he began to mumble the words, 'I'm sorry.' Then facing her once more, and speaking more audibly and more clearly this time, he repeated himself. 'I'm sorry,' he said, looking her in the eye at last.

She didn't move a muscle at first. Then, feeling slightly shivery, she wrapped her arms around her tense body. She'd convinced herself, somewhere between losing Conker and now, that nothing would shock her. So why was she now lost for words? She looked at his face and tried to smile, but his dejected expression and the look of shame was enough to make her want to weep. *Come on Millie, say something, your silence is deafening.* But if it was agonizing for *her*, how on earth would he be feeling? Looking him in the eye, she tried not to frown. Her frown would send the wrong message and in actual fact, she'd be frowning at her own self rather than at him. So what if he had been addicted to heroin? It's no worse than being an alcoholic or a compulsive gambler surely? But despite her reasoning, she just couldn't shift the image in her mind of desperate addicts and a desperate drug that had claimed countless lives.

'That's what 'Golden Brown' is about, isn't it.' Untensing her muscles for a moment, she'd finally thought of something to say.

'Yes,' he replied.

In the voiceless moments that followed, she stared at aching eyes, which gave away nothing to suggest anything was wrong or ever had been. That made sense. He was a survivor, obviously. He wouldn't be here telling her all about it, otherwise.

'What happened?' she asked, unsure what *she* even meant by those two simple words.

'What happened?' he repeated. 'Well…' he sighed, 'it destroyed me… almost. My body, my mind, relationships, my finances…'

She blinked. He must be exaggerating. She wasn't looking at a former junkie whose life had almost been decimated by an illegal substance. Okay, he was a bit on the thin side, but that was no evidence of being a former addict. No, for a moment she just couldn't believe it. If the damage was so significant, how come there were no visible signs?

Following the silence, her mind became flooded with questions. How did he get into it? Was it because he was in that band? How common was it to take heroin? And the biggest and most terrifying question of all - was he now clean?

'I took my first hit at a friend's party in '79,' he said, answering the first question, 'and within a year I was injecting.'

A wave of nausea was suppressed by the steady trickle of the stream. The gentle sound offered much-needed serenity and lightness to a story of tragedy and awakening. A friend dying from hepatitis C, an acquaintance overdosing after a relapse, despair and the fear of never breaking free, recurrent nightmares, battles with anxiety and depression, and so the list went on. *But… but…but.* After he'd said 'but', even though it was followed by a lengthy pause, Millie held on to the word, because surely, 'but,' meant there was hope. And she was right, because he then went on to say he was now on a healing journey, and she continued to listen to the words still pouring out, more positive this time, while his tightly clasped hands rested on his lap.

She was going to be a doctor. She could handle this. She wasn't that sensitive teenager any more, always on the verge of tears every time she heard stories of suffering, or saw something distressing on the news. Yes, she could handle this.

Conker was quiet and surprisingly still. It was as though he could feel the weight of Ben's words.

'Can I ask…' she began, after he'd finished.

'Go ahead,' he coaxed.

'Why did you take it? The first time, I mean.'

There was a pause. 'I've asked myself that question many times,' he said with a tormented smile, 'but I guess the simple answer is everyone was doing it. Gigging and performing went hand in hand with partying hard, drinking hard and hard drugs, but that's not really an excuse…' his voice trailed off. 'You see, when… when there's something missing in your life and something's not quite right…' Stopping again, he turned his body to face her head-on. 'How well do you cope with rejection?' he asked.

That question, which seemed to come from out of the blue, instantly made her think of one thing, or rather one person. Giles. He was the last person she wanted to think about right now, because despite what he'd done to her, he now seemed refreshingly uncomplicated by comparison, and now wasn't the time to go back to feelings of loss and self-pity. Was now a good time to tell Ben how she gave her all, her mind, her body, everything, only for him to scrape her away like filth from under his shoe? No, definitely not. There was enough to contend with right now.

'I don't think I deal with rejection well,' she said. 'It hurts, doesn't it?'

'It does, and when you feel rejected, it's easy to see rejection everywhere you look. It's easy to be always trying to stop it happening.' He smiled weakly. 'I didn't know it at the time, but looking back, I now see my friends became the Dad I didn't really have. I wanted - no, I *needed* their love and respect.'

Her eyelids began to feel hot and prickly, but no, she was *not* going to cry. At this moment, Ben needed her to be strong.

'It wasn't until...' he paused, 'I felt love from someone much better than any friend, or even my dad, that things began to turn around.'

She gave him a blank stare. What did he mean? Feeling tense again inside, she wondered if this was going to be 'it' for her and she'd come to the end of the road. The burning sensation in her stomach reminded her that she had a problem with jealousy which could be irrational. But if there was ever a legitimate reason for jealousy, surely this was it? If a woman was strong enough to get Ben out of that mess, there was no way she could compete with her, or her memory, or could live under her shadow. She just wasn't that strong.

'The 12-step programme.' The corners of his mouth turned up at her puzzled face. 'It, or I should say, Jesus, literally saved my life.'

Her eyes widened and her shoulders relaxed. He was talking about religion, and ironically, *thank God*, were the first words that came into her mind. God wasn't a threat, was he? And plenty of people were religious, although maybe less so these days. She wasn't used to hearing people talk like this, and it felt odd at first. But listening to him share his experiences at Narcotics Anonymous and how it had changed him, brought sunrays of positivity and hope which began to penetrate her soul.

She looked down to see Conker's ears twitch. No wonder he was sleeping. He was exhausted, just like she was. Wrung out but happy, she was hopeful and starting to think that everything might, just might end on a positive note. He was clean, and even more than that, he had just told her he was a new man.

But then, when she turned to look into his eyes again, everything threatened to crash and burn once more. There was an ominous expression on his face, and with a heavy heart, she knew something else was wrong. Perhaps the exorcism wasn't fully complete? Perhaps she'd been too hopeful, far too soon.

'I really like you, Millie,' he began slowly.

There was a 'but' coming, and this time, she sensed that unlike earlier, it wasn't going to be followed by anything good. She wasn't totally sure she could take any more at that moment. These ups and downs were starting to get too much.

'It's okay…' she interrupted, clearing a lump in her throat, convinced that he was about to reject her despite all he'd just said. She'd known it was coming and she braced herself stoically.

He looked away. 'No, it's not okay,' he said, sounding frustrated. 'It's in the past but,' he looked her over, 'I want to… I *need* to make sure everything's right before getting into a relationship. I don't want to be like my Dad,' he shuddered. 'I don't want to be a liability to anybody, least of all you. Do you understand?'

His voice was hopelessly pleading, and she felt sorry for him, almost as much as she was feeling sorry for herself. And then the lightbulb switched on and she could see why, until now, he hadn't tried to make a move. Sure, he was a decent guy, and that had to be partly the reason why, but now, all his slowness, all his hesitation was starting to make perfect sense.

Wrapping consoling arms around her chest in another self-hug, she made the courageous decision to accept everything as it was, to go with the flow and to go easy on both herself and on him.

'Thank you,' she smiled, bravely.

'What for?'

'Your honesty, and for sharing that with me.' The two sat on the log in quiet contemplation, in that hitherto undiscovered wood. Millie felt privileged that he'd made himself so vulnerable, and now her priority was to show him acceptance, even though her disappointment was real and she also had to think about what was best for her. Was a former heroin addict who wasn't ready for a relationship, and who had confessed to having ongoing psychological battles, great boyfriend material? She wanted to become a surgeon, not a psychiatrist. And what about all those warnings that she was biting off more than she could chew? Perhaps she should listen to the likes of Horace. But merely thinking of that cantankerous old man was enough for her to snap her out of all these rationalisations. Looking at Ben, she could see that this was the same guy she'd walked into this wood with and had felt so positive about. He was no different now from the person he was then, and just because he'd told her he was once a heroin addict and needed more time before getting involved, surely it didn't mean she should be ready to write him off just yet.

'This stream,' he said, picking up the map and following its course with his finger, 'looks like it leads to the Pevensey Marshes - not far from where we walked before.'

'So it does,' she said, leaning in. 'But it's tiny. I'm not sure it's even a stream. Maybe it's a brook?'

'Is there a difference?' he asked.

She shrugged, but one thing was certain, it was time to go. Finding their way back might take some time, and Ben had planned to go fishing with Alan - she hadn't forgotten that. Instinctively they began to head towards the lightly flowing water to take one last look.

Watching the clear, rejuvenating, fresh liquid rush across the stones, she bent down and dipped her hand in. Sloshing it around, the sensation was crisp and comforting.

'So, is it a stream or a brook?' he asked, crouching down next to her.

'I think it's a brook,' she said. Then, a smile, which began slowly, then moderately, grew larger and larger, until she almost felt her cheeks ache. 'It has to be,' she beamed, 'it has to be a brook!'

'Why?' he asked, with a baffled smile.

'Look at these stones. Can't you see?'

'Can't I see what?'

'No, you wouldn't, because you don't know, do you? Ben, it's a stony brook!'

'*O-kay*,' Ben said, slowly, but thankfully his bemusement didn't last long. They began to make their way back, through the wooded copse and then through open fields and sleepy meadows, and as they did, he listened to her excited garbled recounting of Amanda and Dean's wedding day, and the reasons why Amanda had chosen the name 'Stoneybrook' with an 'e', for their cottage.

They said their goodbyes, and parted, after which Millie made a slight detour just before reaching Hillbrook Farm, and soon, she was outside Marshywood, Amanda's previous home and where Amanda's parents still lived. At first, when she stopped right outside the rustic, Sussex-style cottage, she wondered why she was there. Then, with a quivering heart, she realised. Despite all the trauma of the day, despite all the crazy revelations, and despite all the uncertainties and issues that were bound to come if she and Ben had a future, she knew there was hope. Breathing in deeply, she closed her eyes, thinking to herself that stumbling across their own Stoneybrook seemed too incredible to be a coincidence.

With a hand still wrapped tightly around Conker's lead, she looked down at him, then across to Marshywood, and finally upwards at low-level stratocumulus clouds. Did God bring Dean and Amanda together? She raised her eyebrows, not knowing the answer, and turning back towards home, that one question kept churning inside her mind. All the earlier talk about religion had got her thinking. Maybe, just maybe, the same God who had perhaps brought her brother and sister-in-law together, for what looked like a lifetime, might be mindful to do something similar for her, and for Ben, for them both, and not only that, maybe God would make better again everything that had gone wrong. But wouldn't that take a miracle? And, what did *she* know about God anyway?

Smiling sadly, she arrived home, not knowing if God was even there, and if he was there, whether he'd listen if she prayed. But passing through the farm gates with Conker by her side, her head full to bursting, her heart even more, she knew there was no harm in giving prayer a try, just this once and just in case.

Chapter 27:

'Our Lips Are Sealed'
- The Go Gos/ Fun Boy Three

Victoria could tell by now that when Millie had that twitchy, awkward smile, it meant something was up. She sat her down and it wasn't long before, 'I'm fine,' became a fretful, 'Don't say anything to Dad,' and when moments later the words began to flow, slowly at first, they quickly turned into an avalanche.

'I'm glad you told me,' Victoria said, relieved to be taken into her daughter's confidence at last. But there was a time in the not-so-distant past when listening to Millie pour out her heart had been far from easy, a time when holding back from offering advice had felt like the surest way to avoid alienating her.

Sitting beside Millie on her bed, Victoria bore silent regrets over not being braver in days gone by. Crossing her fingers and hoping for the best by burying her head in the sand hadn't turned out to be the best course of action in hindsight, and having promised herself never to make the same mistake again, she sat tight, gritting her teeth and waited for her daughter to open up more. 'I bet it feels good to get that off your chest,' she said when Millie had finished, 'but I'm very surprised you didn't tell me straight away.'

'What was I supposed to say?' Millie spat back. 'Hey folks, we had a lovely time, Conker bolted and we stumbled across a beautiful woodland with a brook - oh and by the way, Ben just happens to be a heroin addict in recovery, but apart from that, everything's hunky-dory!'

Victoria's features remained soft, knowing that her daughter's mocking tone and fake smile were just a cry for help, and after waiting for emotions to settle, she felt the timing was right to respond.

'Don't you think your father should be told,' she began tentatively, 'especially after what Horace said, and...'

'No,' Millie interrupted, '*I said*, don't tell Dad, please!'

Everything fell silent once more and while staring blankly at her fingernails, Victoria felt a familiar sense of déjà vu. Cecil was still largely, blissfully ignorant about Giles. He knew, of course, how devastating the break-up had been for his daughter, but even today, he didn't quite know the full extent of it and how at the tender age of sixteen she'd become involved intimately. At the time, Victoria didn't think he needed to know, but now she wasn't so sure that keeping him in the dark had been such a good thing.

Knowing how hot-headed her husband could be, she could appreciate why back then, giving him fodder for fury would've been unwise. But Cecil wasn't stupid or naive, and trying to pretend, especially today, that their twenty-year-old daughter was as pure as the driven snow, was just plain silly.

Just then, both mother and daughter heard the lively barking of the sheepdogs. That Cecil was with the sheep just beyond the farmhouse reminded Victoria how in many ways her husband treated his daughter like a lamb. Millie was still very much his 'Innocent Miss Millicent', and the fatherly sentiments behind his childhood nickname for her, still held true. One thing was certain, he'd be less than thrilled to hear that his Innocent Miss Millicent was seriously thinking about taking up with a former heroin addict, and it gave Victoria the chills just to imagine his face should some brave soul dare to tell him.

'What do you think I should do?' Millie's pleading eyes were strained but undaunted, and before responding, Victoria realised she'd seen that look before. 'Should I stop seeing him? Should I wait for him to get better? Is it *really* such a big deal?'

The questions kept coming, and while they did, Victoria's head spun with questions of her own. *She wants to know what to do. What do I think? What should I say? What to advise? What to do?*

'I don't know darling,' she said eventually, running apprehensive hands across her thighs and smoothing down her apron. 'I really don't know, you see, I've never met a heroin… I mean an *ex*-heroin addict before.'

'Same here, Mum. You and me both.'

There was another hollow and prolonged silence and then Victoria smiled, cautiously, gently.

'Ben says he has faith in God,' she began softly, 'and you trust Ben, but…' she stopped talking and rubbed the back of her neck. 'Supposing he's damaged himself? What if he's still addicted? Have you thought about that?'

On the outside, she was calm, but inside, everything was starting to scream, *think carefully Millie, think, please! Why do you like him so much? He's pleasant enough, at least that's what I thought that brief time I met him, but this heroin thing takes things to a whole new level.*

Sitting tight and waiting for an answer, she could see in the silence, cogs turning in Millie's brain. Was she beginning to see sense? Hopefully. But sighing inside, Victoria feared there would be an awful day of reckoning. When it came, she'd be there of course, ready and willing to comfort and console and to gather up all the broken pieces.

Millie's face muscles began to relax and her conflicted eyes took on a quiet assurance. 'I *have* thought about it, Mum,' she said finally and in a whisper. 'I want to help him, and I feel when he's ready for me, I need to give him a chance.'

Closing her eyes briefly, Victoria kept trying to listen, not just with her ears, but also with an open heart.

'He told me he is damaged in some way,' Millie continued, 'and I don't know how, not yet. But I *do* know he's not addicted any more because he told me he was clean.'

Hey, he told her. Well, that's alright then. It really must be true! Rather than sharing the sarcasm voiced by her inner cynic, Victoria harboured a secret hope. When Millie returned to London the attraction might fizzle out, and then the problem would be solved almost overnight. And what about that nice young man, Zane? She wanted to say. He ticked so many boxes. A fellow medical student, respectful, wealthy, generous, not to mention, keen. Why couldn't Millie just look past his airs and graces and give *him* a chance?

Knowing a little bit of Shakespeare, Victoria's thoughts began to travel in a different direction. Didn't the phrase 'the course of true love never did run smooth' come from *A Midsummer's Night's Dream*? Indeed. True love could be messy, and Victoria knew it was time to accept that Millie had to go with her heart, even if that meant putting it in harm's way.

'You trust him, and I trust you,' Victoria said, finally willing to embrace the unknown, 'and if anything does develop, I really hope it all works out.'

Millie smiled, just a little, but enough for her mother to know she'd been reassured, and glancing up at a bookcase, Victoria saw Bagpuss lying on a shelf. She stared up at the stripy pink and white, pull-string toy, the very embodiment of everything her little girl meant to her. Childlike innocence, sweetness and love oozed from Bagpuss's beady blue eyes, and taking him off the slightly dusty shelf, she handed him over.

'I'm glad I kept him,' Millie smiled, cuddling his squishy body, 'even though he can't talk and he's all broken inside, I didn't want to get rid of him.'

Watching her daughter cuddling the toy in silence, Victoria said nothing. However, inside she was now feeling the weight of words that had led her to a eureka moment. What if *Ben* was broken, just like Bagpuss? What if all he needed was time? And if you truly love something, if you *really* love someone, why give up on them, why throw them away?

I love you very much, and I promise to always be there for you, no matter what. That's what she ought to have said, but since Millie already knew all this, she had other words for her instead. 'Aren't you soppy, you great big baby!' she chuckled, reaching over to give her a massive hug.

Chapter 28:

'Just Got Lucky' - Jo Boxers

'I've got medical appointments all day today.'

Millie furrowed her brow and gripped the phone a little tighter. 'Really? Why?'

'It's nothing,' he said, cheerfully. 'Just routine stuff.'

Everything fell silent, except for the steady sound of his breathing. 'Because what happened to me,' he began again, less buoyantly this time. 'Because of that, I have a medical every once in a while, just to check everything's ticking over okay - and it always is - so there's never anything to worry about.'

'That's good.' Millie sighed, making no effort to hide her relief. Ben loved her honesty, so why play games?

'Gran's home tomorrow,' he said.

'Oh really?' Feeling her heart sink, she couldn't believe the time had gone so quickly. Sadly, their opportunity for alone time at Clover Cottage was over.

'Fancy coming round first thing, before she gets back?'

Now he was talking! Glancing upwards, she clasped the phone to her chest with a wide smile. 'Yes, of course. What time?'

After the conversation had ended, she placed the receiver on the hook and before bolting upstairs, stopped and listened. Was that the *Taxi* theme tune? Yes, but why was it coming from the kitchen radio and not the TV? She continued listening, completely entranced by the sound of a tuneful recorder, crisp and bright, partnered with mellow keyboards and soft cymbals. Everything was jazzy and so mellow, and she breathed in the sound, thinking it was so very Ben and so very gorgeous. "Angela', by Bob James, the theme from Taxi,' the radio presenter said, and knowing that tomorrow couldn't come soon enough, she slid her hand across the smooth wooden bannister, before quietly heading upstairs to her room.

**

The next morning she walked along the well-trodden path towards Clover Cottage, wondering how things would change once Enid was home. Although there were bound to be fewer opportunities to spend time alone with Ben, inviting him back to the farm wasn't a solution. Millie could see her family in her mind's eye right now, descending on him like carrion crows, especially her father – sussing him out, vetting him and firing questions. Clenching her jaw, she thought about how dangerous that would be for obvious reasons, and increasing her pace, resolved to get her own head around things before introducing him to her family.

She arrived at Clover Cottage and reached for the doorbell, but before pressing it jerked her head. 'Arghh!

You made me jump!' Placing a hand across her chest, she couldn't tell if it was his sudden appearance by the side gate, or that 'pleased to see you' look in his eyes that had made her heart melt like a Mr Whippy ice cream by a roaring fire. She did know one thing though, he always looked so fresh, even this early in the morning, which was more than she could say for herself. How could a man this gorgeous be a former heroin addict? It just didn't seem possible, or real.

'This way.' He beckoned her with a bouncy stride and she willingly complied. But why the garden?

After they entered the small courtyard space, he stepped aside to reveal a small patch of grass on top of which sat the upper section of a large hamster cage.

'I'm glad you're here,' he said, 'I caught him last night and he's really active, so I need to let him go.'

Caught who? She approached slowly, curiously, keen to see the captive, and then, a quick movement caught her eye. She looked more closely and tipped her head back with a beaming smile. There, inside the cage was an excitable, tiny brown creature. Its white underbelly was visible through the thin, metal bars and she watched it bounce, long back legs propelling it in the air as though the grass were a trampoline.

'Is that a…?' She paused and tipped her head to one side. 'Actually, I'm not too sure *what* it is.'

'It's a wood mouse,' he said, 'and we're right at the end of the breeding season, so if it's a male, he'll be looking for food to feed his family – although actually, I think wood mice *might* be polygamous.'

'Polygamous?' she repeated, before breaking into a giggle. 'Polly Ga *mouse* – get it?'

He smiled, and after tilting his head affectionately, his eyes began to glisten, as though something suddenly dawned on him. 'Millie the wood mouse,' he said unexpectedly.

'Come again?'

'That's a great name for *you*. Millie the wood mouse – Millie mouse for short.'

Sweeping her hair back, she crouched and peered closer at the cage. 'Once,' she began, with eyes still focussed on the furry little creature, 'a girl at school kept going on about my hair, saying it was mousy brown and boring as hell.' Putting her hand through a small door in the cage, she hoped the wood mouse would jump on it. 'I used to think she was being a right cow - no disrespect to cows or anything,' she smiled, 'but now I know she was paying me a compliment.'

Ben blinked sharply. Then his eyes flitted from mouse to Millie, Millie to mouse and he compared the earthy brown fur on the tiny beast with the deeper hues falling across her shoulders. Her hair *was* mousy, but the similarities didn't end there. Both she and the dainty creature were unbelievably endearing, but while *it* was cute, *she* was stunning.

Millie looked up and their eyes met, and what she saw in that moment was nothing short of deep, rugged affection, and her body tensed with instant feelings of connection, flooding her with joy. Whatever he'd done in the past or whatever people thought of him now, didn't matter at all when the little mouse wasn't the only captive in Enid's garden. Crouching side by side, their eyes still glued, it came to her mind that the word 'Enid' was just one letter away from 'Eden'. While she could see that Enid's tiny, paved courtyard garden was a far cry from a luscious paradise and that she and Ben were fully clothed - there wasn't a fig leaf in sight - just being there with him, together, on their last morning alone, felt like a tiny slice of heaven on earth.

After giving Ben a heated glance, she could tell it was time to release the captive.

'Bye bye, little chap,' he said, lifting the cage.

'Enjoy your freedom,' she called after it.

About to ask how his medical appointments had gone, after the mouse took flight, the distant sound of a car caught their attention. Then, staring at each other with heightened senses and disappointed eyes, they heard familiar voices and footsteps drawing ever closer. Enid was back with Lauren, and their time alone had been cruelly cut short.

'Gran, you're home!' Ben glanced at his watch when Enid and Lauren wandered into the garden, chatting. 'It's not even eleven yet,' he said, trying to sound lively, 'you must've set off early.'

'We did,' Lauren said, 'I wanted to avoid a motorway snarl-up. There were issues on the M1, and 'Convoy GB' was on the radio first thing, so I took it as a warning! Anyway, never mind all that.' She flapped her hand. 'Millie,' she said, with a mischievous smile, 'what a surprise to see *you* here.'

Clearing his throat, Ben opened his mouth, 'Millie was just...'

'Urgh!' Drawing up her leg, Lauren interrupted with a squeal. 'That wasn't a ... there'd better not be a rat on the loose!' She stared at the upturned cage, her eyes bulging.

'Looks like my grandson's been showing off his clever trap,' Enid interjected.

Millie nodded silently.

'I for one, would prefer he kept his bloomin' trap shut,' Lauren grimaced.

'Nice one,' Ben grinned, 'and no, it wasn't a rat, it was a wood mouse.'

Millie chipped in. 'I caught something the other day myself,' she said, quietly amused by Lauren's panic. 'I thought it was just a mouse but Ben thinks,' she paused, eying him softly, 'it was a hazel dormouse, don't you?'

'Yes, and I wish I'd seen it - big black eyes, orangey yellow fur, sounds a lot like a hazel dormouse to me.'

'Well, I'm glad *I* didn't see it,' Lauren exhaled, 'I can't understand why you guys are so into vermin, I mean, you're both flippin' as bad as each other!'

Millie glanced at Ben sideways with an incredulous smile. How could anyone call such lovely creatures, vermin?

'How's about a cuppa?' Enid asked, and with everyone more than happy to take up her offer, all three followed as she slowly made her way to the kitchen. While walking behind, Lauren's glossy, high-heeled court shoes clattered on the concrete surface below. How she'd managed to drive in them was anyone's guess, and within moments, Millie saw the palpable relief on her face when after flopping onto the sofa, she sighed and eased them off her feet.

'The kids keep saying, "*Mum*, when's Uncle Ben coming to see us?"' Lauren said, putting on a whiny voice.

'Tell them, soon,' Ben said, picking up a mug from the coffee table.

In an instant, Millie visualised him with his niece and nephew and although he wasn't a playful, muck-around sort, she could easily imagine him dishing out piggyback rides, hugs and tickles by the bucket load while Hattie and Oscar laughed along with much-loved Uncle Ben. He *must* be doing something right if they're begging for him to visit. Then, while brushing her hand against the velvety sofa fabric, she was reminded of the evening they'd spent together in that same room. She could almost taste the delicious lasagne and hear the saxophone, and she could feel the warmth of her head against his chest while they danced to 'Strange Little Girl'. That night was the closest they'd got physically, and although only days had passed since then, it was already starting to feel like an age.

After Lauren had finished chatting about how the shop was doing, Millie took a sip of hot, steaming tea. It was then she noticed Enid's contorted face when she got up to wash a mug, and how, after stooping at the sink for several minutes, she came back looking exhausted. Had her pain relief worn off? Millie could tell she was suffering in silence. Ben and Lauren also noticed, so everyone offered to help, and when the offer was declined, Ben scrutinized the floor, checking for potential trip hazards. Having suffered major fractures in recent years, five of her spine alone, Enid's osteoporosis was clearly advanced, and everybody was alert, aware that more fractures could happen at any time. Ben's attentiveness towards his grandmother didn't go unnoticed by Millie, and in *her* book, any guy who looked out for the interest of others like that was worthy of her time and energy.

'Do you need me to get some shopping in?' Ben asked, as if to prove her point.

'That would be lovely.' Enid wriggled in her seat, visibly trying to get comfortable. 'I've got three pupils booked for this afternoon so I'd better conserve my energies.' Watching and listening, Millie remembered that Ben had said that Enid could barely manage even light groceries these days.

'Just give me a list,' he said, downing his tea. 'Want to come?' Lifting his brows, he threw Millie an inviting look.

Controlling her movements so as not to appear too excited, she nodded and rose to her feet. She didn't want to say 'goodbye' to Lauren just yet, but not only was this an opportunity to help Enid out, she had an inkling Ben was arranging this shopping trip so they could have some more much-needed time alone. Also, they'd be going by car, which meant the exciting prospect of being his passenger for the very first time.

Enid eased herself off her armchair. 'Best check I've got enough marge and other bits and bobs,' she said, sounding arduously bright.

'I'll get my sunglasses,' Ben said, and as soon as he left the room, Lauren stood up too.

'I'd better get going myself,' she said to the backdrop of Ben's footsteps mounting the narrow cottage stairs. 'Malcolm *hates* being lumbered with the kids and the shop.'

Millie nodded and watched how the muffled sound of Enid's shuffling feet in the kitchen soon melted away Lauren's smile. 'Gran needs to go back to the doctor for stronger painkillers, but she's so incredibly stubborn she won't listen to me. Hey,' Lauren's tense brow relaxed, 'you're going to be a doctor, maybe she'll listen to you!'

'I doubt it,' Millie said. 'I'm not qualified yet.' She stopped talking. Lauren was leaning in, with a face as heavy as thunder, looking as if she was about to say something important and very, very deep.

'That's why I trust you with Ben,' Lauren said, with a wavering smile.

Millie tilted her head.

'You know what I mean, trust me I'm a doctor and all that,' Lauren gestured animatedly with a hand, 'but no, seriously, the reason I know you're trustworthy isn't just because you're going to be a doctor. It's also because you're, you seem...' her voice floated away. 'Oh, nothing,' she said, smiling with her mouth but not her eyes, 'I'm just rambling on as usual.'

Starting to feel awkward, Millie tried her best not to fidget, while sensing all this hesitation must have something to do with Ben's past, and she watched, waiting for Lauren to spill out her words, noticing how she was now looking almost moved to tears.

'You *will* take care of him – won't you?' Lauren said at last, lifting her lowered eyes. 'Taking care of Ben was *my* job before I left home and life got in the way.'

The sitting room of Clover Cottage was stiflingly hot, and Lauren's perfume was heavy, but there was much more to Millie's overwhelming feelings. She was also overcome because Lauren had officially blessed her and Ben's relationship, and since she'd almost certainly won Enid's approval as well, she felt incredibly lucky. Of course, she would look after Ben. She couldn't wait! Taking care of people was her forte, perhaps even her raison d'etre and the very essence of why she wanted to be a doctor. But why all the emotion just now? Ignoring a tightness in her gut, she smiled faintly, convinced that Lauren couldn't possibly be suggesting that Ben was unable to take care of himself. If anything, she must be referring to the old Ben, the addict before he was clean, because no one who was still an addict could hold down a steady job and look after their Granny the way he did. If he was able to look after someone else, surely, he could look after himself.

'Sorry I took ages,' Ben bounded into the room with gold-rimmed, dark shades dangling from his fingers. I couldn't find them.' He stopped talking, and his eyes flitted from Lauren to Millie, and back to Lauren again. 'You two look like you're plotting something,' he said, with a look of suspicion.

'Do we?' Clearing her throat, Lauren glanced sideways. 'I was just telling Millie to avoid you like the plague, that's all – you and your dirty rat traps!'

Ben shook his head and put his lips to Millie's ear. 'One day I'll manage to persuade her that my trap's *way* more exciting than Gucci bags.'

'Dream on!' Smiling, Lauren turned towards the sound of the kitchen fridge door closing, and Enid's voice. 'What was that, Gran?'

'I was only asking if Ben could add a tin of semolina and some Edam to the list,' Enid replied, plodding back into the room. 'Grab yourself some cash, dear.'

Reluctantly, Ben reached up for a metal tin that was sitting on top of the piano. 'You know I'm always happy to pay,' he said, prising open the tin.

'No,' Enid said firmly, 'you pay your keep. I can't have you paying for my food as well.'

After acquiescing, he took the money. 'Well, if you're sure, fifteen pounds should cover it.' Then, picking up a pound note which had escaped from the over-stuffed tin, he popped it in again.

'I hope you've taken what you need to cover the lovely meals you cook.'

'I have Gran, it's fine,' Ben said, reaching into his pocket. 'You look like you're leaving too, Big Sis,' he smiled. Lauren nodded crisply. 'Safe journey then.'

Millie watched him lift his hand to say 'goodbye', but there was no physical touch, no warm hugs, no kisses. Growing up used to hugging her parents and her brothers, she felt the urge to give Lauren a hug herself, even though they weren't sisters - yet, and she told herself it didn't matter too much that Ben wasn't the touchy-feely type. The minute their relationship stepped up to the next level, the moment they became close, she intended to bring out the latent hugger in him and make it shine.

***

Sitting in his car for the first time, Millie watched Ben slide on his shades, and in the rearview mirror, caught sight of the dark, highly reflective glass against his sun-kissed skin. Fastening his seatbelt, he turned to her with a confident smile, ready to move off.

'Stop throwing your Gran's money around,' she chuckled, picking up a stray note that had fallen out of his over-stuffed pocket. But, to her slight surprise, he didn't laugh or even smile. Instead, in silence, he turned on the engine and lifted the handbrake. As the car began to move, her unsettled stomach wondered if he'd pulled away from her, and not just the curb.

'Did I say something wrong?' she said, biting the bullet and swallowing hard.

He smiled, weakly. 'No, I'm sorry if I gave that impression,' he said, picking up speed. 'No, I was just thinking how lucky I am to have a proper job and a fresh start.' Changing gears, he stared starkly at the road ahead. 'There was a time in my life,' he announced, with a heavy sigh, 'that Gran would have been sensible to lock all her money away,' he paused. 'Things were *that* bad.'

There was a long, uncomfortable silence, and feeling her already nervous body jerk when the car drove over a pothole, Millie tried to open her mouth, only to discover she was speechless.

'You don't have to say anything,' Ben said quietly. 'Stealing from your Gran is desperate and disgusting, there's no two ways about it.'

Still on edge but trying not to be, she glanced up at him, managing to smile.

'But that's all in the past now, thank God,' he said.

'Yes,' she said, embracing the warm sunrise of optimism, just over her horizon. 'Yes,' she smiled, "That Was Then But This Is Now'.'

'That's an ABC track isn't it?' he asked, recognizing the song she'd quoted. 'And guess what?'

'What?'

'ABC are from Sheffield.'

'I didn't know that,' she said, with a lightness in her voice, 'do they play blue-eyed soul as well?'

Just the mention of Sheffield led to talking about Yorkshire and its comedy, and sitcoms like *Oh No It's Selwyn Froggitt* and *Rosie*. They laughed together while the Ford Cortina made its way along winding roads with fields, hedges and trees flanking its course, and in no time, it felt as if they were heading off for an exciting *getaway* rather than the boring *Gateway* supermarket in town. But their true destination could more accurately be called, 'Gateway to the future,' a place where the past would be left behind forever, and glancing at a relaxed Ben turn the wheel, Millie believed with all her heart they'd get there soon enough, one way or another.

Chapter 29:

'Is She Really Going Out With Him?'
- Joe Jackson

The Breakfast Club finished and the credits scrolled across the cinema screen accompanied by 'Don't You Forget About Me', by Simple Minds. What a great song and after a gentle stretch, Millie stood up, ready to leave with Ben at her side, but before she did, she had a stark warning for him.

'Don't you forget about *me* when I go back to uni,' she said, wagging a finger.

'Sorry, too late,' Ben said, with a poker face, 'I've already forgotten about you!'

They laughed together, and set off towards the exit. She was desperate to hold his hand, but she hadn't forgotten he'd said he needed time to heal, and so, although it was September already, and they'd been seeing each other, at least in a manner of speaking, for an entire month, she wasn't going to push him. She felt less in a hurry these days, and much more able to wait. In many ways, Ben was refreshing, after Giles, who after just two dates said, 'I would normally have kissed a girlfriend by now.' After that, he went in for the kill, so not being pounced on and pawed was a novel and pleasant experience, even if it did take a little bit of getting used to.

There was something more troubling though. For a few days now, Ben had appeared exhausted and had complained from time to time of headaches and tiredness. But at other times, thankfully, he seemed fine. As a result, it was easy to tell herself it was nothing, although at those times he was also quieter than usual and seemed unsettled.

More than once, she'd ask him if he was okay, and the answer was always, 'I'm fine,' and while not convinced, she knew she had to resist the urge to keep asking. She'd only come across as a worrier or a nag if she did, and that was the last thing he needed after requesting more time. What he needed was space to breathe.

Thankfully, they'd now managed to discuss previous relationships, and so that was one thing out of the way. He'd told her that he'd split up with his most serious girlfriend two years ago and that it was 'for the best'. Knowing that she and Ben weren't officially a couple yet and confident that he'd say more in his own good time, Millie decided not to press for more information despite being very curious. He was focussing his energies on trying to sort himself out in the hope that they might have a future together, and she told herself that was enough for her, at least for now.

Being in the early stages of a relationship, which arguably hadn't even got off the ground meant she had to be cautious when talking about Ben. She hadn't even told Ursula, who had just come back from holiday, that she and he were together - well, sort of.

But one balmy afternoon, Millie sat on Stoneybrook's terrace with her sister-in-law and glasses of R White's lemonade: thinking about the advert, *she* obviously wasn't a secret lemonade drinker, but she *did* have a secret. While she was prepared to tell Amanda, in confidence, that she and Ben were dating if the timing felt right, Millie flinched at the idea of saying anything about his chequered past, and pressing her lips tight, she determined not to.

'How do you tell you've met "the one"?' she asked Amanda, careful not to mention Ben by name while knowing full well Amanda knew exactly who she was thinking of.

'It's hard to say,' Amanda said reflectively, taking a sip of ice-cool fizz. 'If I said, "you just know," it would sound too much like a boring cliché, so I'll put it this way. Somewhere along the line,' she began, with eyes drifting upwards towards the clouds, 'at some point, after you've met someone, the thought of *not* being with him becomes more and more...' she paused, 'unbearable and unthinkable.'

Soaking in Amanda's words, Millie smiled a little, and after leaving Stoneybrook, she walked back to the farmhouse churning the words over in her mind. They *did* make sense, they really did. *The thought of not being with him becomes unbearable and unthinkable.* She wasn't there yet with Ben, at least she didn't think so, but who knows, maybe that would happen one... Her thoughts stopped abruptly as she noticed her father waiting by the cowshed. She knew he'd just got home, and she didn't much like the look on his face.

'You were with Amanda just now, I take it?' he asked gruffly.

Millie nodded, 'Yes I was. How were things at the cattle market? Is everything okay?'

Rubbing the back of his neck, Cecil seemed agitated. 'Horace was there,' he said, 'and Agnes was with him. She has a message for you, Millie.'

'Message?' Millie repeated slowly.

'Yes. She said she saw Ben in the post office yesterday.'

Standing rooted to the spot, Millie felt confused. Why would Ben give Agnes a message? That didn't sound right. News travelled fast around here, and she wouldn't be surprised if everyone knew by now that she and Ben were together. But what exactly happened in the post office yesterday?

'From what I can tell, it's not so much what happened, but what might be going on behind the scenes,' Cecil said. 'Agnes told me that she said, "Hello," but Ben didn't respond. Instead, he seemed jittery.'

'Okay,' Millie frowned, 'what's wrong with that?'

'Nothing, I suppose,' Cecil shrugged, 'but apparently, the next thing she knew, he'd knocked into her and charged out of the shop, looking absolutely furious and for no apparent reason.'

What? Saying nothing, Millie drew back. *Why would he do that? Whatever was behind what he did, it couldn't have been on purpose.* 'Did he hurt Agnes?' she asked, feeling slightly nervous about what the answer might be.

'No, I wouldn't have thought so,' Cecil said lightly, 'I think he just clipped her shoulder from what I could tell, but that wasn't the main issue, you see, Agnes was convinced he was being deliberately aggressive and then,' he paused, 'she said he had this look in his eyes...'

'What look, Dad? What did she mean?'

'"Wild and quite mad," she said.' Raising his eyebrows, Cecil took a step closer. 'Look, your mother told me you and he are just friends, really close friends, but that's all, is that right?'

Millie nodded, then she shook her head, too stunned and too reluctant to explain. 'It's complicated, but yes, we're still just friends.' She thought it best *not* to tell her father that she was hoping for more.

'Now, I don't know what was going on in this… friend of yours' head,' Cecil said hesitantly, 'but I've never had reason to doubt Agnes before. Horace yes, perhaps, but not Agnes. So it's all a bit worrying, don't you think?'

Millie fell silent. It wasn't like her father to call Ben 'this friend of yours,' and she could tell he was trying to distance him from her.

'Ben's not like that at all,' she spluttered, her words sounding hollow, even to her.

'How well do you know him?'

Pausing to think, she repeated the question. *How well do I know him*? She stared at her father, unable to answer.

'Agnes is convinced she knows why he was on edge,' Cecil said, resting his hands on his hips, 'and for both his sake and yours, I *hope* it's not true.'

As Millie was still staring at her father in disbelief, two holly blue butterflies fluttered past, their bright aquamarine, black-tipped wings dancing before their eyes. Within seconds they flitted away in opposite directions, and in that moment, Millie's suspended breathing began to flow more freely again. Being graced by those delicate, beautiful winged creatures at such a critical time, felt like an auspicious sign. It didn't matter what her father was about to say next, she knew she had the power to choose disbelief and suspicion or she could focus on the beautiful, just like those gorgeous holly blue butterflies.

'Apparently, Agnes used to serve down and outs in a soup kitchen,' Cecil began again. 'There, she'd met several people like Ben – unsuccessful performers, singers, actors, that sort of thing. Some were lovely, but others were angry, unpredictable and irritable, just like Ben. And that sort of behaviour was usually a classic sign.' Looking concerned, Cecil rubbed his chin.

'A sign of what?' Starting to guess the answer, Millie's eyes became glassy.

'An addiction of some sort,' Cecil sighed, 'or withdrawal symptoms perhaps.'

Standing in the middle of the farmyard with her father on this balmy September afternoon, everything suddenly felt surreal. She was no longer aware of the familiar and comforting sounds of chickens scratching for food, cows mooing and the occasional buzz of flying insects. Instead, everything was muffled, including her father's voice, and although she could register him saying something about how he'd never forgive himself if something went wrong, she wasn't really listening.

'I take it Ben's friends with Alan Carter,' Cecil said, his words finally jolting her mind back.

'Yes, he is, They go fishing together,' she replied, trying hard to convince her father she still thought everything was fine.

'Well, Alan's just started working for Horace,' Cecil said. 'I'm not sure if you know.'

'No,' Millie said with a faltering smile, 'I didn't.' After a series of casual jobs, Alan had guaranteed work at last, and with a third child on the way, it must be very welcome news for him and his wife. Not only that, everyone knew Horace treated his employees well. But, feeling her body tense, she asked herself why Horace had told her father this, today of all days. Did Horace know Ben and Alan were friends? If he did, she knew he wouldn't like it, not at all, not one little bit.

'I'd better get on,' Cecil said, lifting his hand. 'I'm sorry to bring you this news and I'll leave you alone now to think about it. Oh, and I won't say anything to your mother. I'm sure you'd prefer to do that yourself.'

'Yes, I would, Dad. Thanks.'

After picking up his bucket, Cecil stopped again and turned around.

'It's easy for a man to hide his true colours if he has a goal in mind,' he said, furrowing his brow. 'For all I know, what Agnes said might be complete and utter nonsense. But what *I* want, all I've *ever* wanted for you, is someone good. You know I don't care about his background or what he does for a living or any of that. In fact, I'm not bothered *who* he is, but whoever he is, Millie,' he said with a heavy tone, 'he'd better treat you right.'

The water in the bucket sloshed as Cecil walked away, leaving Millie standing alone, dazed, in the middle of the farmyard. *Wait, Dad, need any help?* By the time she'd thought about asking, he was already walking through a field and she felt too drained to call after him. Should she ring Ben and ask about what happened, or should she wait, hoping he might raise it himself, the next time she saw him? Clearly, telephoning now to cross-examine him wasn't the best way to look like she was giving him space, and if she did that, it would seem as if she didn't trust him. And she *did* trust him, really, she did.

Heading back to the farmhouse, she decided to spend some time alone, just her and the piano. The simple, yet profound act of playing music would provide an escape that could help drown out every blaring and unwelcome noise in her head. At least, she hoped so. She reached the living room and opened the piano lid, and after taking out some music and taking a steady breath, she began to warm up her hands and fingers with some scales. She stopped for a moment and her mind started spinning. 'He said he was clean and he talked about God,' she mouthed furiously. Ben couldn't be a liar and both Agnes and Horace were wrong, but even if they *were* wrong, how could she possibly tell the rest of her family about Ben's drug-taking history now?

Chapter 30:

'Suddenly' - Billy Ocean

She picked up her sequined clutch bag and glanced at her reflection in the mirror, her heart beating nineteen to the dozen. Serviceable cleaning overalls were exchanged for a slinky teal green, off-the-shoulder number and although afraid she'd forgotten how to date, she knew she was doing well. Another wave of terrified excitement rose to the surface, even though this wasn't their first date. She paused to picture him again, and although still not wowed by his thick, black, Magnum P. I. moustache, she loved all the attention he was pouring on her. After a decade of living in an arid, dating wilderness, life was suddenly rich, lush and exciting.

The doorbell rang. He was early, and her feet ran downstairs as though they belonged to an intoxicated youth, not a woman just shy of forty. He was no spring chicken either, and neither of them was perfect. They were just two divorcees, trying to forge a future together and she hoped that with him, she would get it right.

It wasn't so straightforward this time around. This time, they came with children in tow. Sons and daughters, some fully fledged, others still dependent. Her heart bled, thinking of one in particular, wondering where and how that child fitted in. What would she, could she, say about this child? What would her date say, after she told him what she'd done, what she couldn't do, and how she wished she could've been stronger? Would he be nonplussed, would he be surprised, would he care deeply or would he just gloss over her feelings? She hoped he wasn't judgemental and hoped he'd understand. Should she tell him tonight or perhaps some other time? And the biggest question of all was, why did she always make this into such a big deal? Couldn't she just accept and believe in herself, knowing she'd always tried to do her best?

"Bye Mum.' A bright voice rang out like a bell over the sound of the television. 'Have a lovely time.'

Responding with words of thanks and appreciation, the woman paused before opening the front door. She didn't need to be reminded how lucky she was to have an amazing daughter, because she already knew. She smiled at her loved one, the one who was selfless enough to indulge her by caring for the little ones. The one who afforded her mother the luxury of dating like a teenager again, and for that reason alone, Doretta was worth her weight in gold.

'I've got myself a ten-year plan,' he'd said over dinner. 'I'm going to open up a luxury hotel in Spain.' He suggested she might like to join him, and that by then, all their children would be old enough to take care of themselves. That's when nervously, she told him. But the instant she did, she saw how little difference it made. There was no room in his plan for anything, or indeed anyone else, and that was understandable because it was more straightforward for him. His kids lived with their mother and not only that, they were almost grown. *He* would never have to worry about any of his children or be concerned for their welfare. It was different for her.

***

It's cool outside, but warm in the flat where the woman is attempting to focus on the positive. She tries to accept that she and this man didn't work out in the end and she's sad, but she isn't sorry. Sometimes in life, people's pathways cross, only for them to separate again, diverging in different directions. His ambition is to be a hotelier in Spain, hers is to qualify as a nurse in London, and since the day they went their separate ways, she has had time for the dust to settle. Her moods could still oscillate from day to day, but this evening she is happy, and telling herself to stop ruminating over the past, she focuses on the present, because now it's her daughter's turn. The woman can't quite believe how suddenly, as if overnight, her firstborn, her baby is no longer a child. Doretta is sweet sixteen, and this will be her first-ever date with her first-ever boyfriend. They're going roller skating together, and the polite young lad has just arrived and is now sitting in the lounge of the eleventh-floor flat.

The woman talks to him while he waits for her daughter to appear. Just general chit-chat to put him at ease. Has he been rollerskating before? Is he sporty? What's his favourite sport? Ah, football. So, what team does he support?

Soon, Doretta dashes downstairs, her face beaming, her eyes bright.

'Enjoy yourselves,' the woman calls out, as her daughter and her date head towards the door.

'Thanks, Mrs Norcott,' the boy replies. Then, the woman hears giggles followed by her daughter's whispers.

'Don't be so formal!'

'What shall I say then?'

'Just call my mum by her first name, silly, she won't mind.'

'What's that then?' the boy asks quietly.

'Grace,' Doretta says, a smile spreading across her face. 'Her name is Grace.'

Chapter 31:

'You'd Better Not Fool Around' - Haywoode

Waiting for Ben to arrive was agonising. She stared out of the window, chin resting against the palm of her hand, feeling apprehensive. This was the last time they'd meet before she went back to university, and so much was at stake.

Swallowing, she noticed that her mouth felt dry. No wonder. She'd been winding herself up, wondering why, lately, he seemed so tired all the time. She'd put it down to him being back at work, but now she wasn't so sure. As a busy peripatetic teacher, he travelled from school to school offering saxophone and piano lessons to dozens of pupils. 'Peripatetic teacher sounds too much like very pathetic teacher,' he'd joked, making her smile. She made a fist and pressed down hard on the damask tablecloth. If Horace's and Agnes' suspicions were right, pathetic wasn't the word. He was worse than pathetic, he was a monstrous liar, and although she didn't consider herself the best judge of character, she just couldn't believe she could be capable of getting it so very wrong.

It was approaching mid-day, and the tea rooms of The Old Loom Mill craft centre were still quiet. Initially, she wasn't sure about meeting at this quaint spot, just outside of town. It was hugely popular with the blue rinse brigade, and so while having a heart-to-heart with Ben over lunch, she ran the risk of being overheard by a host of village busybodies. But on the plus side, Ben was teaching at a nearby school, and the craft centre was a great place to buy unique gifts, as well as have a bite to eat. She'd found the perfect present for Enid's birthday - a colourful gemstone brooch, which stood out from amongst the other trinkets and hand-crafted gifts. If only she could give it to Enid personally, but there was no time to visit her before leaving for university. The beginning of the clinical years meant the new term was starting sooner, and today would be the last time she and Ben would be together for a while. Her legs felt restless, which was daft. She knew she didn't need to be nervous around him. She knew she could be herself, but somehow, today felt different. It felt like crunch time.

'Can I take your order?' A timid-looking girl was standing by her table with a pencil and a notepad.

'Thanks, but I'm waiting for a friend to arrive,' Millie said, looking at her watch. She didn't have long to wait, because within seconds, she was hit by an adrenaline rush. Ben was dashing towards her. He'd arrived.

'Hi,' he said, pulling out a chair. 'Sorry I'm late, the lesson ran on a bit. Have you been waiting long?'

'No, not really, and seven minutes is hardly late, so you're fine.' She smiled a little, hoping she was coming across as she always did, hoping he couldn't tell she was checking for signs that something was wrong. Surreptitiously her eyes studied him, looking for some indication. Twitchiness, bloodshot eyes, slurred speech, agitation - she expected something. But no, there was nothing to alarm her. Nothing at all.

'Have you ordered for me?' he asked, glancing at the menu and sitting back in his chair. She shook her head, noticing how, in stark contrast to how she probably came across, he seemed completely relaxed. He was also chatty, perhaps more than usual, diving in to tell her about his pupils that morning, and how well several of them were doing. She listened, while at the same time trying to catch the waitress' eye, but *he* only had eyes for her. Not only that, his eyes were playful and more flirtatious than they'd ever been. She gritted her teeth discreetly, thinking how annoyingly disarming this all was when she had some serious bones to pick with him, but when he rested his hand on his chin and gazed at her, no amount of frustration could stop those goosebumps from coming, and those reassuring warm brown eyes penetrating her soul, were far too credible, telling her that there couldn't possibly be anything to worry about. She still needed answers, but unless Ben was some sort of Jekyll and Hyde, he couldn't possibly still be on drugs or be that nasty, aggressive waster certain people made him out to be. With optimistic eyes, she watched him slip off his blazer, and then, like in that moment a building is smashed by a heavy bulldozer, she was hit by something that rocked her world and brought it crashing down.

He turned around to hang his jacket on the back of his chair, and when he turned back and saw her face, his smile melted away. Millie had been taught as a child that it was rude to stare, but when her eyes fixated on Ben's bare arms and realised in that moment and to her stupefaction that she'd never seen them before, she just couldn't help herself. Now, she knew why he always wore long-sleeved shirts on their country walks, no matter how hot it was. Now she knew why she had sensed something was amiss but only subliminally, with her thoughts never quite reaching the level of consciousness. Not until now. Now she had come face to face with a myriad of tiny, red prick marks and scars covering his arms.

'Can I take your order now?'

Jerking her head up to look at the waitress, Millie nodded. 'You first,' she spluttered, extending out her hand towards Ben and within moments they'd cobbled an order together.

'Um, two quiche lorraines with salad, and um, tea and scones for two,' the waitress recapped hesitantly, scribbling with a nervous hand on her notepad before walking away. Millie's eyes met Ben's again and she blinked rapidly, still painfully unsure about what to say.

'I know what you're thinking,' he said, breaking the awkward silence, 'and I really don't blame you.'

Still unable to speak, Millie wanted to say something, *anything*, but unusually for her she remained lost for words. No matter what she was desperate to believe, she just couldn't ignore the evidence that was now right before her eyes.

'I guess I'm unlucky because most people don't see reminders of their past mistakes every single day like I do.' He was smiling, but it wasn't a happy smile. Instead, it was forced and laboured. Millie looked and she listened. *He said past mistakes didn't he? Past mistakes.* Churning those two words over in her mind, she concluded that they could only mean one thing. Despite what she could see right now, right in front of her, Ben wasn't a liar. Somehow, those marks that were terrifyingly real, had everything to do with his past, and nothing to do with the present and how he was today. Absentmindedly she began to rub her own arms, questioning herself. Could she, should she dare to believe him? And if she did, was she a fool just buying into his lies?

'I shouldn't have hidden it for so long,' he said, clasping his hands, 'and this morning I asked myself, why? Why am I trying to hide this? I mean, you're such a caring person and I've told you loads of crap about me and still, you haven't run away.'

Hearing him say how caring she was and seeing him looking so dejected made her want to cry. By accusing him of lying, albeit only in her mind, she felt she'd really let him down. But those scars, what about those scars? Reluctantly, she eyed them again and they looked so fresh, so recent, so new.

'Is it…are those…?'

'Yes,' he interrupted, 'they're needle marks, track marks, whatever you want to call them. My doctor said they'll fade over time, but everything's taking way too long, Millie, way too long.' Hunching his shoulders he stared at the menu again, as though needing something else to focus on.

'Taking too long?' Millie repeated, and reading her face, he could instantly tell what was troubling her.

'Hey now,' he said, lowering his voice when an elderly couple sat down at a table nearby, 'I told you I was clean, and that's the truth.' She glanced nervously at the couple, relieved to see them completely engrossed in conversation. Then, looking at Ben again with eyes full of anguish, she searched his face wanting to believe him. Should she? She knew nothing about track marks and how they were supposed to look when someone had been clean for nineteen months. She shut her eyes briefly, surprised they hadn't faded more, and instantly she was reminded of what she'd been through herself.

'I know what it's like to live with scars too,' she said softly, 'but I've had mine much longer, so it's had more time to fade.'

Ben swallowed visibly, and after seeing relief in his eyes, she watched the waitress approach again. With unsteady hands, the girl dropped the tray on the table, creating a symphony of rattling cups and saucers and liquid sloshing from an overfilled teapot.

'I'm so sorry,' she said, grabbing a napkin from a nearby empty table.

'No, let me get that,' Ben said, soaking up the splash with a serviette. 'Is it your first day?' he asked, having just overheard another waitress teaching the girl how to take orders correctly.

'It is actually.'

He gave Millie a sideways glance. 'You're doing brilliantly,' he said.

Placing a timorous hand to her chest the waitress thanked him and then she thanked him again, before looking giddy but more confident and walking away with a smile.

Millie watched Ben, her throat thick with emotion. Unless he was putting on an act to deceive her, the way he'd treated that waitress wasn't the typical behaviour of an arrogant man. So why then, why on earth did he treat Agnes like that?

'This came in the post today,' he said, interrupting her thoughts. Reaching into his pocket, he pulled out an official-looking letter and handed it to her.

Accepting it quickly, she began to read, and as her eyes flitted from left to right, they lit up like fireworks. 'You've been approved for a mortgage,' she smiled, 'that's terrific news. Congratulations!'

Leaning back in his chair, he grinned proudly. 'It means I can look for my own place, really soon, but when it comes to the timing, well, that all depends on Gran. Me and Lauren want to be sure she's able to take care of herself first and only after that, I'll start to look for somewhere, so it may not be for a while.'

Millie was glad to see Ben loosening up, and although he didn't seem quite as relaxed as when he'd first turned up, it was great to see him smile and enjoy mouthfuls of quiche and crunchy green salad. She tucked in too, and while the food was good, and the news about his mortgage even better, she hadn't forgotten about something unpleasant which still needed to be addressed. It was time to repeat what Agnes had said, and to ask if it was really true.

The instant she brought it up, he stopped smiling. 'So, you heard about that,' he said, putting down his knife and fork.

'Yes.'

'I was going to say something, but you beat me to it,' he said. 'I intended to mention it because it's all tied up with something else I wanted to tell you today. He picked up his knife and fork and slowly cut into his quiche, but before putting the food into his mouth, he stopped. Obviously, there were more revelations to come, and Millie braced herself.

'I could see us going somewhere, ever since our first walk,' he began.

Closing her eyes for a moment, she savoured the quiche as well as his words, but what, she asked herself, was coming next?

'You've known for some time that my life has been complicated.' Feeling tetchy, Millie nodded. 'But it isn't just drugs,' he continued. 'Remember I told you I was serious about someone before I met you?'

'Yes, of course.' Unsure where this was going, her stomach began to churn.

Ben sighed. 'Well, that serious relationship I told you about. I thought it was over – and it is!' he raised his voice. 'But it wasn't until last week when I believed it was one hundred per cent over, that I made the decision about you.'

'About me?'

'Yes, about us. I finally felt able to go deeper with you, and I couldn't wait. But then…' Slowly, he slid a hand across the tablecloth and placed it on hers, 'something happened.'

How bitter-sweet. The first time he was initiating physical intimacy, he was about to say something she was sure she didn't want to hear.

'Nobody deserves to be dated on the rebound,' he whispered, 'especially you.'

Feeling mounting tension, she absorbed the heat of his hand and tried to calm herself. 'I'm not sure what any of this has to do with Agnes,' she said truthfully.

'Well, it was literally only the day after I'd made that decision, about us I mean, that I was in the post office. I went to pick up a parcel, but it wasn't until I got there, I found out that it was from Faye.' The corners of his mouth fell and he gritted his teeth. 'The timing was terrible, just so bad, because I'd felt ready to move on. Look, Millie, it *is* over, but you've got to remember that me and Faye lived together for three years. For me, it felt like we were as good as married although I try not to think of it like that, so when she writes to me out of the blue saying she's coming back to England…' He lowered his head. 'Well, I'm sorry to say, I didn't take it too well, and now my only regret is that I didn't wait until I got home to read her letter because that poor old woman, what was her name again?'

'Agnes.'

'That's it, Agnes wouldn't have got the full brunt… Well, I was annoyed, just put it like that.'

Millie's head spun, trying to get things straight. So, from what Ben was saying, he still hadn't got over this Faye woman, who he'd lived with for three years and who was coming back into his life, and he was only just telling her all this now? *Thanks a bunch, Ben, thanks a bunch!* While her hand tensed, she noticed mounting alarm in his eyes.

'Why didn't you tell me about Faye before - I mean properly?' she asked, dropping her shoulders.

He shrugged. 'Because that time I told you - about her I mean - it was still early days for you and me and I didn't want to dump everything on you. Talking about my…' He looked over to the couple again and lowered his voice. 'Telling you about my addiction was hard enough.'

For a moment, the two listened in silence to the low-level hubbub around them.

'Anyway, she's history,' he said, straightening up and cutting into his quiche. 'After we split I heard she'd moved to the Far East, and settled in Thailand, so telling you all that didn't seem important. That's why I just couldn't believe it when,' he paused, putting down his cutlery, 'she wrote saying she's moving to Hastings to open a shop with a friend.'

Millie stared at him. *Hastings? Hastings? That's so close!* She tried to eat a forkful of food and began to rue how being with Ben felt like having to endure one revelation after another, just when she was learning to trust him. Then, seeing the worry and uncertainty in her eyes, he gripped her hand.

'Don't worry Millie. It'll all be fine, really it will. Oh, and when I see Agnes, if I get the chance to apologise, I will. Wait, do you have her telephone number?'

Millie shook her head. She could tell him that her father had Horace's number, and ask Ben if he'd be happy to risk his arch-enemy picking up the phone. She could also mention that Alan was now working for Horace, but right now, she didn't have the energy to discuss any of this. There were bigger fish to fry.

'Now I've got over the shock,' he said, 'I know Faye means nothing to me - at least not in *that* way, not any more. I only gave her my new address because our lives were so tangled up and there was still so much to unravel.' He spooned strawberry jam onto his scone, then paused. 'I'm not in love with her, but I still *like* her. I hope that's not a bad thing.'

'Why did you break up?' Millie asked. 'And if you don't like her any more in *that* way, why does it matter she's coming back?'

Ben spooned cream onto his scone and looked up again. 'Drugs,' he sighed. 'That's why we broke up and it's also why I'm worried about her coming back. You see she… Faye reminds me of my old life, and I'm scared of her because of it. I really want to forget the past.' He was smiling oddly, and Millie thought she could see fear in his eyes, but only briefly. 'If we hadn't broken up, I don't think either of us would be around today.'

Just when she thought things couldn't get worse, the awful topic of drugs had reared its ugly head again. Why was he so scared though? Surely he could avoid Faye easily enough, couldn't he? 'Apart from what you said about the drugs thing,' she asked with sober eyes, 'do you want to see her again?'

His pause felt overly long and she looked at him intensely, feeling unsettled.

'Well, yes and no,' came the disappointing answer. 'We didn't break up because we hated each other. We tried to stay friends, but we knew we were better apart. But now, she's saying she's changed, and I'm really curious.' He laughed briefly. 'You see, Faye's crazy, at least she used to be. When she wasn't high on drugs, charities and campaigning were her thing.' Pausing, he began to reminisce. 'She was forever bombing about, lobbying, protesting about this and that, or going on some march or another. She's well into CND and nuclear disarmament and she's camped at Greenham Common as well.' He slurped his tea, 'Now she's saying that after travelling to 'spiritually enlightening places' - whatever that means - she's kicked the drugs for good. She sounds so different, Millie, still mad as a box of frogs,' he chuckled, 'but much more - how can I put it? Stable.'

Despite taking in every word, Millie still wasn't sure what to make of Faye, or indeed the whole situation. 'What was in the parcel?' she asked finally, remembering Faye's letter came with a package.

'Spices,' he said, rubbing his fingers. 'Little muslin bags of cardamom and cumin, coriander, some strands of saffron and, what else? Cloves and turmeric I think. I always did the cooking, and she used to say our kitchen smelled like a restaurant.'

Ben seemed as pleased as punch with his gift, and when Millie saw his mouth corners curling upwards into a smile, she tried to keep calm. 'So what happens now?' she asked, taking a deep breath, 'and how can I be sure that when I go back to uni, Faye isn't going to snatch you away and lead you astray?' She forced a laugh, just to lighten things up, but Ben wasn't fooled and neither did she fool herself. She wasn't really in the mood for laughing.

'I'm sorry if what I said makes you think that could happen,' he said. 'Even though in some ways, I'd like to see Faye again, I've no plans.'

Millie felt relieved, not just because he'd said he had no plans to see Faye again, but also because he was being honest about *wanting* to see her, and although she didn't like that one little bit, at least perhaps it was more evidence she was able to trust him.

'Once an addict, always an addict, and the only solution is to stay away from anything that will draw you back.' He took another swig of tea. 'That's why I never see my old bandmates and why I was glad to hear Faye'd moved abroad.' He looked Millie in the eye. 'But if for any reason I *do* see her again, I'd like you to be there with me.'

Those beautiful, reassuring words were so comforting, and realising that their intense lunch date was almost over, Millie was glad it was ending like this. Against all the odds Ben had managed to dispel most of her fears, she didn't quite know how, but he'd done it, and although she loved scones, it was time to go and leave hers behind. After Ben gave the waitress a cheque and tipped her some cash, they left the tea room, neither knowing what to say nor when they'd see each other again.

After reaching the car park, they stopped and faced each other.

'So this is it,' Ben said.

'I guess it is,' she said, wondering what was wrong with her. Despite all the earlier angst, uncertainty and confusion, all she wanted to do now was throw her arms around him and plant a long lingering kiss on his lips. Now she knew he was telling the truth about being clean, all she had to do in addition was to believe that he had no feelings for Faye and trust that he was strong enough to keep his distance from his former girlfriend.

'I'm sorry,' he said, still looking into her eyes.

'What for?'

Looking exasperated, he shook his head. 'I'm sorry my life's complicated and… and that when it comes to my health, there's still some way to go. I feel like crap sometimes and I really hate that.' He tried to smile a little. 'But, with God's help, everything's going to get better, I know it is and when it does, I hope I can make it up to you. If you still want me by then, of course.'

Want you? Millie repeated inaudibly, *of course, I'll still want you, because I'm a massive fool!* But naturally, she held back from speaking her mind.

'Surgeons have to deal with complications,' she said, thinking of something less incriminating to say, 'so if I can deal with you, I can deal with anything.'

Smiling, he took hold of her hand and gave it a reassuring squeeze. Enjoying the moment, she chose not to think about what challenges might lay ahead, then, slipping her hand away briefly, she reached into her bag. With all that had happened, she'd almost forgotten. 'Please give this to Enid and wish her a happy birthday from me,' she said.

'I will, and call me when you get to London, won't you?'

'I will,' she said, wishing with all her heart, she didn't have to go.

Lightly placing both hands on her shoulders, he slowly leaned in. Closing her eyes she waited. Having longed for this so much, her body was feeling weightless, tingly and excited, all at the same time. But, unexpectedly, and disappointingly, bypassing her lips, he planted a soft kiss on her forehead. Trying not to feel cheated, she opened her eyes and looked into his, and there she experienced a warmth and heat that wrapped around her like a fluffy, feathered eiderdown. There was no reason to be disappointed, because his kiss, his touch, was more sensual in that moment than any full-on mouth-to-mouth contact could ever be.

Parting company, they walked away, Ben to work, and her, back to the farmhouse to pack her suitcase, and while pulling her seatbelt across her chest, she thought about how she'd been warned not to fall for Ben. Too many thought he was a wrong'un, and turning the key in the ignition, she reflected on her mother's admonition to take it slow. And things were definitely slow, but only by accident, and only because Ben was setting the pace. But as far as Millie was concerned, it was a matter of slowly but surely. And even though something inside was shouting, 'Run away Millie, quit while you can,' she wasn't going to listen to the voice of fear telling her what to do. No, when it came to Ben, she'd moved past dipping her toes in the water or having a paddle and she'd even gone beyond swimming in the shallows. Right now she was in the deep end of the pool and completely and utterly submerged, and she drove away accepting that she was *In Too Deep,* and there was no getting out now.

Chapter 32:

'Take On Me' - A-ha

'You've landed on your feet there, Ben. A doctor, and she's a great girl. I really like her.'

'I know, I'm amazed Millie's willing to take me on to be honest.'

'Stop putting yourself down, little bro. You're a great catch!'

'Yeah, right.'

There was a pause over the telephone line.

'Are you okay?'

'I am now, but I wasn't on Tuesday.'

'Why? What happened?'

'I went to the doctor's with chest pain.'

'Oh flip, where?'

'Hailsham.'

'No, you twonk, I don't mean where the surgery is. The pain. Where in your chest was the pain?'

'In the middle, pretty central I think, or maybe slightly more to the left side. I thought I was having a heart attack.'

'Bloody hell, Ben, I don't want to have to start worrying about you again. Gran's enough for now.'

'It's fine. Dr Wilson just gave me painkillers, but I still wasn't sure, so I went to Casualty and had an ECG and blood tests. They said it was just musculo-skeletal chest pain coming from rib muscles – intercostal pain they said, although they didn't explain what that was and why I got it, apart from it could be stress-related. They just wanted to kick me out and move on to the next patient because the waiting room was thrang wi' folk, as they say back in Sheffield.'

'So you're none the wiser. Umm, Have you told Millie? She might be able to advise you.'

'Nay lass, she's back in London and it's nothing serious. I might mention something next time I see her though.'

'And does Gran know?'

'You're joking, aren't you? How can I tell Gran I'm worried I've destroyed my body when she doesn't even know I took drugs?'

'I'm amazed you're still managing to hide all that from her, but I see what you mean. You have to be careful, don't you? Your halo won't only slip, it'll smash to smithereens if Gran finds out you're not really the golden boy she thinks you are.'

'You're not going to go on about me being her favourite again, are you?'

'Would I do such a thing? Even though you and I both know it's true. Anyway, how's Gran today?'

'She's doing okay. Those new painkillers seem to be working.'

'Where's she now?'

'Gone out for a paper. You know what she's like and how she always says, "I'm not an invalid and I'll take my time." But it's true, she takes care, and actually, I'm not so worried about her these days.'

'Pleased to hear it. Still, I can't help being scared she'll have another fall.'

'But that could happen anywhere, including here at home.'

'True. We'll keep our fingers crossed.'

'That we will.'

'So, with Gran improving, does that mean you'll be house hunting soon?'

'Aye, I'm thinking it won't be long.'

'By the way Ben, why do you always sound so much more like a Yorkshireman when it's just you and me talking?'

''Aven't a clue, lass. Must be summat to do with us growing up in Sheffield together.'

'Yes, but *I* talk proper now, me.'

'Only because working with antiques has turned you into a snob.'

'Ha ha. Anyway, now you're buying a house, does *that* mean I have to buy a hat?'

'A hat?'

'*Well*, once you've found a place, the next thing you'll be doing is… dare I say it? Getting married?'

Silence.

'You're smiling, I can tell, and like I said, Millie's great, so you've got my approval.'

Silence again.

'Lauren.'

'Yeah, what?'

'I got a letter from Faye last week.'

'Faye?' Pause. 'Oh. You mean, crazy overdosing, almost killed herself Faye?'

Silence.

'That's not funny Lauren.' Pause. 'Yes, I mean Faye, you know, the woman who used to mean everything to me.'

'I'm glad you said, "used to," and you're right, what I just said wasn't funny. I'm worried for you, that's all. Ignore me. How come you've heard from *her*? I thought you'd decided to cut ties.'

'I did. Sort of.'

'Sort of? What does *that* mean? Anyway, scrap that. I'm glad to hear she's alive and kicking. Did she sort herself out in Thailand then?'

'Yes, she's doing really well actually. She says she's clean.'

'Clean at last. That's fantastic news, assuming it's true of course. And by the way, it's nice to hear you speaking proper English again. In fact, you always sounded so la di da when you lived with Faye. Must be because she's got a rich daddy.'

Silence.

'What's up Bruv? You've gone quiet again.'

'Faye's coming back... to England.'

'Is she? Okay, well, that doesn't surprise me. I bet she misses waving placards outside Downing Street and I'm surprised she hasn't whacked Mrs Thatcher over the head with one yet.'

Silence.

'Lauren.'

'What?'

Pause.

'Faye's moving to Hastings.'

'Hastings?' Pause. 'Oh.'

Silence.

'How far's Hastings from Gran's, then?'
'Not very. Not far at all.'
Silence, and then more silence.
'Oh,' a lengthy pause. 'Crap!'

Chapter 33:

'Gotta Go Home' - Boney M.

Such a stupid dream. With her heart still thumping, Millie looked at the glowing hands of her alarm clock. Ten to three. Then, slipping back under the covers she tried to remember exactly what horrors had woken her up.

That's right, she was standing in a registry office with a small group of people, feeling wrought with pain. *I don't want anyone to know, I don't want anyone to see me cry.* Then she looked around to see a bevy of faceless guests. Faceless meant they had no eyes, and that in turn meant no one could see her tears.

'Will you take this woman,' a voice murmured.

'Yes,' was the gurgled and muted reply, sounding like it was being said from underwater, as though coming from the deep. It was reminiscent of Ben, but no way, it couldn't be! But if it wasn't, why was she so fraught with anguish?

'Will you take this man?' the ceremony continued.

'Yes, yes, yes.' The high-pitched, piercing woman's voice sent chills up Millie's spine, and then it was over in a flash.

'You may kiss the bride.'

Millie looked aghast, watching the shrivelled hand with witch-like talons, squeezing, grabbing and clawing at his back as though clinging on for dear life, threatening to never, ever, ever let go. The man's head was buried in the arms of this woman and his back was turned. His fair hair seemed so familiar, but he couldn't be Ben, she was confident of that. But then, he turned around and she was in no doubt. His face was there, for her and everyone to see, if only they had eyes to see. But the bride, that cackling bride, *she* had eyes. But what about Ben? Could Millie catch *his*? Would she get the chance to look, one last time, into those deep brown eyes and say 'goodbye'?

Millie heard herself scream and the sound was piercing, even more piercing than the woman's ear splitting voice. Where were Ben's eyes? Millie began to panic, because all she could see were two empty, hollow holes in their stead. He didn't smile. His eyeless face was expressionless, but his victorious bride looked up at him adoringly before laughing, triumphantly, relentlessly.

'His eyes,' Millie screamed, 'what have you done with his eyes?'

The Frankenbride walked up to her, deliberate and slow, just like a cat that's seen a mouse - a Milly mouse, ready to pounce. She smirked, she gloated and then she opened up veiny hands and revealed two jelly-like optic balls, complete with dark brown iris-shaped discs. Ben stood passively, helplessly and joined hands with his new bride. 'Take me where you want to,' he mumbled like a robotic fool. 'Lead me where you want me to go. I cannot see, I cannot see.' She grinned and began to creep, leading the way, slowly but surely and all the faceless guests stood back immobilised, and began to sing a dirge.

'Put them back now!' Millie screamed, writhing in distress. 'I'm telling you, put them back, now. Now!'

'Back now.'

'Back.'

And finally, *she* was back. Back to the real world, back inside her room at 8 Somerley Street, Tooting. The nightmare was over and with her heart still thumping, all she could think was how much she hoped neither Joyce nor Wahida had heard her cry out. Such a silly dream and it meant nothing. One thing's for sure, it didn't mean she had to rush back home to Sussex to make sure Ben was safe. She pulled up the covers a little tighter, keen, desperate to get more sleep. She needed to be fresh for morning lectures and she wouldn't allow any nonsensical nightmare to ruin her day.

***

'The ischaemic myocardium can gradually be replaced with fibrotic tissue leading to a thin-walled ventricular aneurysm.'

It was no use. Her concentration was weaving in and out again, like a long wave radio signal on an old-fashioned wireless. 'Stop it,' she told herself sternly, thinking she'd moved beyond this nonsense. After all, she wasn't a lovestruck teenager this time around, she was twenty and more able to handle her emotions. Also, wasn't having a long-distance boyfriend supposed to be less distracting and so a plus point for choosing Ben over Zane? But she hadn't factored in how hard it was to miss someone, and not be able to see them for days on end. Study was relentless and practical placements would soon eat into what little spare time she had left, but nevertheless, she *had* to carve out time to see Ben somehow, whether that entailed going back to Sussex at the weekends, or him coming to London to see her. Deep down she knew that by the time she got home, she'd have to turn back again and precious study time would be wasted. Still, the thought of hardly seeing him between now and the Christmas break was unbearable.

Apart from missing Ben, she didn't mind being back in London, and it was great to see the old St George's crew again after such a long break. Not much had changed. Wahida was still crazy for Jonas and the two continued where they'd left off before the summer holidays, spending hours in each other's company but still weirdly without any discernable amorous developments. One breezy Saturday afternoon, Millie joined them on a trip to the very trendy Camden Market, and after watching the pair hover over gothic jewellery stalls, soaking up with their eyes dubious delights such as sterling silver skulls, vampires, dragons and coffins, she chose to make herself scarce. Wahida later came home fanning her face with a hand, but it was excitement and not the weather making her sweat. She proudly showed off a ring on her finger, which she'd purchased. 'Are you engaged?' Millie joked, peering at a metallic bat's head with wings. She knew an engagement between Jonas and Wahida wasn't currently even a consideration, but *if* it ever were to happen, she wouldn't put it past them to seal their romance with a freaky choice such as that.

Inspired by the newly released record by Lloyd Cole and the Commotions, Wahida and Jonas had plans afoot for a 'Lost Weekend' away and Millie was invited. But as she sat in Wahida's room, surrounded by posters of sinister-looking, goth musicians, Millie had other things on her mind.

'Ben and I are a couple now,' she smiled tentatively.

'Oh, really? Cool, congratulations.'

The first time Millie had mentioned Ben to Wahida, she'd told her he'd been in a band. 'Blue-eyed soul's not my thing,' Wahida replied candidly, remarking how she wasn't into groups and artists like Culture Club, Eurythmics or Paul Young, but when Millie told her Sheffield Fusion's style was more Philadelphia soul than pop, she seemed much more impressed.

Wahida liked the sound of Ben, but it was Ursula that Millie worried the most about impressing. Her old school friend had spent most of the summer in Yugoslavia and Edinburgh, so despite the extended break, they had only managed telephone catch-ups. As Ursula had once said though, the two were 'friends forever,' and Millie felt obliged and keen to keep her up to date.

'Ben and I are getting closer,' she'd said nervously, 'but we're taking it slow because there are a few practical things to sort out.'

'Like what?'

'Um, like me being in London most of the time and him being in Sussex.'

Surprised that Ursula seemed to buy into this, Millie felt relieved, because the time wasn't right to be totally transparent. She knew that saying, 'Ben's a drug addict in recovery who's not long come out of a serious relationship and is slightly stressed because his ex is moving nearby,' wouldn't have gone down too well, and there was little doubt in her mind what Ursula's curt response would have been. 'Are you absolutely crazy, Mills? Don't be an idiot. Run a mile!' or something on those lines for sure.

Thankfully, Victoria wasn't quite so outspoken and Millie felt confident she could confide in her mother without fear of chastisement or looking foolish. Still, when she'd mentioned Faye at the end of the summer, as predicted, there was a doubtful, heart-sinking look on Victoria's face which Millie would have preferred not to see.

'Ben said he doesn't have feelings for her any more,' she'd said, casually taking an apple from the fruit bowl. When doing so, she'd noticed the way her mother's eyes widened, just a fraction. That, together with the silence which followed were clear indications that Victoria was worried, although very adept at holding her tongue. Biting into the apple, Millie had kept quiet herself, and let the moment pass by, hoping that one day, her mother would come around to Ben and would be as certain of him as she was.

For now, Millie decided it was sensible not to say too much about him, even though she wanted to scream his name from the rooftops. On the other hand, Wahida wasn't family. She was a friend, and far less protective than Ursula, but even with Wahida, Millie wasn't ready to reveal the full truth.

'Ben's been through a lot, but I can't go into details.' That's all she was prepared to say.

Wahida responded with an understanding nod and repeated how she hoped it would all work out. But she *did* have just one comment to make.

'Zane's going to be heartbroken,' she said, in her usual dispassionate way.

'I hope not,' Millie replied, mentally crossing her fingers and aware that Zane had been acting cooler towards her recently. Was his coolness because they hadn't seen each other for ages, or perhaps because he'd sensed someone else was soaking up her affections? Either way, he was showing early signs of giving up, and Millie was surprised by her mixed feelings about that. On the one hand, she was well aware that stringing him along, keeping him waiting in the wings like some sort of insurance policy, was grossly unfair. But on the other, she was reluctant to let him go. Recently, she'd jealously watched him spend more and more time with Sara, a bubbly and attractive girl who didn't seem to mind his airs and graces, while knowing her slight resentment was highly unreasonable when she didn't really want him that way herself. But perhaps she wasn't being a complete meanie. She still valued Zane's friendship, and after spending so much time with him, sometimes daily for the last two years, perhaps it was a simple matter of being jealous for their friendship and being loath to give that up. She was glad they'd continued to have regular lunches together, and in true Zane style, he'd still laugh out loud, although sometimes he'd sound more forced and have a soft, sad look in his eyes as though he'd sensed he'd lost her. So, perhaps Wahida was right. Maybe he *would* be devastated when she told him about Ben, and even though she knew she didn't owe Zane anything, she also knew she really didn't want to hurt him.

'Sounds like you had a good summer,' Wahida said at the end of their chat.

'And next summer will even be better,' Millie smiled.

'Why?'

'Because in May I'm going to be an aunty. Amanda's pregnant!'

Millie left Wahida's room and closed the door behind her with memories of how Dean and Amanda had turned up at the farmhouse with big smiles, just before she'd left for London. When Amanda announced she was expecting, Dean jumped up and pumped his fists in the air and after Millie gave her radiant-looking sister-in-law a big kiss and a squeeze, she watched her mother bounce from foot to foot with joy. The happiness at the farmhouse was palpable. Even Cecil, her father couldn't contain his excitement, slapping Dean on the back and smiling, while knowing it would be inevitable that he would have to take on more work, despite Amanda insisting she would carry on as normal. 'I only need a short break after the baby's born,' she said. 'Maybe just a week or two.'

'She's looking for one of those sling thingies so she can strap the baby to her back,' Dean winked before cracking a joke about growing tea and rice in the fields so that Amanda truly looked the part. Laughing, Amanda said again that all she wanted to do was pull her weight, and after Victoria attempted to be witty by saying something about losing baby weight, the laughter and celebratory mood began to die down and smiles became muted as everyone realised what everyone else was thinking.

Who would tell Stuart? Would he be excited about being an uncle? Would he and his wife come down to visit after their niece or nephew was born? And finally, when might *they* become parents themselves?

'He's in the army now,' Victoria often said, whenever the family suggested including him in anything while knowing full well he was unlikely to participate. Being in the army wasn't a credible excuse for his absence, not any more. But nobody wanted to add to Victoria's heartbreak, by cruelly verbalising the truth.

Millie focused on the positive, happy days ahead. Aunty Millie had a nice ring to it, and she pictured herself with Uncle Ben, both of them grasping the tiny hand of the newest member of the Appleby family and spending time in play parks, at the Zoo or on trips to the seaside. She couldn't wait to have a little one to fuss over and someone other than Conker to spoil, and by the time all this came about, she had but one big desire. She hoped Ben would finally be free of everything and every*one* that was now holding him back and by then, it might just be *her* turn. He'd be there for *her*, by *her* side, supporting her through long working hours, encouraging her when she'd made a clinical mistake or had a difficult patient and holding her hand when she felt overwhelmed and close to tears.

Back in her London room, she pulled away the net curtains and spent a moment or two gazing at the Edwardian houses across the street and watching a few pedestrians stroll by.

'You *will* take care of him – won't you?' That's what Lauren had said, and though too overcome to respond in the moment, her heart had answered back with a multitude of yeses. But now that same heart was speaking a different, more unpalatable truth. 'If you keep pouring out without ever filling up,' she heard a voice inside say, 'then one day your emotional well will run dry.' Arguing back, she told herself to shush. Ben needed her, and while she had more than enough love for them both, she was happy to carry the can. Letting the lace curtain fall back into place, she reminded herself that this was only for a season, and best of all, she knew she could trust him. And there was nothing else that mattered more than that, nothing else at all.

Chapter 34:

'See You' - Depeche Mode

November and early December went by in a heady, passionate blur and whenever Millie caught sight of Ben, 'Run to You' by Brian Adams, described her behaviour perfectly. Whether meeting him at the train station or seeing his car pull up outside her London home, or arriving outside Clover Cottage, she'd run to him, she'd jump on him, she'd wrap her exhilarated arms and blue-jeaned legs around him, and they'd kiss. Oh, how they'd kiss, because now they'd kissed properly for the first time, she didn't want to stop. 'Kiss Me', by Stephen Tin Tin Duffy was a song with words of passion lifted straight from the bible, at least that was the case according to Ben. 'Really?' Millie had said, raising her eyebrows and certain he must have been having her on. Only when he'd whisked her off to Ave Maria Lane, a street name so beautifully reminiscent of the Schubert classical piece, she'd finally seen the evidence, because there, inside the Christian bookshop, he'd opened a bible and shown her Song of Solomon.

'Believe me now?' he asked quietly.

On this particular day, they passed the honey-coloured magnificence of the Houses of Parliament and Big Ben flanked by the sparkling river Thames. Then, they watched the changing of the guard at Buckingham Palace, standing with arms wrapped around each other, in front of its gold and black heraldic gates. Then, after splashing out on afternoon tea at the Ritz hotel, they visited the Tower of London and gazed at the crown jewels before ending their day kissing under St Paul's Cathedral's famous pillars and dome. Time was limited, so they took in as many sights as they could, and at the end of the day, Ben had just one word to say, which, although not quite in keeping with the romantic ambience, totally summed up how they were both feeling while at the same time, paying tribute to their love of sitcoms. 'Cushty,' he grinned, kissing Millie on the cheek, knowing he'd be hard-pressed to summarise the day's experiences any better than Del Boy from *Only Fools and Horses*.

When she finally got home, alone and feeling pleasantly worn out, Wahida remarked how handsome Ben was, adding with a completely straight face that he was 'almost as good-looking as Jonas.' Laughing, Millie felt very much at ease, so much so that she regretted the chilly weather had meant Ben's arms had been hidden under sleeves. She wanted Wahida to see his scars, in fact, she now wanted the whole world to see them. She wasn't ashamed, and neither should he be. He should be proud. She'd moved beyond embarrassment to recognize those as war wounds, just like hers were. But she also realised that unveiling them to Wahida, and explaining why they were there, wasn't quite the same as revealing it all to the people back home. Reminded that Ben was still officially yet to meet her family, apart from that brief encounter he'd had with her mother, her heart beat a little faster. Still, progress had been made because a date had been set. Ben would be spending New Year's Day at the farmhouse and everyone was looking forward to meeting him. Nervously she anticipated them all enjoying one of her mother's delicious roasts while getting to know each other and loosening up. Then, in the evening, they might play a game of Trivial Pursuit, or even take part in an after-dinner singalong session at the piano. She sank back into the sofa, thinking U2's 'New Year's Day' would be an excellent choice for a Hogmanay singsong, if only some miracle were to occur and she managed to learn how to play it on the piano between now and then.

While it still remained that her mother was the only family member who knew about Ben's drug taking, there came a day when Millie finally decided to bite the bullet and reveal all, well, almost all, to Ursula. Again, it was a matter of being half disappointed and half relieved that she was telling her over the telephone. But when the words: 'Ben used to take heroin, but he's now totally clean,' left her lips, she immediately experienced an unexpected, heavy dose of regret.

'Being in a band, that's why he fell into it. Everyone was doing it, pretty much.' In desperation, she tried to cut through the ensuing silence, wishing she could see Ursula's face, while also thankful that she couldn't. The seconds seemed to pass slower than ever, and she could almost hear the cogs in Ursula's brain turning, before she finally opened her mouth.

'You're a big girl now,' Ursula said at last, 'but I really hope you know what you're doing.'

'I do Urs, I really do… he's…'

'He's what?'

'He's different now.' Millie moved away from her intended trajectory, changing her mind in a split second about telling Ursula that Ben was a Christian. Something inside was warning her that sceptical, cynical Ursula would immediately be suspicious. An ex-addict was one thing, but an ex-addict who was now a bible basher, as Ursula liked to call Christians, was another. No, perhaps best to reveal things in stages and leave that bit of information for another time. Now feeling conflicted, Millie acknowledged to herself that it was odd that Ursula felt more like a strict parent than a mate sometimes, but still, she'd always been a great friend, and even though they were both busy and now lived miles apart, she didn't ever want to let the friendship die. Ursula was the only one who had stood by her through thick and thin including through some very tough times at school. And more recently, she'd protected her from seeing Giles in the pub that day. 'Friends forever,' Ursula had said afterwards, and Millie would never forget that.

Perhaps it'd been too early to say anything about heroin, but it *was* definitely safe to tell Ursula about the first time she and Ben had kissed, and Millie did so with glee. 'It happened in our special place,' she said, her pulse quickening at the memory. 'The place we call Stoneybrook.' Going slightly off track, she then mentioned how they were standing near the water and her excitement when they saw a water shrew, the first she'd ever seen. She said they crept up and managed to get a glimpse of its cute snout, long whiskers and silky grey fur before it disappeared into some vegetation. Ursula grunted a little, pretending to sound bored, but Millie guessed she was smiling really. Then came the more exciting bit. She told Ursula what it was like to feel Ben's arms around her and his lips touching hers for the very first time. If only she and Ursula were in the same room, it would be just like the old days when they were schoolgirls, talking about Giles and Gregory together, only this time, Ursula had nothing romantic to report, and as for Ben, well, he wasn't Giles, and for that reason alone, Millie couldn't be happier.

Ursula didn't need to know how understanding Ben had been when she'd told him how far she'd gone with Giles. Initially concerned about bringing it up, Millie was fearful he might judge her, whilst knowing deep inside, that Ben wasn't like that at all. Then, after squirming a little, and cracking a lame joke about the song 'Like a Virgin', she felt him take her hand, and then she heard some words she didn't expect. 'Your Dad's right to call you Innocent Miss Millicent. And as for me, well,' he paused, giving her a solid look, 'I don't care about any of that, because like your Dad says you are to him, you'll always be Innocent Miss Millicent to me.'

Squeezing his hand tight, they'd kissed again, and later that day, separating from him was like having a piece of her ripped away. She'd never felt love like this before, and couldn't wait for the day when they didn't have to part and go their separate ways.

Something else she didn't tell Ursula on this occasion was that she felt more than ready to take things further with Ben, but as ever, he seemed to be in no rush. And neither did she tell Ursula that she could tell he continued to struggle. Some days he looked really exhausted. On others she'd occasionally touch his hand, only to discover it felt clammy. Then, there were the days he was jittery, or seemed out of sorts in other odd ways. But despite his history, she refused to question him, or even doubt him. Her insecurity and fears had driven Giles away, she was sure of that, and she didn't want to repeat the same mistakes and besides, thanks to Ben's openness and honesty, she already knew he had psychological problems. All she needed was to be patient, all she had to do was wait things out. And there was one more thing that was very encouraging. He'd not mentioned Faye for a while, so there was no need to say anything about her to Ursula and the last thing he'd said was that he'd heard nothing more from her, which was very good news indeed.

Before putting the phone down with Ursula, Millie changed the subject. She told her how upset she was that her Great Aunt, who was downsizing to a flat which didn't take pets, had given Conker away without warning her. 'I didn't even get the chance to say goodbye,' she sniffed, and Ursula, being a dog lover herself, understood her pain. But she also confessed it was hard to feel down when she was hopelessly over the moon about becoming an aunty, and she also felt that her family, or rather her future family, was growing now that she was getting to know both Enid and Lauren better.

After she'd hung up, she remembered the afternoon spent at Clover Cottage when Enid had opened up about her late husband, Percy. What Enid had said gave a whole new meaning to Double's 'The Captain of Her Heart', and with Ben sitting next to her on the green velvet sofa, Millie once more admired the old photograph of a beaming bride in an elegant 1930s gown with her besuited groom by her side. Moments earlier, Enid had eased herself onto her feet, taken the photo out of the display cabinet and gazed at it fondly. 'Percy was such a good man,' she mumbled, dejection in her worn grey eyes, 'a very good man.' Then she sat back down without saying a word, but after a few moments, she was ready to talk again, this time, about what happened the day she'd heard that Percy's Merchant Navy ship was lost at Sea.

'It feels like a long time ago now,' she said, her voice perking up a little, 'but then again, I suppose forty-five years *is* a long time. Still,' she paused, her lips pursed tightly, 'it still hasn't been long enough for someone to find his ship, or tell me exactly where my Percy was brought down.'

Millie swallowed hard, and when Ben offered to make tea, Enid said she'd rather play the piano for a while before lying down. So, Millie left the cottage with Ben, her eyes prickling, thinking she was beginning to feel Enid's loss almost as though it were her own. 'Why didn't you tell me about what happened?' she asked Ben.

He shrugged, 'I'm not sure and it didn't really cross my mind. But I suppose, thinking about it now, it's probably good that I didn't. Gran likes to be the first to tell people what happened, and it's good you heard it from her.'

Millie nodded, thinking Ben's family were different to hers, and that was fine. If her grandfather had been lost at sea, she couldn't imagine not telling Ben by now.

'How did Enid cope? Did she get a telegram?' Nodding, Ben said he supposed she did. Millie had other questions in her mind. *Did Enid believe it straight away or did she spend years waiting for a knock on the door that never came, hoping that Percy would eventually turn up alive and well?* But in quiet contemplation, she guessed from the way Ben had shrugged his shoulders earlier, he wouldn't know.

As they walked hand in hand, Millie's curiosity about his family and her keenness to spend time with them grew. She hadn't seen Lauren for a while, but they'd spoken on the phone recently, and Millie was looking forward to meeting Ben's parents, despite there being a few obstacles in the way. Going to the Shetland Isles to see his mother would have to wait until the summer for practical reasons, and his father, although closer geographically, wasn't nearby either. Also when it came to *him*, Millie got the distinct impression that Ben was in no hurry to introduce them.

Just before they'd left Clover Cottage, Ben had shown her a picture of his mother, a smiling woman in her fifties, standing outside a remote croft, oceanic winds blowing through her thin, fair hair. But when he presented her with a different photograph, this time a Polaroid picture of his father, his face was looking a little more flushed.

'He's a big wrestling fan and models himself on Giant Haystacks and Big Daddy,' Ben had said with a narrow smile. Millie stared at the photo of the dark-haired man holding a can of 'Special Brew' in one hand and a big bag of monkey nuts in the other, his hairy chest and bulging belly visible through a worn and greying string vest.

'Lauren's got your Dad's hair and you've got your Mum's,' she smiled, having thought of something to say.

'I know what else you're thinking,' Ben said, 'but not so fast, young lady. I hear string vests are in vogue.

Plenty of punks wear them, Rastas too in fact, loads of cool dudes - just because it doesn't look so great on my Dad doesn't mean he's not 'with it'.'

Millie looked at Ben's wry smile and mentally relaxed. 'I think he looks… well, it doesn't look *bad* on him. Ah, I see your Dad reads *The Sun*.' She pointed to a black and white tabloid newspaper in the foreground with characteristic red and white lettering.

'Aye Lass, it's his favourite.'

'Nothing wrong with that I guess,' she said.

'Nay, nowt wrong wi' 'at, but equally, 'tis something not quite right about a fifty-five-year-old man ogling a sixteen-year-old girl on page 3 i'nt it?'

Ben had gone all Yorkshire on her again, which was probably something to do with him talking about his father, and notwithstanding his Northern phraseology, Millie knew exactly what he was talking about.

'Sam Fox isn't sixteen still, is she?'

'She *was* when she started that topless stuff though wasn't she? I'm surprised her parents allowed it. It's a bit of a shocker don't you think? I mean, some of my pupils are that age.'

This set off a conversation about page 3 in general and whether it was harmless fun like so many people believed it to be, or was pernicious and dangerous. That in turn led on to a conversation about TV shows like Benny Hill, where scantily clad women ran around in front of dirty old men. Both being fans of comedy, they agreed Benny Hill could be funny, but that didn't mean that they were blind to the fact that a lot of the jokes and material could be unsavoury.

Millie wasn't sure if it was because Ben was a Christian or not, but on matters like these, he was refreshingly different. She looked at him with admiration, thinking how wonderful it was that he wasn't into stuff like that, and although she sometimes felt like grabbing him and in frustration, shouting out aloud the title of the Bow Wow Wow song, 'Do You Wanna Hold Me?', she was immensely glad that he seemed to have oodles of respect for her, and for women in general.

As they continued their stroll, hand in hand, in step with each other in more ways than one, Millie felt a slight chill when Ben casually mentioned that Alan wasn't in touch with him any more, and she could guess why. Horace, she seethed, it had to be Horace. Now that Alan was working for him, his mind had been poisoned, you can bet your bottom dollar. Turning her head, she glanced up at Ben's doleful face and felt a mixture of helplessness, sadness, fury and concern. He and Alan had got on *so* well, but now, whenever Ben called Alan's home, his wife always answered, and Alan was never in, and despite always leaving a message, he never called back. How cowardly, Millie thought. She'd always liked Alan, but if you were going to snub someone, the least you could do was be polite enough to own up to what you were doing. But listening to herself, she knew she was being naive. By its very definition, snubbing was a nasty act, because it meant ignoring, spurning or rebuffing someone, and what true friend would ever do that?

Smiling through gritted teeth she told Ben that if she ever bumped into Alan again, she'd try to be pleasant. She'd also be very tempted to put the record straight and tell him that Ben was a good guy, but she refrained from telling Ben that. But perhaps, instead of trying to heal Ben and Alan's broken friendship, she'd be better off focusing on trying to help Ben get out and about to find new friends. She gazed up at him again, knowing that despite her worries, he was more than capable of taking care of himself. He wasn't a child any more, and neither was he an extrovert, desperate for social interaction. Over these past months, if she'd learned anything, it was that he liked his own company and the Animal Nightlife song, 'Mr Solitaire', could easily have been written for him. While she hoped he'd soon make new friends in the village - her brother Dean being one of them - she was just happy that for the time being, he already had the best friend he could ever want or need. She held his hand and her face brightened with optimism. He'd make more friends soon enough, and none would ever be more loyal than she was.

***

It was never going to be easy saying goodbye. Although she ought to have left yesterday, and couldn't afford to do this too often, getting on this train meant she'd still make it for Monday's afternoon lectures. She stood on the platform with light precipitation in the air, feeling just a little bit disappointed that Ben wasn't the type to go in for public displays of affection. She definitely could have done with more kisses, but aside from his shyness and reticence, he needed to get to work, so their goodbye had been short but sweet. Missing him already, she peered down the platform to see the train in the distance and soon it had pulled up at the platform and she was morosely opening the door. After she slammed it shut again, she stepped into what she thought was an empty carriage, but the moment she lifted her eyes, they quickly lit up.

'Dr Wilson!'

'Millie, hello. How are you?'

Millie sat herself down opposite the cordial-looking family doctor, who had kindly provided her with work experience during her latter days at school. His surgery was also the one where her sister-in-law had worked before the scandal that rocked the family had changed all that.

'I'm guessing you've got the day off work?' she smiled.

'You guessed correctly,' he said, 'Mary and I had breakfast at a hotel in Eastbourne, and being the kind merciful wife that she is, she released me afterwards, rather than subjecting me to a day's shopping.'

Millie chuckled. 'How are your lads?' she asked.

'Chris and Alex? Oh, they're fine - too fine. They're eating us out of house and home.'

'They must be - what, at least 14 and 10 now?'

'Chris is nearly sixteen and Alex's twelve actually. I can't quite believe it.'

'Neither can I.'

He paused. 'So, how are all *your* family? Presumably very healthy, because I don't recall seeing any at our surgery for a very long time.'

Millie smiled. Even though she'd very much hoped to fit in some study on the train, she was happy to be catching up with Dr Wilson instead. She told him she was going to be an aunty and when he asked with a tongue-in-cheek smile, 'How is she who shall remain nameless – the one who left us high and dry?,' she also filled him in on how things were with her other brother and sister in law, telling him they were both doing well, 'At least as far as we know,' she added, for the sake of accuracy.

'So you've started your third year at medical school, how are you finding it?' he asked.

'Tough, to be honest.' The honk of a passing high-speed train almost drowned out her voice.

'How on earth do you find time to come home at the weekends then?' he asked, tilting his head.

'Well,' she breathed, 'I don't *really* have the time, but my boyfriend lives in the village, so I travel down to see him whenever I can.'

'Boyfriend, eh?' Dr Wilson smiled. 'Who's the lucky chap?'

'His name's Ben. Ben Bradshaw, and he's a music teacher.'

Dr Wilson's face froze for a moment, and feeling puzzled, Millie watched his features change before adopting a more nonchalant expression once more.

'Well, I wish you and Ben all the best and of course Millie, I hope everything continues to flourish for you at St. Georges.'

The doctor smiled quickly and glanced out the window. 'We've almost reached Lewes. Hasn't time flown? I'm staying in a hotel in London tonight because tomorrow I'm at a Royal College of General Practitioners' conference and it's an early start. But first, I'm stopping off to visit my parents.' He cast his eyes upwards. 'They're both in their seventies and ridiculously fit and well, but it's amazing how one's family suddenly develops all kinds of ailments once you're a GP.' He smiled, warning Millie that one day, everyone and their aunt would be showing her their verrucas or moaning about constipation and allergies, even if she was a surgeon and not a family doctor.

The train pulled up at the station and he stood up to leave.

'I'll bear that in mind, Dr Wilson,' she smiled, 'and I hope the conference goes well tomorrow.'

'So do I,' he said, opening the door after the train had ground to a halt. 'All the very best Millie, and do say hello to the family for me.'

With the clatter of the slam-door train resonating behind him, Dr Wilson slowly began to walk towards the station exit. Ben Bradshaw. Was it the same man? How many local Ben Bradshaw's were there? It had to be. Stepping onto the pavement outside, he wondered how well Millie knew her young chap. Was she aware that he lived in constant fear and was a regular at the surgery, terrified that every benign symptom was serious, constantly taking himself off to casualty and getting a name for himself at the hospital? And did she know why? Did she know many of his fears were based on legitimate concerns because of what his body had been through after his intravenous heroin abuse in the past? And what about the other thing? What about what he'd mentioned about his ex-girlfriend and everything else he'd told him in confidence? The doctor sighed, hoping for Millie's sake that everything worked out for her in the end, and he dismissed that gut feeling that her happy, excited smile was an ominous sign that she was oblivious to what might lie ahead.

It wasn't always easy being a doctor to patients you'd known so long they almost felt like friends. But one thing was certain, if neither she nor her family were aware of any of these things, they wouldn't be finding anything out from him. He was a professional clinician, bound by the strictest rules of patient confidentiality, and buttoning up his rain mac, he sighed and headed out of Lewes station, silently making his way towards his parents' home.

Chapter 35:

'Don't Dream It's Over' - Crowded House

Before our love came to an end
I never guessed it was a lie.
I truly thought you were a friend
and never knew I'd say goodbye.

I loved you much but now I know,
Broken hearts and severed ties.
Treachery, can it be so?
Best endeavours, wicked lies.

Ice winds blow, I feel a chill,
I should have heeded those who cared,
But even so, I love you still,
And that's what makes me feel so scared.

A time to laugh, a time to grieve,
I shall not e'er see you again,
A man so able to deceive,
I loved you so, I loved you, Ben.

***

There are people who leave a bad taste in your mouth – figuratively speaking of course. You don't actually taste anything, but you know these folk have left their mark when they leave behind something nasty in their wake.

Déjà vu, going around in circles, ever-decreasing circles, dying. Call it what you may, say what you will, but terrible truths can't be denied. She'd been here before, not long enough ago, and she didn't know how she was going to survive this time.

There had been signs but no forewarnings, fears but few doubts. When Millie met Lauren in Harrods, London, that mid-December day, it'd felt like she had a new sister and a friend. 'I'll be at Gran's on Boxing Day,' Lauren said. 'Come round, I'd love you to.' She tucked away her Access credit card, her 'flexible friend', and told Millie she'd wrap her gift and give it to her then.

The two parted, Millie to lectures, Lauren to an antique dealers' conference, her hands laden with bags of extravagances.

'Your sister's invited me on Boxing Day,' Millie later boasted.

'I know,' Ben smiled down the telephone line.

The start of the holidays was beautiful. Winter walks in the country and Stoneybrook in the snow. Buffeting winds propelled them forward, strolling hand in hand by the sea. But then without warning, he detonated a bombshell. He looked uneasy, and then he blurted out, 'Faye's coming Boxing Day.' While wringing his hands just a little, he stopped her in her tracks. Surely, she hadn't heard him right, so she asked him to repeat himself.

Ambushed by reality, she listened to the ensuing words. She heard an explanation, hoping for some damage limitation. Wide-eyed and open-mouthed she tried to follow, trying not to panic, trying to understand. Faye had turned up one day at Clover Cottage. Noted and understood. Enid had let her in, 'tick'. Ben wasn't home, 'tick' and Enid had always liked Faye even though she hardly knew her. No tick. Enid often said she'd never understood why Faye and Ben parted. Much worse than a 'no tick'. That last piece of information needed a big black cross by it.

'I'm in Hastings over Christmas, my parents are abroad, would you like to see my new flat?' Apparently, those were Faye's words, and Enid thanked her kindly.

'I find it easier to stay home these days. Perhaps you might like to come here instead?' Only later did Enid realise the implications, and when Ben came home, she apologised. 'I know Faye is just a friend to you now, but I ought to have checked with you first.' Above all she hoped Millie would forgive her misjudgement. She'd had no idea that Lauren had invited Millie, she went on to say, but was very glad when she'd heard.

Though still struggling to believe it, Millie could exhale at last. She was going to be there, what could go wrong? And anyway, she hadn't forgotten Ben's words that emotional day. 'If for any reason I *do* see her again, I'd like you to be there with me.'

Boxing Day came all too soon. Cascading curls on a flirty girl, relentlessly running fingers through her golden mane. Ben had said Faye was larger than life, but he hadn't said how incredibly healthy she looked. With full rosy cheeks and bright eyes, how could this girl ever have smoked a cigarette, let alone taken heroin?

And personality-wise, she wasn't that odious either. It might have been easier to hate her had she been. She was lively, friendly, vivacious and fun, but Millie wasn't fooled, *she* knew her game. She knew exactly why she was there and what she was after. No amount of 'I'm here to see Enid' would wash with her, and only a brazen hussey would impose herself like that. Neither Lauren nor Ben could protest. Enid believed Faye was just a friendly ex, and nobody was about to tell her that behind that smile lay a frightening past. Dependency, addiction, drug abuse.

Enid *did* try to make Millie the centre of attention, as though it were her way of saying sorry and Faye acted as though impressed by what she'd heard. 'Millie, you play the piano; Millie, you're a medical student; Millie, is there *really* no end to your talents?' And then, obviously hungry for the limelight herself, she proceeded to open her mouth and refused to close it. She spoke at length about her months in the Far East and how much the culture had inspired her. She droned on about her business partner and their soon-to-be-opened shop. Everyone politely listened to her enthuse about transcendental meditation, healing crystals and Celtic deities, and not until after she'd speculated how the age of Aquarius might affect all their star signs did Enid step in, offering a proposal.

'Talking of stars, what about stargazing instead of a walk? I don't want to slow everyone down.' Little did Enid appreciate when she said those words, how fateful that suggestion would turn out to be.

Venus' intense brightness and the constellation of Orion were leading lights amongst billions of stars. They gazed, hands wrapped around steaming mugs.

They took warming sips of frothy hot chocolate and stood shivering in the cold night air. Every now and then, someone would excuse themselves. Someone, other than Enid, would slip inside the house. Millie kept a jealous eye on Ben, after all, wasn't it *her* job to make sure he and Faye were never alone? But there came a time when she failed in her mission. It happened around the time that Ben went inside to heat some mulled wine. Faye said she needed the bathroom just at that moment, and when minutes later Ben emerged, not looking guilty at all, Millie's knotted stomach unravelled again. Faye returned a little later, and making sure there was always someone to keep Enid company, Millie waited until Lauren had finished a telephone call with her husband and kids before visiting the bathroom. After that, everyone had had enough of being cold, and the decision to enjoy their mulled wine inside was unanimous.

'I should never have had that Baileys plus two glasses of mulled wine. Now I've got to drive back to Hastings, all alone and in the dark.'

Millie looked aghast. What was Faye angling for? For Ben to give her a lift? Surely, now, everyone could see her true colours? She'd sounded so rehearsed, so insincere, and her feigned innocence was beyond belief.

'Why not stay the night?'

Now Millie was faced with something else she couldn't believe. Something even worse. What did she just hear?

In the silence that followed and with speechless faces staring back at her, Enid knew her efforts to accommodate had gone too far. But there was *one* person whose face had lit up, one person who looked happy and relaxed. There was one soul in the room trying to hold back a smile, and now the offer had been made, it couldn't be revoked.

'Are you sure?' Faye gushed, 'I've no nightie.' She gave Ben a devious glance, one filled with evil promise, and before anyone could say Jack Robinson, Ben was relegated to the sofa and she was offered night clothes, a toothbrush and *his* bed.

This cannot be happening. Millie took a steady breath. There was no need to panic, of course there wasn't. Then, she remembered the nightmare, that harrowing, vivid dream, which was all it took for the panic to return. How could she keep an eye on Ben now? How could she make sure he and Faye were never alone? How, when the Jezebel was literally sleeping in his bed? Millie jerked her head towards him, desperate for a sign, some measure of reassurance to calm her down. But Ben just looked tired again, only this time cornered. He looked defeated and helpless, and she felt like screaming.

She couldn't stay all night, even though she wanted to, she needed to. Enid liked to retire early, so Millie knew she had to go. 'Let me sponsor your mother for her charity walk.' Enid stood up slowly when Millie was ready to leave.

'There's no need to give me the money now.'

'You're going back to university, I don't want to forget.'

Everyone watched Enid walk towards the piano and they all knew where she kept her money. After piano lessons had finished, she'd place her earnings inside a tin. She'd done it for so long, it was always so reliable. But today, she was in for a shock. Prising the top off the tin she looked inside. Then her eyes widened and her posture crumpled.

'What's the matter, Gran?' Lauren bit her lip.

Silence, then perturbation, dismay and disquiet. So many questions. Enid's head twisted slowly towards each questioner. Are you sure you haven't spent it? Could you possibly have put it somewhere else? How could £70 go missing just like that? Who was your last pupil? When did you last see the money? It's a heck of a lot of cash: are you positive you had *that* much in there?

Enid was so sure and then questions were replaced by uncomfortable stares between the guests. Only Faye had something more to say. 'Who's the most hard up in this room?' She laughed, glaring at Millie with a comical smirk. 'Sorry, bad joke.' Then she said how she knew first-hand how tough it was to live on a student grant.

How funny. Ha ha ha. And apart from her disbelief at the false implication, Millie also had suspicions of her own, but she reigned them back. Faye was clean, wasn't she? And for a moment Millie was mystified again. Then, like the reel of a horror film, like the sound of a clanging death knell, ominous words replayed in her mind again, and she lifted her eyes towards Ben.

There was a time in my life that Gran would have been sensible to lock all her money away. Things were that bad.'

She kept looking at him. Why was he looking away? He was visibly tired but it wasn't *that* late. She needed to leave, she needed some air. She needed to get away from Clover Cottage and away from Faye. And more than anything, she needed time alone with him, she needed answers and her trust restored.

***

He walked her home and she kept her cool, and as they strode together the fresh night air worked wonders. Soon, she couldn't believe she'd doubted him, about the money, about Faye, about anything. He wasn't going to be alone in the house with Faye tonight, but even if he was, she knew she could trust him. She felt it in the touch of his hand, in the rhythm of his breathing and in the light of his eyes. Still, should she try to be funny and dish him a stern warning, just in case? Should she wag a finger, or sing a line or two from an appropriate song? What about Heaven 17's 'Temptation'? That would be good. Resist her, or else, Ben! Resist her, or else! But while almost managing to make light of the situation, she couldn't rid her head of a different song. Being a lover of R&B, Soul and funk, Ben would know only too well Gladys Knight & the Pips' 'Baby Don't Change Your Mind'. Did *he* realise that their love was on the line? Was *he* strong enough to move away from the past - to leave it all behind? She didn't know the exact lyrics, but the raw sentiments were filling her head.

> *The ex was back so what was Ben going to do?*
> *Now she's started to do her act*
> *In order to be taken back,*
> *Will their love remain,*
> *Or will he choose her?*
> *Will he change his mind,*
> *Or will he stand firm?*

The walk, so refreshing for them both, helped steady her emotions, and by the time they arrived back at the farm, she felt reassured once more.

'Ben.'

'Yes?'

Pause, 'Do you still want Faye?'

'What? Don't be ridiculous.'

Silence. 'And Ben.'

'Yes?'

'What happened to Enid's money?'

Another pause, then nothing. Then the words, 'I don't know,' were quietly, softly spoken. Those three simple words were plenty enough. She believed him, she *had* to believe him.

They embraced and then they said goodbye. It wasn't just her sleepy body that was heading for her bed; she was resolute about putting her fears to bed too. The night would soon be over, she'd wake in the morning, Faye would be gone and that would be that.

'Parting is such sweet sorrow,' Ben said. 'Bye bye my Millie Mouse.'

And then it came to mind, filling her heart with joy. It was a beautiful pet name for an irresistible lover. A name inspired by Shakespeare, and one which paid homage to nature. It was a name befitting of lovers of all creatures, furry and small.

'Bye bye my Benvolio.'

Pause. 'Benvolio? Who, or should I say, *what* is Benvolio?'

'Benvolio was – Benvolio *is* Romeo's cousin and his friend, and I think it's the perfect name for you.'

'Really? Why?'

'Isn't it obvious?'

'Um… because it starts with Ben?'

'That, and because there's a vole in it. And we love voles, don't we, Benvolio?'

'Very good. Actually – it's perfect – only, instead of Benvolio, wouldn't you rather I was your Romeo?'

Face to face beneath a myriad of stars, Millie Mouse had just one more thing to say and she had to admit, it was full of cheese.

'Gorgeous Benvolio, you should know by now, you already *are* my Romeo, my love.'

Chapter 36:

'Heartache Avenue' - The Maisonettes

'Millie, Sweet Pea – are you okay?'

Victoria's heart took a dive when she walked past the open door and spotted her daughter sitting upright on her bed, looking dazed.

There was no answer, but Victoria knew what was coming next. She'd seen something like this before and in the not-so-distant past. The rapid blinking, the splotchy skin and then the quivering chin. But this time, she sensed she was about to witness a deluge, a flood, like none seen before.

Even worse – she'd been anticipating for some time that something like this might happen. She squeezed her eyes shut, asking herself why. How had she managed to fail, yet again? Why hadn't she done everything in her power to try to prevent it this time?

Walking into the bedroom, she quietly shut the door and as she approached her daughter she noticed a letter on the bed with scrawled handwriting, written in a hand she'd never seen before. She sat down in silence, noticing Bagpuss. Soft and squidgy, he sat motionless on a pink, button-backed chair, his cute but worried-looking face, staring starkly at them. Wrapping comforting arms around her daughter, she held her tight, then, lightly cupping her head, she brought it down onto her lap and began to stroke her hair.

With her head resting against her mother's Toile du Jouy apron, Millie's tears began to flow steadily, relentlessly and silently. Very soon, bucolic scenes of French farmhouses, courting couples and peasants harvesting hay were dampened with copious tears, drool and a not insignificant quantity of mucus - all the sorts of things that a loving mother is happy to accommodate when her devastated child is in desperate need of solace.

This moment marked a pinnacle that had been building for a while, four days to be exact. Four days since Boxing Day, and four days since the last time Millie had seen or heard from Ben. She'd called since, but hadn't been able to reach him, despite leaving messages. She'd walked to Clover Cottage and stood outside, hoping, wondering why, thinking she might see him standing by the window, gazing out, looking lost, the way he'd done last winter, which now felt like such a long time ago. She'd stopped herself from opening the black metal gate and refrained from stepping up to the painted red door. She'd held back from peering through the sunrise-stained glass or lifting a hand to reach for the bell. Instead, she turned around and walked home again, finding the strength to wait until tomorrow, the strength to wait, just one more day.

With Millie's head still resting on her lap, Victoria glanced at the letter again, knowing that *it* must have been the catalyst that had finally burst the banks of the river. 'Hush, Millie, hush.' Sighing, and feeling an ache inside, Victoria was comforted by one solitary thought. Whatever that letter said, horrible as it was, it must have provided answers, which would finally bring to an end days fraught with uncertainty, mad questioning and helpless anxiety.

'Darling, I'm here for you,' she whispered, 'and whatever's happened, you will get through this – I promise, you will.'

Still waiting for words, Victoria listened to more quiet sobbing, still wondering what had gone wrong. Millie had come back from Enid's smiling, hadn't she? She'd said she and Ben had enjoyed their time there, despite Faye's presence. She'd said Faye came across as flirtatious, annoying, even calculating, but Ben hardly noticed her. He had no interest in her whatsoever. So, what on earth had happened since? Surely he hadn't done a 180-degree turn and decided to go back to his old flame? Victoria's heart beat a little faster, desperate to know, but keen not to push. *All in good time*, she said to herself, *all in good time*.

Unexpectedly, Millie lifted her head, looking ready to speak at last. 'I don't…' she said, before heaving in a breath and trying to formulate a sentence.

'I know. I think I understand, darling.'

'Do you, *really*? How? When even *I* can't understand it!' Immediately regretting her outburst, Millie rocked back and forth a little, and while she and her mother listened to the faint creak of mattress springs, her eyes grew softer. 'He seemed…' she began again slowly, 'I don't know, I mean, he hasn't been right lately, but he didn't seem sick, not really and I didn't think for a second…' Her voice cracked and she twisted her head to look her mother straight in the eye. 'He couldn't still be on drugs, could he? No, no, he can't be.' Shaking her head vigorously, she bit down on her lip. 'Something happened between him and her. Something *must* have happened in the night.' She said these words with fresh tears welling up in her eyes.

Catching her breath, she froze when they heard Cecil's footsteps outside her door, but the sound quickly passed, so it was safe to speak again. 'He couldn't have taken the money, could he, Mum?' she mumbled. 'It must have been *her*, but she's supposed to be clean.' With her face contorting, Millie shook her head until other parts of her body also shook. 'I don't think I'll be able to cope,' she cried, 'I really don't think I can cope!'

'You can and you will,' Victoria said, looking sagely at her daughter, her eyes pleading for her to calm down. 'I know you said money went missing, but are you *now* saying someone stole it, from Enid, in her own home and on Boxing Day?'

Millie shut her eyes tightly, feeling too weary to say anything more, then, picking up the slightly crumpled letter, she handed it over to her mother to read.

Dear Millie,

I don't know what to say except – I wish I wasn't writing this and I love you very much. My sweet Innocent Miss Millicent, I've got to go away. I have to pay for my past sins, my past mistakes and I need you to understand that you deserve someone better than me. Some people thought you were too good for me and now I can see they were right. No matter how much you want to help me become a better person, I'm no good for you, I now know that for sure.

I don't want to hurt you and I appreciate it's probably too late for that, but hold your head high and forget about me. I've found a room to rent nearer the coast, where most of my schools and pupils are. That will make my life easier and your life will be better too when I'm out of your hair. No more travelling back and forth for my sake, or missing out on your studies, just to be with me.

If you really love me Millie, please, let me go. I really think, for your sake, a clean break is best. And when you come back to Sussex in the spring, I won't be here any more. That will mean I'll have made life easier and not harder for you for the first time ever.

Can I also ask one other thing? If for any reason you see Gran, please don't say anything, not yet. She doesn't know I'm planning to move out, and telling her won't be easy. I want to break the news gently and explain that although she doesn't know it now, she'll soon realise it's best for everyone if I go away. I do feel bad about leaving her so soon, especially after she lost all that money. I think it's left her a bit shaken up and confused, but at least she seems stronger in her body these days.

And as for that money, please believe me, I still have no idea where it went. I just hope Gran's been forgetful and somehow misplaced it, and I pray it turns up again. If she's mistaken, that's terrific, and luckily, her mistakes will never have the same awful consequences that some of mine have. I wish I could turn back the clock, but sometimes the past catches up with us no matter how hard we try to leave it behind.

You're probably blaming Faye for all this, but please don't. She isn't the reason I'm going. And I hope you'll never blame yourself either. It goes without saying you're innocent, Miss Millicent. If anyone's to blame, it's me. God has forgiven me. Will you do the same? I know you will, you have a good heart. But please, once again my Millie mouse, I don't want you to come after me. I'd like to spare you the heartache. I can't tell you why I'm telling you this right now, and in many ways, I hope you'll never know.

Always and forever,

Ben x

Chapter 37:

'Take It Away' - Paul McCartney

Thank you, journal, for being my sanity. Thank you as well for reminding me there is so much to be grateful for, and so many people to love and who love me. Thank you for being my friend when I wake at 3 am and can't get back to sleep, when the house is quiet and I can't phone home and when my head is full of memories, and my heart's full of pain. Thank you Jonas for giving me this idea and telling me that writing things down helps. If it wasn't for your suggestion, I don't know how I'd have managed these first weeks of term. But I still struggle, it's still hard, I still sometimes don't know where I am or where I'm going. But it's early days isn't it, journal? It's very early days.

Jonas, you told me to start with a gratitude list. That did help, quite a lot, and today I'm making a 'thank you' list, for all the people I like and love. Where do I start? With Mum, obviously.

Mum - thank you for being my best friend. Not just a shoulder to cry on but a constant in my life, never judging me, always loving me, always there when I need you. I love you.

Dad - Thank you for letting me be Daddy's little girl and for being the best Dad any kid could want. Thanks for giving me a fab home - the beautiful farm which you work so hard to maintain. Thank you for keeping wolves at bay, not just from the sheep, but also from me. No wolves in Sussex, I know Dad, but still, you're like a shield from those who try to hurt me.

Dean - Thank you for making me laugh! For being a big brother who knows how to crack a joke that will always raise a smile. Thanks for bringing music and fun into my life and for marrying Amanda, my sister, my friend.

Amanda - Thank you for being a good listener and for being kind. Thanks too for being quirky and loving trees. You love trees so much you're calling your very first baby Holly if it's a girl and Rowan if it's a boy. That's so funny and I love you for it!

Ursula, my best and oldest friend. Thank you for flying down from Edinburgh, just to be with me when you heard the news. Thanks for stopping me from trying to see Ben, for talking sense into me and for suggesting we forget about men and head over to the Hungry Monk restaurant in beautiful Jevington, in the South Downs. It _was_ great, wasn't it? Scoffing banoffee pie like there's no tomorrow, in the very place it was first invented - or should that be, 'created'? You looked flippin' hilarious, crossing your eyeballs and licking fresh cream off your nose, but then again, you always knew how to cheer me up. And I laughed, just like I used to. Well, almost, I think.

Can I ask you something, Urs? Something that's been bothering me ever since I saw you, and something that just won't shift from the back of my mind? Why did I catch you with a smirk on your face? Why did you look at me once or twice in a weird way, in a way that made me feel uncomfortable? I don't believe for a moment you're enjoying my sadness. Why would you? Right now, I'm just really sensitive, thinking the worst about everyone because I've been hurt by a man again. And that's exactly it Urs, I know you understand my pain, because you've been there yourself. And while I'm not sure I can agree with you when you say all men are filthy, worthless bastards, I do think you're right about one thing. It's no accident that Ben did this to me after he and Faye'd spent the night together (although not literally, I hope). I don't care what he said in his letter, it can't possibly be a coincidence, can it? Still, I haven't lost hope in mankind, not yet. The words 'man' and 'kind,' reversed is 'kind man', and it's true, there <u>must</u> be a kind man out there, there's got to be. Don't forget, you yourself said Zane might be one of those, and it sounds like he's worth a try.

Ben once said, 'Nobody deserves to be dated on the rebound,' least of all me, and I think it's true. I'm perfectly able to see him for the liar he is, and still see the truth in his words. So, because I agree that dating on the rebound isn't nice, when it comes to Zane, I don't know what to do. He knows I'm free again, I can see it in his eyes and I'm sure he's heard. He's not talking to Sara half as much these days, in fact, now it's obvious they're just friends. So, Zane's gone back to being dead keen on me, and when he took me to his posh mate's dinner party, I was his 'plus one'. I hate to admit it, but it felt good to be wanted again, after not being wanted. So incredibly good.

So Urs, when Zane makes a move, would it be terrible, would it be so wrong to just go along with it? Just go with the flow, even though I don't feel anything for him, not in that way, and never have done? Everything's still raw with Ben, and I can't say when, or even if I'll ever stop loving him. Does that really matter and should that stop me from living again? I have to live again, even if I never love again.

Love. Isn't that a loaded word? I'm not even sure I know what it means any more. All I know is I keep hearing it, especially in songs. Altered Images 'Don't Talk To Me About Love' is always in my head. I'm sure you can guess why. And then there are songs about love that don't even mention the word. 'Have you Ever Had It Blue?' Have you heard that one yet? It's the new one by the Style Council, and I think you already know the answer to that question. Sometimes, I feel as if I have more than the blues. It's actually physical sometimes, like a pain in my chest that won't go away. It only disappears when I'm asleep, and that's why I go to bed early, to forget. But then I wake up again in the middle of the night, and can't get back to sleep, and when I eventually do, I wake in the morning wishing I hadn't, wishing I were still dreaming, because when it's been a good dream, that pain in my chest is no longer a forever pain. Instead, it's a 'just for a while' pain, like the one I used to get after me and Ben said, 'Goodbye.' The sort of pain I once felt, knowing that very soon I'd be seeing him again.

Everyone's been trying to take this pain away. I know you've tried, and Wahida has too. She's been lovely, doing my share of cleaning at Joyce's when I've been too wiped out to lift a finger. I know she's a clean freak, but she doesn't have to do that, does she? The other day, she went out and bought me orange fluorescent leg warmers and a Jane Fonda video. She said doing a workout might take my mind off things. It might 'channel my energies,' she said. Energies? What energies, Urs? I didn't tell Wah, but I have no desire whatsoever to 'feel the burn'. And as for, 'no pain, no gain', well at the moment it feels like I've had enough pain to last me a lifetime. But what have I gained from it? Nothing, or as Ben would say, 'Nowt.'

Anyway Urs, I've got one more person to thank - and that's Jonas. Hold on, have I thanked him already? These days, even when I write things down, I'm not sure if I'm coming or going. But it's no big deal to thank him twice, is it? Because it was his idea to keep a 'thank you' journal after all. Lately, Wahida and Jonas keep giving me 'I'm so sorry for you' looks. That's why he told me it helps him to write things down when the going gets tough. Weird isn't it, Urs? I start writing in a journal and I end up talking to you - in my imagination. Says a lot about our friendship, doesn't it?

Friends forever, Urs, and I hope by the time I see you next, I'll be laughing just like I used to. Yes, one day, Urs, I promise, I <u>will</u> laugh again.

Chapter 38:

'Halfway Up, Halfway Down' - Dennis Brown

Looking back, was visiting Enid all those years ago a good thing to have done? Of course it was, and until now, Millie wouldn't have entertained a question like that. However, today, looking through the blurry lens of life and with the raw benefit of hindsight, she played hostess to a plethora of mixed feelings and emotions. The experience had taught her that giving to someone else was one of *the* best ways to take her myopic eyes off herself, but she couldn't pretend she'd come out of it completely unscathed. Had she not befriended Enid, she doubted she would ever have fallen in love with Ben, and had she never fallen for him, she'd have less pain and sadness in her life right now.

Despite this internal struggle, the lessons of self-sacrifice hadn't failed to make their mark and when the time came to choose a third-year project, she knew exactly what criteria to apply. She needed something people-orientated, something that would pull her away from her internal struggles, redirect her focus and help her forget. Nothing theoretical or clinical would fit the bill, instead, she wanted to give her time and energy to someone, *anyone* who needed her, and after discussing the options in a morning seminar, it didn't take long to find something suitable.

'Child psychiatry. Good choice,' Wahida said, sitting opposite her at a refectory table in the canteen. 'Sounds less tedious than pharmacology.'

'I guess, but your choice isn't bad either - the effects of nicotine on… what was it again?'

'Memory and learning.'

'That sounds interesting.'

Wahida looked at Millie as though she'd grown two horns. 'An interesting third-year project? Come on, there's no such thing.' She cut into her leathery-skinned jacket potato. 'The real reason I chose that topic is because I wanted something that'd put me off turning to ciggies myself next time exam stress hits me hard!'

'Seriously?'

'Nah, I can't see myself resorting to fags, no matter how stressed I end up, but seriously, don't you think projects are boring? What *I'm* really looking forward to is our elective. Everyone acts so virtuous, don't they? Pretending they don't give two hoots where they might end up. Not me,' Wahida shook her head crisply, 'I'm bagging somewhere hot and tropical if I can.'

'And why not?' Millie said, all the while thinking Wah made the elective sound more like club 18-30 than an opportunity to serve as a medic in a poor country. Perhaps she had a point though. Wouldn't the Caribbean, or a beautiful island in South East Asia be much more pleasant than a trouble spot, or somewhere that didn't attract tourists? Sure, finding a good hospital for sharpening her medical skills was what mattered most, but if that hospital also happened to be somewhere lush and beautiful, it would definitely be a bonus.

Mulling on that thought, she peeled a banana and reminded herself that electives were famously either hard work or an absolute doddle and she wouldn't know which hers would turn out to be until she was right in the middle of it, and sadly by then, it would be too late. Taking a bite of the mushy fruit, she was tempted to dream about a tropical escape to distract her from those everyday feelings of dejection that were always bubbling just under the surface. But trying to find fulfilment in something that was almost two years away wasn't sensible. She needed something that would satisfy now, and the sooner it came, the better.

***

When Millie began her first weeks of clinical practice it was just the start of what soon turned out to be an incredibly steep learning curve. There were many words to describe being on a hospital ward - confusing, busy, stressful, disorientating to name a few, and for several days she looked completely lost in her little white coat with an Oxford Handbook of Clinical Medicine in her pocket and a stethoscope around her neck.

She'd watch people rushing around, and whenever she *did* have hands-on clinical experience herself, she'd suffer from a serious case of imposter syndrome and feel totally out of her depth. Thankfully, though, the general medical ward wasn't all chaos. Occasionally, she'd get the chance to enjoy a chat and a cuppa with a friendly nurse, or she'd laugh with a fellow team member, whether that was a house officer, senior house officer, registrar or consultant, otherwise known as a firm. But most days, all she could find time for was dealing with a daily onslaught of heart, lung, kidney and liver disease, cardiac arrests, resuscitations and the like, and this was something she found incredibly challenging.

Luckily for her, as an unqualified but keen medical student, she was usually relegated to the role of an observer rather than the main clinician and that meant performing more basic procedures such as putting in cannulas and taking blood. What could go wrong? Everything, and what's more, much to her disillusionment, after several weeks in a clinical setting and with all that activity, she *still* couldn't shake off the pain, or cease to remember the hurt, so much so that at night, she'd cry herself to sleep with a heady and toxic mix of despair and exhaustion. But, things were about to improve, because only when she started spending time with Theo, did she finally come close to forgetting.

Chapter 39:

'Let's Hear It for the Boy' - Denise Williams

When she first stepped into Redwood Lawn, the long corridor with its polished parquet flooring made it more reminiscent of a school than a children's home. The sound of her footsteps clattering across the solid wood added to the rhythmic, sometimes irregular and occasionally strange noises which could be heard all around. There were periodic shouts and laughter, intermingled with wailing, grunting and clapping. From one area came a variety of sounds, and then, while passing a noiseless room with an open door, she noticed a teenage lad rocking in a seat, with arms tightly wrapped around his upright body.

When invited into the manager's office, she was greeted by an official-looking woman wearing a wide shoulder-padded jacket.

'You're here for your project on autism, is that correct?'

'Yes, that's right.'

The middle-aged supervisor's mouth morphed into a broad smile. 'I'm very pleased to meet you, Millie, and thank you for coming today. I've already assigned you someone to work with and he's a lovely lad, so I'm confident you'll both learn a lot from each other.'

Rising to her feet she walked towards the door. 'Come this way Millie, and let me introduce you to Theo.'

***

Over the ensuing weeks, each visit to Redwood Lawn brought Millie a step closer to something, although she didn't quite know what. What she *did* know was that as the weeks turned into months, she found herself feeling calmer and more balanced, with greater clarity and elevated hope. Progress wasn't linear, but meeting new people outside the frenetic clinical and college environment brought with it a newness and optimism. Life at Redwood Lawn wasn't all roses. Some of the children were aloof, others could get angry and aggressive, but when observing challenging behaviour, Millie was inspired by staff who were gifted with oodles of patience.

It was lovely to witness children with special needs communicate in their preferred way. Bright-eyed Lynn, fourteen, with a happy-go-lucky smile demonstrated fortitude in the face of a congenital abnormality that limited her learning, and Kirsten, a fun-loving teenager with Down's syndrome frequently cracked jokes, especially knock-knock ones, and took to Millie straight away. 'Cornelious is my boyfriend,' she beamed, 'I love him very much.' Millie later found out Cornelious was the tall, smartly dressed lad who paced the corridor, every time his parents were due for a visit.

There was one young person Millie felt especially drawn to. Thirteen-year-old Alfie had dark skin that hinted at a Caribbean background and a melting smile which spoke volumes. Because of his cerebral palsy, he had very limited movement in his wheelchair, but despite this, his playful, sometimes cheeky eyes communicated immense joy. Millie looked forward to seeing his smile each week and soon, she counted the days until her next visit. Every young person at Redwood Lawn warmed her heart in some way. All had unique characteristics and all were special.

'You wouldn't believe the horrors I've seen in places I've worked in before,' said an energetic and fast-talking member of staff called Denise one drizzly afternoon, 'but here, we're a small team and management are decent, and for what it's worth, I think that's what makes all the difference.'

Millie had seen the truth in that statement from the very first day she met Theo, the same day when that friendly manager led the way along a corridor to the TV lounge, and even though weeks had passed since then, her mind often went back to that moment.

'Theo is much more verbal now than when he first came here,' she remembered the manager saying.

'How long ago was that?' Millie asked, ripe with curiosity.

'He was seven when he first arrived. He didn't find communication easy then, but now, he enjoys a chat, especially about his favourite subjects.'

When they approached that day, Theo's back was turned and all Millie could see was a mop of brown curly hair, a tall body and a bright green T-shirt, with a Muppet Show logo on the back.

'How are you doing, Theo?' the manager asked, after waiting for an ad break to start.

Theo turned his head, and in that instant, Millie saw a boyish face with a mellow expression and just a mere hint of curiosity. Then, turning around again, he returned his attention to the screen.

'Theo, this is Millie. She's a medical student at St Georges and she's here for a project. She'll be visiting every week for three months and would like to get to know you. She might ask one or two questions, if that's okay with you.'

Again there was no answer and after the manager gave Millie an 'over to you' gesture, she quietly slipped away. Standing in silence and unsure what to do next, Millie opted to sit down to enjoy whatever Theo was watching. That first day, not many words were exchanged, but it proved to be only the beginning, and now, after several weeks had passed and after spending many hours by his side, an affinity had slowly begun to develop. The best opportunities for communication tended to occur during ad breaks, and when programme credits finished scrolling, Theo's hunched shoulders would indicate that he was now amenable to conversation. However, Millie soon learned that it wasn't until all children's programmes had ended for the day, that a golden hour of undivided time with him could finally begin in earnest.

While getting to know Theo, it was inevitable that she would become acquainted and re-acquainted with many entertaining characters. There was *Little Blue* the cartoon elephant, and *The Munch Bunch* – a colourful motley crew of fruit and vegetables. There was also *Dr Snuggles* the inventor, and Mr Spoon in *Button Moon*. One afternoon, Millie told Theo about programmes *she'd* enjoyed as a child - *A Handful of Songs, Pipkins,*

The Clangers and *Mr Benn* - he seemed to know them all, and his eyes lit up like stars amidst grunts and smiles at the mention of each one.

There was a programme they both enjoyed watching together that felt particularly special. *Storybook International* had opening titles featuring a friendly anthropomorphic fox, a companion to a Robin Hood-like minstrel who strummed on a lute and morphed into different ethnicities as he sang. His song ended with encouraging, yet poignant words:

> *Sometimes there are tears*
> *Sometimes there is laughter,*
> *But always, a happily ever after.*

Theo didn't always verbalise his preferences, but judging by the way he rhythmically flapped his hand and gazed at the screen, smiling with rapt attention, Millie thought she could tell this programme was a particular favourite, and when, without warning, *her* eyes filled with tears, she felt glad she was able to gather herself unnoticed, while *his* eyes remained glued to the television screen. *Sometimes there are tears, sometimes there is laughter.* Still crying silent tears of her own, she heard a voice inside her head asking a painful question. What about Theo? What about *his* future? Will *he* have a 'happily ever after'?

Thankfully, such times of highly charged emotion were rare and far outweighed by lighter moments, especially once Theo began to open up. Encouraged by Denise, Millie soon discovered how much he loved maps and his incredible knowledge of populations in countries and major cities. She'd sit with an open

Encyclopedia Britannica on her lap, asking questions like 'Name all the countries in South Asia,' or, 'Which European countries have the highest population densities?' or 'Which cities in South America are the largest?' Theo was usually able to give the correct answers immediately, and after realising this was no fluke, she gritted her teeth, amazed but at the same time, frustrated. Surely there had to be a way to capitalise on this genius. It was as though he had entire sections of the encyclopaedia etched into his mind. Everyone needed to see how gifted he was, but try as hard as she might, she couldn't think of a way.

'I've racked my brains over that conundrum myself,' Denise told her, 'but apart from pub quizzes and TV game shows, I haven't managed to come up with anything yet.'

When Theo wasn't talking about geography, he loved chatting about food, and whenever he did, his enthusiasm was contagious. But, there was a problem. He had an aversion to a wide variety of meals and snacks. Raspberry ice cream was perhaps number one on his most hated list, closely followed by coronation chicken, Welsh rarebit, mushy peas and a whole lot more. Although he didn't fully articulate why he hated these foods, Millie gleaned from a number of sources that it was a combination of the look, the smell, the texture and the taste that made him want to retch. Denise let Millie in on another important bit of information. She said that when Theo was served meals, the cook had to make sure *all* signs of congealed fat were removed and if not, he simply wouldn't touch any of it. 'Thank heavens for Yorkshire puddings,' she said, '*that's* something we don't have any trouble getting you to eat, is it Theo?' Turning to Millie, she cupped her hand around her mouth and whispered, 'He wolfs down Yorkshires like there's no tomorrow and nobody else would get a look in if we didn't put our foot down!'

While the image of a ravenous Theo scoffing down Redwood Lawn's limited supply of Yorkshires made Millie smile, the sinking feeling that followed hot on its heels was just too disheartening for words. Yorkshire. The mere mention of Ben's former home was enough to set her off, and she closed her eyes tight, hoping that her primitive automatic response would soon pass. Being reminded of Ben was not going to set off another negative spiral. She was determined not to let it, because up until then, she'd been doing so well.

***

When the time came to sit down and write up her project, Millie dawdled in her room and opened her desk drawer. She gazed down at two bars of Bitz chocolate. Mint crunch or orange sugar crisp? What was she in the mood for, right now? Finally having made her choice, she peeled back the shiny green wrapper and took a bite of velvety chocolate with crisp peppermint clusters. *Mmmm, delicious,* but it wasn't just the chocolate elevating her mood. After twelve rewarding and educational weeks at Redwood Lawn, she was in a better place emotionally and she felt confident that growing feelings of solace, peace and restoration were finally here to stay. She'd got over Giles, and the same would happen with Ben. It had to, and technically, things ought to be easier this time, because the complicating and entangling issue of sex wasn't part of the mix. Although initially frustrated by this, she could now see how Ben's slowness had turned out to be a good thing. Regrettably, as always, life wasn't that simple. Picking up her pen, she had to admit her emotions had gone deeper with Ben. Her connection with him was more solid than anything she'd had with Giles, regardless of how physically intimate things had become.

Opening her exercise book she began to gather up and assimilate her notes under various headings. Spring term project 1986, Redwood Lawn Children's home and links to a South London study of Autism and Aspergers Syndrome. Landmark study involving 173 children. Dr Lorna Wing, psychiatrist, Dr Judith Gould, clinical psychologist. Study became a major contributor to the field of child psychiatry. Conclusions. Broad set of traits identified, including a 'triad of impairments…'

She paused and laid down her pen. Despite this and other major advances, so much about Autism remained a mystery. On a personal level, she was finding it almost impossible to treat this as purely an academic exercise. She'd met many special people at Redwood Lawn, staff and residents alike, and she'd only just scratched the surface of autism and other conditions that made some people different and unique. What was also important was how neurological and developmental issues made an impact on personal lives, and not just of those who were affected, but also their loved ones and others in their communities. It was clear that Redwood Lawn grappled well with challenging conditions when providing full-time and respite care, but the role of parents and why some of those parents whose children were residents lacked the will or ability to cope, was still unclear to her.

After finishing her chocolate bar, she sighed deeply. She was going to miss Redwood Lawn - Theo in particular, and if she was going to miss him after such a short time, did he have loved ones who missed him even more? She picked up her pen and began to write again. Time to re-focus, because the truth was, she'd probably never know.

Chapter 40:

'Why Can't This Be Love' - Van Halen

There could be worse things to be doing than walking with Zane in a busy London street at the beginning of June. Summer had begun in earnest, and Billy Idol's 'Hot In The City' felt like a fitting anthem, not least because Zane himself was hot, but only in the sense of having pearls of sweat dripping onto his collar. Tugging at it, he shot Millie besotted glances as they strode side by side.

He'd offered to accompany her home earlier that day. 'I've never been comfortable with you walking on your own in London, especially after dark,' he'd said. 'You could come across all sorts of trouble.'

'I'm used to it,' she'd said, accepting his offer, even though warm sunshine was still streaming through the seminar room window.

Was that the right thing to do? Probably. Boyfriends were supposed to walk their girlfriends home, weren't they? It didn't matter they weren't officially a couple, because Millie had given Zane enough indicators that after three years of being pursued, she was finally ready to relent. Spending more time alone with him, giving him more attention, going out for a meal, just the two of them, and seeing *Chess* at the theatre together. All these indicators he lapped up readily, and the result?

According to Wahida, he was now going around the college telling people how happy he was with how their relationship was progressing.

'What relationship?' was Millie's quick retort.

'*He* clearly thinks there's one,' Wahida replied. 'He says you're the prettiest girl in the whole year even though you don't realise it, and he feels honoured.'

'Oh.' Despite the compliment, that was all Millie could muster, and now, eight days later, whenever she thought of Zane and his keenness, she still couldn't manage more than a flat, unemotional 'oh'. But still, she hadn't quite given up on getting excited yet. She liked Zane a lot, and so she was determined to keep trying to fall in love with him.

'Better not lead him on,' Wahida had said earlier that week. 'He's not chilled like me and Jonas. He acts cool, but he gets emotional, so be gentle with him.'

Millie agreed that she would. Of course, she wasn't going to hurt Zane, and flattered and bolstered by his rapt attention, she wasn't going to be put off by her own indecision either. He didn't usually walk to and from college, but since his 'Silver Dream Machine' Porsche was being serviced today and she usually declined his offer to drive her home, she decided to say 'yes' to an after-college stroll. But then, feeling uneasy, she remembered what had happened when he'd driven her home from the pub that night. Attempting to kiss someone was hardly a crime though, and what's more, if he were brave enough to try it on again this time, she might just surprise him with a very different response.

***

The red and yellow signage of a recently opened McDonald's stood out on the approach.

'Can I get you anything?' Zane asked keenly.

'Oooh, I'm tempted,' she looked at her watch, 'but it's not even five o'clock yet.'

'Go on, you know you want to.'

'Okay, if you insist. I'll have a Big Mac and…' she stopped short and looked across at a young homeless man, sitting near the entrance, a sleeping bag and rucksack by his side.

'What about him?' she asked.

Zane raised his eyebrows.

'I mean, do you think *he* might want something to eat?'

They both looked at the man who seemed limp and exhausted, his once finely honed mohican hairstyle growing out at the sides, with the dyed pink central spike floppy rather than upright.

Standing stiffly, Zane continued to eye him and then turned to Millie. 'You've got the right idea,' he said under his breath.

'About what?'

'About giving him food and not cash.' He raised his chin. 'I'm guessing he'd much rather have money than food, but I'll ask anyway.'

Before Millie could respond, Zane sauntered over to the young man.

'Hello,' he began, clearing his throat, 'would you like us to buy some food for you from this establishment?' Awkwardly extending out his hand, he directed it towards the fast food outlet while Millie stood there, cringing and wondering why he had to put things *quite* like that.

The man looked up, his eyes dazed and confused. 'Say what, mate?'

'Would you like us to purchase a meal for you?' Zane repeated, louder and slower this time.

'Can we get you a burger or a drink or something?' Millie smiled, stepping towards them. having decided to wade in.

'Oh cheers, Miss,' the man said. 'I'd love a burger; in fact, I could murder a quarter pounder with cheese.'

Giving a thumbs up, she glanced at Zane who was peering down his nose at the man in that unfortunate way of his, but the guy *was* sitting on the ground, and everyone who took the time to get to know Zane would soon realise he wasn't a snob. With parents who were renowned in their fields of medicine, and an elite education at the world-famous Eton College, Millie knew it'd be more surprising if Zane *didn't* occasionally give off a whiff of snobbery, but thankfully, he made up for it by being generous. After saying she would have been more than happy to pay for hers and the man's meal if her student grant wasn't almost entirely eaten up, he insisted on hearing nothing of it, and without a moment's hesitation said he'd place the order.

'Hey Miss?' the rough sleeper called out as they were about to leave.

Millie turned around.

'A root beer would also go down a treat.'

'No problem.'

'And Miss.'

She turned around again.

'Thank you, beautiful,' he said, drawing his feet towards him, 'oh, and you too, mate,' he added, giving Zane a perfunctory nod.

'What's your name?' she asked.

'Derry, Miss.'

'Back soon, Derry.'

There was an uncomfortable pause and acutely aware of the tight expression on Zane's face, Millie offered up a weak smile, watching him march ahead silently and push his way through heavy glass doors.

***

After eating their McDonalds, the lack of connection and hand-holding during the remainder of their walk was disheartening, and each time Millie looked at Zane, her energy felt sapped. How can that be, when this was the day she'd planned to take the relationship further? She certainly hadn't intended to revisit the past, but now, try as she might, she couldn't stop reminiscing over days gone by.

She remembered how different it was, walking through London with Ben. They'd amble along, and she'd grip his hand. They'd gaze at each other and they'd laugh. They'd snatch a kiss when they stumbled across quiet, hidden places and they'd soak up the sparkle of the Thames or the majesty of historic buildings. Inside restaurants and cafes, she'd mostly jabber on while he'd listen, or they'd sit in silence over their meal, like a boring old married couple.

But today, with Zane, not only was there no sparkling river, there was also no laughter or stolen kisses either. There was no hand-holding, no touch, or desire, but there were faultless manners and laudable attentiveness, chivalry, charm and a warm covering of care and protection. But, was that really enough, when there was no passion, no inspiration, no excitement, nothing?

Actually, there *was* something. There was irritation. She thought it started when he'd flared his nostrils, just as a teenager, who looked as if he could be in the band Musical Youth, sauntered past with a ghetto blaster, blaring out Kool & The Gang's 'Straight Ahead', at full volume. It *was* loud for sure, but Zane complained so much that in the end, she asked herself why it had annoyed him to such an extent.

And now, all he kept talking about was the homeless man, repeating how most likely he squandered money on narcotics. 'You should have kept your distance,' he muttered, 'people like him can be manipulative and the last thing you want is a fellow like that taking a shine to you. What *he* needs is a job, but he's probably forgotten how to do a decent day's work - assuming he's ever done one in his life.'

Zane's negativity took her by surprise. Was he letting his guard down now they were getting closer? Or conversely, maybe he could sense she was starting to pull away, and that was making him even more irritable. Whatever it was, underneath all that irritability, he *did* have a point. Maybe she ought to learn to keep her distance and be less trusting. Maybe, if she'd had more discernment with Ben, she would be in a better place today.

Zane didn't only have an expectation that she wouldn't talk to the homeless. Earlier, he'd also made it clear that any future wife of his would stay at home with the children, 'unless,' he clarified, 'we send them to boarding school.' Feeling strained, Millie told herself that prospect was too far ahead to fret about, but even so, his words came as a minor blow. Surely he appreciated that just like him, she was working towards becoming a surgeon, so why then, did he expect her to give it all up to stay at home? The boarding school solution or 'compromise' as *he* saw it, felt too much like the other extreme. She needed some middle ground, but the more she was getting to know Zane, the more she could tell he wasn't one for half-measures.

In retrospect, it didn't seem such a wise move to have spread the word about her 'new relationship' when she went home for the Easter holidays. But at the time it'd felt necessary, because she reasoned that if Enid heard on the grapevine she was dating, then Ben would too, and only then would he know she was totally over him. It didn't matter that the news was premature, not when Zane believed she was giving him the green light, even though she knew deep down she was only flashing amber.

Walking in semi-silence, she found herself repeating again and again that she was over Ben and despite her best intentions, her mind began to zone out Zane's words, as past thoughts flooded her mind. Did Enid ever find that missing money? It couldn't have been stolen but if it had, it must have been Faye. But that didn't make any sense because Faye looked healthy and fit, and there wasn't any obvious reason she'd steal unless she was still on drugs. Then, with a tightness in her gut, the same haunting image of a tired, sick-looking Ben came to Millie's mind. But he'd said God had saved him, hadn't he? If he was hiding an addiction, that meant he was a liar, and if he wasn't lying about that, there could only be one other explanation. He was a cheat.

A familiar shudder swept through her body when that thought came to mind. He must have been ashamed after something had happened between him and Faye that night. The likely scenario was that he'd decided to take the blame after Faye had come on to him, and because he was weak, he'd responded. Afterwards, he was so disgusted and ashamed of himself, he'd had to move away. 'Nearer to the coast,' he'd said, which obviously meant Hastings, where Faye lived, but why would he say his move wasn't because of her if that were true? She tried not to shake her head in front of Zane while thinking. Nothing made sense.

Zane kept talking and she nodded along, while her inmost thoughts wished Ben all the best. Being filled with hate would achieve nothing and would only hurt her. Then, an improbable notion crossed her mind for the very first time. Had Faye blackmailed him? Perhaps she'd threatened to tell the schools he worked for about his drug use unless he went back to her. So many questions, but had this been Ben's trial, the evidence to convict him was scant. On the contrary, much of it pointed to his innocence. Millie couldn't deny that Ben had been respectful towards her, despite her own impatience to get physical with him. He never came across as a man who lacked self control or was incapable of resisting a woman's advances. But Faye wasn't just any woman, and at one point he'd lived with her, as though they were married, for three years. So perhaps that in itself made it all too easy for him to slide back into old habits.

It wasn't until they'd reached a Zebra crossing that Millie realised Zane had stopped talking for some time. Immediately feeling embarrassed, she tried to initiate conversation and fished around for something to say. Her hospital placement was a guaranteed, easy thing to talk about, and after repeating how gruelling it was, she sighed with relief after successfully getting the conversation rolling again. Thank goodness Zane hadn't realised she'd only been half-listening, but soon, all the talk about working in a clinical setting led to her thoughts drifting again. She thought about how concerning yet hilarious it was that Ben would act like a nervous wreck after he felt an ectopic heartbeat, or panic over a tickly throat. But, even all his silly hypochondriac tendencies couldn't detract from his strength of character. No man who was weak in either mind or body could drag a weighty deer across the road and hurl it into a ditch. No weakling could stand up to an angry posse of men, just to protect a helpless hare.

None of that mattered any more. Despite loving the song, 'You'll Never Know' by High Gloss, the lyrics felt too close to home these days, and now, she was close to her real, physical, bricks-and-mortar home. Stepping into the street where she lived, she knew Ben would never know what he'd done to her, how much she loved him and how hard she'd tried. Likewise, *she'd* never know what happened that night at Clover Cottage, what had led to their cruel separation, and ultimately, what would become of him. He'd made sure of that.

She and Zane were now standing outside Joyce's house and he was looking down at her with more than a hint of dejection in his dark brown eyes. Flooded with guilt, she gazed into those same eyes, which hours before were jovial and bright. Things could change in an instant, that was something she knew only too well, and her prior resolve to pucker up and not turn her face away had long since melted away. Giles, Ben and now Zane, she'd said to herself earlier, third time lucky, surely? But the words inside her head were very different now. *Forget it, Millie. Don't even try.* That's all she could hear right now.

'See you tomorrow then.' He sounded firm, distant, and in an instant she knew this time, there'd be no kiss. Zane could certainly be formal and reserved at times, even aloof, but up until then, never with her.

'Goodbye Zane.' When she said those two little words, she felt a mix of relief and devastation. It made her feel lighter to face the truth at last. She couldn't have her cake and eat it, and that was okay. But where would she go from here? What would she do now? That was a problem for later - right now, she needed to focus on Zane and stop wasting his time. He needed to be unleashed to look for that woman who not only appreciated his generosity and good manners, but was also happy to accept his quirks, and above all else, give him the love he deserved.

Extending out his arm towards her he hesitated and drew it back. Then, after taking a deep breath, he reached out again, took her hand, raised it to his lips and gave it a slow, tender kiss.

'I knew a long time ago,' he began, allowing her hand to fall limply. 'I knew I couldn't quite be a match for some handsome rock star. But Millie, I...' he paused and clenched his jaw, 'I *did* try.'

Millie had never seen Zane close to tears before, and with a knotted feeling in her stomach, she watched him walk away, not knowing what to do or say. *He wasn't a rock star, he played Blue-eyed Soul, but none of that matters because _he_ doesn't matte*r *to me any more. I tried to love you Zane, I really did. Come back, maybe we, I mean, maybe _I_ could try again, but, I'm sorry. Even as I think those words I know trying would be pointless. Still, I hope when I see you tomorrow, things won't be too awkward. I still like you and hope we'll stay friends.*

None of these desperate thoughts reached her mouth. Instead, drawing in her bottom lip, she watched him shuffle away, turn a corner and disappear out of sight.

After taking out her key and noticing the lounge curtain move, her irritation at knowing Joyce had been watching was soon supplanted by grief. She opened the door and, by-passing her landlady who was pretending to dust the furniture, she rushed up to her room with a head full of noise. What was she going to do with all these loud, intrusive thoughts now? *Ben loved Faye but he didn't love you. You will never be able to keep a man. No man will ever want you, ever.* And the one fallback that had been guaranteed to halt the tears was now lost forever. *Zane wants me, there's always him.* Until today, those words had kept her going, providing a counterbalancing rhetoric to keep her from despair. So what was she going to do now?

Her eyes settled on the aqua-blue towel lying on her bed and picking it up in quiet desperation, she held it to her chest. Soft, fluffy and made from terry cloth, it wasn't nearly as cuddly as Bagpuss, but after focussing on its comforting fleeciness for several minutes, she finally felt her heart rate begin to slow. She wasn't going to cry, not again. But what was she going to do, now there was nobody in her life? No one special to hold on to. No one at all.

Chapter 41:

'Higher Love' - Steve Winwood

Opening her eyes, Millie could hear distant fireworks crackle and whizz beyond her tightly shut sash window. No need to check the time then, but with nothing else to do, she felt her neck muscles ache when she turned over to look at the numbers glowing red on her bedside digital clock. 00:04. She turned away again, thinking she really ought to be feeling more excited that 1988 had just begun. Yet, here she was, tucked up in bed. How uncool was that?

How many twenty-two year-olds would say no to a night out with pals? But now, she could see it'd been a smart move declining Jonas' invitation to a friend's party in Slough because she'd felt so run down. Let's face it, when you're burning up with a fever, standing in a stranger's home, linking arms and singing Auld Lang Syne isn't much fun. Still, she thought, turning over again in her sick bed, you could almost guarantee Wahida and Jonas were enjoying themselves, and good for them.

For her, there was no better place to be right now than back at the farm. That's where her mother poured green, syrupy 'Night Nurse' into a measuring cup, and brought warm bowls of salty chicken broth on a tray.

Much nicer than waiting for loud party music to stop, before crashing out on somebody's floor.

Sitting up, she breathed in slowly, noticing she wasn't shivering as much and her head hurt less. Maybe she'd be well enough to meet with Ursula on Sunday, but feeling tense, she acknowledged she needed to be cautious. Was now a good time to share her latest news with her old school friend? Guessing how Ursula might react, perhaps it was wise to think carefully about what she was going to say first.

After switching on her bedside lamp, Millie poured Lucozade into a glass and watched the tiny orange bubbles bounce around and rise to the surface. Just after midnight felt like a funny time to be wide awake after having slept for hours, especially because there was no one to talk to. She didn't fancy reading, and the radio might wake her parents up, so all she had for entertainment were her thoughts. With an old year just gone, and a new one just beginning, now was a relatively easy time to be entertained by a head full of past memories and future hopes.

She tried to remember her feelings this time last year, and while unsuccessful, she *was* able to sum up the whole of 1987 in just a single word - survival. And survive she somehow did, because whenever she was at breaking point, she always managed *not* to break.

Her clinical placements had kept her busy. It was a wonderful distraction, but at the start of the year, there were some things she couldn't forget - anniversaries, for instance, and January 1987 marked a whole year since Ben, six months after Zane, and an incredible five years after she and Giles had split. How ironic that instead of making New Year resolutions she was doing her utmost to forget old flames, although admittedly, Zane's flicker never did turn into a proper, full-on burn.

Now Zane was on her mind, she thought back to their unhappy parting back in 1986 after he'd walked her home that awkward summer afternoon. Although the following days and months weren't easy, she smiled a little, thinking that always the gentleman, he hadn't once been nasty, or used what had happened as an excuse to make her feel bad. *Thank you, Zane.* One of her greatest concerns for her years at St George's had been a failed love affair with a fellow student, and the thought of losing a friend was also unbearable. But thanks to Zane, none of those fears had come to fruition, and even though she'd done nothing wrong, not every man would've been so gracious. She took another sip of Lucozade, thinking about how they hardly saw each other these days, but whenever they did, their friendship was still underpinned by a foundation of mutual kindness and respect.

The unique but artificial taste of the drink lingered on her tongue and she rolled her eyes, feeling the sockets ache. Eye-rolling was often automatic whenever Millie thought about Wahida and Jonas, and she was rapidly losing hope, now that her mates only had six short months left to get their relationship act together before leaving university.

Even that 'Lost Weekend' away, just the two of them, albeit to a hotel in Paris rather than Amsterdam, couldn't seal the deal, and when they arrived back on English shores there was still no inkling of romance. 'Talking of all things French,' Millie had said after Wahida came home looking besotted, 'do you like 'Voyage Voyage' by Desireless - get it? *Desire* less.' Met with a wall of silence, she initially thought the joke had fallen flat, especially as it wasn't apt since there was oodles of desire, at least on Wahida's part. But, following a delayed reaction, Wahida surprised her with a muted smile.

'We're warming up slowly,' Wahida said, 'and the slower the burn, the hotter the flame.' Then after enthusing about how she and Jonas danced to Euro-pop greats like Ryan Paris' 'Dolce Vita' and Modern Talking's 'Brother Louie' on the banks of the river Seine, Millie remembered being amazed they'd given anything other than Indie music the time of day.

Still thinking of fun times, her thoughts switched to her little nephew's first birthday and how, despite looming exams, she was compelled to head home for the weekend to celebrate. With russet-red hair, just like his mother's and a cheeky grin like his dad's, she could spend ages listening to him say ma-ma or da-da, or feeling his watery dribble, every time he bit down on her finger to ease his teething.

Casting her mind back to when he was newly born, she remembered Amanda explaining why she and Dean had decided against the name Rowan and had chosen Ewan instead. 'It sounded almost the same but we preferred it, and when I found out Ewan means "born of the yew tree", I couldn't believe it, and that was it!'

But then, what Millie heard her sister-in-law say next, although innocent, hit her hard. 'Ben's sister - wasn't her name Lauren?' Amanda had asked, rubbing Ewan's back to wind him. 'That's a tree as well...' Amanda stopped short and almost immediately, Millie could tell from the look in her eyes she'd realised she must have said something wrong. 'I'm really sorry,' she apologised, explaining she'd only mentioned Lauren because she came across the name in her baby name book and didn't know it came from Laurel, as in the shrub.

'No, it's okay,' Millie remembered saying. 'It's my fault for being so touchy about Ben in the first place.'

And now, with her mind back in the present, she was looking forward to seeing her nephew later that day, even if giving him a cuddle wouldn't be a great idea until she was sure she wasn't infectious any more. How could it be that Ewan was now nineteen months and Stuart *still* hadn't seen him? Realising that even her mother was now losing hope of a family reunion, Millie sighed. If being an uncle couldn't entice Stuart back for a visit, with or without his wife, then surely nothing would.

Breathing in through an aching chest, she tried to think of other good things that had happened during the past twelve months. Passing all her exams for instance, and managing to win a surgical prize - now *that* was something she still couldn't quite believe. Even more incredible was that she'd impressed her professor with her honesty and not just her clinical abilities. Sitting up in her bed, she shook her head, remembering how the sly surgeon had led her to believe she should be able to detect an aortic aneurysm in a patient's abdomen. Standing in the clinical room, palpating for several minutes but feeling nothing, she recalled the rising feeling of terror inside her gut and that voice of temptation in her head saying *pretend you can feel it or you'll fail*. When she finally decided to do the right thing and admit to the truth, she clenched her teeth and prepared for the inevitable marking down. But then came words from her professor's mouth that she didn't expect to hear.

'Miss Appleby,' he'd said, hiding a smile, 'the patient doesn't have an abdominal aortic aneurysm, he has a thoracic aortic aneurysm, and since it's located in his chest, it cannot be palpated.'

Even now, when reliving the experience, she wanted to break out in a sweat, but in retrospect, she would have been extremely disappointed in herself if she had failed this integrity test. Doctors should be trustworthy, shouldn't they? And furthermore, she'd learnt from Ben some time ago, that lies only lead to pain.

In the semi-darkness of her room with the orange glow of her bedside lamp casting shadows on the walls, she began to reflect on how 1987 had been a year of disasters.

January had started with The Big Freeze, and with up to thirty inches of snow, many places were cut off for days, including parts of London. But for her, it wasn't so much the icy conditions and disruptions that were hardest to deal with, it was being forced to slow down and sit inside her room with nowhere to go and nothing to do, except listen to relentless thoughts of loneliness and loss.

Just two months later, not long after she'd considered taking a short break to Belgium, the *MS Herald of Free Enterprise* capsized near Zeebrugge, killing 193 people. Then in August, while enjoying a well-earned summer break, she heard the news that sixteen people had been gunned down and massacred in Hungerford. The crazed gunman who later committed suicide had watched 'video nasties', according to the papers. *I've heard enough* she remembered thinking at the time, rekindling her resolve to stop watching the news.

Drawing her blankets up to her chest, she now thought back to how The Great Storm in October had perniciously sucked her back into watching the news again, and this time, not only were lives lost, but so much nature too. Forests, parks, roads, railways - everywhere was strewn with fallen trees, and it was hard to forget her mother's voice when she'd rung to say the farm had lost ancient specimens and Amanda was incredibly upset. As bad as it was, Millie remembered shutting down her emotions that day. With her mind and body already shattered, she was simply unable to take on anything more.

While slurping the last of her Lucozade, it dawned on her that the reason some tragedies felt like yesterday was because they'd literally taken place only weeks ago - the barbaric bombing of civilians in Enniskillen by the IRA at a Remembrance Day parade, followed by the fire at Kings Cross underground station. Trying not to berate herself, she recognised it was only days ago she'd managed to pluck up the courage to get back on the tube, and even then, she had needed to take deep controlled breaths when using the escalators.

Being reminded of all this led her to think of something else terrible but also quite different. Something that was arguably an ongoing disaster which had been casting a shadow all through the year, infecting every month with menace. The burden it posed to society was so strong, that a leaflet entitled 'Don't Die of Ignorance', had been dropped through each and every letterbox.

The scourge of HIV/AIDS was a worry for would-be doctors, and she was no exception. Medicine could feel like a high-risk occupation when accidentally getting pricked while taking a patient's blood, or being contaminated by their bodily fluids, could literally kill. She pulled the covers up tighter, wondering if despite all the many reassurances from teaching staff, there were risks nobody yet understood.

It wasn't just students who harboured rational or irrational fears. When an elderly man had peered at Jonas through a monocle like Patrick Moore's, and shouted, 'Get me another doctor, please. This one looks like he might have that infernal homosexual disease!', Jonas just made light of it.

'I wasn't expecting that,' he laughed, 'especially now I don't wear make-up!'

AIDS was no laughing matter, though. People dying after blood transfusions, babies contracting it in the womb, married people with cheating spouses - it all felt like a very dark time. Millie shrank back in her bed, thinking how the unhealthy focus on lust, not love, and obsession with condoms and 'safe sex,' felt here to stay. All it did for her was to reopen old wounds and thoughts about how Giles had treated her, the first and only person she'd slept with. But despite all the negativity, she hadn't given up hope that one day she would enjoy a solid, permanent relationship, just like her parents' or Amanda and Dean's. Placing her hands behind her head, she lay back, gazing into a void and giving Ben his due. At least he'd respected her body, even if in the end, he'd ended up leaving it for someone else's.

National disasters, a global epidemic, exam stress, clinical pressures, loneliness, doubt, exhaustion, fear -

she wasn't at all surprised that one thing piling on top of another slowly but surely turned into a huge boil, a ripe pustule fit to burst. And then came the straw that *did* finally break the camel's back, the thing that completely shattered her fragile world. Looking back at that intense, defining moment, she felt heat flowing through her, and she sat up again, quite unable to believe it had all happened a mere fortnight ago, because in many ways, it felt like forever.

The day she witnessed the death of a young, fit and healthy woman would never leave her memory. She could see in her mind's eye right now, clinical staff dashing around the ward at St Helier hospital, fraught with activity, having had a clinical emergency declared. She remembered thinking it looked like organised chaos, and wondering if and how she could assist. 'Female, twenty-eight years, admitted to the ward, twenty-four weeks pregnant, unconscious, heavy blood loss from a suspected placental abruption.' This much she knew, but what could she do to help? She didn't have a clue.

She hated the way moments like these forced her to be an observer rather than an active participant, but very soon, she realised there was nothing *anyone* could do. Nothing, nothing at all.

Harried staff began to depart, one by one, while the senior registrar who was the last doctor to remain, explained to her, 'The placenta separating from the womb was what caused the profusion of blood.'

She remembered nodding along, her head feeling strained, then watching him walk away while nurses set to work, gathering up bloodstained sheets as best they could without disturbing the body. In stark contrast to all the activity leading up to this moment, everything now felt calm and unhurried, and when she dared to look across at the departed woman, she had to take a step back. Ashen cheeks and eyes closed as in a deep, deep sleep. Millie remembered feeling mesmerised at how the terrifying stillness and finality of death was tempered by the beauty of a woman lying, delightfully at peace.

At that point, Millie had failed to anticipate how things were about to get even harder, but when the husband arrived, his countenance dark, disbelieving and tortured, she began to see. Knowing it was high time to leave the room, she arose but turned to watch him sit next to the bed, the life sucked out of him and his chest caved in, so stunned he couldn't move. Then, with feet heavy as though dipped in quick-drying cement, she shuffled along the corridor, blocking out thoughts of what he might be feeling, not wanting to imagine the depth of his brokenness. Only moments before, he'd been at work and his wife was home, full of life, carrying his child. No doubt she was laughing, and doing the things everyday people do. And now, she and the child were both gone, taken away before he'd had the chance to say goodbye.

Then, while still feeling on high alert, the sound of haunting sobs reached her ears and she turned a corner to see a visibly shaken grey-haired man trying to keep a mature-looking woman upright, her mournful cries muffled by his tear-soaked shirt. There was no question in her mind who these people were, and how unthinkable and impossible it must be for them to accept that their daughter and grandchild were gone forever.

After she'd finally thought she'd seen it all, there came the awful moment when she remembered that seeing someone putting on a brave face could hit just as hard as witnessing their unbridled distress. She could almost see herself, leaning up against the coffee lounge door and trying not to break while watching a boy around Ewan's age, sitting by the foot of a sparsely decorated hospital Christmas tree, munching on a mince pie. His father and his grandparents were smiling at his antics, and she found herself laughing along silently. But she also noticed that even then, their faces were contorted and she continued to watch, painfully aware of the father's dilemma. How was he going to decide whether or not to let his toddler see his mother, one last time? Beginning to lose track of time, she watched the little lad's bright eyes and chubby hands build a tower from colourful wooden blocks, so happy, so oblivious, and thankfully, far too young to realise he'd not only lost his mother, but after the failed emergency caesarean section, his unborn sister too.

While thinking she'd managed to get to the end of the day unscathed, she lacked the energy to walk home and so from the vantage point of the top deck of a red London bus, she peered through a window at the winter darkness lit up by city lights. She remembered how her muscles felt weaker by the time she'd arrived home, and how she'd opened her mouth to tell Wahida what had happened, but was worryingly dumbstruck.

Once inside her bedroom, it was as if a release valve had been opened, with every bit of agitation that had built during the day slowly beginning to leak. Had she eaten lunch? At this point, she couldn't even remember, and although her stomach felt empty, she was too sick to eat. But still, she needed something to fill her, something, anything to take away the emptiness she was feeling and dizzily, she delved into her bag and drew out a bible. She'd taken it from the hospital on a whim, spotting it by an empty bed, and although this wasn't the first time she'd come across one in a similar fashion, it *was* the first time she'd considered borrowing it or taking one home. Now all the noise had died down, bizarrely, annoyingly, all she could hear was Ben's voice. She could hear him talking about hitting rock bottom and about the 12-step programme, she heard him mention Carl, his mentor, and how he'd told him to read Mark's gospel, saying it was the shortest. 'I read it in two hours but you should try Luke,' Ben had said to her with a chuckle, 'because Luke was a doctor, just like you.'

Even through her mental fog, she couldn't forget how his eyes had sparkled, and how at the time she'd thought *I wouldn't mind some of that myself.* But where should she start? With Mark perhaps? Or should she listen to Ben's recommendation to read Luke? How about starting right back at Genesis, at the beginning? Or maybe she should just open it and see what she stumbled across? Doing just that, she quickly spotted a thin piece of paper nestled within its pages, and with shaky hands, she unfolded it, to see handwritten scribble in dark blue ink at the top. 'Comforting scripture verses', the heading said, and she closed her eyes, knowing that was *exactly* what she needed, right now. Comfort, comfort, she needed comfort.

John 14 verse 27 was the first reference. What does *that* say? Where *is* John? Ah, there. Running her finger across the page she found the verse.

Peace I leave with you, my peace I give to you. Not as the world gives do I give to you. Let not your hearts be troubled, neither let them be afraid.

Instantly aware of something rich and deep, and hungry for more, she flicked through to Revelation remembering from school assemblies that it was the very last book.

God shall wipe away all tears from their eyes; and there shall be no more death, neither sorrow, nor crying, neither shall there be any more pain: for the former things are passed away.

Ten minutes later, having read all the scriptures in the handwritten note, she looked around through a watery gaze and laid the bible down together with the piece of paper on her bed, before her weary body slid down next to it. She felt weightless, as if floating, buoyed with words that had pierced her, lifted her up, filled her, even as her empty stomach growled, and as she lay on her bed, feeling something she'd never felt before, she began also to sense she may have stumbled across something she'd been searching for all her life. It felt like a warm embrace, a love so complete and a love that no man had ever been able to give her before, or perhaps ever could.

When a hot, salty tear fell down her cheek, followed by another and another, she could tell, even as her body began to tremble, she wasn't crying tears of sadness. She *did* feel sad though, sad and sorry for all the time she'd spent, fruitlessly trying to bury her pain, losing herself in hard work and struggling alone, all by herself.

Had she been missing out on love? Had she been searching for something all her life, totally unaware, until now? Lying there, still feeling this love, she began to question how she'd ever believed any man, any earthly man, no matter how wonderful and no matter how much he loved her, could've poured into her this way and made her feel as if there was a chance, even a distant hope of being utterly complete but at the same time, utterly broken.

But then she began to realise that the truth was, she'd always known him. Because she'd felt him in the sincere but imperfect love of a humble farming family, and she'd sensed his presence while spending hours amongst sheep and cattle in the beating heart of a rural idyll, and she'd sensed him from her earliest days, learning about why he came to the world through a Christmas carol, or soaking up his words of love while watching *Jesus of Nazareth* at Easter time.

And now, in the here and now, in the early hours of 1988, she rolled over in bed, alone in her room back at the farm, appreciating, perhaps for the first time ever, that she wasn't alone, and not just because Mum, Dad, Dean, Amanda and Ewan were nearby.

Her pulse quickened with excitement. In less than two weeks she'd be flying out to Belize for her elective, and there, she would have the privilege of using her medical skills to make a difference in a less affluent place. Then afterwards, she was looking forward to an exciting adventure exploring America for three weeks. Before her awakening, this had felt daunting, but now, she was no longer afraid of being alone and so far away from home, because she knew she was never alone.

Laid up in bed, recovering from the flu on New Year's Day she couldn't have been happier. Yes, she was *still* overworked, boyfriend-less, prone to worry and exhaustion, and yes, she was still clueless about so many things, with no idea of what the future held. But, despite all this, she knew that at last, the tortuous feelings of despair, of losing her mind and a constant terror of not being able to cope, were finally and beautifully put to bed. For now, it was time to settle under the covers for the night, and to fall asleep while thanking her saviour, her father in heaven, her best friend and the lover of her soul.

Chapter 42:

'Livin' on a Prayer' - Bon Jovi

9th February 1988

Dear Mum and Dad,

Still having a great time, mainly because the family I'm staying with are so lovely. Mr and Mrs Sanchez have done everything to make me feel welcome and I have to say, I'm starting to like Belizian food, even though I prefer your dinners, Mum. Conch fritters are quite tasty, especially washed down with Belikin beer, and I was surprised when I liked hadut which is a sort of fishy stew swimming in coconut milk. I'm not so keen on cassava pudding, though, as it's dead sweet and kind of rubbery, but that might be entirely down to Mrs Sanchez's baking of course (I hope she doesn't see this!)

Last weekend the family took me to Secret Beach on Ambergris Caye and although judging by how popular it is, it's hardly a secret, it was incredible. Please tell Amanda she would have gone crazy for all the mangrove trees, and when I swam I spotted incredibly colourful fish. The sea was clear turquoise blue and shallow for a long way out, and the sand was powdery and white. I spent a lot of time swimming, which is quite daring when there are sharks (but please don't worry, Mum!) and I stupidly left my factor 8 behind (oops) but luckily it was cloudy so I didn't get burnt.

That same day I couldn't believe it when I first came face to face with a massive, bright green iguana sitting on a rock back home in the village, but Mr Sanchez says that's totally normal. Since then, I've also spotted a pelican with a seagull sitting on its head (hee hee) and I've seen toucans high up in the trees, plus so many cute bugs - more than I've seen in my entire life!

Working out here in the heat of Central America tests my character and concentration, but at least here, the people are as warm as the weather (boiling heat in February takes some getting used to, by the way!).

When I leave, I'll definitely miss the Belizeans and their laid-back attitude, and being here has also taught me what it's like being a minority.

The hospital work keeps hotting up, almost as much as the weather, and I've been in some fascinating clinics with top paediatricians from Miami and other parts of America. I must say though, some of the Belizean junior doctors are a bit *too* laid back for my liking, and when things go wrong, a few don't feel they need to tell patients what's going on. Also, the way some of them practise medicine has been an eye-opener and not in a good way. Still, most doctors here know what they're doing and are super friendly plus keen to make sure I have a good experience. I really am grateful for that.

Last week I did some clinical work at a children's home. You know me, so you can imagine how I cried (when no one was looking) after seeing so many orphans. Some looked so dull and lifeless I almost burst into tears there and then, and I wanted to do something, anything when I joined them all for their simple meal of rice and beans. I asked the manager about sending money to help, but in not so many words she said don't bother, because it won't reach them. How terrible is that? Belize is beautiful, but like so many places where real poverty exists, life can be tough. I can see why Wahida was dead keen to go for a tropical Island. I wonder how she's finding Mauritius? She was lucky to get a placement in a tourist destination, although I'm not sure it'll be all luxury, in fact, I'm guessing she's linked with a missionary hospital or something like that, so like everyone, she's bound to have her work cut out. Did I tell you Zane's in Cameroon and Jonas is in Borneo? I imagine they're facing some challenging situations too.

How's Dean and Amanda and my sweetie Ewan? I can't believe he's going to be two in May. Where did that time go? Is Amanda coping better with morning sickness this time around? Tell her I'm still miffed she left it until two days after I flew to announce she's pregnant! Seriously though, I'm counting down the days to seeing my new niece or nephew in September. Also tell Amanda that while I'm happy if it's another nephew, I'm kind of hoping I'll get a niece, at least at some point. Ewan needs a sister to keep him in check when he's older!

Anyway, better finish now. How's everything back home by the way? Can't wait to see you all when I return. Dad, I'm really glad you suggested making the most of my stop-over in New York and I hope you realise that it's all your fault I'm doing a full-on Trek America trip as well. My first taste of the US and I'm super excited, so much so, I keep humming 'New York,

New York (So Good They Named it Twice)' and 'From LA to New York' around the house, and I expect I'm really annoying all the Sanchez's in the process!

One last thing, I have to say I'm not looking forward to the flight home, but I am glad I've started reading the bible and praying. I don't know how else I'd have coped when I literally thought the plane was falling out of the sky during that awful turbulence, not to mention losing all my luggage at the airport. I still can't stop thanking God it turned up so quickly.

Bye, all (for now). Love you to the moon and back, write soon, and see you in April.

Millie x

Chapter 43:

'That Certain Smile' - Midge Ure

The pace at St Helier Hospital was slightly more manageable, even on the busiest of days, and Millie was still trying to work out why.

Maybe after returning from the adventure of a lifetime, she had a new perspective and could see things through fresh, rested eyes. Or perhaps it was simply a matter of getting better at what she was doing, or could it be that after encountering the many challenges of clinical life abroad, things seemed easier here by comparison? Whatever the reason, it was fortunate that her workload had eased a little, because final exams were beginning in earnest in less than eight weeks, and the last thing she needed was additional stress.

She was graduating from St George's as a fully-fledged, qualified doctor in just over three months. How could that be real? The road ahead felt daunting, terrifying even, but also very, very exciting. Feeling she could do with another coffee, which was always a tell-tale sign of approaching burnout, she headed for the kitchenette on Walnut Ward, the best children's ward she'd worked on so far.

After stepping inside, she opened the cupboard and reached for a spoon. The work involved in applying for house officer jobs and preparing for exams while keeping up with clinical placements could easily lead to emotional exhaustion, unhappiness and physical burnout. Stirring a spoonful of Coffee-mate into her mug, she closed her eyes, instantly aware that for days, instead of turning to God, she was turning to coffee. Perhaps she ought to have added caffeine to her list of addictions, together with chocolate and hard work, that day she, Ben and Conker had gone for a walk and he'd opened up about taking heroin.

Stirring her coffee, she was beginning to regret going several days without finding the time to grab a minute or two to read the bible. How silly, when she knew that whenever she did, it always seemed to set her right.

'This is the coffee room, isn't it?'

Millie turned her head quickly, to see a friendly face standing by the door. 'Yes, it is.'

The woman who walked in was simply dressed and in her early forties, her dark hair loosely secured, as though tied back hurriedly, her warm eyes lively and compassionate yet slightly weary. 'I'm new to this ward,' she said. 'It's actually my first day here.'

Millie shook her head slowly. 'Nobody told you where the coffee room is? How mean!' With a welcoming face, she pointed to the mugs. 'How have you been finding it so far?' she asked, taking another sip of Mellow Birds.

'Hectic,' the woman said, 'but Sister Rawlings has been showing me the ropes, and she seems lovely.'

'She *is* lovely, and paediatrics is a great area to work in, especially on this ward,' Millie said. 'I love it here.'

The woman smiled pleasantly, and when she did, Millie thought something about that smile felt familiar. It was a 'Magic Smile', as in the Rosie Vela song, and it reminded her of someone.

'I've always wanted to be a nurse,' the woman said, 'especially a children's nurse, so I can't believe I'm actually here.' She turned her face towards the door. 'I'm looking after Tommy right now, he's a super lad.'

'Tommy?' Millie glanced up, 'Is he the one who came in this morning with the burst appendix?'

'Yes, and he's also very special.'

'Special?'

'He is, because he has autism.'

'*Has* he?' Millie's eyes ignited with interest. 'I didn't know that.' There was a short pause and the woman reached for the kettle. 'I did a project at Redwood Lawn Children's Home on autism, two years ago,' Millie said.

The woman froze, then after putting the kettle down, she turned around slowly. Her eyes were wide and her body stiff. Somehow, with a look of surprise, Millie slowly began to realise.

'Theo,' the woman said, as if out of the blue, 'Theo Norcott.'

'Yes,' Millie said, sounding amazed, 'I knew Theo. I'm guessing you're his mum?'

The woman nodded and gently bit her bottom lip. 'Theo doesn't talk much, although he does have his moments,' she laughed lightly.

Millie nodded, understanding exactly what she meant.

'Of course, you already know how excited he gets when he talks about his favourite things, don't you,' his mother continued. 'Cartoons, countries of the world and all that, and you also know he doesn't say much otherwise.'

Millie nodded again.

'But even so, he told me over and over that someone called Millie, I'm sure he said Millie - came to talk to him. Was that you?'

'Yes,' Millie said, 'yes, it was me.' She gazed at the woman, wondering, keen to know something.

'How is Theo now?'

'Fine,' the woman said, 'and right this minute, I'm guessing he's watching Roobarb and Custard. Doretta, my eldest, is home with him today.'

Millie chuckled, then her face softened. 'He's not at Redwood Lawn any more?'

The woman's eyes glistened. 'No, he isn't. Theo's back home with me and his brother and sisters, where he belongs.'

Staring, Millie swallowed hard.

'You see, Millie,' the woman began, 'I needed time to find my feet. For years, I worked and I got by, and during that time, I couldn't,' she paused, her voice cracking. 'I *tried* to see him as often as I could - I would have visited every day but...' she stopped and the drooping corners of her mouth began to smile again. 'I used to tell myself I was the luckiest Mum in the world to have a kid that could literally sit and read encyclopaedias for hours.' She laughed a little. 'And because he loved TV so much, at one point I asked myself, why on earth didn't I just leave him home plonked in front of the box all day? At least that way,' she sighed, 'he'd be there, with me. But then I realised I was only kidding myself, because I was hardly there, was I? I had to work, and while you might be able to get away with leaving a 14-year-old lad at home by himself, you can't do it when he's little, can you, especially when he needs you more than the others?'

Millie shook her head and listened to the clink of a metal spoon against the side of the woman's mug.

'Redwood Lawn gave me breathing space,' the woman said. 'It did what I couldn't do, and the staff, those lovely people, *they* met his needs 24/7, while I learned how to survive.'

Millie's throat felt tight listening to the woman's story, a story about financial struggles following a divorce, right up until she began to work as a ward orderly at St Helier after her youngest had started school. 'I can't believe I'm finally here,' the woman repeated, her eyes flitting with excitement.

At first, Millie wondered why this stranger was telling her so much, but the answer soon became obvious. Very quickly this woman wasn't feeling much like a stranger at all, and Millie also sensed she felt the same about her.

'If I had even an inkling everything would turn out alright in the end, I think I would have cried a lot less,' the woman said.

'I'm sure your tears weren't wasted,' Millie said, 'and I'm sure you did your best.' The words seemed to come from nowhere, and Millie knew she was speaking in ignorance. However, a still, small voice, deep inside, reassured her that she'd said the right thing.

Turning away briefly, the woman brushed a hand against her cheek and, looking down, clutched her mug and tried unsuccessfully to hide the tears. Millie understood, at least in part, because her first day at St Helier had been exhausting and emotional as well. But she'd been lucky, she only had herself to worry about and despite all the stresses she'd felt then and still felt now, she could see she had it easy in so many ways. 'I'm afraid I have to go,' she said reluctantly, after noticing the time. 'I'm moving on to geriatrics on Monday.' She stopped talking and tilted her head. 'It's amazing our paths crossed like this: I can't believe how easy it would have been to have missed you today, and I am so glad we bumped into each other.'

'Me too.'

'And I'd love to see Theo again.'

'I'm sure he'd love to see you too. Hey, guess what?' the woman said. 'We're moving to a garden flat in the summer. It's still small, but it's bigger than where we are now, and we've never had a garden before, so I can't wait. I'm going to have a housewarming garden party or maybe a barbecue, something along those lines, and Millie,' she smiled, 'I'd love you to come if you can make it.'

They hastily exchanged telephone numbers and Millie turned to leave the room. Looking at the number scribbled on the piece of paper, she realised there was something very important that she'd forgotten to ask.

'Sorry, I don't know your name. I mean, I can't keep calling you Theo's Mum can I?'

The woman paused, her worn eyes lit up with brightness. Then, putting down her mug, she beamed. 'Grace,' she replied, gently, joyfully, 'my name is Grace.'

Chapter 44:

'Whenever You Need Somebody' - Rick Astley

Why was she here again? On the surface, the answer seemed obvious. She'd snatched one last weekend back home before the onslaught of exams hit heavy and hard. But why was she *here*? Was it because as much as the River Wandle provided her with a slice of nature and had kept her sane throughout her five years at St George's, it just wasn't the same as sitting in bucolic noiselessness, with burgeoning birdsong bursting through the broadleaf trees and evergreens?

But that *still* didn't answer the question. Why was she *here* again? There were plenty of other places she could be instead of sitting on the oak log by Stoneybrook, where the gentle rhythm of trickling water mimicked the tempo of a plethora of songs.

'Phew Wow' by The Farmer's Boys, for instance, because being at home was always a relief, and because *she* was a farmer's daughter. That was a happy song, but disappointingly, others that came to mind, had the sour top notes of Ben flowing through them, just when she'd thought she'd managed to forget him.

It had all started in London when she'd been triggered by hearing Blue Eyed Soul artists, Swing Out Sister and Simply Red on the radio. However, the belief that running home to Sussex would help her to escape the memories had turned out to be 'Twilight World' thinking.

Now she was sitting by the brook, she was reminded of Julian Lennon's 'Valotte', with its classic tune and melancholy undertones. To Millie's mind the words spoke of loss and trying to find some way – any way - to hold on to the other person's heart. She knew she'd failed to do that, but while she most definitely felt like a failure, she didn't think *everything* in the song matched her situation. Instead of a pebble, she was sitting on a log, and rather than being by a river, she was by a brook. And last, but not least, unlike the person in the song, she wasn't playing the guitar: - instead, she was playing the fool, because only a fool would remain stuck. Only a fool would struggle to move on like this.

This used to be her happy place - correction, this used to be *their* happy place. A place where they'd revelled in their love for the natural world, and where, in between wildlife observations, they'd steal a tender kiss.

'There might be water voles here,' he'd once said, while sitting right by her side on this very same tree trunk. Upon remembering that, she let out a sigh. At last, she'd found a good, legitimate, solid reason for being here. She was yet to see a real-life water vole, and today might just be the day. Thanks to living rurally, she was already au fait with another of the vole species. Last winter, in a bid to occupy herself at the farm, she was clearing up, only to pull back a sheet of corrugated iron to reveal a furry creature. She didn't have long to identify it, because as soon as its hideaway was uncovered, the grey ball of fluff darted away as fast as its little legs could carry it. Despite the fleeting glimpse, there was no mistaking a field vole, because she'd seen one once before as a child while making daisy chains in a meadow with her father. She'd never forgotten that rounded snout, tiny eyes, furry ears and stubby tail, and was delighted to see another, thirteen years later.

Similarly, she was unable to forget Ben's enthusiasm when he'd said she'd almost certainly caught a dormouse in his trap. Neither could she forget the sweet wood mouse he'd captured, or the shrew they'd stumbled across that clement summer's day before they went on to recite the words of Shakespeare on the bridge. Other memories of Ben also stuck, like the way he'd stood up for a helpless hare against a hateful Horace, his delectable cooking, and his penchant for roadkill and humane hunting. Before they'd met, she'd never known anyone quite like him, and following their separation that fateful, or rather *Faye*-full Boxing Day, she hadn't met anyone like him since.

What would she do if she saw a water vole right now? How would she feel? Thrilled, excited, ecstatic? Perhaps. But how could she possibly experience the richness and depth of her first water vole sighting without Benvolio sitting by her side? If she were to spot one this very minute, what else would spring to mind except, 'He needs to see this too!'

If Ben were to see his Millie Mouse today, what would he think? One thing was certain. The man she'd once dubbed her Benvolio was unlikely to be the same today as he was back then. She didn't even know his whereabouts.

'Where's Romeo?' The singer from CaVa CaVa asks in his rather odd, but characteristic voice, but when it came to *her* Romeo, or rather her Benvolio, *he* wasn't such a good boy, was he?

Millie had wondered recently if feelings of isolation had partly led to Ben fleeing the village. Had Horace threatened Alan, causing him to fear losing his job unless he shunned Ben? If Ben had been ashamed after stealing to feed his secret drug habit, and had slept with Faye, could he also have been lonely? He'd left Magham Down at a time when his girlfriend was away at university for literally weeks on end. Not surprising then, that if, after losing the only male friend he'd had, he felt isolated and alone.

If Horace *did* have a hand in the break up of Ben and Alan's friendship, he was wicked, but after what Ben had probably done himself, what right would *he* have had to point the finger? Lost in her thoughts and soothed by the gentle trickle of water, Millie concluded that Ben should count himself lucky. At least he'd fared better than old Jerry who'd lost his barn - again, assuming those rumours were true.

Why should it matter to her if Ben had been lonely? He'd chosen to leave, and right now, he probably wasn't giving her a second thought. Even so, it was impossible to toss aside her abject curiosity. Was he well and finally free from addiction? Were he and Faye still together? Could they be married? She felt a restless flutter in her stomach, thinking he could even be a father by now.

But there was a possibility of something far, far worse than him marrying his ex and fathering her children. Even as the mid-May sunshine warmed her bones, she felt a chill, recalling how Ben had talked far too much about death to take anything for granted. Feeling suddenly panicked, she steadied her breathing, telling herself not to be ridiculous. She could always call around the schools if she were *that* worried about him. He wasn't a normal teacher based in one location and it might take some surreptitious detective work to find out where he was, but there were ways and means to check if he was still alive. Then holding her horses, she accepted that doing something like that wasn't just unnecessary, it was also very unwise. It would achieve absolutely nothing except rub more salt into the wound, because he was bound to be fine.

Whatever he was doing now, she hoped he'd learned his lesson. She hoped for his sake, as well as Faye's, or any other woman he was now with, that he was no longer a cheat or a liar. She'd recently heard Level 42's, 'Lessons In Love', its jazz-funk smoothness so richly aligned to that cool, king of all things jazzy - the saxophone. That infuriatingly delectable golden instrument, which she found herself missing so very much, and which was so reminiscent of Ben.

Forget about him. He was gone forever and that was a good thing. Horace and Agnes were probably right, she'd dodged a bullet. But if she really was better off without him, why then, despite all her best endeavours, could she not forget her sister-in-law's words? Why did her stupid head keep repeating those words, over and over? 'Somewhere along the line,' Amanda had said that day, on the terrace of her own Stoneybrook, 'at some point, after you've met someone, the thought of *not* being with him becomes unbearable and unthinkable.'

Millie shook her head and told herself it was no use trying to hold on to something that had died. When something or someone disappears, there's often nothing anyone can do. She and Ben had loved mammals, and some of those furry creatures, once commonplace in the United Kingdom - bears, wolves, elks for example - were here no longer. But even as she thought about all these losses, she felt a wave of positivity. Thanks to meat farmers not unlike her own father, the wild boar, once hunted to extinction, was back, and if it could happen with that species, perhaps there was hope for others.

Would the bob-tailed lynx, which had roamed Britain until 1300 years ago, ever return? Massive deforestation had destroyed its habitat. *Destroyed, destroyed.* She sat by the brook, repeating that word. It sounded so very final and so very hopeless. But if there was any lesson she'd learned from her spiritual awakening just six months earlier, it was that no matter how bleak everything looked, there was always hope.

Thinking about lynxes, the group Lynx had the hit, 'So This Is Romance', and as far as Millie was concerned, romance went hand in hand with her and Ben's love story. You couldn't get more romantic than two lovers reciting a Shakespearian sonnet together in the middle of the countryside, but if perchance someone transformed their story into a play redolent of the Bard's, it would fall into one genre and one genre only. A tragedy.

Often when she remembered Ben, she had questions about so many stupid little things. Had he finally seen sense and swapped shorts for long trousers to avoid getting stung by nettles on country walks? Was he still wearing those gorgeous, aviator top gun 'Take My Breath Away' glasses? Did he 'Find The Time' to tune into the latest episodes of *Only Fools and Horses*? Had he learned not to panic at the first signs of a tickly cough or sore throat, or was he still just a massive wuss? She smiled bitterly, knowing she'd never know, and aware that made the not knowing so much harder.

And now, dear old Enid couldn't help with answers either. Feeling depleted, Millie was still unable to believe what had happened earlier that day. After driving right past the spot where Ben had stopped to help after she'd hit the deer, she decided to take a detour past Clover Cottage. But the moment her car turned into the lane, she not only saw the row of two-up two-down cottages, but also something so unfamiliar and unexpected it made her stop, take her hand off the wheel, cover her mouth and gasp. There, fastened to the wall of Clover Cottage, that same wall against which Conker had cocked his leg, was a big SOLD sign. And in the front garden was a man and a child, two people she'd never seen before, the little girl sitting on the brick wall, eating an ice lolly, the man with garden shears in hand, vigorously cutting back the passion flowers. Her heart had almost stopped until she registered that Enid couldn't have possibly passed away without it being common knowledge. She'd only moved on to pastures new, that's all.

How could it be that three and a half years had flown by since Conker had made that racket and she'd looked up to see Ben 'Looking Through The Window'? It felt like yesterday but in many ways, it also felt like ancient history, because so much had happened since.

'Mum, why didn't you tell me Enid's gone?' she'd asked Victoria after heading straight home. With empathetic eyes her mother sat down before responding. She'd said she'd only found out herself a few days ago and explained that because Millie was only home for the weekend, she didn't want to put a dampener on her stay and she'd planned to say something, 'the moment you got back to London, Sweet Pea.' Disarmed by her mother's considered response, Millie had nothing to say, and now, all she had was Stoneybrook as a reminder of her and Ben's relationship, and so here she was again.

Enid's leaving had felt so ill-timed because it happened just when Millie was so close to plucking up the courage to drop by after a frosty two and a half years. But wasn't the actual truth that even if Enid *hadn't* moved, nothing would have changed? In reality, Millie knew she would have preferred to have avoided reconnecting with her old piano teacher, if that meant staying ignorant, rather than hearing that Ben was happy, thriving and still in love with Faye. And anyway, there was another compelling reason she ought not to have gone round to see Enid. Ben had asked for a clean break, and even after all this time, she still needed to respect that.

Enid's move was a turning point that marked the end of an era. Where would her pupils go now? Had she finally conceded that living alone was too much and that she needed help? Perhaps she'd taken up Lauren's offer to move in with her, but the sad thing was, Victoria said she'd asked around for Enid's new address but nobody in the village seemed to know.

It wasn't just Enid she was going to miss. Lauren had felt much like a sister and had made her laugh out loud with her expensive tastes and love of game shows like *Sale of The Century, Play Your Cards Right* and *321*. Ben had once said that his sister only watched these programmes to drool over the prizes, but despite being a gadget-mad person who could talk endlessly about soda streams, Breville sandwich toasters and coffee percolators, Lauren wasn't just all about stuff. She also had a big heart, a heart which Millie was going to miss connecting with.

Back beside Stoneybrook, she looked around and filled her lungs with air rich with the aromatic smells of vegetation. Since her arrival over an hour ago, she'd picked up on a scent evocative of pines, eucalyptus and cedar but it was only now she noticed the freshly cut evergreen logs that lay on the woodland floor, just beyond the brook. Was it spruce? Maybe it was cypress? No doubt Amanda would know. And who was the woodsman? Millie concluded that whatever tree had been felled and whoever had done it, Stoneybrook was as beautiful and as peaceful as it had ever been, and although it was unlikely she'd be lucky enough to spot a water vole today, it didn't matter, she was just so very glad to be here.

'These stones,' she remembered Ben saying as he crouched by the brook, 'they remind me of my life, or maybe I should say, how it once was.' He picked up a handful of large pebbles and she stared down at the smooth, grey, tan and ivory-coloured rocks.

'I'm going to sound really weird now,' he'd said, 'but sometimes… just sometimes, I feel as if I've got these stones right here.' Her heedful eyes watched him place a hand on his chest. 'There's stuff inside me I wish I could get rid of, but I know I can't, because I'm weak. But I've learned to live with it, and not only that…' he stopped abruptly.

'What?'

'Just like the way the water flows around these stones and keeps them clean, I know my rockiness, my broken pieces keep getting washed away, and although I hope one day eventually all the fragments inside will wash away for good, I also know that even if they don't,' he paused and opened his hand to reveal a smooth, pearlised stone, 'God will cleanse them, polish them and make them beautiful.'

The moment he'd finished, that autumn day, she remembered hearing a riot of birdsong so incredibly welcome after the silence of the summer hiatus. She also remembered seeing clusters of crimson-red hawthorn berries dangling close by. But most of all, she couldn't forget the look in his eyes and the heady feeling of being in love with a poet, and how she couldn't possibly imagine loving him any more than she did right then.

And today, *this* day, it was time to leave Stoneybrook behind, both literally and figuratively. It was time to make her way back home, to get back to everyday life, to plough through the busy days ahead and to face the unknown. It was time to face a future without her poet and fellow believer, without her lover and her friend. It was time to say, 'Goodbye.'

Chapter 45:

'Let Me Know' - Maxi Priest

It was a mild morning in June. Jolting to attention at Joyce's hollering, Millie reached for the tap and turned off the shower. It was just gone half past ten, so who could be calling and for what possible reason? She had an exam to sit that very afternoon, and those who knew her well, knew not to call during the daytime when she was tied up with revision. But what if it was an emergency? Her heart thumped while she dashed towards the stairs. *Oh, no, not now. I really hope nothing bad's happened, not today.*

'It's for you,' Joyce said, when she reached the hallway.

Resisting the urge to respond with a caustic, 'I know', Millie calmly asked who it was.

'Some woman,' Joyce muttered, covering up the mouthpiece. 'I didn't ask for a name. I don't like to pry.'

Too preoccupied with anxiety to respond, even with an eye roll, Millie took the handset and put it to her ear. 'Hello,' she said, watching Joyce skulk off to the lounge. For what felt like an overly long moment, she stood waiting in her fleecy dressing gown, a white towel wrapped around her head and Joyce's Axminster carpet absorbing the occasional drip from her saturated legs.

'Hello Millie, it's Lauren.'

Silence.

The words at the end of the line were crisp, clear and unmistakable and when Millie pressed her hand against the chair in a bid to steady herself, Joyce appeared again from nowhere.

'Is everything okay?' Joyce asked, watching Millie as she sat with an ashen face.

'Fine, everything's fine.'

'I'll leave you to it then, shall I?'

'Yes, please, thank you.'

Dumbfounded at hearing Lauren's voice, Millie failed to register an unspoken gratitude for her landlady's concern, and saying nothing, she watched her walk away for a second time.

'Sorry about that, Lauren,' she said, uncovering the mouthpiece and hardly able to believe the words coming from her own mouth. Was it really Lauren? Was it truly Ben's sister calling, after goodness knows how long?'

'I hope you don't mind me phoning…'

'No, no, not at all.'

'And how are you doing?'

Millie's confused eyes looked up towards the ceiling. How *was* she doing? High up, she saw a spindly daddy long legs spider whose messy web seemed to reflect her own tangled insides.

'I'm fine,' she said, with a series of frustrating thoughts racing through her head at breakneck speed. In the weeks since she'd returned from that weekend back home, she'd managed to leave her brooding behind in Sussex and with it, her associated memories of Ben, at least enough to focus on the onslaught of

exams that were hitting hard. And now, *and now...*
this happens.

'It's really lovely to hear from you after all this time,'
she flustered. She wasn't lying either, she genuinely
meant it, especially as the sound of Lauren's bright,
easy-going voice had already helped settle a multitude
of fluttering butterflies inside. Lauren couldn't have
known she'd picked probably the worst time to ring.
She hadn't done it deliberately or to be annoying and
inconsiderate.

'I imagine I'm one of the last people you expected
to hear from,' Lauren said, 'and I'm sorry I haven't been
in touch for so long.'

Biting her bottom lip, Millie nodded, annoyed at a
sudden and unexpected emotional response to Lauren's
apology. Exam time always left her feeling emotionally
ragged, and so anything was capable of setting her off,
and it often did.

After briefly replying to Millie's questions about
how Hetty, Oscar and Malcolm were doing, Lauren
changed the subject. 'I'd really like to see you, if that's
okay,' she said keenly, warmly.

Swallowing hard and gripping the telephone that
bit tighter, Millie readily agreed.

By the time the call had ended, they'd decided on a
time and place, but only after Millie had apologised for
their meet-up not happening sooner. She'd mentioned
that she was taking exams, but didn't try to explain
that only after those were finished would she feel able
to focus or have spare capacity for anything else. She
wanted to say how exhausting it was to be in the middle
of her finals, and to tell Lauren that it wasn't easy

finding the time to eat, let alone meet someone for a drink. But much more than that, if only she could share her deepest truth. She was emotionally vulnerable, and coming to terms with losing Ben. Was Lauren about to stir up a hornet's nest? *Please don't drop it on me that something bad's happened to him,* she would have said if only she'd had the courage, *and don't tell me either that he and Faye are finished and he wants to crawl back.*

Staring blankly at the phone on the hook, her jaw was tight. She had her dignity and her standards. She wasn't desperate or lonely, and rising to her feet, she reminded herself that if she gave much more mental energy to this, she risked failing, not just the paper set for this afternoon but also all the others that followed. What would happen if she *did* fail? She could kiss goodbye to that hospital house job she'd managed to secure just a fortnight ago, that's for sure, and the worst-case scenario following that would be the prospect of saying goodbye to her entire future career. She un-tensed her muscles and tried to stop catastrophising. She and Lauren had always got on well, so maybe she just wanted to rekindle their friendship. But knowing this was highly unlikely, Millie decided to strike a balance between panic and downplaying the situation. There was no time now for speculating on the reason for Lauren's call. She had to compartmentalise somehow. She *had* to find a way to put everything to the back of her mind, and quickly.

Back in her room, and still unable to toss her troublesome thoughts to one side, it felt as if she was already falling at the first hurdle. Lauren's call was inexplicable, irritating, maddening even, but frustratingly Millie registered it was also everything she could have wished or hoped for. Well, almost everything, because deep down inside, she knew that had it been Ben on the telephone line, her heart would be beating even faster than it was right now.

Oddly, Lauren didn't mention Ben at all during the call, not even once, and in many ways, Millie was grateful. The chances were that hearing news of Ben would have messed with her head, but Millie did walk away from the conversation with one regret. She wished she'd asked about Enid, only remembering after putting the phone down that she'd somehow forgotten to ask how she was. *Lauren, please don't be ringing me because something's happened to Enid or anyone else.*

Whatever the reason for Lauren's call, mystifying and disconcerting as it was, Millie recognized there *was* something that brought a lightness to the whole situation. The phone call was vexing and unintentionally ill-timed, but she felt more than a hint of excitement and optimism peeking through the fog, even though she'd rather not admit it to herself. Reaching for her rose-scented moisturiser, she untwisted the lid and released the natural aroma of rose oil. Although Lauren had sounded more sedate than usual, she didn't seem distressed, so perhaps the news wasn't bad. Scooping out some cream and rubbing it into her bare arms Millie sighed tensely, knowing that if Lauren *did* have something important to tell her, it was just going to have to wait.

***

A mere four days and six exams later, Millie was sitting opposite Lauren at a wooden table inside a

Wandsworth café. 'The lady's not for turning,' might be a suitable phrase for Mrs Thatcher, but it didn't ring true for Millie, who shortly after that phone call with Lauren, began to waver. Should she get the meeting out of the way, and risk jeopardising things, or should she wait and endure yet more tense, agonising days of self-questioning and uncertainty? Crossing her fingers, she reluctantly chose the former, and today, despite being slightly on edge, she had no regrets. It felt wonderful to be face-to-face with Lauren again, and after ordering drinks, they sat quietly, as though needing to warm up after so much time.

The first thing that struck Millie after not seeing Lauren for so long was a subtle change in her demeanour. Still warm and friendly, her vivid smile was initially more subdued, making Millie wonder if guilt and embarrassment due to leaving things so long might be the reason. Her hair was looser, and instead of the black velvet cameo choker she'd often wear, a lightly secured blue silk scarf matching her eyes, rested against her collar bones. Always so elegant and forever chic, but now more sagacious and a fraction more reserved.

Another surprise came prior to the meeting itself. The first and only time they'd met in London before now was inside Harrods in the run up to Christmas, back in 1985. Lauren had glowed, knowing she was about to splash the cash in that famous store and Millie still couldn't forget the sparkle in her eyes.

Now, while sitting in this South London café, Millie observed a slightly shabby interior, yellowing net curtains across the door, and a dog-eared laminated menu resting on the tablecloth. She smiled inquisitively at Lauren, amazed she seemed comfortable in such a humble environment. Since she'd said she was happy to go budget 'for a change,' Millie, wondering if she'd heard right, suggested a venue just around the corner from Joyce's. Exam season wasn't the time for travelling around or for being one of those 'West End Girls', but rather for keeping things local and low-key.

'I know you're in the middle of exams so I don't want to keep you long,' Lauren said, stirring her black coffee with a silver spoon.

'Not quite the middle. I only have four papers left, thankfully.'

'What are you listening to, by the way?' Lauren asked, looking curious.

Slightly baffled, Millie tilted her head.

'I saw you in the street, just before you arrived, and you had a Walkman over your ears.'

'You saw me?' Millie laughed, shifting awkwardly. 'Oh, it's just a classical cassette, I find classical relaxes me around exam time.'

Lauren nodded, blew her coffee, sipped and then put her cup down slowly. 'Well, I really appreciate you finding the time to see me when you're so snowed under.'

'I was... I *am* very happy to.'

There was a pause and Millie poured from a small milk jug. 'How's Enid?' she asked, looking up.

'Gran? Gran's doing very well. I'm not sure you've heard, but she left Magham Down in May.'

Millie responded with a delayed nod. 'Yes, I knew she'd moved, but I only found out recently.'

There was another pause and when Lauren spoke again, she told Millie that Enid had moved to a warden-controlled flat in Eastbourne. 'Somewhere smaller and more manageable and where there's always someone to keep an eye on her.'

Millie knew Lauren had always loved her Gran, but today, she thought she could detect some extra emotion in Lauren's eyes when she spoke of her. If Enid was doing well, why was Lauren suddenly looking so serious, so heavy?

'Gran's living in Eastbourne now, not far from where Ben lives,' Lauren said quietly.

Feeling her heart jolt at the mere mention of Ben's name, Millie felt annoyed with herself. She'd been fully expecting to hear something about him sooner or later, so why the moment it happened did it feel akin to being hit by a brick?

'How *is* Ben?' she ventured to ask, casually raising her cup to her lips.

There was an excruciating pause while she waited, silently ignoring her churning insides.

'Ben's doing well,' Lauren said reservedly. 'Still working hard and loving life by the sea, but I'll come to that in a moment,' her face grew sombre again, 'because I'm not just here to talk about *him*.'

Now feeling more confused than ever, Millie sat tight. Ben was doing well, and there was no mention of Faye. But there was also something else Lauren wanted to talk about. With no choice but to listen and wait for all to be revealed, she tried to remain patient.

'Everything okay with your order?' The genial-looking Greek Cypriot proprietor of the café was now standing over them.

'Yes, good, lovely thanks,' they both replied, almost in unison.

'Can I interest you beautiful young ladies in some food… maybe some cake? And we now do custard tarts and pasties.'

Millie and Lauren glanced at each other and after thanking him, explained they were in a hurry but perhaps another time. 'Sure thing,' he said, walking away with a spring in his step.

With everything quiet again, Lauren looked Millie directly in the eye. Then, tight-lipped, she began to do something inelegant and very unlike her. She was rubbing the back of her neck and had averted her gaze again. Feeling the growing tension, Millie wondered if Lauren had changed her mind. It certainly came across as though she was no longer sure about saying whatever she'd planned to say.

Then she said it.

'I took the money.'

What? At first, Lauren's words failed to register in Millie's consciousness. But soon, memories of what had happened that Boxing Day, married with the pained expression in the crystal blue eyes now staring back at her, made everything suddenly, dramatically and unexpectedly clear.

Opening her mouth to speak, Millie closed it again, and instead, half shook her disbelieving head.

'Yes,' Lauren continued, '*I* took Gran's money.' Smiling oddly, she looked away briefly, before focussing on Millie's face again. 'Ben didn't know until recently, but Gran and Malcolm, they've known for...' She stopped and gave a dull, weighty sigh. 'I don't deserve my hubby,' she said, 'and I'm sure he's built differently from other men. I mean, he still loves me, despite everything that I put him through. He loves me even though his 'Posh Missus', as he calls me, stooped so low.'

At first, Millie didn't blink, and then, cognisant of her rigidity began to blink rapidly.

'Lauren,' she said finally, 'I…I really appreciate you telling me all this. Can I, I mean, is it okay to ask… why?'

'I'd assume there was something wrong with you if you didn't,' Lauren tried to smile.

Dropping her shoulders, Millie eased up, not just for her own sake, but also for Lauren's - in fact, especially for Lauren's. She listened, and listened some more, because Lauren had quite a lot to share. She began by saying how Malcolm trusted her with their finances and how for months he had no idea a tax payment on their antique shop had been missed. She explained how her secret spending on 'that stupid credit card' had snowballed out of control, and how a poor investment decision had made a financial dent in their once thriving business, leading to a knee-jerk re-mortgaging of the house swiftly followed by rising interest rates.

Stunned into silence, Millie wasn't sure what to say. What could she say? 'I'm sorry you had to go through all of that - it sounds like a lot,' or 'I hope things are better, I'm sure anyone could've fallen into that trap,' maybe. That was it. *That's* what she should start by saying.

Lauren shrugged. 'I'm not sure I agree, actually,' she replied, after Millie had suggested it could happen to anyone. 'Not too many folk would let things spiral out of control or bury things under the carpet the way I did. I look back now, wishing I'd nipped things in the bud sooner, but like they say back home, ee by gum I'm a daft 'ap'orth sometimes.'

Relaxing in Lauren's self-deprecating humour, Millie found her Yorkshire speak a bitter sweet reminder of Ben.

'And I didn't just lie to Malcolm, Gran, Ben, my parents *and* my kids, Millie, I lied to myself. I convinced myself I was only borrowing Gran's cash, and that when I'd paid off the credit card and sold a few antiques for a profit, I'd pay it all back.'

The two sat with their arms resting on the table, briefly watching pedestrians and traffic go by in contemplative silence.

'I grew up wanting stuff,' Lauren said. 'Dad took away everything Mum had, even the roof over our heads.' She breathed deeply, gazing out of the window once more. 'So when I got my first paycheck, it felt as if I'd won the pools. Spend, spend, spend, that's what I decided to do, and I didn't stop, but when I got that damned credit card, my spending mushroomed before I even knew what was happening.'

Sitting opposite, with not much more to offer than a warm smile, Millie thought about taking hold of Lauren's hand, but she didn't want to give the wrong impression, knowing Ben's family weren't touchy-feely. Hearing Lauren talk this way was quite a revelation, but what about Ben? There were so many unanswered questions there. At least now she knew *he* hadn't taken the money, but that didn't mean he was innocent of all charges, and for all she knew, he could still be in a relationship with Faye.

'When Gran sold the house,' Lauren said, 'you wouldn't believe what she did.'

Millie's focussed gaze communicated her keenness to find out, and she watched Lauren's face melt into the saddest of smiles. 'She paid off all my debts. *That's* how she punished me when I told her what a low-down toad I'd been to her. I told her I'd pay her back one day,

I told her not to do something so ridiculous, and do you know what she said?'

Biting her lip and blinking hard in a bid to stop the tears, Millie whispered, 'No'.

'She said, "Why wait until I'm dead? It's time I moved on from this place and I've made a good living teaching piano, and even if I give you your inheritance now, I still have my pension and savings to help pay the rent. Just promise me one thing Lauren dear, just promise me you'll look after your money this time, and that you'll never, ever lose it all again."'

With hands clasped around her cup, Millie absorbed the heat of her beverage, and the warming, rich aroma of filtered coffee was comfort indeed. But even good coffee was no match for the incomparable affection and love that was now seeping through Lauren's words.

'And you know what's funny?' Lauren said, laughing a little.

Millie shook her head.

'I was always convinced Ben was Gran's favourite.'

Sitting quietly, they listened to the chiming of the cafeteria's front door bell and watched a man and woman enter, wearing shiny, his and hers, shell suits.

'Talking of Ben,' Lauren said.

'Yes?'

'I mean, I couldn't come all this way without saying a word or two about my baby bruv, could I?'

'Couldn't you?'

Lauren gave Millie a wry smile as if to say, 'Stop pretending you're not curious about him,' but rather than saying those words, she told Millie that Ben wanted her to pass on a message. 'He'd really like to talk to you,' she said plainly.

Feeling confused and looking away, Millie pressed her lips together tightly.

'When I told him you're still taking exams he insisted that I let you know that if, and that's a big *if,* you're willing to see him again, he doesn't want you to get in touch for a month or two, until after your last exam. He said he's waited years to speak to you, so he can wait another month or two.

Narrowing her eyes, Millie didn't know what to make of what Lauren had just said. So *he's* dictating to *her* when she should get in touch? And what did he mean by *he's* waited years? Wasn't *he* the one who had left Magham Down with no explanation? Didn't *he* say he wanted her not to get in touch? Wasn't *he* the one who did the dirty? For goodness sake, is he for real?!'

'I get my results mid-July,' she said, her amiable voice giving away nothing of her internal outrage, 'and after that, there's a graduation ball and then I start a full-time job, but I'm sure I'll manage to find time to see him at some point.'

Ben was lucky that she was as good as agreeing to see him, and because she was a woman of her word, she was now committed, but did he really deserve that commitment? Did he hell! Then suddenly, without warning, a word started to flash inside her head, a new word, a new concept, that meant much more to her these days. Forgive, forgive, forgive. And who on this earth *deserves* forgiveness? Who?

'Here's his address and telephone number,' Lauren said, sliding a piece of paper across the table.

There it was again. The same scribbled handwriting which had composed that devastating letter, she'd since destroyed. *32 Seaside Crescent, Eastbourne. So that's where he lives.* Having secured her first hospital job at Eastbourne District General Hospital just weeks earlier, with her heart now beating nineteen to the dozen, she couldn't help but wonder if this was a sign.

Dipping again into her Gucci bag, Lauren drew out another paper object, this time, square and colourful. 'And he wants you to have this too,' she said.

Millie stared at the 7-inch record sleeve lying in front of her on the table. At first, feeling indignant about having her emotions messed up like this, she wasn't quite sure how to react. Then, feelings of regret began to set in. Why did she ever agree to this meeting before finishing her exams? How unbelievably stupid of her, how incredibly, unbelievably stupid. Then, with heavy eyes, she contemplated the cover. 'I Won't Let You Down', PHD. Yes, he'd chosen 'I Won't Let You Down', a song about promising not to let someone down again, basically an apology song. She looked at the photograph on the sleeve and the colours of the artwork, black, red, blue – two men, two band members, one holding up his hands as if to say 'guilty as charged', or perhaps 'stop'. That was it, 'Stop'. Her sentiments exactly. She'd had enough. She wasn't up for manipulation.

'Please take it,' Lauren said, prodding Millie's hand with the sleeve. 'I could say more, but really, it's not my place. *He* needs to explain himself.'

After some hesitation, Millie accepted the record and drawing in her breath, slipped it into her shoulder bag.

With an expression that seemed to exude 'mission accomplished', Lauren rose to her feet. 'Whatever you decide to do, Millie, please keep in touch,' she said.

'I will,' Millie replied as they headed for the door, then she turned to Lauren with an earnest expression. 'Yes, I'd love to keep in touch.'

Outside the café, the warmth of the day's heat and the ringing of a nearby pedestrian crossing filled the air as the two women parted company, one smiling, feeling lighter and relieved of a burden, the other, encumbered as though weighed down by the world, despite returning home with only the extra weight of a brittle, black vinyl disc.

Chapter 46:

'Don't Forget Me When I'm Gone' - Glass Tiger

Our days are like shadows. They're always there, wherever you are. And then, when you think they're with you forever, suddenly... they're gone.

***

Despite being about the end of the Falklands War, Captain Sensible's 'Glad It's All Over' doubled up as a fitting anthem to describe Millie's sentiments when she walked through the glass doors of St George's and out onto the street for the very last time. Medical school was over, and after years of dreaming and hard graft, life as Doctor Millicent Appleby was truly about to begin. How daunting was that? But at the same time, how very, very exciting!

Goodbyes are never easy, especially after five years - which can feel like an age when you're only twenty-three. Although glad to see the back of exams for the time being, saying 'Adios' to university life wasn't so easy and having to say 'Ciao' to her fellow students was going to be harder still. She'd even miss her professors, not just the friendly ones, but also the formidable and grouchy academics, who would strut around their clinical spaces like pompous peacocks, or stand stiffly behind polished, wooden lecterns to deliver their masterly pearls of wisdom. Annoying as some could be, she was grateful to them all, because had it not been for their inspiration and dedication, she had a sneaking feeling she might not have got through, let alone passed with flying colours.

But her success wasn't just down to her tutoring, not by a long shot. Sheer dedication, hard graft and prayer, lots and lots of prayer, were equally, if not more significant for laying the foundations for victory. Amazingly, she'd found herself able to put that meeting with Lauren and thoughts of Ben to the back of her mind, and even though she'd been determined not to let any emotional disturbance stop her from meeting her goals and had ramped up her efforts, she knew that despite all that, things could have easily gone the other way.

Celebrating with the rest of her year on a Thames river cruise had felt like a fitting goodbye, and the perfect way to say farewell to all the friends she'd made. But when she found herself aboard that floating vessel, in her cerise organza ball gown, no amount of pumping disco music, food, drink or bright London lights could stop the encroaching melancholy and awareness that she was losing her little St George's community forever. That evening she stumbled across something that temporarily cut through her feelings of loss, something that brought instant cheer, something unexpected which delivered an encouraging message that perseverance pays.

On the way to the toilet when the night was almost over, she stumbled across two people, tucked away in a dark corridor. A tall figure of a man with familiar-looking dyed black hair had one hand pressed against the wall while his other hand gripped the shoulder of someone soft and petite, her ebony barnet several shades darker than her azure blue dress. The couple were instantly recognisable, and although it felt incredibly awkward to be listening to the amorous, muffled smacking sound of smooching lips, Millie's footsteps were temporarily suspended while her mind processed what she was seeing and hearing in that surreal moment.

Was it really five years ago that Wahida's eyes lit up when she saw 'Goth Guy' for the very first time? Could it be that long since she and Jonas first debated whether or not Duran Duran's, 'My Own Way', was better than 'Planet Earth', or bonded over Elizabeth Frazer's unique voice in 'Pearly-Dewdrops' Drops'? Millie's gaze drifted away at the memories. How incredibly strange to think they were all *Absolute Beginners* back then. Finally finding her feet she tiptoed away towards the lavatory, intent on remaining unseen, determined not to disturb them, and when she came out again, they'd gone.

Later, when catching up with Wahida, she wasted no time with her congratulations. 'You and Jonas are together!' she gushed. 'My goodness, talk about leaving it to the last minute, you must be over the moon!' She stopped talking when she noticed that rather than garnering a favourable response, the positivity in her words disappeared faster than rainwater down a drain.

Sounding detached, Wahida casually explained that she and Jonas weren't in a relationship and Millie went quiet for a while. 'You're pulling my leg, Wah,' she eventually said, trying her best to sound light-hearted, trying hard to smile. But Wahida wasn't usually the joking type, and tonight was no exception.

'It was only a goodbye kiss,' Wahida said, swaying lightly to the music with a faraway look in her eye, 'and that's perfectly okay with me.'

Until now, Millie had always been amazed by Wahida's carefree and 'I'm cool with anything' attitude, but this time, she wasn't fooled. Right now, she could clearly see a chink in her friend's emotional armour, and despite being frustrated that Wah was lying to herself, Millie also felt her pain like never before. What sane woman would be happy with a kiss and a grope after yearning for something more for all that time? Wahida might be determined to give the impression she was insouciant and laid back, but once Jonas returned to beautiful Northern Ireland, the place The Adventures dubbed a 'Broken Land' on account of the troubles, Millie knew her friend would mourn her loss like any normal, healthy girl would, albeit in her own, atypical way.

Millie hoped her soon-to-be erstwhile university pals would stay friends at the very least, but Belfast and Leicester were hundreds of miles apart and separated by the Irish Sea. Even now, Jonas was on the other side of the room, laughing with other students and not paying attention to Wahida. Millie cringed, remembering how earlier that evening, he'd joked in front of others that he was thinking of leaving Wahida with a 'parting gift'. Then afterwards, he casually invited both her and Wah to visit him in Northern Ireland, and at the time, she questioned why he was treating them both the same. Now, looking across the room at him, the answer seemed obvious. As far as Jonas was concerned, that earlier, passionate encounter with Wahida was of little or no significance and it was safe to assume that Wah was now relegated back to friendship territory - if, of course, Jonas had ever considered her to be more than just a friend.

Looking on the bright side, Millie was glad that if anything happened between these two in the future, she'd be the first to know. She and Wahida had a growing friendship and planned to keep in touch always.

Zane was also a friend, but Millie knew it was unlikely they'd be seeing each other again after *they'd* gone their separate ways, and that was all right. People move on. The latest she'd heard was that Zane had managed to secure a prestigious house job in their very own St George's hospital, and now, watching him striding purposefully towards her, all decked up in his tuxedo, patent leather shoes, black bow tie and with a champagne glass in hand, she could tell he had something important to say.

'I'm engaged,' he announced with gusto, radiating happiness that warmed her to the core. Only recently she'd listened to him waxing lyrical about a sweet-sounding Antipodean nanny, whom he'd met while walking in the countryside near his parents' second home in the Cotswolds. And now, after only a few short months, he'd popped the question. 'I asked for her hand on a gondola in Venice last weekend,' he said, 'and we're getting married next September.'

'Wow, what a whirlwind!' Millie said, full of smiles and warm congratulations. 'How incredibly romantic, I'd love to meet her. Will she be at the graduation ceremony?'

'Perhaps, if she can get the time off work.'

Millie had another question. Now Zane was getting married to an Aussie lady, did he have any ambitions to emigrate to 'A Land Down Under'?

Zane shot Millie an incredulous look. 'You know me,' he said, 'I'm an Englishman through and through, and my dear fiancée, despite being Australian, is also a rabid anglophile, so I have to say, a move to Oz is not on the horizon.'

Feeling incredibly happy for them both, something inside her made her want to reach out, to touch him - not too effusively because notwithstanding his good spirits, he was as stiff as ever. So instead of an embrace, she touched his shoulder gently, just enough to communicate that she'd miss him and to indicate how she'd always appreciated his way with words, his politeness, his super sharp brain and his gallantry. But then, feeling uneasy, she dropped her hand, noticing his countenance had completely changed.

'I wish you all the best and I *really* hope things work out with Ben,' he said suddenly.

His words hit like a thunderclap. 'Ben?' She said, staring at him with her mouth open. Why had he brought up Ben's name? She hadn't breathed a word to anyone - not at university. At first, she'd talked too openly about Ben, and the word had got around that he'd done a dirty on her, but determined to be more private this time, no one knew he was back on the scene, so how come Zane did?

'It's obvious you've always loved him,' Zane said, breaking the silence, 'and with someone like you, it would be impossible if he didn't love you back, whatever he'd done. So,' he paused, sighing heavily, 'so you can almost guarantee he'll see sense and come crawling back one day. And when he does, I really hope it all works out for your sake, because you're a beautiful person Millie, and you deserve a true gentleman who'll be good to you.'

The seconds turned into minutes as she stood, hands limply at her sides, watching convivial students taking photographs, exchanging addresses and wolfing down food and drink. What a relief to be able to watch Zane walk away, with everyone else far too preoccupied to see a tear, followed by another, slide towards her chin. The party was over for her now, but no matter how desperate she was to go back to 8 Somerley Street to spend her final night in her London lodgings in silent contemplation and tears, she couldn't, not yet. She was on a cruise, and as much as she wanted to, she couldn't just say to the skipper, 'Stop the boat, I want to get off. I need to go home to blub my eyes out.'

Knowing she'd let someone as keen and as kind as Zane get away made her question why she hadn't tried harder to love him. But then, she remembered Amanda's words. 'Somewhere along the line, after you've met someone, the thought of not being with him becomes unbearable and unthinkable.' Taking in a deep, courageous breath, she accepted an uncomfortable truth. Those sentiments had only ever applied to one person she'd known, and sadly, that person wasn't Zane.

***

The following day she awoke to the gentle heat of the July sun penetrating her open window, and a few hours later, she and Wahida had packed up all their belongings and were waiting with suitcases for their respective parents to arrive.

'Come back and visit, won't you,' Joyce murmured, giving them both a big, surprise hug. Squeezing her soon-to-be former landlady's squidgy body tight, Millie didn't anticipate feeling an emotional lump in her throat. How could she possibly be sorry to see the back of a blatantly nosy woman who'd infuriated her so much over the years? But by now, everything was starting to feel like a wrench, and before waving goodbye, she'd promised effusively to look in on Joyce next time she was in old London Town.

Thankfully, this wasn't just a season of endings and goodbyes. There was also newness, excitement and hope, and Millie was hard-pressed to recall anything more heartwarming than when, after returning home to the farm, she'd watched with delight her brother Stuart, fully fitted out in his all-terrain army gear, playing rough and tumble with his nephew Ewan. Not only that, but by the time Stuart was ready to leave after his flying visit, he'd also promised to return with his wife when Ewan's new baby sister Holly had arrived.

For the stunned Applebys it felt like all their best Christmases had come at once, and the tingling feeling Millie had, watching her mother rush from kitchen to dining room and back, fussing and hardly able to contain her joy at having all three of her children back home again, was second to none. Best of all, the negative repercussions of the scandal that always lurked at the back of everyone's mind were successfully put aside and forgotten for a whole afternoon, and while no one ventured to ask Stuart what had finally made him come home, one thing was crystal clear, at least to Millie. No matter how bleak a situation appears to be, never say die. Even her father's reserved eyes were sparkling, and he'd always had a rather complicated relationship with his eldest son. Looking up towards the ceiling, Millie whispered words of thanks, knowing that at some point she must have prayed for Stuart to come home.

Little did she realise, however, that now she was back in Sussex, there were more unexpected things to come. Had she known what was ahead, she would possibly have braced herself and been better prepared, but when you desperately want to believe something and when you're keen for things to go a certain way, it's so easy, so tempting to ignore all the warning signs.

She'd been looking forward to spending time with her old school pal in town after they'd chatted on the phone that previous evening. 'Mills, I can't wait to see you so I *have* to squeeze you into my lunch break.' Ursula's throaty laugh sounded familiar and comforting, and as well as a lunchtime meet up, she also suggested tripping the light fantastic at a local pub that coming weekend.

Ursula was suited to her new job as a local authority Environmental Health Officer in nearby Hailsham and, proud of her oldest and most established friend, Millie strode towards the park to meet her, feeling it was an age since they'd last spent quality time together. So much had happened since, so many important developments that she was yet to tell Ursula about, and trying to ignore the nervous tension in her stomach at the thought of revealing all, she consoled herself with a comforting realisation. If after five years of not seeing each other regularly, three of which were spent with Ursula miles away in Edinburgh while she lived in London, if after all that, their friendship was still strong, there was absolutely nothing to fear. At least, that was her thinking before she passed a dule of hungry doves pecking food off the ground. Now reminded of Thrashing Doves and their hit record 'Beautiful Imbalance', Millie smiled nervously, hoping the doves weren't a sign that she was about to get a thrashing herself after telling Ursula the latest.

She soon spotted her wavy-haired friend and they rushed towards each other and hugged. Then, after grabbing some food at a nearby bakery, they headed to a park bench and it wasn't long before Millie began to open up. When she'd started, the words kept coming, and although she stopped short of sharing the sensitive and personal things Lauren had said about taking the money, she knew that at the very least, Ursula needed to be put in the picture about Ben's appeal and attempt to woo her back, the seven-inch record and everything.

Watching Ursula silently tucking into her lunch, seriously unimpressed, Millie made sure to tell her that despite how it looked, she wasn't prepared to take him back just like that. She made it clear that his blatant audacity was more than a turn-off, in fact, it made her furious. Yet, she was also raw enough, honest enough to admit to feeling pathetically indecisive and in not so many words, she confessed to having a desperate need to be understood by her friend, explaining why she felt inclined to see him, despite everything that had led up to this and despite everything he may have done.

At last she'd finished, and with trepidation she watched Ursula's eyes morph from incredulity to an icy, grey coldness. That was okay and hardly surprising.

After all, it would've been weird if Ursula *had* been happy, impressed or won over by what she'd had to say. So, having fully prepared herself for a negative reaction, she waited for the words to come. Ursula would always tell it like it was, and feeling a little anxious, Millie began to imagine her reply. After an initial telling off, she would end with something on these lines, 'Gosh, Mills, you must be an absolute moron to even consider giving that jerk the time of day, but you're a big girl now, and even though I don't agree, I'm right by you.'

But when after several minutes Ursula still hadn't spoken, Millie began to fidget while she watched her friend lift a Cornish pasty to her lips to take a bite.

'Is everything okay, Urs?' she asked.

'Fine,' Ursula said, sounding jaunty, 'and I'm sure you know exactly what I've got to say to all of that.'

'Um, I guess.'

'Good, so let's move on, shall we?'

'Move on?'

'Yes, I mean, what's the point talking about that jackass when you're going to ignore him?'

Smiling weakly, Millie blinked. 'Ignore him?'

'Yes, Mills, *obviously* that's what you're going to do, isn't it.' Ursula took another bite of her pasty. This time, her tone of voice was firm and Millie was left in no doubt that she wasn't being asked a question, Ursula was making a statement.

Having hardly eaten anything, Millie wrapped her fingers around her lunch and felt the warmth of a sausage roll through its paper bag. 'I know it's a bad idea, Urs, but,' she paused, trying to sound assured, 'I've thought about it, and I believe I need at least to hear him out.'

Ursula almost dropped her pasty. 'Hear him out?' she bit back, breathing furiously. 'You must be off your rocker. Hearing him out would be like…' she twisted her head briefly, 'It'd be like getting out of a bath and sticking your dirty knickers back on!'

Overhearing that last comment, a woman pushing a child in a buggy sauntered by and after tutting, dished out a disapproving look. Stunned into silence, Millie didn't know what to say, which was just as well, because Ursula hadn't finished yet.

'If you go back to him, that junkie or ex-junkie or whatever - don't forget who I'm talking about by the way, the guy who walked out on you the minute his ex waltzed back, then lied through his teeth, pretending that sodding off had nothing to do with her. And then he even tries to make you question your sanity by brainwashing you into thinking it's *him* that's been waiting for *you* all this time, just so he can hook you back in again…' She paused and stared at Millie hard. 'If you fall for that crap, you'll be a bigger fool than I thought you were, and you wouldn't just be desperate, mate,' she scowled, 'you'd have no flippin' self-respect.'

Twisting the lid on her Corona cherryade, Millie was glad to have something to do with her hands. 'I'm *not* desperate. I'm really not.'

After those hollow-sounding words rushed past her lips, neither said anything for a while. Instead, they listened to the irritating sound of a fly buzzing around their heads and while shooing it away, Millie tried to take stock of Ursula's words. Was she right? Was she desperate? Was desperation the reason she was even considering giving Ben another chance? She couldn't deny she'd had some pretty intense moments of missing him, but she also knew that with her newfound faith, she was happier now than she'd ever been before. She wasn't the same person today, as she had been after she'd broken up with Giles. Nowadays she was much more together, more whole and more stable, and there was a reason for that. Now was the time to tell Ursula exactly why she wasn't desperate. Now was the time to share the news about her spiritual awakening. Swallowing hard, she mentally geared herself up.

'I actually think,' she said after the prolonged pause, 'I'd be a bigger fool not to give him a chance to explain himself. You're right not to trust him. I mean, I don't either, I don't trust him as far as I can throw him, not any more. But what if... what if he asks me to forgive him, Urs, and he's genuinely sorry?' Looking her friend earnestly in the eye, she smiled softly, reticently. 'The Bible says if we don't forgive, we won't be forgiven. I know I can't keep forgiving him for ever if he keeps breaking my trust, but if I'm not willing to forgive him, even just once, wouldn't *that* make *me* the one in the wrong?'

Ursula stopped abruptly after bringing her orange juice drink to her mouth. Then, lowering her hand, she placed the carton on the bench in between her and Millie. Her eyes were averted, but her tense, clenched jaw, spoke volumes.

'The Bible!' she blasted, letting rip. 'What the... what's happened to you? Are you turning into some Bible bashing lunatic? Look,' she said, turning to Millie with narrowed eyes, '*you* can do what the hell you like, but I... I never thought any friend of mind could be so unbelievably stupid.'

There was a heavy silence, and for some time, not much was said. But soon, in her own, stilted way,

Ursula tried to make amends for her unseemly outburst. Smiling, she changed the subject, 'I hear there's going to be a live band at the Old Sussex Tavern on Saturday,' she said. 'Oh, and next time, lunch is on me, I promise.'

Too stunned to nod, Millie had a growing sense there wasn't going to be a next time. There was no malice on her part, nor desire for revenge or punishment, but it was hard to snap back or return to normal after such rage, especially when there wasn't even a hint of an apology. They spent most of the remaining time eating in silence, then soon, the lunch hour was over and it was time to say goodbye.

Although she felt despondent watching the solitary figure of a friend she once knew and still loved make its way slowly towards the main road and back to the office block, Millie felt strangely relieved. For too long she'd been trying to keep things going for old times' sake, and now she didn't feel the need any more. Heading in the opposite direction from Ursula, she decided that facing reality wasn't so bad. The person who was once her closest friend, a fellow scholarship winner and social misfit in a fee-paying school, the girl who'd stood up for her against malicious classmates and who'd cried with her when they shared the hurt of being dumped, it was finally time to accept that no matter what they had in common then, today, they were miles apart. Not only that, the friend who'd always had her back and probably still did to this day, had overstepped the mark. Sadly, this time, her protectiveness had been a bridge too far.

Leaving the park, Millie felt freer, lighter and more determined to do what she had to do. 'Friends forever,' Ursula had once said, but Millie walked to the car knowing that friendships didn't have to last a lifetime to be of value. She'd always hold a special place in her heart for her once-forever friend. Always, no matter what.

***

Late that evening, Millie stood alone on the grounds of the family farm, staring up at an expansive night sky. It was too cloudy for star gazing, but the heavens looked magnificent nonetheless, and absorbing its wideness and gradients of deepest blue and grey, she couldn't help but admire the way the outlines and shadows of trees of differing sizes interrupted the sky's vastness. The future felt as open-ended as the skies, and she stood, wondering again which area of medicine she'd end up specialising in after she'd finished her house jobs. She'd wanted to be a surgeon for so long, and part of her was still drawn to that specialism, but if there was anything she'd learnt during her five years at St George's, it was that swapping stress for peace and striving for calmness, ultimately brought more happiness, deeper joy and greater fulfilment.

Smelling the sweetness of night-scented stock, she thought about how being a surgeon came with a great deal of kudos and prestige, but she knew she wouldn't need a high-status career and all its associated sacrifices to be content. The time spent navigating at least six more years of intense study and the energy needed to fight her way through the competitive channels to become a consultant might possibly be better spent helping patients with their health issues and everyday ailments in an ordinary town or village surgery. Choosing to swap the excitement of surgery for what many of her associates considered to be a run-of-the-mill life as a GP wasn't a decision she was going to make lightly, not least of all because as Doctor Wilson himself had said, doing so could mean enduring a future of having to listen to folk drone on about verrucas and allergies and the like. He was being facetious of course, and chuckling silently, she acknowledged that Zane wouldn't have approved of her wanting to be like Doctor Wilson and his ilk, but she knew that in many ways, their work could be just as fulfilling as any surgeon's. She had to listen to her gut, and that not only applied to her career choice, but to other matters too, including affairs of the heart.

Still gazing at a rapidly blackening night sky, there was a problematic question that kept pounding on the doors of her mind. *Do I want him back, do I really want him back?* At this eleventh hour, she still didn't know the answer to that question. Yes, she'd missed him terribly and still did, but now the opportunity to be with him again had presented itself, she wasn't so sure she wanted to take it. After over two and a half years, and bearing in mind all that had transpired, would Ben now feel like a stranger?

She watched the silhouette of trees slowly vanish in the encroaching darkness, their gradual disappearance in some way symbolising her diminishing resolve. Then, once again, some of Ursula's words came to mind, crude but also true. After a metaphorical bath, it was time to get dressed in fresh, clean underwear. It just wouldn't do to go back to the dirty ones.

But just like clothing, people can be washed clean, and no matter what anyone said, she knew deep down, she'd always trusted Ben. What happened that Boxing

Day night was still a painful mystery, but for closure and to make sure she understood everything, she needed to hear him out, even though her pounding heart was telling her she was taking a major risk. She feared she was potentially opening herself up to more lies, deceit and manipulation, but she had to give him one final chance to tell her the truth and if necessary, to ask for forgiveness.

It was time to believe and trust that just as the heavens above were far out of reach, likewise, her joy and her peace were untouchable. She slowly made her way back into the farmhouse for the comfort of her bed, and she headed to her room, hoping with a silent prayer on her lips that not a soul, not anyone, not even Ben, could snatch away her peace and happiness, ever again.

Chapter 47:

'Eternal Flame' - The Bangles

She was going to ring, but she had to see him first. She couldn't just call to arrange a date. That would feel far too familiar, too 'all is forgiven', far too weird. When you haven't seen someone for such a long time, and when you were devoted to that person, and still, they left you high and dry, when they cruelly walked out without so much as an explanation, you can't just instantly take up where you left off.

She needed time and everything had to be slow and steady. The first step was to suss him out from afar to gauge where he was at. Did he seem the same? Did he look healthy? Not until they met face to face would she be able to read his body language properly, not until then could she tell whether or not he came across as honest and sincere or shifty and unreliable, but surely glimpsing him from a distance would give her a head start. Maybe she'd catch him doing…goodness knows what, or perhaps she'd even spot Faye lurking around.

Feeling frustrated, she kept her head down and her eyes fixed on his front door from her safe vantage point. Why was she being so melodramatic, so obsessed? If Ben wanted her back, Faye was unlikely to be in the picture still, so was there any justification for this pathetic stakeout, or even stalking, behaviour? Shifting uncomfortably, she concluded there was, and the reason? Good old-fashioned anxiety.

She'd always been able to be herself with Ben, but she wasn't the same person today as she had been back then. Leaning back in her parents' car, her shoulders resting against its upholstered seat, she closed her eyes and drew in a breath. Yes, she was different today, and actually, that was a very good thing. Ben had said back then that God had pulled him out of a pit, and if he were to say the same today, she would be able to do far more than merely nod and listen. Today, she could genuinely relate and say, 'Ben, it happened to me.' But there were some things she couldn't understand, like how, despite saying he loved God, he'd done what he'd done. Was he genuinely sorry now, or was he about to lambast her with more lies? If he pleaded, grovelled and begged, how should she react? All this uncertainty was enough to make anyone break out in a sweat. That's why she was hoping that seeing him before actually *seeing* him, would somehow lessen the strain.

He must come out, he must. It's the school holidays and Lauren didn't say he was going away anywhere. She looked at her watch. She'd been sitting here for almost an hour. Parked some distance away, in the opposite direction to the seafront and shops, she felt confident that her hideaway wouldn't be discovered. Thanks to her binoculars, she'd get a good view the moment he left the house, but there was a problem. This was now day three, and she still hadn't seen him. A jaunty-looking postman came and went each day, but there was no resident landlord and no sign of Ben. In an attempt to release pent-up energy, she began to tap frustrated fingers on the dashboard. If he didn't emerge soon, she conceded, she was ready to give up.

Ben was an early riser, and loved nothing better than to head out for a morning stroll. It just didn't make sense then, that this was now the third lie-in she'd sacrificed, just to wind up with no results.

A stroll. The more she thought about a stroll, the more appealing it sounded. Until now, to avoid detection, she'd driven straight home, but she was sick of all this and more than ready for a leg stretch by the sea. After opening the car door, she resolved to bite the bullet, put on her big girl pants and ring him later that day. There was no point waiting any longer, was there? It was high time she stopped messing about.

Heading away from the pebble-dashed, terraced cottage, she felt the sea breezes tickling her face and drawing her forth. Soon, she gathered speed, wondering why she'd left it so long. She needed this. It felt so good to leave that cramped space for just a while to take in some views and clear her head. It'd been months since she'd spent time at the beach, and although today wasn't the best day to hang around, at least she could grab five or ten minutes to watch the waves lapping at her feet.

She anticipated passing Barbarelli's, an amazing Italian ice cream parlour that sold delectable flavoured ices. Wouldn't it be something if she had a little more time to indulge? Ginger and Rhubarb had turned out to be unexpectedly delicious when she'd tried it, and the last time she was there, she'd spotted an unusual-looking Mississippi Mud Pie offering, which was a totally new one on her. Pistachio, rum and raisin and bubblegum - those three were next on her hit list, and of course there were all the usual suspects - strawberry, lemon and chocolate. It was a good thing she didn't live right on Barbarelli's doorstep, otherwise, she'd be stuffing her face with gelato all the time and...'

'Millie.'

The instant she heard his voice, her heart almost flew out of her mouth. She turned around and there he was, panting just a little and slightly out of breath. He must have been running. How had she not heard him? Had his footsteps been masked by the sharp shrill cries of herring gulls gliding above their heads, or perhaps drowned out by scores of babbling school-aged kids and the convivial greetings of a lollipop lady ushering them across the street towards a summer camp?

'Can I walk with you?' he asked, looking meltingly at her.

She swallowed hard. 'Feel free.' After a slight hesitation, she continued ahead, her heart beating furiously. Of course, he could walk with her, how could she refuse him, even if she'd wanted to? After all, *she* was encroaching on *his* territory and he'd rumbled her good and proper. For that reason alone, she was afraid to look him in the eye, but as they strolled ahead and the seconds ticked by, she gradually began to loosen up.

'It's good to see you,' he said.

'And you.'

'You look great, by the way ... I mean, you're looking really well.'

'Oh, thanks.' Unwilling to return the compliment and still hardly looking at him, she'd seen enough to tell he wasn't looking too bad himself. In fact, she was loath to admit it, even to herself, but he looked fantastic, and not only did he seem on top form, he was sporting that annoyingly attractive stubble on his face. He didn't shave daily in the holidays, he didn't need to, and after her stomach did a backflip, she felt vexed with herself for being such a sucker for stubble.

'How did you know I was... I mean, how come you ran after me?' she asked, briefly turning her head to see his face glowing.

'After I saw your parents' car, I guessed you'd be around somewhere.'

Millie felt her cheeks grow hot. How had he managed to spot the car after her attempts to park far enough away to avoid detection?

Still mirroring each other's footsteps, he glanced at her with a twinkle in his eye. 'At first, I thought, no, it couldn't possibly be *your* Ford Fiesta, but then I saw those pink, furry dice.'

She could tell he was trying not to laugh, but *she* wasn't amused. Those dang-blasted furry dice. She'd have hidden them if she'd had any inkling they'd give her away.

'I thought my best bet would be to head this way because it's the opposite direction to my house,' he smiled.

She raised her eyebrows. '*Your* house?'

He nodded.

'So... you're not renting?'

'No, not any more.'

In silence, they came to the end of the side street to find pedestrians and vehicles on the main road ahead and an inviting expanse of shimmering aquamarine seawater just beyond.

'So, you bought a house,' she said, stating the obvious.

'Aye.' His Yorkshire twang was like music to her ears, ringing out like the dulcet tones of his smooth, serenading sax. 'I bought it with a leg up from Gran. Did Lauren tell you where Gran's living now?'

'No, not exactly, but she did say it was a warden-controlled flat in Eastbourne.'

'Well,' he pointed a finger, 'Gran lives just a few streets down that way, and guess what.'

'What?'

'When she sold up and left the village, she insisted on giving me a lump sum for a deposit. "Benjamin," she said, "you've come into your inheritance early."' He paused, and Millie thought she could tell by the way he gulped that his heart was overflowing with gratitude. 'She always calls me Benjamin when she's being deadly serious,' he said. 'Anyway, thanks to my amazing, wonderful Gran, I don't have a big mortgage.'

They stopped for a moment and this time she dared to look him in the eye. Those mid-brown eyes so reminiscent of cinnamon, drew her in like they'd always done, and silently she shook sense into herself. He hadn't even explained himself yet, but just as the sea breezes were stronger now, so were her heartbeats, even though the heavy pounding had begun the moment he'd called out her name.

'The pier,' he said.

'What?' Feeling annoyed with herself yet again, she could tell she was sounding dazed.

'Would you like to head to the pier? It's been ages since we went on it. Or, maybe you'd prefer to come back to my place, but,' he paused and held out his hand, 'I understand if you'd rather not...if it's too soon that is...'

'The pier would be just fine.'

'Great, but first, can I get you something to eat, or what about a coffee?'

'No, I'm fine for the moment, thanks.' With thoughts of ice cream now long gone, it wouldn't do to admit that feelings of apprehension stopped her from wanting food or even a beverage. Right now, the only thing she craved were his words, and all she truly thirsted for was an explanation. Why, *why* did he choose to ride roughshod over their relationship? Was it just because of Faye he'd flattened and demolished their love, like a heavy-duty bulldozer being driven over rocky ground? She deserved an answer, she *demanded* an explanation, and keeping calm while allowing him to lead the way, she knew it wouldn't be long now.

***

When they arrived at the Pier just minutes later, hardly a word had been exchanged. It was as if Ben was saving everything up and waiting for the best moment to dump the truth on her, at least she hoped it would be the truth. When he did start to talk, would it result in an emotional overload that would be too much for her to take in? Was she even going to be able to cope? Suddenly, she felt unsure.

They found a bench overlooking the sea, and for a while, they sat and admired the grandiose Victorian and Edwardian architecture of Eastbourne to their left, and the open sea, dotted with small fishing and pleasure boats to their right.

'So, how's things?' he asked, cutting into the silence.

'Fine. What about you?'

'I'm alright. Better than ever in fact, because Lauren told me you took the record.'

Millie gave him a brief but stern look as if to communicate, 'Only just.'

'Have you played it yet?'

'Yes, I have.'

'Sorry if it was a cheesy thing to do, but I needed to let you know…' Looking slightly embarrassed, he shook his head. 'It doesn't matter. Anyway, I didn't expect to hear from you straight away because I knew you were busy with exams, so I still can't believe I found you today.' He turned to her. 'I hope everything went well, by the way.'

'With my exams? Yes - yes, it all went well, thanks.'

'And you're a qualified doctor now?'

Feeling conflicted by his attention, she nodded. It was great that he was interested to know how she was doing, but at the same time, it was frustrating to be talking so much about herself when all she wanted was for him to get on with it. But there was one bit of news she simply had to share.

'I've got a hospital job here in Eastbourne,' she said, trying to sound more muted than she was feeling.

His soft brown eyes lit up and grew wide. 'No. Really? Wow! Congratulations.'

'Thanks.' There was a short pause after her deliberately deadpan reply. It was time to stop all these pleasantries and get down to business. 'So…' she began firmly, 'Lauren said you wanted to talk to me.'

His face grew serious and for a while, they watched a cormorant perched on a rock, stretching out its sleek, black wings.

'I didn't just want to talk to you, I *needed* to talk to you. You see, things haven't always been easy the last couple of years, since we were… you know… together, but I'm happier now than I've ever been. Work's great,

I've bought a house, and best of all, I'm fitter and healthier than ever,' he smiled at her momentarily, 'but of course, there's been something missing all this time.'

'Let me guess,' she said, resting a sardonic forefinger against her chin. 'A woman perhaps?'

'Not just any woman, Millie.'

'Oh really?' she said.

'Yes, and I think you already know what I mean.'

'Oh, you think that, do you?' she said, unable and unwilling to hold back any longer. It was time to give it to him and to make it clear she was unimpressed by his pitiful attempts to worm his way back in.

'I never wanted to leave you,' he said.

Now wasn't that taking the biscuit? 'That's interesting,' she spluttered, 'because *I* was under the impression that leaving me was *exactly* what you wanted to do!'

'Actually no, it wasn't.'

Feeling her blood pressure still rising, she couldn't quite believe her ears. 'No,' she began again, sounding bitter, 'I suppose you're just a helpless man who can't resist another woman. You couldn't say 'No,' is that it?'

Looking confused, he paused for a moment. Then he looked her in the eye with a tentative, crestfallen smile.

'You mean Faye?'

'Well yes… of course.'

'Even though I said in my letter I hadn't left you for her?'

'Well, didn't you?' she asked, starting to feel a smidgen of shame.

'No, Millie. I said it before and I'll say it again, I didn't leave you for Faye.'

There was silence, and now suitably reprimanded, she gazed out over the sea at a sailing boat floating on the water, feeling her tensions evaporate to the rhythm of waves lapping against the shore.

'So, nothing happened between you two that night.'

'No.'

'And you've not seen her since?'

He dropped his shoulders slightly. 'Well, when she'd heard I'd left the village and that you and I weren't together any more, I did see her just once, for a date, because she was keen for us to try again.'

'And so you did try again with her?'

'No, never. I told her I wanted to stay friends but I just couldn't be with her again, for too many reasons.' Pausing, he looked into Millie's eyes. 'And the main reason was, I was still in love with you.'

She blinked hard, and then blinked again. Nothing made sense. 'Was it drugs?' she asked, turning to face him again, 'even though you didn't take the money?'

He shook his head. 'Lauren said she told you all about that and no, it wasn't drugs.'

'Then what happened?'

He closed his eyes for a moment and tried to smile a little. 'By 'eck, did I go insane.'

Millie sat tight. 'What do you mean you went insane?' she frowned.

'Something *did* happen with Faye that Boxing Day night.'

His words felt like a kick in the teeth. She knew it! He watched her eyes widen and he held up his hand. 'Nothing like that,' he said. 'No, but Faye *did* tell me something that night, and it fed into my deepest fears and terrified me.'

Wondering how she'd managed to fall into the trap of mistrusting him, yet again, Millie searched his face and waited patiently for an explanation, and this time, she didn't have to wait long.

'Faye told me a friend of ours, Freddie, had AIDS,' he said quietly.

There was a heavy pause while she tried to process what he'd just said.

'That night we stayed up and talked for hours. When she came downstairs after Gran and Lauren had gone to bed, I didn't think it was to talk, not when she'd been flirting with me all night. When I saw her walk into the living room in just a nightdress, I thought to myself, oh no Faye, please, you're not going to try it on with me, surely?'

Swallowing uncomfortably, Millie gritted her teeth.

'The first thing she did was to beg me to come back upstairs to my room just so we could talk. She claimed she didn't want Lauren or Gran to stumble across us downstairs. and even though I didn't trust her, I think she was probably being honest about that.'

Running a hand nervously through his hair, he paused. 'Like I said, she'd been flirting, so I knew going upstairs to my room was out of the question. So, we sat on the sofa and before I knew it, she was telling me about Freddie.' His body froze. 'I… I felt *so* confused and so upset, my brain went to mush, so much so, that I even considered going upstairs, just so we could talk all night without being discovered.'

Millie smiled briefly and nothing more was said for a moment. Then, he spoke again.

'I was already convinced I was seriously ill, because for weeks I'd been feeling sick and exhausted, so the minute she told me about Freddie, I knew it was all over for me.'

Millie drew her eyebrows together, remembering how poorly he'd looked in the run-up to Christmas. 'Yes, I was really worried about you,' she said, 'but… but you didn't think *you* had AIDS, surely?'

He nodded. 'Yes, as far as I was concerned, I now had a diagnosis, and I remember silently bawling my eyes out on the sofa after Faye'd gone back upstairs. Right now, I can't remember everything that went through my head, but I *do* remember feeling torn to pieces with guilt.' He smiled awkwardly. 'Looking back it sounds so mad, doesn't it, but at the time, it seemed so real. I didn't get a wink of sleep that night, knowing I was a literal killing machine and that because of that, I could never spend the rest of my life with you. All I could see was you, Innocent Miss Millicent, watching me getting sicker and sicker, slowly but surely, until I was gone. Even though I knew you'd love me and look after me, until the end if necessary, because that's the sort of person you are. I never wanted to put you through that. I didn't even want you to know I was ill.'

Biting her lip, she knew he was right. Had he been dying she would have cared for him, no questions asked, and it would have devastated her.

'Why were you so convinced you had HIV?' she asked after a long pause. Then, no sooner than the question had left her mouth, she knew the answer. 'Heroin,' she whispered, thinking it was obvious, 'it was because you'd injected heroin, wasn't it?'

He raised his head in agreement. 'Freddie used to hang out with me, Faye and the gang, and I'm pretty sure we never shared needles or anything like that, although I've no idea what Freddie did when he was with other addicts. For some reason the thought of sharing needles disgusted Faye, even though we didn't have a clue about AIDS back then. I guess I was lucky. It would've been so easy for me to end up like Freddie.'

'Is Freddie still alive?' she asked, sounding hesitant.

Ben's eyes became duller. 'I think so, but I've heard he's going down fast and hasn't got long. Millie,' he said, his voice cracking, 'it still feels unbelievably close to home. How did *I* manage to get away with it, but Freddie didn't? I suffered in other ways, I know, but at least I escaped with my life.'

Everything was quiet for a moment. 'What about Faye?' Millie asked, eventually. 'Was she ever worried… I mean, about herself?'

'Not at all. She was mega-confident and never afraid. She said, why would the Celtic deities rescue her from a heroin overdose, only to let her die from AIDS? Even in my mad hysteria, I didn't get how she could believe stuff like that. But at the same time I felt ashamed, because Jesus saved my life and she trusted her Celtic gods more than I trusted him.'

Saying nothing, Millie touched his knee, briefly and gently. 'Would you believe, not long ago, God saved me too, and I'm also learning to trust him.'

At first, he stared back in disbelief, then, seeing her unchanging smile, his face morphed into an expression of indescribable joy. 'Really?' he gasped.

'Really.'

With their eyes fixed on the horizon, both wanted to rest their head against the other, to hold them in their arms, and to make up for lost time. But it felt a little too early for that and besides, Ben had more to say.

'Weeks after I left the village, I managed to pluck up the courage to get tested. That's when I found out that although I didn't have AIDS, I *was* sick.'

Millie's heart skipped a beat. 'But you're okay now?' she asked, feeling apprehensive.

'Aye, Millie, I'm better now, but I tested positive for glandular fever, and it took me months to recover from it.'

Millie's body went completely still. 'Glandular fever?' she repeated.

'Aye, lass.'

She sat back while the jigsaw pieces began to fit together. No wonder he'd looked so ill back then. Tiredness, a sore throat, night sweats - he'd had them all, and as a newly qualified doctor, she could now appreciate that these were all symptoms that could be mistaken for HIV, especially if you were an anxious type. Then she began to think about herself and how ill *she'd* felt after their relationship had ended and during the weeks that followed. She'd put it all down to the stress of breaking up and her heavy workload, but now, looking back, she wondered if she'd caught the infamous so-called kissing disease from Ben. It was impossible to know.

She looked at him hard, feeling wracked with guilt and sorry for ever having doubted him.

'Why did you wait so long to tell me all this?' she asked, her voice pleading and incredulous. 'I would have understood, you know that, and while I can see why you felt you needed to leave, why didn't you get back in touch the moment you knew you didn't have AIDS?'

Ben blinked as though she ought to know. 'When I heard you and Zane were together, I thought I'd blown it forever, but then Alan told me that…'

'Whoa, hold on a minute,' Millie said, her jaw dropping. 'Zane and I were never together.'

'That's not what I heard.'

Falling silent, the horrific realisation dawned on her that her efforts to spread the word about her and Zane had been rather *too* successful. She'd been so desperate for Ben to find out, and now look what had happened as a result. Two and a half wasted years.

'I thought you said something about Alan just now,' she said.

'I did. We're going fishing next week, by the way.'

'But didn't he stop talking to you?'

'That's what I believed until I spotted him at the petrol station a couple of months back. I was about to drive off and I almost didn't get out of the car to speak to him, but I'm unbelievably glad I did. It must have been God whispering in my ear, because if I hadn't spoken to Alan, I doubt I'd be here with you, right now.'

She looked vacantly at him. 'How come?'

'He told me why he hadn't been in touch, and then he asked if I knew you and Zane weren't together any more.'

Millie's mind was now on fire and she was finding all of this almost too much to take in. 'That's strange,' she said, 'and like I said, I was never with Zane. Alan must have heard I was single, but how?'

Ben lifted his eyebrows. 'Doesn't he know your brother and your Dad?'

Millie nodded, 'Sort of, well they're all part of the farming community, but I can't imagine Dad blabbing about my relationship status. Dean's more of a talker, so it's possible he may have said something.'

Ben began to smile broadly. 'Well, if it *was* Dean, I'd like to shake him by the hand, because knowing you were single was just what I needed to give me the confidence to ask Lauren to call you.'

Millie watched the crashing waves and the sun glistening on the horizon. The sea was spectacular and the beach inviting, and she had a sweet inkling she'd be spending a lot more time here in future. 'So Alan wasn't avoiding you?' she mumbled.

'No. His dad was seriously ill and sadly he's now passed away, but just before I left the village, Alan was spending most evenings at his parents' house and often staying overnight. He told me the kids were too boisterous to take with him, so Wendy kept them at home, and that's why she always picked up the phone. He'd been meaning to get in touch with me for ages, but was going through a lot. Then, when things began to settle down, someone told him I'd moved with no forwarding address.'

Sitting back on the pier bench, Millie listened to two women chatting and eating nearby, the enticing smell of their vinegar-covered chips wafting towards her and Ben. *So Horace wasn't to blame after all*, she mouthed silently, *Horace wasn't to blame*. She felt bad about her hostile attitude towards Horace, but at least she hadn't misjudged Faye. She'd known all along that Faye was out to get Ben, and she'd been proven right.

'How's Faye now?' she asked.

'Oh, Faye's still… Faye.' He sighed a little. 'She's been to visit Gran in her new place, but because I've kept my distance and she's been in…what - two relationships in the last couple of years, we're hardly in touch these days. I do know her shop's doing well though, but it sells tarot cards and…' he paused and looked up, 'mystical rune stones, I'm sure that's what she said - stuff like that. I'm dead happy she's doing well and finally kicked drugs and everything, but what she's into these days does worry me.'

Millie looked fixedly at him, her heart filled with warm admiration. 'Why worry when you can pray?' she asked, softly.

Quietly sitting by his side, she felt safer than ever, safe enough to leap ten feet in the air or to grab her unsuspecting lover and wrap her entire being around him. But there was no getting around a disconcerting truth. False beliefs had kept them apart for a long time. She didn't know whether to laugh or cry, and while leaning into him and grasping his hand, she slowly began to realise there *was* a funny side to all of this. Soon, a broad smile became a chuckle, which gradually turned into tender laughter.

'I'm so sorry,' she said, placing a hand over her mouth.

'What's so funny?' he asked, looking bemused.

'You are! *You* and your bloomin' hypochondria!'

He gazed at her silently. 'It's a good job you're a doctor then, isn't it?'

Still giggling, she rolled her eyes, 'Umm… maybe. Still, there's only one more thing to say.'

'What's that?'

Breathing in, she arched an eyebrow. 'You Plonker Rodney!'

He swallowed a smile. 'And you know what *I've* got to say to that?'

'What?' She shook her head slowly and waited.

After pausing for effect he delivered his rebuke. 'Shut up you tart!' He grinned.

There are moments in life when only the words of a great philosopher like Del Boy Trotter from *Only Fools and Horses* will do, and feeling the warmth and comfort of his arm slowly wrap around her eager shoulders, she snuggled into him as they laughed together. Then, lifting their heads to watch black-headed gulls gliding above, they listened gleefully to their squawks which sounded a lot like laughter.

'They think it's hilarious too,' Ben said, gently kissing her on the nose. Pressing her forehead against his cheek, she gazed up at him and smiled. It felt good to be back. So, so good.

'Oh, there's just one other thing,' he said, pulling away and reaching into his pocket. After taking something out, she watched his clenched hand open to reveal an item made from silky, peach-coloured fabric.

'My scrunchie!' she exclaimed, recognizing it instantly. 'I'd wondered where it was. I lost it a while back.' She tilted her head and smiled. 'How come *you've* got it?' she asked, eying him curiously.

'I found it.'

'Where?'

He shot her a knowing look. 'In the grass by the log next to Stoneybrook.'

Everything was quiet and she looked at him aghast. 'You mean to say… you've been back to Stoneybrook?'

'Many times.' Lifting her hand, he gently stroked it, then, after taking the item she wrapped appreciative fingers around it and held it tight.

'I knew it was yours,' he said, watching her intently. 'I could easily imagine how pretty it looked in your mousy hair.'

Feeling her eyes prickle, a desire to turn away to hide soppy tears was countered by an even stronger urge to gaze back at him. 'I lost it ages ago,' she said, staring in disbelief. 'How long have you been carrying it around?'

'I've kept it in my pocket ever since Lauren told me you were willing to see me again.'

Lifting the scrunchie and slipping it into her hair, she turned her head to show off a soft ponytail.

'Beautiful,' he said, 'just beautiful.' There was a pleasing, loving pause, then arising, he reached for her hands. 'It's time, Millie Mouse,' he said, lifting her onto her feet.

'Time for what?'

'It's time for me to introduce you to 32 Seaside Crescent, my very humble abode, although I have to say, it's not exactly a castle fit for a princess.'

She held her head in her hands in mock despair, and then lifted her hazel eyes. 'But is it fit for a house mouse?' she asked.

'A house mouse?'

'Yes. We both know a mouse would much prefer a cosy nest over a draughty castle any day, so then, is 32 Seaside Crescent good enough for a Millie Mouse?'

'Um let me see…' Tapping his chin with playful fingers, he glanced up as if in deep thought. 'D'you know lass, I think it could work quite well for a Millie Mouse.'

Holding his hand tight, she gave it a tender squeeze. 'Then,' she smiled, 'I can't wait to see it. Let's go, Benvolio.'

The End

I hope you've enjoyed 'A Visit to Stoneybrook' and thank you for taking the time to read it. If you could spare a few moments to post a review I'd very much appreciate it, and for updates of future novels, you can follow me on Amazon, Goodreads or sign up via marinamclune.com

Best wishes,

Marina McLune